the home trilogy

finding home

Book One

ami van

AUTHOR. DREAMER. WANDERER

Table of Contents

- 1 -

Frankie

With eyes rolling upward, she throws her hand in the air in exasperation as she listens to her father firing off question after question on the other end of the phone. He gives her no time in between to answer, so she remains silent until he pauses to take a deep breath.

"Are you finished? Do you want me to answer any of those questions?" She inhales deeply before answering. "Dad, it's almost eleven p.m. so of course, it's dark outside. Employee parking is in the alley so I have no choice but to walk through it to get to my car. And yes, other people are walking with me to their cars too."

She quickly glances up to make sure she isn't walking alone. Two of the waiters who work with her each give a quick wave before getting into their own cars.

"Calm down before you give yourself a heart attack, would ya? Look, I'm at my car so I'm going to get in and lock my doors and let the engine warm a little, okay?"

"Ahh, Frankie, I worry about you is all. You're so far away. If something happens, who will be there to help you?" her father speaks with a hint of sadness. "I'll let you go. You really need to call more often and maybe even visit too. Drive carefully and send me a text when you get home all right?"

"Of course, Dad. I love you. Good night." She checks her phone to make sure he hangs up properly and stares at the picture on the screen.

Smiling to herself, she briefly recollects the day the photo was taken five years ago, on her father's fifty-seventh birthday gathering in bright and sunny Tucson, Arizona.

"And here I am five years later, in foggy and cold Portland, Oregon." *Sheesh.*

She puts her car in gear and begins slowly moving down the alley onto the main street.

Driving through the neighborhood, she hums quietly along with the radio as restaurants and shops begin to fade behind her in the fog. It looks as ominous as it feels and gives a little shiver.

She quickly snaps out of her mood as she approaches the all too familiar neighborhood she had fallen in love with almost five years ago. She counts her blessings frequently that she had found a nice little apartment above a small coffee shop located in Southeast Portland.

The coffee shop owners, Paul and Beth Lehman, also owned the apartments above, which happened to have just been freshly painted after their last tenants had moved out. Luckily, she had stopped in for a fresh cup when she was exploring different neighborhoods and saw an employee posting the flyer.

She saw the price and immediately called the number to ask for an appointment, pleasantly surprised when Beth Lehman said that she and her husband could come down immediately if she had the time.

Five minutes later, they were cheerily chatting up a storm with her as they walked the set of stairs to the apartment.

It was cozy at approximately 650 square feet, and other than not having enough windows, she had immediately pictured herself at home inside. There was a second apartment next door that the Lehmans resided in, but they had both assured her that privacy and personal space were respected.

They had upheld that promise until they retired a little over a year ago and moved two hours away to be closer to their children and grandchildren. They had also closed the coffee shop at the same time; however, they notified her about four months ago that they had leased it out to someone who will be opening a cafe/bookstore. Though there has been some movement in regards to renovating the place, there have been few signs of the place opening up soon.

"So much for the 'Private Property' signs," she says to herself as she rounds the building in search of parking. She rounds the block several times before snagging a parking spot a block away.

The Lehmans had been worried about her safety when they decided on their move. They took extra steps to make sure that she would be okay, giving her a list of emergency contact numbers in case they couldn't be reached.

There had been an active security system; however, the service has been temporarily suspended during the renovations or until the new shop tenants figure out what kind of system they will be using. Beth had often suggested that she adopt a dog as an extra set of ears since they knew she isn't actively dating.

Sure, she's gone on a few dates, used a few dating apps, and set up profiles on a few dating websites. But all in all, she hasn't met anyone worth the time. No one with the spark that would ignite her inner fireworks. She enjoys being on her own, for the time being anyway. When the time is right, the right person will come along and change that for her.

- 2 -

cole

"Way to go, you fucking dipshit! I told you we didn't have time. *Fuck!*"

"Quiet down," he hisses at brother.

His brother, Nick, is pissed and about ready to rip the head off of their traveling buddy, Dusty who is obviously high as a kite and oblivious to what just happened or what's even going on.

"We've gotta keep moving in the dark. It's only a matter of time before more of them show up and start going down street by street," he growls. "Dusty, you say you know these streets. Get your shit together and start moving, man."

"Uh, yeah. All right. All right. We, uh, we'll just keep in the shadows of this alley. There are a bunch of abandoned places not far up ahead," Dusty says, speaking for the first time since they ran from the pawnshop he'd suggested they hit. "How the fuck was I to know cops would show up so quickly at this time of night...er, morning or whatever?"

"Dusty, keep moving, man," Nick barks with a shove.

"We've gotta move faster. I can see more lights behind us," he growls at both Dusty and Nick.

"A few blocks from here, there's a coffee shop we can duck into. Maybe even for the night. It's empty," Dusty says as he signals for everyone to back up into the shadows when a car slowly drives by.

After a minute, they begin moving again.

"Right here. This one," Dusty says as they reach the coffee shop. "There's a side door that should be easy to get through."

"Wait. Look, they have a security system. Stay here, give me a minute to check it out," he instructs before quickly moving within the shadows to the other side of the building.

He returns a few minutes later after he finishes his assessment. "Are you sure it's empty?" he questions Dusty.

"Yeah, man. The owners moved away and the new tenants are renovating. Look, no lights on inside anywhere."

"The security system isn't hooked up. It's just a blinking light. I can see through the window that there isn't anything on the keypad," he replies.

What a night it's been so far. So much for giving Dusty the benefit of the doubt and the chance to redeem himself of his many fuckups as of late. It took him more than the usual effort to convince Nick not to ditch the guy the last time.

Truth is, he'd thought about leaving Dusty behind too. But in the condition that Dusty is in, if he gets busted, he isn't sure Dusty wouldn't rat them all out. Dusty needs help, more help than he can give, and definitely more than what Nick is willing to do.

He continues moving down the hallway as quietly as his six-foot-five frame can to the left into what he thinks should lead into the kitchen area of the shop. More lights flicker on. He turns around, noticing that Nick and Dusty are smart enough to hang back by the staircase.

They nod at him in unison when he gives them the hand signal for them to stay put.

As slow and as quietly as possible, he begins the task of moving from light to light, disconnecting the cord, then signals back to the guys to let them know it's clear.

As the other two men join him in the kitchen area, he checks his watch.

"We can lay low here for a few hours. It's almost three in the morning. Renovating or not, no one should be coming in on a Saturday morning till at least sunrise."

The other two men nod in agreement and begin to quietly scatter and check out the place.

"Hey," he says still barely above a whisper. "Let's not take our chances and stay down here, all right? Let's leave the upstairs alone."

Nick gives him a thumbs-up. Dusty nods, looking like shit.

"I'm gonna find a place to get some shut-eye. I think maybe you guys need to do the same," he says in an attempt to avoid having another talk with Nick about Dusty. *And Dusty needs to sleep off whatever it is he's coming down from.*

Dusty paces the area like he doesn't know what to do with himself. He can see the guy's sweat-covered shirt even in the dim light shining from Nick's small flashlight.

Nick heads off into what might be a pantry or small closet with what little light they have. His brother comes back out a few minutes later with a nearly full, opened bottle of Captain Morgan and a few dirty covers.

"We need to talk, baby brother," Nick says as he offers a drink.

He waves it off. "Later. I'm tired," he grunts out.

- 3 -

Frankie

What was that? She slowly wipes the sleep from her eyes and glances over to her nightstand. *4:08 a.m.* She thought she heard a noise but isn't sure if she was dreaming or not. She's only been asleep a few hours.

The curtains slightly billow and her window is still cracked open. She must have heard a noise from someone passing by outside. She slowly sits up in bed, contemplating if it's worth the walk on the cold floor to go and close the window. She huddles in the comforter for a few more seconds before getting out of bed. The early morning chill makes the goosebumps rise almost instantly and the shivers come just as quick as she reaches the window and pushes it down.

She turns around just in time to see what she thinks is a shadow move past her doorway. Now her chills aren't just from the cold of the air but from something more.

She hears a faint click. Barely audible but it's a click she knows all too well. It's the click of her front door closing. Her heart rate begins rising. *Is someone in her home or are they leaving?*

Shit. Shit. Shit. What do I do?

Her eyes dart around her bedroom. Should she make a dash for her phone on the other nightstand and then run into the bathroom to call for help? Her other option is to open the squeaky window back up, climb onto the fire escape, and get down the stairs as fast as she can, screaming bloody murder the whole way.

Her feet slowly and quietly back up to the window. She turns around and slowly pulls the curtains apart.

"Don't do that."

She freezes as a man's voice confirms her fears. There's a stranger in her house, in her bedroom. She can feel her own heartbeat picking up speed.

This is your only chance, Frankie! Her inner voice is right.

She has no way to defend herself. Her only chance is to open up this window and jump out. So she goes for it.

Before she is even able to lift the window more than a crack, her scalp is burning as the man pulls her hard by the hair. The force causes her to stumble back into him, where he manages to turn her around and back slap her across the face and then throw her onto the bed.

"I told you not to do that, you stupid bitch," the man slurs, apparent anger in his voice. "You might've had a chance if you had gone for the phone," he chuckles before putting his knee between her bare legs and slapping her across the other cheek hard enough for her to see stars.

She instinctively reaches up to touch her flaming hot cheek.

"Please don't hurt me. I don't have much. My purse is on the table in the kitchen. I won't call the cops. Just take what you want and go," she pleads.

"Don't worry. I plan on taking what I want," he replies menacingly.

The intruder suddenly slams his hand over her mouth, muffling her cry. The smell of his sweaty palm and the salty taste of it makes her gag. She can barely breathe over his hand and over his stench. He must have heard the same barely audible creak she just heard seconds before. She knows the sound well and knows where it's coming from.

He snaps her to her feet, still with his hand over her mouth. His other hand wraps tightly around her hair as he begins to shove her hard and fast toward her bathroom.

"Get in the tub or I'll snap your pretty little neck right here," he whispers angrily into her ears.

She complies as he twists his hand tighter around her hair.

He gets in after her and maneuvers himself with his back now against the shower and her in front. With his dirty hand still in a vise grip over her mouth, he lets go of her hair only to tightly wrap his whole arm around her, pinning her body to him.

"One peep and you're dead," he whispers icily.

It seems as if she stands there with him for months when she knows it has been only but a minute, maybe even two. She feels moisture through the back of her shirt, can smell his nauseating stench even more now that they are in a more confined space.

Oh god.

She can feel something else in the small of her back. The thought alone makes her cringe, causing him to tighten his grip, squeezing her body to him even closer.

The son of a bitch is getting hard. She can feel him, can feel *it*, growing against her back. Her mind now focuses on his other hand. At only five feet tall, she's a lot shorter than him. His other hand isn't just holding her arms pinned against her but he is groping the side of her breast too.

She hears another noise at what must have been the same moment he hears it. The sound of her door opening. Someone else is coming into her home. Is it this asshole's partner? Is she about to get raped by two men and possibly be killed tonight?

Wait. Wait. Think, Frankie! If it's his partner, why is he hiding in the tub too? Why is he afraid to be seen? No. It has to be someone else. Someone's here to help!

Her eyes dart downward.

His grip around her arms is loosening up as his fingers slide in through the sleeveless opening of her shirt. He's distracted by his contact with her plump flesh. *The sick bastard.*

"Oh, you like that, don't you," he whispers right next to her ear.

She answers by leaning the back of her head onto him and pushing her back up against his erection.

He responds by reaching further into her shirt, but for him to touch more of her he has to let go of his grip. At the exact second he lets go, she slams her elbow into his rib and jerks her head up just enough to give him a good hit to the bottom of his jawline.

"HELP!" she screams as loud as she can the moment his hand comes off her mouth. "HEELPP!"

Her hands push open the shower curtain as her legs whip themselves over the side of the tub. Not looking back, she rushes for the door as her eyes try to look around the bedroom for another person.

No one.

Instinctively heading toward the door as fast as she can, she turns around to see if she is being followed. She can hear his footsteps in the dark. Right before she turns her head back around, she runs into something.

Hard.

No, not something. *Someone!*

"Oh god! Help me! There's a man here and he's trying to kill me!" she screams breathlessly up at the giant she just ran into.

She looks up only to see the silhouette of a very tall and broad man, not able to see any real features in the dark.

He doesn't say a word as he reaches down to grab her wrist and pulls her behind him like a chivalrous knight ready to do battle for her.

She grabs onto the back of his jacket with one hand, staying hidden behind him. Her other arm now wrapped tightly around him as if her life depends on it.

"What the fuck are you doing?" the giant speaks for the first time in a loud whisper, barely containing his anger.

How did he...

She attempts to slip her arm off of him as the truth dawns on her but he's too quick. He grabs her wrist and pulls it back where it had been, keeping the rest of her still hidden behind him.

"I said we leave the upstairs alone!" he continues on.

"Sorry, man. I...I just didn't want the night to go to waste," the scumbag replies. "I didn't get a chance to go through much before that slut woke up. But hey, now that you're here, we can go through the place faster together."

"Please, just take whatever you want and go. Please," she pleads from behind the giant, trying to wrench her arm free.

"What the fuck is going on?" another voice booms from behind her.

Before she can turn around to see who it came from, a large hand shoves the side of her head, *hard*, into the frame of her bedroom doorway.

And then she is falling...and falling...but never hitting the floor.

- 4 -

cole

He turns around just in time to catch his little damsel in distress before she hits the floor.

Swiping her hair away from her face, he gets a chance to take a good look at her for the first time with what little light there is in the room.

Fair almost pale, small, and round face. Her cheeks are red on both sides and a small cut was on her lip. The blood is barely visible next to her plump pink lips. *Dusty hit her. That piece of shit.* Her hair is long and dark brown, maybe even black.

Ravishing. Beautiful.

He finds himself wondering what color her eyes are.

"Well, what the fuck is going on?" Nick repeats.

He ignores his brother and picks her small body up with ease and walks past Nick to the couch in the living room. "Ask the genius over there," he says, nodding his head toward a nervous-looking Dusty.

As he lays her down on the couch, he notices her legs and her body in its entirety. She's small, a whole lot smaller than him, but then a lot of people are smaller than his six-five frame.

She can't be more than five feet tall and a hundred pounds, give or take. Wearing what she's wearing probably didn't help her in the situation either. She would have been no match for Dusty even if she tried. He gently swipes her hair behind her ear and checks her head.

He decides to sit her up since she isn't appropriately dressed and moves to sit next to her. Her head flops onto his chest and the smell of her hair flows straight up to his nose. Damn, she smells amazing. Floral. Fragile.

Snap out of it, Cole.

He reaches into his pocket and pulls out a bandana. He senses her coming around as he ties it around her eyes, wondering what they look like again.

"Nick, man. I just didn't want the night to go to waste, ya know. I came to check the place out. See if maybe there is something we can use. I didn't even know she was in here. The other rooms are all empty," Dusty tries to explain.

"And now we have to deal with another problem," Nick finishes.

Nick walks over to the closet by the door and switches on the light inside. His brother peers in and then closes the door halfway, dimming the brightness. Nick walks over to a dining table and digs inside the purse sitting on top to pull out a wallet, quickly going through it. Nick pockets the cash and pulls out her ID.

"Francine Grace Hoang," Nick says aloud to no one in particular. "Maybe she's married."

"It's four in the morning and there's no one else here with her," Dusty adds. "What...what do you think we should do, bro?"

Nick moves to sit on the other side of Francine. "She doesn't look like no Hoang," his brother says as he touches her leg.

He watches as Nick's hand slowly continues upward.

"But she does look delicious," Nick disgustingly says. "I think I might like a taste of whatever she's serving."

"But...I'm the one who found her, man," Dusty's squeaky voice comes from the kitchen area. "We were about to have a good time before Cole came. She was just getting hot for me, wanting me to get a handful of her big and soft tits," the asshole says with a smirk.

"No," he calmly says and slaps away his brother's hand.

"Baby brother wants to go first, does he?" Nick laughs.

- 5 -

Frankie

As she starts to regain her senses again, she realizes that the muffled bickering isn't just in her throbbing head. She's blindfolded now and it has her panicking. She strains to see through it but can only make out silhouettes.

There aren't just one or two, but three strangers are arguing about who gets a turn with her first!

Her body shivers ever so slightly as she begins to comprehend the dire situation she is in. Whoever she is leaning up against must have felt it; his hand pulls her closer to him. She keeps as still as possible, breathing as silently as she can, listening for anything that might save her.

She hears the tall one calling the first slime ball Dusty. Now listening to their conversation, the one that she is leaning against is Cole and the other sitting next to her is Nick. Cole hasn't said much but she can remember his voice. He is the one she ran into earlier.

He shifts his position so she falls forward into his left arm, as his right one swoops underneath her knees. He stands up, carrying her, walking quietly in the direction of what she can assume is her bedroom.

Fighting to keep her breathing slow and steady so he doesn't know she's conscious, she prays for help. He's a big guy. Even if she manages to fight him off, what could she do to save herself from the other two savages? This man, who she had moments earlier thought was her knight in shining armor, is about to rape her in her own bed, in her own home. They are *all* going to take turns raping her!

"Oh, don't be shy now, Coley," Nick taunts. "Leave the door open," he commands.

She feels Cole inhale sharply.

Cole gently sits her down on the bathroom counter, her head still leaning against his chest. He turns on the light but what light she can see is dimmed thanks to the blindfold. She hears him open the drawer and digs around.

"Can you sit up?" he asks in a whisper. He grabs both of her wrists and ties them together with a cord.

She sits up unsteadily.

It feels like an eternity of silence between the two of them there in the bathroom as he binds her wrists. She can hear her couch squeak like someone either sitting or lying down on it. She can also hear drawers and cabinets being opened. One of them going through her home searching for valuables most likely.

"Are you going to rape me?" she manages to whisper.

Stillness follows.

Seconds later she hears him rummaging through the drawer again. The sound of a medicine bottle being rattled and then the lid being popped off follows shortly after.

"Take these," he commands, not answering her question.

She closes her lips tightly, shaking her head no.

"They're just Advil, Francine. For your head. It's gonna hurt and these should help," he whispers patiently.

She nods her head.

"Will you need water?" he asks softly.

She answers by shaking her head.

He puts the pills up to her lips one by one and waits for her to swallow them. Softly into her ear, he says, "I've never raped a woman in my life and I'm not going to start with you, okay, Francine? I'm not sure how but I promise you that those two out there won't be getting their hands on you either. Just trust me a little, okay? Please?"

He has a slight twang to his speech and her mind begins to wander and wonder what he looks like and where he's from.

"Am I going to die tonight?" she asks, her voice shaking.

He softly chuckles. "No, Francine. Not if I can help it."

He lifts her off of the counter, helps her stand up, then turns her around so that her back is against him. "I think you need a warm shower. I'll help you but I can't untie you, okay? I'm going to have to cut your shirt off though, I'm sorry."

She nods her head. He could easily have ripped it off of her even if she had said no. At this point, she is putting blind faith into this man, who is either a knight or a jester about to slit her throat after he...*they*...are done with her.

His hands grip the bottom hem of her shirt and begin pulling upward and over her head before settling the bunch on her wrist. Next, she hears the cut of the fabric before feeling it fall to the ground next to her feet. Other than her panties, she is now standing naked before this stranger.

Her arms instinctively come up to cover what she can of herself.

"Here," Cole says as his hand leads her toward the edge of the tub. "Get in first. I'll give you a few seconds to warm up," he says gently.

She finds herself shivering under the very warm shower, alone. For now. He said for her to get in *first*. He hasn't hurt her and she doesn't want that to change. So she's following his instructions in hopes that the situation doesn't change. But her mind just can't *not* think about the worst-case scenarios.

This guy is nice to her. He seemed sincere when he said she isn't going to die tonight. *He also said he didn't know how he was going to help.*

She didn't realize that tears had started falling. How the hell did this night turn into such a nightmare? One minute she's scrolling through her phone looking through happy social media posts and now she's standing in her bathroom, naked...with three strangers in her home. One of whom is probably undressing himself to get in the shower next to her and do God knows what.

She feels the shower curtain open and tries harder to cover herself, moving closer to the wall as she feels him stepping in the tub behind her. His presence feels as if it engulfs the entire space.

"Hey," he whispers. "Just keep close to the wall so I can't see. I'm sorry I'm in here too, but you needed a shower, I need a shower, and I can't leave you alone out there."

She nods her head.

- 6 -

cole

Well, he wasn't lying. He did need a shower, especially since it helps him buy her some time, hoping Nick will fall asleep soon.

He looks down at the tense figure standing a mere inch in front of him. Even with the blindfold on, he can tell she's crying.

He doesn't know what to do but turn her around and wrap his arms around her in the most non-sexual way he can, pulling her closer to his chest.

"I'm sorry, Francine," he says. "Shhh...." She stands still but he can feel her softening in his arms. "I'm so sorry," he repeats.

He holds her for a moment before she shoves away from him. He loosens his hold on her as she takes a step back and tilts her face upward as if she can see him. What a beautiful, round, and fair face it is. Her eyes. He's still trying to imagine what her eyes might look like.

"Cole, right?" she asks quietly. The first time she's ever said his name. Without waiting for him to say anything, she continues. "Please stop calling me Francine. It's Frankie. My mother was the only person who ever called me that."

"Frankie," he repeats. "I like that. I think it suits you better than Francine. And that Hoang. That's a surprise," he says with a chuckle.

When he looks back down at her face, still tilted upward, she's actually smiling a fraction. That smile makes her look almost angelic with her long dark hair flowing down her back.

Before he knows what he's doing, his lips have reached hers like a magnetic pull that he had no chance of resisting.

And he's lost to the kiss...to her.

Maybe it's the moment, the warm shower, the adrenaline, the emotional rollercoaster of the night, that causes her to react unexpectedly as well. She should be shoving him off yet her lips mold themselves onto his. Soon she's kissing him back as tenderly as he's kissing her. Long, deep kisses. Her still-bound hands turn from balled fists to open palms touching his abs, roaming slowly upward.

As their kiss continues to grow in intensity, a feeling sprouts. It's a feeling of warmth, of being needed. It makes him feel like he could be the guy standing in front of a loaded gun for her. That's never anything he's ever felt before. It should be alarming but it settles inside of him nice and warm.

Her fingers touch his face softly. His senses are lost and he deepens their kiss.

He breaks the kiss for a few breaths before he picks her up, turning her so that her back is against the wall and the warm shower rain flows in between their bodies.

She follows his lead and wraps her legs around his torso, pulling her tied hands over and around his head. As she rests her arms on his shoulders, her fingers play with his hair.

"You're so beautiful," he whispers. Even without completely seeing her face, he knew. She's fucking gorgeous.

This time, she leans down and initiates the kiss. It takes him by surprise but he follows her lead, the only beat skipping was that of his heart.

He's so lost in her that he doesn't hear the door opening. His eyes closed, savoring her taste until the shower curtain swooshes open.

"Damn, Cole! She is fucking fine." Nick whistles.

"GET the fuck out of here!" he growls.

Frankie tense up even with his own body blocking hers from Nick's view. Before he can turn around, Nick grabs the edge of her lace panties and rips them away.

"What are these still doing on her?" Nick asks as he lifts them to his face for a sniff.

He unwraps her and puts her down behind him before whipping back to face his brother. He shoves Nick and roars, "WHAT is your fucking problem? Get out!" He gives Nick a hard shove toward the door.

"Stop taking your time dating her or I'm fucking her first," Nick replies in a tone he recognizes all too well. The tone that always told him to back down from whatever disagreement they're having at the time.

When Nick leaves, he turns back to the tub to find Frankie sitting curled up shivering with her arms wrapped around her knees. Her face is flustered and her skin is flushed.

"I'm sorry," he says again as he reaches to turn off the shower and yanks her robe off the hook on the door. "Stand up," he tells her.

She complies and he quickly throws the robe over to cover her. As much as he wants his eyes to get their fill of the sight of her amazing body, he doesn't want her to feel so completely exposed.

He sees his brother's smug face on the couch when he carries Frankie out of the bathroom. That means that Dusty was the one he heard leaving a few minutes ago. Good riddance.

He lays Frankie down in the middle of the bed and pulls the cover over her.

Never one for modesty, he lies next to her on top of the covers stark naked. Not that she can see through the blindfold anyway. For all his years dealing with all types of women, at this moment, he doesn't know what to do. She's so fucking quiet about this.

Of course, the other women he's brought to bed didn't have to be bound and blindfolded either. If they were, it was usually by choice.

The silence in the place is broken by the sound of a creak coming from the couch. Nick is either moving or getting off the couch. Not wanting to take any chances, he quickly lifts his body up, pulls the covers out from under himself, and glides under them. He quickly positions himself so it would look as if he is on top of Frankie if Nick comes in.

"Damn quiet in there! You need me to come help make her moan?!" Nick yells from the couch.

He looks down into Frankie's pale face. "I'm sorry," he whispers yet again.

Her lips tighten. The same luscious lips he was just kissing earlier.

Losing his ability to think freely again for the second time tonight, he bends his head down and gently touches his lips to hers. Not pushing, but waiting to see if she would respond like before.

It takes a few seconds for her lips to move under his, softly inviting.

Breaking his will, he pulls away from her and gets out of the bed. He walks to the bedroom doorway still naked, looks Nick straight in the eyes, and closes the door, leaving it only an inch open before returning to her.

Damn it!

He thought his brother would be passed out by now. But for whatever reason, Nick is still awake and waiting. He's getting less and less optimistic about his brother's need to be with a woman right now. To be with *this* woman.

He reaches the bed and crawls back in next to Frankie.

"I thought he'd be passed out by now," he says to her in little above a whisper.

- 7 -

Frankie

"What should we do?" she asks quietly.

His body is warm and hard next to her. Yet his voice is soft and comforting. What a strange mix.

She feels lightheaded. Is it from the hard knock to the head from earlier? Or is it from the shower? Their shower. His kiss moments earlier had been brief, but she can still feel the tingle on her lips.

She absentmindedly licks her lips, confused at why she's reacting to him this way. *Chemistry, that's why,* her inner voice answers. How fucked in the head is she to think about chemistry with a stranger who's broken into her home?

He doesn't answer her but she feels him lean over her again, can feel the heat coming from his lips. From his whole body. Then he moves up and places a sweet kiss on her forehead, followed by one to her temple, then on the bridge of her nose before he whispers, "I don't know."

She finishes what he's started by lifting her chin up to meet his lips with hers.

And then she is lost.

Chemistry.

Where did the nightmare end and this dream begin? She doesn't know. She isn't afraid of Cole like she was of Dusty. She isn't repulsed by the scent of him and doesn't flinch at the touch of his hands on her skin.

Her body melts under his trail of kisses while her mind prays for a different kind of help now.

He lifts her bound hands above her head. Almost immediately, she feels the sensation of him kissing the hollow of her neck. Then kisses on her collarbone. He continues trailing soft, sensual kisses until he reaches the top of her right natural, plump breast. Then the warm kisses include small wet licks trailing over to the top of her other breast.

She inhales sharply as her body anticipates more.

Her anticipation is paid with the sensation of his hot tongue slowly gliding over her nipple. Her body aches and arches in response, silently asking for more.

He answers her body's traitorous plea by gently squeezing a hand around her breast and wrapping his lips around, taking a mouthful. Suckling and twirling his tongue around her nipple. First one side then repeated on the other.

It's been too long since she's felt like this. Her skin tingles, her mind swirling with emotions, and her body needing more of what he is doing to her.

She lets a soft moan escape her throat. With each of his hands having a handful of her now swollen breasts, his lips leave them as he continues with his trail of kisses.

His stubble tickles her skin as he places a kiss between the hollow beneath her aching mounds. He continues down her torso until he reaches her navel. Slow, caring kisses are placed downward until reaching just right above her mound.

She doesn't realize she is holding her breath, waiting for what may come next. She can't see what he is doing. She can't see him at all. She doesn't know what she's thinking, but before her thoughts run further away, she feels him gently lift her left thigh up just high enough to brush it with light kisses. Her legs react by slightly coming apart, allowing him better access.

He rolls himself fully between her legs now, placing tender kisses from one inner thigh slowly to the other. Lingering his warm breath a few seconds in between, teasing her freshly shaven mound. Heightening the anticipation. Her legs tense as her body wriggles, asking for more.

He answers her desire's call by kissing her at the apex of her legs. His warm, smooth tongue delving in, tasting her.

She moans louder this time as he dives in deeper, as if hungry for more. His finger enters her and she gasps. The gasp turns into a loud aching moan as his thumb finds her sensitive nub and begins teasing it. Both of her legs move over his broad shoulders as her hands come down from above her head and into his hair.

"Oh god," she moans.

cole

He can't get enough of her taste, like vanilla and light cream. Her scent alone is driving him mad, attacking his logic. He wants to devour every drop of her but reins in every ounce of willpower to move away from her bare mound.

His trail of kisses ascends back upward, although quicker than the descent. As he reaches her stomach where her tied hands are resting, he unties her. Gentle little pecks at each fingertip as he works the knot with one adept hand.

He isn't sure what might happen once the cord comes off, but right here and right now, he doesn't care.

He gently raises one of her arms back above her head as he glides his body up along hers, controlling his weight so he doesn't crush her small frame.

Her other hand immediately comes up to her eyes, wanting to remove the blindfold too.

"Frankie, please don't," he whispers.

She nods her head in compliance without question. It would have really been a turn-off for him if he had to remind her of their situation. It's for her own good. She hasn't seen any of their faces, therefore cannot identify any of them even though at that very second, he wishes with all his might that she can see him. But Nick probably wouldn't appreciate that and who knows what his brother would do.

Frankie moves her hand to his face instead.

He doesn't stop her as her hand moves gently around his face. Feeling the shape of his jawline, caressing his cheek before running her thumb over his lips. She pulls his face to hers for another kiss.

"So fucking beautiful, baby," he whispers. "May I?" he softly asks.

Frankie

Baby. It sounds amazing and endearing coming from his lips.

She knows what he is asking of her. She can feel the weight of his cock resting on top of her mound and he is all man. Big, like every other part of him.

She answers by pulling her legs up and wrapping them around his waist.

He crushes her lips hungrily as he positions himself at her moist slit. Her hips lift up a fraction to encourage his entrance.

He lifts his lips off of hers as he slowly pushes through her hot, moist folds.

"Oh god," he hisses.

"Ahh," she lets out unexpectedly at the pressure. Her arms quickly hug onto him, holding her breath and waiting for her body to yield to him.

He slides in a little deeper, not all the way at once. He's long in length and thick in girth, thicker than she's ever had, and it isn't even all of him.

She moans as he pulls back out, wrapping her legs around him tighter, lifting her hips pleading for more.

Kissing her neck, he enters again. Deeper this time, as she gives him an even wetter invitation. And still, she pulls him in deeper with her legs as he tries to leave her again. He stretches her more than ever before and her body is begging for more.

This is crazy.

And then he's deep in her. Not fully but as deep as her body can handle. It's pure ecstasy.

"You feel fucking amazing," he whispers to her, kissing her face, nibbling on her ear.

He uses slow, measured strokes, allowing her body to accept and adjust to him. He feels like nirvana, burning her in the best way possible. With each pull and thrust, she stays in sync with his rhythm. Her hips move in just the perfect way to meet his thrusts. Her every action inviting him to lose himself within her. She can feel her peak building up as their rhythm begins to pick up its tempo.

She doesn't know when the kissing stopped, replaced by moans that she doesn't even attempt to keep quiet. She's too lost in the feeling and intimacy. She needed more. She wanted more of his touch, more of his warmth.

She wants all of him.

She pushes him to the side and onto his back and she rolls on top to straddle him, literally sitting on his throbbing cock.

She leans forward for a kiss, lifting herself off of him.

His rock-hard cock springs up to meet her at just the perfect angle. She lifts her lips off of his and rests her face on his chest before sliding her wetness down on him as far as she can with one stroke. It's now her own hiss that she hears as she inhales deeply, loving the feel of him inside.

"You're killing me," he whispers with his sexy drawl before she sits up, pushing off of him and then sliding down again, deeper. Building a new rhythm each time, he lets her have control for the first time since they've met.

She rides him with deep, long strokes, and reckless abandonment. His hands kneading her hips every time she comes down on him.

He sits up, one of his hands leaving her hips as it travels up to her breast. He wraps his hand around it, thumbing her perked nipple as his other arm wraps around her waist and pulls her down on him even deeper each time.

He sends her closer and closer to the edge as he wraps his hand harder around her breast and begins to suck on it.

She nearly loses what little control she has as his tongue flicks her sensitive nipple. Throwing her head back, she feels his hand wrapping itself with her long hair, still careful not to move the blindfold.

Her moans grow louder as she continues riding, floating into space, and all she wants right now is to be lost there. Lost in pleasure and some sort of sick kink she didn't know she had.

"Tell me, Cole. Tell me what you want," she hears herself whispering into his ear as if the words came from a stranger.

His lips come off of her breast. His hand leaves her hair and his arm unwraps from around her waist. He puts both hands on her hips, pulling her down on his fully engorged cock even deeper as she rides him faster.

"Come for me, baby," she hears him softly demand. *Baby...how did he make that sound so fucking seductive?*

The second he utters the words, she wraps her arms around his broad shoulders and comes fully down on his throbbing member. She lets herself go, riding him as she continues riding the waves of an amazing orgasm. The first non-self-induced orgasm she's had in years.

Only a nanosecond later, Cole thrusts himself deep within her one last time as the undertow of her waves pulls him along with her and he fills her.

She continues bucking and riding him, taking every last drop of him, letting herself flow all over him again and again.

Spent and sated, he collapses onto the bed taking her along with him in his arms. Still attached, her on top, they lie there in silence as she waits to return from her utopia.

- 8 -

cole

5:25 a.m.

He turns his head away from the clock on the nightstand and looks to the window. He can see through a small gap that it's still dark outside, but civil twilight is approaching in an hour or so. This moment, this feeling of content...*this happy place...* is minutes away from coming to an end.

He feels like he is on an amazing high, the highest of highs. *She's fucking amazing!* He'd nearly blacked out when he felt her orgasm around him as she kept riding him all the way through his own as he spilled into her.

He can still feel her energy around him, can feel the energy of what they've done floating around the room, and he isn't the most sensitive guy to be feeling this type of way either. There are parts of her lingering on him, everywhere her skin touches his.

He peeks down at Frankie, who fell asleep not too long after the most amazing sex he's ever had the pleasure of experiencing. And he's done a lot of experiencing through the decade.

Her head rests on his bicep, her arm draped over his chest, as the rest of her body snuggles warmly next to his even with the blindfold still over her eyes. Her breath softly and steadily caressing the hollow of his neck.

He never cared for this part of sex, or rather, after sex. He isn't what women would call a cuddler and frankly, he's always been turned off by women who wanted to do it. He's used to his women always picking up and leaving whatever shitty motel they're in immediately. Probably to get back home before their husbands missed them. Or he was the one asking them to leave. There isn't ever any semblance of a connection to want their companionship afterward.

But this is different. Frankie is different. He can feel it.

He knows next to nothing about her. He knows her name is Francine Hoang, though she doesn't look close to being a "Hoang." So maybe she is married? Divorced? Maybe she's seeing someone too. All that passion brewing just beneath the surface, someone has to be helping her tame that.

Jealous?

He rolls his eyes. Those things never bothered him before. He never cared enough about who he's fucking for it to be a bother. And he never stayed in one place long enough to care.

There's just so little he knows about her to be feeling this way though. This feeling of wanting to stay exactly where he is at this very second.

Be real, Cole. What can you give her?

This time his inner voice sounds like his brother. The sober Nick. Probably because it's something Nick would be saying to him.

He's a crook, a criminal who's broken into this building. He's broken into her home. It may look like he saved her from the likes of Dusty and even Nick, but she never should have been in this nasty situation to begin with. He is, in part, at fault for that and yet she put her trust in him, had given herself to him.

He suddenly feels guilty, like he's taken advantage of her vulnerability.

No. He can't think of it like that. She hasn't shown she was afraid of him. She surprised him by taking charge in leading them both on a high that gave him more satisfaction than anything he's ever had before.

In that room, with just the two of them lying side by side, it's he who feels vulnerable. *What the fuck is going on?*

She stirs next to him and he holds his breath, not wanting to wake her. Instead of moving off of him, she nestles even closer, moving her head off of his arm and over to his chest. Her hand travels down over his abs, her leg drapes over him, her thighs moving up over his own.

He's rock hard for her again even before her small and soft hand reaches for him.

"Shit," he hisses as her hand wraps around him, his body sinking into the bed.

"*Mmm...*" he hears her hum drowsily. He can feel her tilting her head and he places a kiss on her forehead. "*Mmm...more,*" she whispers even more drowsily as she continues stroking him.

More?

Oh god. Yes! He would love nothing but more of her. More with her. All of her.

His fingers are under her chin, tipping it up so he can taste those wonderful lips again. Her tongue is eager to dance with his. Her hand leaves her hold of his stiff dick, moving up his abs and reaching for his, interlacing her fingers with his own even as she continues kissing him.

She pulls his arm around her before her lips leave his as she turns her body around, pulling him to spoon her as she snuggles up against him, her round globes pushing up against his stiffness.

He can't tell if she's still asleep or not but she's the ultimate tease right now and he needs more. More of her. His hand travels down the length of her body, down in between her legs to find her hot, already wet, and ready.

He kisses her bare shoulder, trailing over it all the way up to her ear before his finger slides deep into her.

Her loud gasp satisfies him as her back arched against his chest, her moans filling the quiet room again.

"More?" he whispers into her ear.

"Please?" she whimpers.

Fuck! This tiny bit of a woman is going to end him.

Her soft whimpers, her squirming ass up against him, drive him crazy. Her wet heat around his finger just about pushes him over the edge.

Her legs part and he's more than ready to position himself at her entrance. Giving her one second to prepare herself, he glides smoothly inside her as far as her body will let him in that first stroke.

"*Shit,*" he manages to slip the words through his gritted teeth as he holds himself still, afraid if he moves, he'll spill into her with just the one thrust. "So tight," he says before placing another kiss on her creamy shoulder.

"Mmm…" she purrs lazily even as she begins moving on to him.

Fuck! She's so soft…so sexy…

The arm she's lying on top of bends, folding across her chest, interlacing his fingers with hers again. His other hand travels down her stomach, holding her tight as he begins moving. Thrusting in and then pulling out of her.

"So good," he barely hears her whispering, encouraging him to take deeper and harder strokes.

Shit! He's already so close to losing it. *How?* He's been in whole-day fuck fests that didn't feel this amazing.

"Promise, every time someone puts their lips on you, you'll think of me. Only me, Frankie."

"Cole? Please?" she pleads as her fingers tightening over his, her body moving so in sync with his own. Every time he thrusts, she pushes back on him.

"I wanna fuck you hard till your body is marked," he growls into her ears, slamming into her with each thrust now. "But I won't, sweetheart. I'm gonna let you burn me slow and deep. So you'll never forget me because I'll never forget you."

He doesn't even know where all these promises are spilling from. It doesn't fucking matter though. It's his truth. He's never forgetting her.

"Let me feel you, baby," he tells her. "Come for me."

"Cole," she breaths out.

Her heat rains and burns him from the tip of his dick and all around him. Her loud moan followed by her sexy whimpers and the trembling of her body against his sends him over. He can feel himself pumping into her. *Three...four ...five...pumps.*

She's taking him. Draining him...and he's loving it. Proof by his loud grunts and groans filling the room while he tries to hold himself together.

"Stay," he thinks he heard her say.

Amid the silence long after she's fallen asleep again, he hears a tiny squeak.

Shit! Nick!

He looks to the gap of the bedroom doorway, waiting for it to open but it never does. He only sees a shadow passing by. He smoothly slides out from under her arm and out of bed, silently moving to the door. He steps out into the living room to see Nick giving him a hand signal, saying that he'll be waiting downstairs.

Nick mouths the words "hurry up" as he closes the door.

He turns around and steps back into the bedroom. Frankie is still asleep. He can hear the sound of her steady breathing. The temptation to crawl back into her warm bed and wrap his arms around her is strong. Too strong. But daylight is coming and he knows what has to happen. So he tiptoes silently to the bathroom to retrieve his clothes.

He already knows this is the wrong choice to make and he's made a shit ton of wrong choices in this lifetime. But this one? This one is the one he's going to regret the most.

She yawns and opens her eyes, expecting to be blinded by the morning sun. Instead, she feels her lashes swipe up against something and the light is very dim.

The blindfold.

Her foggy brain begins to clear as she rips off what's wrapped around her eyes.

Her blurred vision comes into focus quickly as her head whips from one side of the room to the other, expecting to see someone in there with her.

The curtains are still closed. She looks at the clock. 9:17 a.m.

How long has she been asleep? How was she even able to fall asleep?

She shoves off the covers and sits up only to find that she is still naked and pulls the covers back up to her chin.

She holds on tightly to the covers with one hand, the other hand gripping the cloth that once blinded her. She holds her breath, listening carefully to see if he's still here.

Five minutes pass before she is sure she is alone in the apartment.

- 9 -

Three Weeks Later

Frankie

"Aye, Frankie, you need help up there?" Sam yells up from the hallway below.

"I'm just finishing up!" she replies to Sam. All done," she says to herself and steps back to look at her handy paint job.

She sits down and looks around her freshly painted bedroom then lies down on the floor for a quick breather. Involuntarily, her mind wanders back to the events of the past few weeks. The aftermath of that night.

The first week slugged by with paranoia and sleepless nights. She imagined herself looking like some sort of crazy woman glancing over her shoulder every few seconds when she was out running errands. At work, she'd been jumpy when friends and coworkers were too close.

The nights were the worst. She found herself checking the locks and windows several times a night before falling asleep, only after she was physically and mentally exhausted. And even then, she would wake up not much later thinking she had heard someone walking around.

Things began getting back to normal midway through week number two after that night. Renovations downstairs finally started picking up their pace so she wasn't alone in the building as often as before. Half a dozen crew members were working throughout the day and sometimes into the night as well.

She also met the new shop tenants, Rebecca and Sarah Stenzil. They are vibrant sisters about her own father's age. Both strong-minded, single women who retired early, thanks to a recent inheritance, and are now pursuing their dream of opening a think-space/bookstore/cafe.

Along with Rebecca and Sarah came their nephew, Sam Greenberg. He's their shop designer and the head of the renovation crew. Sam is in his late thirties. Never married, no kids, charming, and very easy on the eyes with his light brown hair and welcoming chocolate eyes. Sam is always very much a gentleman to her and an easygoing, good-hearted boss toward his employees.

Sam was very helpful when she asked him about possibly redecorating her place. He had, on his own time, helped her with color schemes and taught her how to paint as well as gave pointers on the best way to make use of the space she has along with her current furniture to save money. He's even asked a few of his crew members to help her move the furniture around.

Memories of the morning after that night flash through her mind.

It's still hard for her to grasp the reality of what she went through and how much worse things could have been for her.

The first thing she should have done when she was finally sure that she was alone that morning was to pick up her phone and call the police. But she hadn't done that. In fact, she'd done quite the opposite. She'd gotten off the bed, wrapped the covers around herself, tiptoed to the bedroom door, and looked around her living room, which she found mostly still intact except for some trash and a few open doors and cabinets. She wasn't sure what she had expected to find.

Cole. Her inner-self answers her again now as it did that morning.

Cole. That's who she was looking for that morning. Like some sick form of Stockholm syndrome, she was hoping to find a man who had broken into her apartment to be sitting at the table sipping on coffee with breakfast already made for her.

What was wrong with her?

Face it, Frankie. You didn't call the cops because you wanted him.

Damn inner voice. But it's true.

Even after she finally was able to go through her home and found that not only was her laptop gone but some of her jewelry was missing too, she still didn't call the police to report anything.

"Where did you go?" she asks out loud and turns her head to the open bathroom door.

On the counter, where she left it, lies the only thing Cole left behind. The bandana he had used to blindfold her.

"Did you call for me? I didn't hear anything," Sam's voice comes from the doorway.

She didn't realize she'd spoken that out loud. She was so lost in thought and didn't even hear Sam coming up the stairs.

She sits up, turns around, and shakes her head. "Nope. Just talking to myself," she tells him.

Sam whistles loudly. "Wow! You did a great job here, Frankie!" He admires her handy paint job as he walks over to the wall for a closer look. "What do you think of the colors now?" he asks.

"I wasn't sure of a gray palette at first but you were right. It looks great and I love it," she answers proudly.

"This paint shouldn't take long to dry at all," Sam says.

"Well, I hope not. Hey, Sam. I'm gonna go grab some lunch. What about you? Wanna go grab a bite?" she asks.

"My treat," he says.

"No way! MY treat!" she declares. "I'll go grab my wallet and you can figure out where you wanna go," she says before walking back inside.

Sam.

She's fucking out with Sam again! This is the third picture she's posted with this guy in just as many days. This guy who came out of nowhere. Who walks in and out of her place at all hours of the day. Who shows up in her pictures smiling with hands on her. Who the fuck does he think he is?

"*I came first, Sam!*" he yells to no one.

"*Are you fucking this guy too, Frankie?*"

"*Fucking whore!*" he hisses before slamming the laptop shut.

- 10 -

cole

"Cole. Cole! Are you even listening?" Nick yells into the phone.

"Yeah. Sorry, people are walking by," he finally answers.

"Dusty doesn't need to be there but if you want him to be, you can call him yourself," Nick grumbles at him.

He hangs up the phone and shoves it into his pocket without saying goodbye. He continues to skim through the local newspaper, checking to see if anything they've done has caught any attention. The less attention the better.

He hasn't seen his brother in almost two weeks. When they arrive in a new city, they rarely stay together. It's easier for people to ignore one new guy walking around than it is a group of three new guys, one of whom definitely looks like a junkie. So they always make an agreement to stay in different motels without disclosing their chosen locations to one another. They keep in touch with burner phones that can be bought at the gas station and then tossed once they move on.

He'd opted to stay near Southeast Portland without his brother's knowledge.

Because of Frankie, he admits silently to himself while staring at the scenes in front of him.

In the park where he now sits, he's watched many scenes unfold.

He watched a couple jogging together, challenging each other. He saw a group of guys tossing a football around, horse playing as longtime friends should. He watched a family having a nice little picnic with their very young kids. And right now, off in the distance, he can see a man walking on the trail while tossing a ball for his dog to retrieve.

He wanted to do all of these things without having to always be looking over his shoulder for someone they may have jilted in the past. He wanted to be able to live a carefree life without the karma of his past catching up to him. And now he wants to be able to do all of these things with her. With Frankie.

Like a fucking obsession, she never left his thoughts after that night. He couldn't shake her if he tried. Many times, he's been tempted to go back to her place and see her but he had just enough self-discipline to talk himself out of it.

Is it possible to fall for someone after just fucking once? Except, it didn't feel like the usual fuck with Frankie. His head's all twisted up over her.

How would he face her? What would he have to say to her? Most of all, he's afraid. Afraid that if he sees her one more time, he won't be able to walk away from her again, and that could cost him everything he's worked too hard for.

Even if she can overlook his past and can get past how they met, what kind of life would he have to offer her? Moving from city to city, breaking and entering, stealing to survive until the next best thing comes along.

Frankie deserves the kind of life that he only wishes he can have. The kind of life that he's been watching these other people live.

He can't give that to her.

Frustrated, he lets out a loud grunt and stands up to walk away.

This is just crazy! Why is he having all these crazy thoughts, these crazy hopes and dreams about her, anyway? He doesn't know anything about Frankie. Well, except for her name and where she lives. He knows the softness of her skin, the invigorating smell of her hair, and the gentle strength she has in her. She trusted him that night when anyone else would not have.

He also knows how she feels against him.

How can he ever forget that?

And her eyes. His curiosity had gotten the best of him and he succumbed to finding her through social media posts for a glimpse of her eyes. Mesmerizing, round green eyes. Francine Hoang. *What a crazy and hypnotic mix of surprises you are.* A cocktail for disaster for the likes of him.

He looks down at his watch before starting the timer for his quick jog around the park. It's warm today with the sun shining brightly, bringing out more people to the park than any other day that he's been here previously. He normally doesn't like jogging while having to maneuver around so many people, but today he doesn't mind the distraction.

His mind wanders back to Frankie again.

He's been diligent about checking the local papers and online to see if there has been any news of her reporting the incident. So far, nothing. He isn't sure something like that would have been reported to the public even if she had.

He looks up just in time to avoid crashing into the two women running in his direction. As he passes them, he hears one whistle and the other one giggle. He shakes his head and smiles as he keeps on his trail.

Eleven minutes later, he's sitting on a bench, stopping the timer on his watch and catching his breath.

"Hey! Excuse me," an excited voice yells his way.

He looks up in the direction of the voice to see a pretty blonde jogging over to him. She pulls off her earbuds as she approaches him.

"Hi. I'm Melissa," she says as she comes to a stop in front of him, hand out, ready for a handshake.

"Hi," he answers as he stands up, purposely not introducing himself.

She's a lot taller than Frankie. *Christ, are you comparing everyone to Frankie now?* He shakes her hand and she holds on a little longer than necessary.

She's definitely pretty, the type he used to have no problem inviting back to his bed for some play. Her dark blonde hair is perfectly tied into a ponytail. Blue eyes set perfectly on her porcelain pale skin. Her body is what you would call "in shape" and she knows exactly how to pose herself for the attention she seeks.

"Are you new around here?" she asks as he takes his hand back.

"Just passing through, ma'am," he answers her.

"Ma'am? Makes me sound so old," she says, giggling. "Call me Melissa, would ya? So, what and when can I call you?" she asks.

"Cole," he finally answers nonchalantly.

She's clearly used to getting her way, so he obliges, hoping she will be appeased enough to not ask for his last name, birthdate, or family history.

"Not one for chitchat, are you?" She smirks. "Do you have any plans for tonight, *Cole*?" Before he can say anything, she continues, "A friend of mine is having a gathering at a bar not far from here. Want to come for a few drinks?"

Before he answers, she reaches for his hand and pulls a pen out of thin air. As she scribbles on his palm, she continues chattering without missing a beat.

"The Bronze Gastropub at seven o'clock. See ya there," she says before winking at him and walking away, making sure her "asset" is on perfect display to catch a few catcalls and whistles.

"You look great already but I wouldn't mind if you cleaned up just a little bit!" she turns to yell back at him and waves.

He isn't sure if this is who she is daily or if she's just looking for someone to keep her bed warm for the night. Strangely, he doesn't feel any sexual attraction toward her. And she's definitely what he normally wouldn't mind spending an hour or two fucking.

Until Frankie.

Fuck!

Maybe Melissa is what his cock needs to get his head straight and shake *whatever* this bullshit is.

He looks down at his watch. It's almost two o'clock already. He decides to head back to his motel room to wash up and start making his way to meet with Nick.

- 11 -

cole

"Hey, baby brother," Nick says as he slides into the booth. "I don't know how you can find your way around new places so quickly," Nick gripes, sounding sober yet frustrated.

Nick waves over the waiter. "I'm starving. You order anything yet?" his brother asks.

"I ordered. The place is pretty busy. Didn't want to wait too long," he answers as he watches his brother settle in.

He notices Nick's outfit. Clean and ironed gray t-shirt, clean jeans, new boots, clean-shaven, and a fresh haircut. *This is different.*

"So, what's up?" he asks.

"I talked to Elliott last night. Not much more and not much longer before we're done," Nick says, taking a quick drink before placing his order with the waiter who finally comes over.

Once the guy is out of earshot, Nick continues. "I sent over another payment this morning. Are you still good?"

"Yeah, I'm good," he answers.

Nick is referring to money. He never really spent much of anything that he made. Other than a place to sleep and a meal or two a day, there isn't room for much else for a nomad like him. He had to pack light and exit quick, so it's just more convenient to not buy much of anything.

"Medium rare, New York, with twice-baked potatoes and broccoli," the waiter announces as he slides his dinner plate onto the table. He tops off the glasses of water before heading off to the next table.

"Steak? I guess you are doing good!" Nick teases.

"Look who's talking," he retorts as his knife makes a cut into the steak. "What's with the new look?" he asks, waving his fork at his brother before stabbing his steak with it.

"I don't know, man. I got bored. Quit the bottle weeks now and doing that gym thing you kids been doing. I just feel better. That's all," Nick says.

He gives his brother a blank stare before shoving a piece of steak into his mouth.

Good. Nick's drinking was getting to be a problem. He wonders why the sudden change in his brother but doesn't want to push the subject, since Nick is obviously trying not to make a big deal of it.

"Here's your Chicken Milanese, sir. Would you like more grated parmesan on top?" the waiter asks once he returns.

Nick shakes his head and waves him off with a "No, thank you," before sinking his fork into the chicken.

Manners? What's going on here?

First, Nick picks this nice restaurant, not some sandwich shop like usual but a nice actual restaurant. Then he shows up like this new person, talking about not drinking and going to a gym. And now he's even thanked the waiter.

Nick notices him staring. "What?" his brother asks with a smirk before forking a piece of chicken into his mouth.

He holds both of his hands up in surrender. Hey, if positive change is what Nick is doing for himself, why question that?

They finish their meals quickly and silently. At least that hasn't changed.

After the waiter clears their table and fills his coffee cup, Nick leans back into the booth and exhales. He looks out the window into the bustling sidewalk before starting the conversation they've held off for too long.

"Dusty. You heard from him?" Nick asks, not meeting eyes with him.

He takes a sip of his coffee, placing his elbows on the table, before answering with the same lackluster tone. "Not for about a week now. He hasn't called. I checked around locally and he hasn't been picked up."

"Maybe it's time, Cole," Nick says with resignation.

"Maybe," he responds dispiritedly before sipping more coffee.

It's time to have that talk with Dusty about them parting ways. He feels sympathy for the guy but right now, his troubles are more than they can help him with. He's in too deep and they are too close to what they've been working so long to get.

"Let's try to get ahold of him and get it done soon," Nick says quietly before sliding out of the booth.

He nods his head in silent agreement as he watches his brother exit the restaurant and disappear into the crowd.

He stops and looks through the huge window from a distance, wanting to check out the scene first.

He can see Melissa with her crowd of friends. They seem loud, and not from cheering for the game on the screen.

He decides to turn and walk the other way. He isn't in the mood for that kind of crowd. He's looking for something else. He doesn't know what it is, but it isn't that.

Hands in his pockets, he crosses the street and continues heading in the direction he originally was heading, not exactly sure where he's going.

Lost in thought, he almost walks into a door that swings open. He catches it and lets a couple come through as they pass him to turn into the alley.

He looks up at the sign. *Vinny's Place.*

"Vinny's it is," he says to himself before walking in.

He takes a quick look around inside. This is definitely more of what he's used to. It looks like a busy night but it isn't crowded and it isn't full of rowdy drunks. All the seats at the bar are taken by patrons watching the game. A few of the booths are filled as well.

He stalks toward the back of the place, where it's quieter with smaller tables. He chooses one close to the corner and sits down. There are a few college kids throwing darts and they all give him a quick nod of acknowledgment.

He surveys the place as he waits for one of the waitresses to stop by his table. One has already seen him sitting down and gives him a wink to let him know she'll be over soon.

Almost everyone inside seems comfortable with one another. He sees one older gentleman standing behind the bar, talking to a couple. There is a younger guy, also behind the bar, who is cheerfully taking orders and filling cups. Over to one corner of the place, he notices an area that is sectioned off with a big "Reserved" sign.

"Hey, doll, what can I get for you?" the waitress asks once she gets to him.

"Is this place about to be packed?" he asks, nodding his head in the direction of the empty space.

"Nah. That space is reserved for a later time. At least a few more hours from now," she answers.

"In that case, can you bring me a pitcher of your best ale, please?"

"One glass or someone joining you?" she asks.

He holds up one finger and she nods her head before heading to the bar.

"Refill on the pitcher?" the waitress asks yet again.

"No thanks. I'll take a bottle though. I see people are starting to fill up. My cue to get out of here," he says, smiling back.

"Oh, that? It's a birthday party for a friend. The owner helped put it together. He's right over there." She points to the old gentleman standing behind the bar.

The man waves at them with a smile.

"There shouldn't be too many more showing up. You should stay a bit," she says before walking away.

He watches as three people enter the establishment and head to the zoned off area with balloons and a cake to join the growing number of people already there. The section is getting packed. People have steadily come into the place since he's been sitting here. It's a nice crowd. Good music and friendly service. He can see why people would come back here.

"Here ya go. On the house," the waitress says as she slides two bottles on the table to him.

He looks up to see the owner smiling and waving at him. He holds one bottle up in gratitude before taking a swig.

He looks over to the section with the "Happy 29th Birthday" banner and balloons floating above. Everyone seems fucking happy. He wonders who the birthday person is and thinks about what it would feel like if he had a celebration like that.

Ten minutes pass as he continues drinking his beer, tapping his foot to the music, and actually enjoying everything going on around him.

The lights in the party section get dimmer a few minutes later, but the music seems to have gotten louder. He doesn't pay it any more attention. He leans back in his chair and pulls out his phone.

Absentmindedly, he opens the Gallery section and taps on the only Album. He opens the only picture inside. It's a picture of Frankie. A picture of her that he saved from one of her social media posts. She's sitting on a park bench with the sun shining down, creating a halo-like effect above her. She's smiling ear to ear. A beautiful and genuine smile with those captivating eyes.

Lost in thought and lost in her beauty, his thoughts are interrupted when the music suddenly cuts out and the crowd of people is screaming, "SURPRISE! HAPPY BIRTHDAY, FRANKIE!"

- 12 -

"What the..." is all she can say as she is ambushed with a barrage of bells ringing, people whistling, and friends cheering.

Both hands come up to her cheek as she looks around to see Alice, Chef Katrina, Vince, and other friends and co-workers, all here surprising her for her birthday. Her birthday isn't until tomorrow and she did not expect anything like this at all.

"Gotcha!" her best friend, Alice, says as she steps forward to embrace her.

"How? How did you guys even do all of this?" she asks as she is ushered into the crowd of friends.

"Vince and Alice are the masterminds," Sam explains from next to her. "And Alice there had the guts to ask your boss to partake," he finishes while handing her a glass of champagne.

She reaches Vince in the middle of the crowd and gives him the biggest and warmest embrace she's able to muster up.

"So, you're saying there's no emergency?" she asks since that was the excuse he used to get her to come here less than ten minutes ago.

He shakes his head and laughs.

"In that case, I'm out of here!" she jokingly says, heading to the door.

"Hey! Hey, kid!" he exclaims while yanking her back into the crowd. "You only turn twenty-nine once, right? Next year you're gonna be an old maid so we had to do this now while you still have the energy." Vince lets out a hearty laugh. "Drink up, kid! You're at a party!" he says as he pushes her champagne glass to her mouth.

"Everyone, let's show this kid a good time, huh! Aye, Donnie! Turn the music back on!" he yells over to the counter.

"Sam! How long did you know about this?" she scolds him as he walks back to her.

"Alice told me about it last week when she came over to your place," he says, smiling.

Still, in disbelief, she goes from friend to friend giving hugs, air kisses, and thanks. After some time, tons of picture taking, a few champagne glasses, and four shots later, she's feeling the effects of the drinks and the music.

"Karmen!" she screeches at the sight of her other best friend.

"Happiest of birthdays, doll," Karmen exclaims as they exchange hugs and kisses.

"I'm so mad at you! Why didn't you tell me about this?"

"It wouldn't have been a surprise if I did," Karmen replies with extra sass. "It's a busy house tonight, but a guy over there sent you a birthday shot." Karmen hands her the drink and points over to the corner by the darts.

"What is it?" she asks, looking into the glass. "Is it safe?"

"Oh, Frankie," Karmen says, smacking her lips. "Donnie made it per the guy's order. A Pineapple Upside Down shot. Fitting for a birthday drink, don't you think?" she says before bouncing away.

"There you are," comes Alice's voice before she can try the drink.

"Hold this for me." She hands Alice the drink as she shrugs out of her jacket. She's starting to sweat with all the drinks and the crowd. Alice takes the jacket from her and hands her drink back.

"That smells freaking awesome. What is it?" Alice asks.

"A Pineapple Upside Down shot someone ordered for me," she answers, looking into the direction that Karmen pointed to earlier.

"Hey, kid, you have a drink! Perfect!" Vince's booming voice comes from behind her.

"Speech! Speech! Speech!" her guests chant and cheer.

"Donnie, let's turn off the music a second," Vince screams over the counter.

Donnie complies and the crowd begins to quiet down some. Vince puts one arm around her shoulders and gives her a quick peck on the top of her head before looking into the crowd.

"Hey, everyone. Give an old man a second to say something, all right!" Vince yells into the crowd.

Everyone quiets down some more as he pulls her to stand next to him.

"Some of you may not know this," Vince continues. "But five years ago, this wonderful establishment that you're standing in almost closed its doors permanently. Years of serving and drinking with you fine people finally caught up to me and you guessed it! The IRS came knocking!"

A round of laughter erupts.

"I bet they didn't expect for five feet of a ferocious fireball known as Frankie to answer the door that day!" Vince shouts amidst the laughter and whistling.

"Frankie. There were times when I didn't know how I was gonna pay you. There were times when I couldn't pay you but you stuck with this old man anyway. I never regretted letting you walk through the doors on that Sunday morning and letting me know you were my new employee." Vince is getting choked up and it makes her get teary as she smiles back at him. He turns back to the crowd, beer held high.

"The best beers you all are guzzling down and the best sandwiches this side of Portland are all due to this kid right here," he says, squeezing her shoulder as she leans her head on his. "Frankie, the man upstairs hadn't blessed me with a brat of my own but he did send me an angel," Vince says loudly. "Happy birthday, kid! To Frankie! Salud!" he shouts as he drinks his beer.

"Thank you, everyone!" she yells over the cheering and clapping.

She holds her drink up before downing the shot and wiping her mouth with the back of her hand.

"Damn! *THAT* is good!" she yells as her friends burst into laughter and howls.

She looks amazing tonight. He just can't stop looking at her picture. Too bad fucking Sam is here too. But his chance will come soon. Tonight will be perfect.

He turns his phone off and takes another drag of his cigarette. Tonight, Frankie. All these motherfuckers will know who you really belong to.

- 13 -

cole

One minute he's staring at her picture on his phone and the next minute her name is being screamed throughout the bar. He still can't wrap his head around what's happening. He should have left as soon as he realized what was going on but he didn't. Instead, he stayed planted in the chair in the dark corner and watched her.

For weeks, he's wanted to see her again. To touch her soft skin and fill his lungs with her amazing scent. Seeing her standing here, having a good time, is beyond unbelievable. It takes all he has in him plus a couple of shots to keep him in that corner and not walk up and wrap his arms possessively around her.

From his seat, he's able to get a nice view of her and who she speaks with. He saw a guy walk up and hug her from behind but she removed herself quickly. Is that her boyfriend? Her husband? There are at least two other guys who are always hovering close by. Is she seeing one of those guys? He doesn't know and can't tell.

"Like it matters anyway," he says out loud to himself.

He can't approach her. He can't risk her remembering him. What if she screams bloody murder right then and there? And if she doesn't recognize him, that might hurt just as much.

Fucking hell.

He finishes another bottle.

He isn't sure how long he sits and watches her. He isn't complaining. He can watch her all night long. He sees her taking a few drinks as well as putting some down when no one is looking.

He volleys his bottle from one hand to the other as he watches Frankie dance with her girlfriends to some pop tune. She laughs and tosses her hair around jokingly. She stumbles back a few steps before one of the girls catches her by the hand and they all burst into laughter.

The song ends and a slower tempo country tune plays immediately replaces it. She's walking to the bar when a guy hugs her from behind, grabs her hand, and spins her quickly around.

He stops volleying his beer and leans forward to watch.

The dirtbag is holding her close to him. Too close. The guy leans down closer to her ear to whisper something. Frankie shakes her head to whatever it is he says. She attempts to put some space between them by putting her arms up as a barrier. Instead of taking the hint, the drunk bastard wraps his arms tighter, lifts her up off of her feet, and spins her across the room before they stop a couple table lengths from where he sits.

Hand wrapping tightly around his beer bottle, he nearly walks over but sees from the corner of his eye, another of Frankie's possible admirers quickly coming over to separate the guy's arms from around her.

"Hey, I think maybe you need to go sit down, Footloose," he hears the new guy say to the dirtbag.

Dirtbag puts his hands up and walks back to the crowd.

"Thanks, Sam," she says. She sways to the side and holds on to the back of a chair. "The rooms still spinning," she says to the Sam guy.

"Yeah, take a seat. I'll go get you some water," Sam says, holding a chair out for her.

"I think I'll go to the ladies' room and take a breather," Frankie says as she takes a step to pass the chair that is offered.

"I'll send one of your friends to check on you," Sam says after her.

She responds by giving him a thumbs-up without looking back.

He watches as she walks slowly toward him. Of course, of all the tables available, he *had* to pick the one by the restrooms. He shrinks back into his seat, hoping she doesn't notice him. He bends his head slightly to avoid eye contact. Just a few more steps and she'll be past his table now.

A few more steps.

*And...*of course, just like every other curveball he's been thrown when it comes to Frankie, the college boys who've been having a friendly game of darts this whole fucking night pick *that* very moment to start pushing and shoving. One hard shove and a second later, one of them stumbles right into her, causing her to topple sideways.

She slams her palms onto his tabletop to brace herself from falling.

Instinctively, he reaches out and grabs her wrist to help her steady herself.

The look on his face tells the frats to get his friend off of her and to do it fucking quick.

One of them tugs his buddy up and he turns around to profusely apologize as another one helps her sit down. Another one runs to the bar.

The music must have been too loud for any of her friends to hear because no one from her group comes over to help her. Which is fine. This is the wrong time for a bunch of people to be crowding around his table.

He looks down at his grip around her wrist and slowly unwraps his fingers. He sees the piece of cloth that is underneath. Black bandana. Is it...*his*? It can't be. Hundreds of black bandanas are sold daily so it can't be the same one. *No way.*

"Thank you. Do you mind if I just sit here for a second?" she asks him as she tilts her head back, eyes closed.

"No," he stammers. Afraid she'll remember his voice, afraid she will look up and recognize him even though she was blindfolded that night.

"Thank you for that drink earlier too," she says, eyes still closed.

"Uh-huh. Happy birthday," he says. *She knew.*

He wanted to punch himself. Their first real conversation after wanting this moment to happen for three weeks and he sounds like a complete imbecile. Thankfully, one of the boys runs over with a bottle of water for her and another beer for him.

"We are so sorry," Frat Boy apologizes to Frankie.

"I'm okay. We're okay, right?" she asks as she turns and looks at him for the first time.

He shrinks into the seat a little as the kid backs away from their table.

"Have we met before?" she now asks him, brows furrowing. "You seem...familiar."

"Don't believe so," he answers, hoping the volume of the music helps mask his voice.

"Yeah. I'd definitely remember if I ever met someone as hot as you. Maybe I've had too much to drink," she says before giving him the most radiant smile he's been blessed to ever receive.

If melting into a chair is possible, all two hundred and fifty pounds of him might be a puddle at that moment.

- 14 -

cole

"Hi, everyone calls me Frankie," she says with a smile and a hand outstretched for a shake and proper introduction.

"Pleasure meeting you," he says, shaking her hand, holding on a few seconds longer than proper and deliberately not giving his name.

Thankfully, she lets it slide and doesn't ask.

"Can you tell me what time it is?" She nods toward the watch on his arm. "I don't know where I left my phone."

"Yeah. It's a quarter ta two," he replies.

"Oh shit!" she exclaims. "I have to work tomorrow!"

"No, you don't. You have the day off," an older lady says from behind her.

"Chef, I'm scheduled for lunch service and dinner prep," Frankie says as she fails in an attempt to stand up.

"I'm your boss and I say you have the day off, Frankie. And when I give an order, what is the proper response?"

"Yes, Chef!" Frankie responds with a smile. "Thank you. Are you heading out?"

"Yes. I'm getting too old for these kinds of festivities," the woman says, stifling a yawn with the tips of her fingers.

"Please drive carefully. Oscar, make sure she gets home safe?" Frankie speaks to the gentleman standing patiently behind the chef.

Oscar nods to her with a smile as he guides the woman to the doorway.

"So, you've met my boss," Frankie says, turning back to look at him. She rolls her eyes upward and giggles. "I swear she really isn't as...*stiff*...as she presents herself to be."

"So, you work *in a restaurant*?" he asks with a chuckle, relaxing a little.

Frankie stands up, bends one hand behind her back and the other in front, before slightly bowing.

"*Oui*," she says in a silly French accent. "You're looking at the chef de partie of Katrina's Bistro." She quickly sits back down in her seat. "Don't worry. It's just a fancy name for a line cook," she laughs.

What a fucking obnoxiously beautiful sound, he thinks to himself. He must be smiling like a kid in a candy shop but he doesn't give a rat's ass. He's loving every second of this, something he didn't think could or would happen between him and her. But here she is, sitting in front of him with her long dark hair and luminous green eyes in a beautiful dress.

"Feeling better?" he asks to break the silence.

"Well, the room isn't spinning as fast as it was anymore. Thank you for letting me sit here. I didn't mean to invade your space."

"Pleasure's mine," he says before taking a drink of his own beer.

"Would you like another one?" she asks, pointing to his empty bottle.

He shakes his head as a group of her friends approach their table.

"Hey, Frankie, we gotta head out now. *Some* of us have work tomorrow," one of them says, poking her back. Another kisses the top of her head.

Frankie stands up unsteadily to give each of them hugs and thanks for coming. They all wave at him before walking away.

The place has emptied out by more than half the crowd present earlier. Probably because the sign out front says the place closes at three a.m. The college boys look like they are getting ready to head out also.

Sam, that's his name, stands next to their table now.

"Frankie, I'm gonna head out too. Alice disappeared. You want me to drop you off on the way? I don't think you should be driving," Sam says.

He looks at the placing of Sam's hand on her shoulder. His jaw clenches at the sight but he keeps it together.

Sam looks at him, eye to eye. Both men determined to not lose the staring contest between them.

"Go, Sam. Don't worry about me. I still have time to clear the fuzzies," Frankie says. "Besides, I'm having a great chat with my guy here." She waves her hand toward him.

My guy? He can deal with that.

"You sure?" Sam asks, still not looking away.

He wants to stand up and knock the look off of the guy's smug face but that probably won't make the best impression. What he wants with Frankie is impossible but he doesn't need to make an ass out of himself for her to see either. He isn't inclined to stand up and make manly introductions with this guy anyway.

"Yes!" She stands up and shoves at Sam. "Vince is still here. Go! You have a far drive, so get there safe, all right?"

"Sorry, I didn't catch your name," Sam says and moves around her to stand directly in front of him with his hand out for a shake.

"I didn't throw it," he retorts.

Frankie looks at him before she grabs Sam's hand and pulls him back.

"Go already!" she says with a final shove and a loud laugh.

Jaws clenching even tighter, he watches Sam turn and head to the exit. He returns his eyes to Frankie, who mouths the word "sorry." He smiles at her and shrugs. He isn't sure how to start the conversation again but luckily, he sees the waitress heading over to their table.

"Aren't you glad you stayed?" she asks. She picks up his bottle and shakes it before putting it on her tray. She lifts two mugs off the tray and places them in the middle of the table, followed by a carafe of coffee and walks to the next empty table to begin clearing and cleaning it.

"So, why's a guy of your...*caliber*...in a bar, alone, tonight?" she asks, starting the conversation again.

By now, he's accustomed to and frankly bored, with the women who haven't been subtle with their compliments and their innuendos. *This* coming from *her* is different.

"A guy of my caliber?" he asks. Fuck! When was the last time he's blushed? High school?

"I'm sure you own a mirror or maybe walked past one a time or two," she teases him with that captivating smile and those amazing, dazzling green eyes. Pulling him in without even touching him.

"Let me pour that," he says, shifting the focus. "I don't trust your unsteady hands," he jokes.

- 15 -

cole

Who would have thought the two of them would be sitting here having coffee? She'd probably dial 911 quick if she figured out who he really is.

The waitress walks by again and slides a bowl of cream and sugar on their table without stopping.

"Thank you. Cream and sugar?" Frankie asks him.

"Nah. I like mine dark," he says. "How about you?"

"Well, normally, I do both. But right now, dark might be what I need," she answers before taking a sip.

Music is playing softly now. Only three patrons are left sitting at the bar and a couple of tables remain occupied. The bartender is wiping down the counter and restocking drinks. Vince, the owner, is walking in and out of the double doors behind the bar.

"Do you live around here?" she asks him.

"Not really. I'm just passing through," he answers.

Not this shit. He's hoping there won't be a Q&A session about himself. He doesn't want to lie to her.

"So where are you from then? Are you sure we haven't run into each other before? You really seem familiar."

Maybe the coffee is clearing her mind a little too fast, he thinks.

"I'm pretty sure I would *definitely* remember running into someone so beautiful," he answers one question, avoiding the other altogether. It isn't a complete lie. She's the one who ran into *him* that night.

She rolls her eyes at his compliment.

"I love this song," she says as she sits her chin above her hands with elbows resting on the table as she enjoys Madonna's "Crazy for You." If anyone asks how he knew the song, Vision Quest was a fucking awesome movie. He'd dick punch anyone that disagreed.

"Dance with me," she says, surprising him.

"I have two left feet so I don't think that's a good idea," he says, trying to save himself.

"Oh, come on! You're not much of a talker. There aren't many people here to see your *two left feet* and it's really my birthday now so..." and before she finishes, she's standing up and tugging on his hand.

Feeling defeated and wanting to make her happy, he stands up. Not wanting to overcrowd her space, he doesn't take another step.

"Holy cow! You're like a whole oak tree taller than me!"

"I don't mind sitting back down," he says and tries to sit.

"No way!" she says as she tries to pull him closer.

Knowing it's useless for her to try and move him, he concedes. A few steps with her hand in his, he lifts it to spin her slowly. The contrast in their size probably attracts what's left of the bar patrons. He can feel eyes looking at the two of them.

Frankie takes a step closer and he looks down at her, but not before he catches the old man behind the bar reaching up to turn up the volume a slight notch.

He's never considered himself to be a romantic guy. Far from, actually. The last real relationship he had was ten years ago. That probably ended long before the night he even decided to hit the road. But this moment is probably one for a chick flick. He's okay with that.

"You're not so bad," she says, looking up at him.

He's careful not to step on her small feet and makes sure there's a decent gap between them. "Just following your lead, little lady," he says, smiling down on her.

"So where are you staying?"

"Not too far from here," he says. Short and simple.

"*Okay?* Where are you from?"

"Montana originally," he says. That isn't a lie.

"I'm originally from Tucson," she says. "Ever been there?"

"I've passed through there. A lot different than it is here," he answers.

"What brought you in here?" she asks, looking around.

"Just out for a walk and somehow ended up here. Nice place," he answers.

He checks and sees that they are the only two left on the floor other than the one guy sitting at the bar. "They're going to kick us out soon," he mumbles.

"Are you trying to get rid of me?" she asks with a feigned look of hurt.

"No way!" he says, pulling her a little closer. This night would end on the perfect note if he can just wrap his arms around her and appease his lips with the feel of hers, right here and now.

They continue dancing to the slow tune though. He can feel her body ever so close to his, her energy pulling him in with each passing second. Then...he can feel someone else standing next to them.

It's the goddamn bartender.

What a way to ruin the fucking moment. He wanted to shove the guy into the next dimension. Maybe further.

"Hey, Frankie, we're about to call it a night. But before that, will you do me the honor?" Bartender Jjerk asks, bowing politely.

Frankie looks at the guy and smiles. She looks back at him and asks, "May I?"

He doesn't answer. He doesn't want to answer. But he puts the few steps in between them and passes her hand over to the guy.

"Thanks for all your help, Donnie," she says as he stalks back to his seat to retrieve his jacket so he can make his exit. As he reaches the table, the owner walks out of the restroom.

"Hey there, young man!" he says, reaching for his hand. "I'm Vince. She's beautiful, isn't she?" the man asks, nodding over to where Frankie and the creepy bartender guy are dancing.

"Can't argue that," he replies, again avoiding the proper introduction.

"She's special, that one. You don't find many like her. If only I were a decade or three younger," Vince says with a chuckle. "Let me go make sure she gets home safe tonight. How about you? Need me to call you a cab?" he asks.

"I can manage, sir. Thank you."

"Come back anytime, all right?" Vince says.

He isn't sure if the song ended or if the waitress turned it off. He can hear Frankie laughing at something the bartender must have said. Vince's jolly laughter follows while giving Frankie another paternal-like embrace as the bartender walks back behind the bar to flip off some of the lights.

He puts on his jacket and heads toward the exit.

Frankie rushes over to him before he makes his escape though. "You know it's rude to leave without saying goodbye," she chides him.

"I didn't want to interrupt," he murmurs.

"In a rush to get back to the wife and kids?" she teases.

"Yeah. I have one needing diapers and that was four hours ago."

She gawks at him blankly.

"Kidding!"

And there it is, that beautiful smile again.

"Do you need a ride to wherever you're going? My car is just parked right in the alley here. It's no trouble."

"Are you sure you should be driving?"

"Probably not." She smiles. "I'm hoping some fresh cold air can help me. I'm only a few minutes from here."

He didn't realize they were so close to her place.

"So do you need help getting home?" she asks him again.

"No. I'm good. I'm more concerned about you."

They absentmindedly start walking together to the door. He opens it for her and they're both blasted by the rush of cold air.

"Frankie! Your stuff." The waitress runs out after them and hands the jacket and clutch over. She gives Frankie a quick kiss on the cheek and waves her farewell.

"Let me help you with that," he says as he takes her jacket and helps her into it, again noticing the black cloth she still has tied around her wrist.

She touches it lightly once she gets her arm through the sleeve. "Oh, thanks." She fumbles around the pockets to find her keys.

"I really don't think you're in any condition to drive. Can I get you a cab?"

"You're probably right. I can walk from here though. It's less than ten minutes to my front door."

"Okay, not to sound like a chauvinist, but that's not much safer than you driving," he says with a grin.

She gives him a soft punch to the gut and he jokingly bends over as if the air was knocked out of him.

"Okay, okay. You can take care of yourself!" he says as she tries to keep from laughing.

"Well, I'm walking in this direction," she says, pointing her thumb behind her.

"I'm going that way." He stands up and points behind him. Of course, they'd be moving in opposite directions. Why would that be a surprise?

They stand awkwardly in silence for who knows how long because he just couldn't get his big feet to move away from her.

He holds his hand out. "It's nice meeting you. I really had a great night."

"Maybe we can do it *again* sometime?" she asks softly, shaking his hand.

They both hold on a little longer before he doesn't fight it anymore. He pulls her into his arms. It's what he's been wanting to do all night. He bends down and smells her hair. *Intoxicating.* Familiar. Just how he remembers.

"You don't think I was really going to let you walk home alone, did you?" he asks her.

Her body shakes against his with laughter. She pushes herself off of his chest but not out of his arms which is a good thing. He wasn't sure if he could let her go just yet.

"And I'm supposed to let a stranger walk me home? I don't even know your name!" she exclaims, looking up at him.

They stand in front of Vinny's Place for what feels like the perfect amount of forever. Unable to resist the urge any longer, he bends his head lower and closes the distance between their lips.

Her lips are just as perfect as he remembers. They move against his own, inviting him. Her hands rest against his chest for balance. He's getting lost in her just as quick as he did the first time and any time they've kissed after that.

For that moment, he doesn't care how they met or where they currently are. It's just him and Frankie.

"COLE! Hey, Cole!"

The moment instantly gone, he snaps his head up.

Fuck.

He watches as Melissa runs across the street toward them.

- 16 -

Frankie

She's wanted to kiss this stranger since their dance inside. Something about him pulls at her. His energy is comforting and familiar. Being so close to him sent her senses in hyperdrive over the edge. She'd wanted so much to place her head on his chest and hear his heartbeat, to let its rhythm lull her for comfort but he seemed to always keep her at arm's length. Not just literally.

When he finally pulled her into his arms, she's hoping and ready for more.

She throws reason out the window the moment he put his lips on hers. Standing there in his arms, her lips making her invitation obvious, she doesn't care about anything that's fuzzy in her head or everything that's fading in the background around them. It's pure freaking insanity.

The moment his lips touch hers, all is lost. Lost in the best way possible. Lost just like she'd been with—

"*Cole!*"

And just like that, the moment disappears.

"Hey, Cole!"

She thought she'd said his name in her head, but no. Someone is calling *her* stranger by *that* name. The butterflies that were fluttering in her stomach just seconds earlier are now cinder blocks settling in her stomach.

She looks up at his face, deep into his gorgeous blue eyes. "*Cole?*" she whispers.

Seeing the expression on his gorgeous face confirms who he is.

The whole night, she felt how *familiar* he was, but she let it slide because she was so intent on forgetting everything about him and that night. She thought she would never see or hear from him again. *Why?*

Because he's a stranger who broke into her home in the middle of the night with two other men who wanted to take turns raping her.

Yet...she'd—she'd yield to him. Given herself freely. Oh, fucking shit!

She tries to shove him off of her but he locks his arms, preventing her escape.

"Hey, handsome. Where were you? We were just down the street," the woman says, pointing somewhere.

Who the fuck is she? How do they know each other? He said he was taking a walk and ended up at Vinny's but it sounded like she'd been expecting him.

"You could have brought your *friend* too, ya know. I don't mind the competition," the woman keeps yapping on, clearly not caring about her presence.

Her head is pounding now. She isn't sure if it's from the alcohol or from the shock of him standing here. The shock of him being here with her for the past few hours.

Again, she tries to shove him off of her. She needed some air, some space between them. Everything is spinning. And this woman standing next to her just won't stop talking.

Shut up. Shut up!

She stumbles forward into him.

"Melissa, we really have to get going," she hears him tell the woman.

"Oh, okay," Melissa says, giving her an ice-cold look. "I'll catch you in the morning for a jog then." Melissa tries to give Cole a kiss then but he turns his head. The woman looks down her nose and walks away, ass swaying like a cat in heat.

Once Melissa is a good distance away, she looks up at Cole. His face becomes a blur and the ground seems to fade away from beneath her for a few seconds. He tightens his arms around her to keep her from falling.

She rests her forehead on him for a few seconds to regain her composure.

"Woah. I got you," he says.

You got me? she screams silently.

With every ounce of will that she has left in her small body, she gives him another shove. He unlocks his arms from around her unexpectedly and she stumbles back a few steps, almost falling right off the sidewalk.

"Frankie, are you okay?" he asks her as he attempts to close the gap between them again.

She holds her hands up to stop him.

"Am I okay, *Cole*?" she hisses, deliberately enunciating each word as intensely as if she were throwing daggers at him.

She backs up a few more steps away from him, into the opening of the alley. "Did you follow me? Have you been following me?"

"No," he says, shaking his head. "I didn't even think I was going to see you again."

"You knew who I was the moment I walked in there and you said *nothing*. We had a whole conversation, Cole! We danced. We had coffee. And the whole time you deliberately didn't tell me your name!"

"What was I supposed to say?"

"Oh, I don't know...how about a 'hey, I'm Cole,'" she answers sarcastically.

"I was afraid, Frankie. What if you—"

"What if I freaked out and called the cops on you in a bar full of my friends?" she cuts him off with the same sarcasm.

"Yes!" His answer booms over her while he rakes his hands through his *blond* hair. "I just didn't know what to say, Frankie. I didn't know what to do. I'm sorry," he says in a softer tone.

He's right, of course, she admits. What could he say with the circumstances of their first meeting? After all the days and nights of wondering about this man standing before her, she never thought about what they would say to each other.

Frustrated with what the night has turned into, she quickly closes the few steps between them and shoves him before turning down the alley toward her car.

"Where are you going?"

"Home!" she yells.

"I thought it's that way."

She stomps back out of the alley past him. She's so pissed that she doesn't hear him walking up behind her to snatch the keys from her hands.

"I still don't think you should be driving," he says with concern.

"Ugh!!!" she growls.

She's so angry. But she isn't sure what she's really angry about. How is someone supposed to react in a situation like this? *Normal people would probably call the cops, Frankie.*

Her throbbing head isn't helping her think clearly. She just needs to get home. She wraps her arms around herself to stop shaking. She isn't even sure if she is shaking from anger or if her body is cold. She doesn't seem to know anything at the moment.

She walks a block when she feels a jacket being wrapped around her. She looks up at him.

"I just need to make sure you get home. I need to know you're safe," he says tenderly.

Safe? Suddenly she remembers Dusty.

She frantically looks around and stumbles.

Cole catches her before she falls and she holds onto his arms.

"Is Dusty and—"

"No. It's just me," he answers before she finishes.

He pulls her close to his side and steers her, never letting his arm drop from her shoulder. She feels safe next to him, bizarre as it may seem. Just like she felt safe that night.

They walk in silence, her still leaning on him, for another block.

"Francine Hoang. Is that from being married?" he asks.

"No," she answers curtly.

"You don't look like a 'Hoang,'" he murmurs.

She looks up to see how much farther they have to go. *Does he really want to talk about this now?*

"My dad is part Vietnamese. It's his family name," she says with a little less anger. "My mother is Irish. Guess her genes were the more dominant one."

He remains silent.

"Is Cole even your real name?" she snarks.

"Yeah." He stops suddenly and releases his grip from her arm. He turns to face her. Looking at him, she can see he's struggling for the right words.

"Frankie, I really am sorry," he says, hands in his pocket.

"For not telling me the truth or for breaking into my apartment?" she asks, sounding cold as steel. More so than she intended.

"Nothing went the way it was supposed to *that* night. It was never my intention to—"

"Break into my apartment," she finishes for him. "What *were* your intentions then?"

"We just needed a place to duck into. Look, I really am sorry about everything that happened. If there were a way for me to change things, believe me. I would."

"Do you make it a habit of breaking into apartments and seducing whoever you find sleeping inside?"

"Shit! NO!" His voice rises. "I was just trying to buy us...buy you...some time. I thought that they'd just leave if I stalled long enough. You were...*are*...just so beautiful and I got caught up in you. I just..." He doesn't finish. "Then tonight, one minute I was thinking about you, and the next minute you were there. I should have left but I couldn't. I just wanted to watch you. To see you."

Her anger subsides a fraction at his sincerity. She's mad at the situation more than she is mad at him. There's so much she doesn't understand and her pounding head isn't making it easy to do that.

Both hands pressing against her throbbing temples, she shakes her head to try and clear it. The action only makes the gongs sound off louder inside. She looks up at him in defeat.

"That night, you asked me to trust you. And I did, Cole. Couldn't you have put some of that same blind faith in me tonight?"

She can see he doesn't have an answer for her. She isn't going to wait for one. Whatever answer he gives isn't going to change anything that happened anyway.

She shrugs off his jacket and tosses it back to him. Breaking eye contact, she turns to cross the street, her arms coming up to hold herself together rather than keep herself warm this time.

"Frankie, I—"

"You want to make sure I get home safe. Yeah! Well, I can cross the street on my own," she yells without looking back at him.

The front of her building is dark so she tries to force her feet to move faster. She hears the sound of a car starting nearby but doesn't care to look up. She just wants to get home and into her bed. This night needs to end already.

Tires screeching.

"Frankie! Wait!" Cole shouts.

Before she can turn around, the force of someone tackling her takes her down as they begin their collapse onto the street. Tumbling a few rounds only to be stopped by the impact of her back against the curb of the sidewalk.

"Frankie! Frankie!" She hears Cole's voice yelling amidst the ringing in her ears. It takes a minute to let the blur fade and her sight returns.

"What happened?" she asks.

"That fucking asshole didn't even try to stop," he says, looking her over.

His face starts to become clearer. The ringing in her ears begins to subside too.

"What?" she asks, confused.

"Don't move," he tells her.

She doesn't listen, of course, and shifts out of his arms onto her elbows. "I shouldn't have moved," she groans.

The stinging on the left side of her head now feels like someone's smacked her in the head with a hot skillet. She feels something trickling down the side and touches it. *Blood.* What the hell just happened? She remembers the sound of a car starting before being slammed into the ground. She didn't realize it was so close to her and she didn't see oncoming headlights from either direction.

"You've got some cuts that have to be cleaned. I don't think anything is broken." He looks over her. "Baby, you're bleeding." His voice is gentle as he tilts her chin up.

"Ow," she says, lifting her hand to her head.

"Can you get up?"

"I think so." She moves to a sitting position first. "My back really hurts."

"You hit that curb pretty hard. Good thing you didn't hit your head too," he says before sliding one arm underneath her knees and picking her up as if she were the weight of a leaf.

"I can walk. I'm okay."

"Let's not take any chances. I think you should get checked at a hospital to be sure." He continues walking with her in his arms, heading down the side of the alley.

- 17 -

cole

Her small kitchen is easy enough for him to navigate. Everything is where it should be and labeled properly. While waiting silently for the kettle to whistle, he tries to recall making tea for anyone else and comes up short. Never.

Five minutes later, he pours the boiling water over the ball-shaped tea infuser filled with loose tea leaves he found. Proud of himself, he walks over with the hot mug.

"Here," he puts it on the side table next to her.

"Thanks."

"You look like you need to rest. I think I should go."

"Wait," she says. "Can we talk? Before you disappear again?"

He doesn't know what to say but sits down on the opposite end of the couch anyway.

"I guess I owe you some answers," he says, subdued.

"That night. You said before that you all were just looking for a place to 'duck into'? Duck from what?"

He knew this question was coming and he knows there is no easy way to answer it. He isn't sure what it is he feels for Frankie, this beautiful person. She's someone he most likely doesn't deserve to even know, let alone have the opportunity of sharing some very intimate moments with.

One thing he's sure of is that she deserves the truth from him.

"I suppose from a job gone wrong," he answers, knowing it's going to bring more questions he doesn't want to answer.

"Define *job*."

"Dusty didn't do his homework nor follow directions and we ended up having to get out of the situation fast when we saw flashing lights and sirens heading our direction."

"Are you saying you were breaking into someone else's home?" she asks incredulously.

"No. A high-end pawnshop." He looks away in shame.

"Is that what you and Dusty and...is that what you all do? The reason why you said you were just passing through?"

"Yes. Dusty's someone Nick and I found along the way. Nick is my brother."

"Your brother," she repeats flatly. "The guy that had his hands on me, *wanting* to *rape* me, is your brother?" She looks at him in disbelief. "And Dusty, the repulsive motherfucker who hit me and...and *groped* me is just someone you found along the way? A byproduct of your...your lifestyle?"

Her words cut. He deserved them.

He nods, not able to tell her any other way and at the same time, wondering what she thinks of him. What words is she going to use to describe him? He waits for her next round of questions but they don't come.

He chances a glance at her only to find tears rolling down her cheeks. It's the last thing he expected to see.

"Frankie, I'm sorry. Dusty is who he is even before we found him. And Nick? He was drunk. It's no excuse but it's the truth. He wouldn't have said and done those things if he were sober."

She stares at him, not saying a word.

"We do what we do. That's just how things are."

"Why? You look like a smart guy. You couldn't have found a legit job in all the places you've passed through?" she asks vehemently. "How many other homes and women have you plundered and pillaged?"

"No. Not for the kind of money Nick and I needed at the time. And one job just turned into another." He pauses. "We don't do houses so there have never been any others before in your...situation."

"*My situation?*" she repeats with contempt in her voice. "MY situation was that I was asleep in MY bed, inside MY home!"

This isn't going well at all. *How well was it supposed to go, dumbass?*

"Dusty said this place was an abandoned shop. There weren't any cars outside and we didn't...I didn't know there were apartments up here." He glances at her fisted hands. "Frankie, if I paid better attention, Dusty wouldn't have been able to slip past me and found you."

"None of you should have been here in the first place," she says with a scowl. She takes the bag of peas off of her knee and takes her leg off the table.

"You should probably leave that on longer," he says.

"It's better. I need to change out of this," she says, standing up.

She limps a few steps before he rushes over to give her a hand. She accepts his help as they walk into her bedroom. She flips on the light switch and he sees the changes in her room as well.

"You've been busy," he says as he helps her sit down on the bed.

"I needed the change," she murmurs.

"Do you have anything I can put on that knee?"

"The medicine cabinet should have something."

He turns to the bathroom but she grabs his hand to stop him.

"Actually, can you help unzip me? My back is really hurting and I need to go. I'll just change in there."

She stands up and turns around for him. As she shrugs out of her jacket, he sees the redness and bruising that's already forming between her shoulder blades on her pale skin. It probably isn't the right time to be thinking about her flawless skin, but he can't help himself.

He unzips her dress and she holds it in place with her arms. "Thanks," she says.

"I'll...uh...wait out there," he says, heading to the couch.

- 18 -

cole

How did I fall asleep? The last thing he remembers is sitting on the couch and waiting for Frankie. He sits up and feels the blanket draped on top of him slide down to his lap.

He finds Frankie moving in the kitchen.

How is it possible that she is even more beautiful now than she was earlier in the night? She's wearing a loose pink T-shirt over a pair of comfortable-looking lounge pants. Her hair is knotted on top of her pretty little head. With no makeup, the redness and little cuts and scratches on her face are more prominent. It looks like she changed the bandage over the cut on her temple too.

"I think I better get going." He looks at his watch as he stands up. *4:10 a.m.* About the same exact time, she came running out of the bathroom into him all those weeks ago.

"Sit down, Cole. We're not done talking," she says nonchalantly.

She limps his way with a tray in her hands and he rushes to take the tray with one hand, offering his other for her to keep balance. She heads over to the couch and sits down.

He sets the tray on top of the coffee table and takes his first look at it.

Whoa. On top are two plates, each piled high with amazing-looking sandwiches and garnishes. Between the two plates are nestled three small bowls filled with pickles, olives, and peppers. He looks away from the tray at Frankie, who is watching him.

"Sit. I'm not sure when you last ate but you've gotta be hungry. I'm starving! Sorry I didn't have much else ready to make except for sandwiches. I hope you like turkey," she says.

"Thank you. I probably don't deserve this, but thanks," he says.

He picks up half a sandwich and takes a bite of what has to be the best turkey sandwich he's ever bitten into. If he were being honest with himself, it's probably the best sandwich he's ever eaten. Period. But what can someone expect from gas station sandwiches?

"That's *not* mayonnaise," he says after finishing his first bite.

"No," she says after she finishes chewing.

She stares at him now, her eyes bright and sparkling with a smile that probably lets her get away with just about anything.

"What?" he asks her.

"Say that again."

"Say what?"

"Mayonnaise," she says, mocking his slight twang and laughing.

He can't help the laugh that comes after and gives her a light shove for teasing him.

"It's an avocado aioli."

Not sure what that actually is, he continues eating. He didn't realize he was hungry until his first bite. He practically devours his sandwich and she's barely had half of hers. He washes it down with a big gulp of cold water.

"You're really from Montana," she starts.

"I am."

"Why did you start...doing this?" she asks quietly, not looking at him.

"Long story," he answers briskly.

"We have time," she says as she leans back onto the couch with her bottle of water.

He can't figure out why he cares so much to tell her. As if it will change anything.

"My family owns...owned a small farm there. My grandpa worked his ass off to buy it decades ago. Nick and I were raised there after our mom dragged us around the country trying to find herself."

"How old were you when you went to live there?"

"Both Nick and I were born there. I was eight when she left me there permanently. She took Nick with her because he was older. Social services brought him back six years later when our mom got killed in a crossfire between her boyfriend and the police. They'd found my brother drunk and alone in a motel room somewhere."

"I'm sorry that happened," she says sadly.

"Nah. It was a long time ago."

"So, what led to this?"

"Gramps took it hard when she died. He blamed himself. His health started deteriorating and so did the farm. My uncle wasn't much help. He just kept pressuring Gramps to sell but the old guy kept refusing. Gramps used to tell me that the least he could do for our mom was to provide her shelter whenever she needed it. He was intent on doing that for Nick and me."

She moves next to him and rests her head on his arm. She snuggles so perfectly next to him as if she's done it a hundred times before.

"Go on," she says once she is comfortable.

"Around my senior year of high school, my grandpa took a turn for the worse. First went the cattle and the horses, then we eventually had to sell off acres after acres of the land. Both Nick and I were working odd jobs, trying to keep it together, but it wasn't enough. So Nick reached out to some of our mom's 'friends' to see if they could help him earn."

"And you went along too?"

"No. Not right away. Nick insisted that I finish out high school."

He looks down to see her making a stink face.

"The guy actually has some redeeming qualities," she says more to herself than him. "So how did you get sucked in?"

"I was twenty when Gramps passed away. His final expenses were equivalent to the cost of selling the rest of the land, except for twenty acres and the house it stood on. Our uncle immediately started pitching the sale of that before Gramps's grave was even covered.

"Nick and I got him to agree to sell it to us, except he wanted us to buy cash. Nick being hot-headed borrows the money from his *associates* without questioning the interest. So we give the money to our uncle, only to find out that he had already sold everything right out from under us later."

"What the...was that even legal?" she asks in disbelief.

"The courts say so. My uncle was left as the estate trustee."

"So you guys just lost the farm *and* the money? You couldn't have sued him to get the money back?"

"No. Nick was twenty-two years old and used to dealing with cash buys because of what he'd been doing to earn it in the first place. He handed the cash to our uncle in a duffel bag without question or record of the sale. Nothing. Jimmy, our uncle, walked away with $380,000 tax-free plus the money he got from the legit sale."

His hands turn into fists above his knees. She covers them with her own hands, small and beautiful hands full of strength and compassion.

"I'm sorry," she says, not moving.

"Don't be. It's our own dumb fault."

"What happened next?" she asks.

"Through public records, we were able to find out who bought the place. Turns out, it was the owner of the neighboring farm, Liam Elliott. He started farming at about the same time my grandparents did.

"The old man bought it because it didn't sit well with him that Gramps's legacy was being sold off piece by piece. He agreed to sell it back to us at cost with the condition that we allow his family to continue to run the place until we pay it off. Other than the main ranch house, there are a few empty trailers, cabins, barns, and plenty to do to maintain it."

"Hope you guys got that in writing."

"Yeah, we found a lawyer that helped us put the paperwork together along with the payment plan."

"So you're doing all of this to buy back your family's legacy?"

"Sort of. While I stayed on the farm and continued working it, Nick was off doing job after job. He had the burden of paying not only Elliott but the money he had borrowed. His luck ran out and he got busted when he was twenty-six. He did five years of hard time. When that happened, I had to pull my weight.

"Working on the farm and odd jobs around town wasn't going to cut it so I took up where he left off a few years later, against his wishes. He wouldn't talk to me or see me almost a whole year after that," he says, chuckling, remembering the time. "I guess he figured since he couldn't stop me, he could help me. He used the time he had left inside to network and made connections, learned things, and then passed them on to me."

"Did you do time too?" she asks.

"No," he answers.

"Should I be proud?"

He can't answer that.

She punches him softly on his rib with her free hand. "Kidding!" she exclaims. "How old were you when you *picked up* where he left off?"

"Twenty-seven," he says, suddenly feeling weary about the time that's passed.

"How old are you now?" she asks, weaving her little, nimble fingers into his as he watches.

"Thirty-six."

It's been a long time since he's been living like this. It's been even longer for Nick. And here she is...just turning twenty-nine.

"So how long do you plan on doing this?"

"We're almost done," he says, remembering his last meeting with Nick.

"How long do you usually stay in one place?" she asks slowly.

"Depends on how long Nick wants to stay or where we need to go. He makes all the contacts and finds out what we need to do."

- 19 -

cole

The pitter-patter of raindrops tapping on the window is soothing.

He opens his eyes slowly and sees not much light coming through. He lifts his arm off of his forehead to check his watch. Just past eight a.m.

He's been up about twenty minutes now but didn't want to move and wake Frankie, who is settled on top of him, sound asleep. From all the events of the previous night, he figured she needed all the rest she can get. Besides that, he's completely content with just lying there beneath her tiny frame.

How the fuck did this happen?

He's still in disbelief that he's here on the couch with her. After everything that has happened and everything he told her, she didn't run for the hills...or to the nearest police station.

She'd shown him compassion and acceptance. Neither of which he thought he deserved nor asked for.

Last night, he told her the truth and she listened with understanding, not judgment. And when they were done talking, he looked down only to find that she'd fallen asleep right on him. Never once did he *not* want her to be there.

"Guess you're gonna miss your morning jog with *Melissa*," he hears her say through a yawn.

He smiles and reaches down to pull the blanket completely over her head. "I need some privacy to call her and apologize," he teases.

The retort he expects never comes. Instead, he feels her hand creep under his shirt, touching his bare abs, setting his skin on fire with every slow trace upward.

"Are you calling her yet?" she asks from under the covers.

How can he answer when he feels her lips on his skin? As if that wasn't enough for her, he feels the warm wetness of her tongue gliding slowly across. He holds still, trying his best to keep his composure. It's near impossible to do, especially this early in the morning, and definitely even harder when he feels her leg swing over his side to straddle him.

She sits up, the blanket still covering her.

"I don't hear any talking," she says as she leans forward and begins kissing his neck.

He finally pulls the blanket off her as her lips trail kisses along his jawline and over to where their lips greet.

Even this early in the morning, she tastes heavenly. Alluring.

His mind randomly ponders if this was why hummingbirds on the farm are out so early. Looking for nectar. Her kisses are hypnotic, inviting him in for a better taste. He accepts the invitation by meeting her tongue with his own. Gently at first, his tongue enters for their dance.

She breaks away, giving him a chance to catch his breath.

"Since you're not going anywhere, might as well get comfortable." She tugs and tries to pull his shirt over his head.

He assists her, never breaking eye contact. "Frankie, you really think we should be doing this?"

"Nope," she says right before her lips crash back down on his.

Frankie

She uses her body to push him back into the couch, where she guides him to sit. She kneels between his legs and slowly begins the task of taking the rest of his clothes off of his gorgeous body. Seducing him with soft touches, never breaking eye contact with him as she pulls the last leg of his pants off.

She leans in, turning her head and kisses his thigh.

He reaches out one hand to find hers and her fingers automatically entwine with his. He leans his head back on the couch, closing his eyes as she places another kiss higher up. She takes the opportunity to glance at his erection and her eyes get their fill.

It lies hard on top of him, hefty and chiseled in perfection. Her body remembers the satisfaction of him being inside of her and it aches for him now.

She makes a big move forward and kisses his navel, purposely letting her breasts cradle his member.

His body responds with a slight jerk as she hears what sounds like a hiss escape.

She moves lower this time, letting the bottom of her tongue slide over the slit of his erection before twirling it around him. Her lips wrap around his cap and his fingers tighten around hers.

She removes her lips just as quick and then slowly glides her tongue from the top of his shaft all the way down and then back up again, wrapping her lips back around his tip. His throbbing gives her much satisfaction.

She feels him move and her eyes look up at him through her lashes, the tip of him still covered by her lips. His jaw twitches before he sits back and pulls himself out from under her.

He swiftly reaches down and pulls her up to stand in front of him. His eyes locking and burning her with his apparent desire.

"Do you want me to come down that pretty little throat of yours, sweetheart?" he asks with his throaty baritone before kissing her belly button. Nibbling on her skin. "Any more of that and you won't have a choice."

Holy fuck, is this man sexy or what?

She smiles at his admission with glee. It's been a very long time since she's wanted to do that, to taste a man like that. It had been long even before she moved to Portland.

He turns her around and kisses the small of her back as he slips her pants off and onto the ground. He moves closer, and her skin can feel the heat his body is projecting.

She leans back, wanting his flesh against hers again. Wanting to melt into and onto him, she lets him pull her onto his kisses as one of his hands fills with her breast, fingers lightly squeezing a sensitive nipple, and the other exploring the moist flesh between her legs.

She inhales a big gulp of air when his finger enters her, his arms pulling her back and sitting her down on him. She leans her head back and turns it to find his lips with hers as he builds her excitement with his adept finger.

Her body shifts and writhes, begging for more. With a mind of its own, her hand reaches down over his hand, letting it rest to feel the motion of his movement before sliding further down and doing some exploring of her own.

"*Baby*," he hisses.

Mmm...the way he says that. It's a fucking turn-on all on its own.

Her small hand wraps around his hot and throbbing cock. She smiles with satisfaction at his pulsing before he crushes her lips with his, kissing her fervently. Her back arches, her body wanting more.

His finger leaves her sensitive folds and she feels him shifting her up to meet him. She reaches her own hand down in her impatience to guide him and her body slides over him.

His entry sends a shock of sensation through every cell in her body. Parting their lips, they simultaneously inhale a breath of pure ecstasy.

His hands grip her hips to hold her in place. Knowing that euphoria isn't too far out of reach, she lifts herself off of him before she slides down again, letting more of him in this time. And each time after.

She folds her legs under her to get better support, allowing her to better feed her carnal needs.

Cole matches her pace, letting her take as much of him as her body can. He slips his arms under her legs, giving her riding a break and letting her head fall back so their lips can touch again. He effortlessly lifts her on and off of him. The thought of their erotic position brings her closer and closer, the feeling in the pit of her stomach growing tighter each time he brings her down on him.

"You're gonna kill me," he says breathlessly, bringing her down again.

"I can say the same," she says right before he swiftly maneuvers their position so that both her knees are now on the couch and he's standing behind her, one knee placed alongside hers.

He leans back and the air cools the sweat off her back. She lets out a louder moan as he eases back inside her, her wetness allowing him in deep. He pulls out and goes in a little deeper each time, never to the point of hurting her but bringing her even closer to bliss with every thrust.

His pace picks up as his hands grip tighter on her hips. She feels him leaning forward to kiss her between her shoulder blades. She plants both palms against the wall, resting her face in between, needing the coolness of the wall to bring down the heat of the moment as he thrusts a little harder each time.

She's close, so close, too close.

Her body can't handle it anymore. Her moans grow louder before turning into whimpers, begging for release. He places a hand alongside one of hers on the wall and feels him lean forward.

"Let go, baby. Come for me," he demands into her ear.

As he pulls her onto him and him into her, she erupts.

Soon after she feels Cole spilling into her, filling her, taking her to an even higher plane of euphoria where she floats and tumbles in a cycle she doesn't care to break from.

- 20 -

He walks to the window and looks down into the street below.

People are starting to appear as the rain lets up. He can hear cars driving by and people chattering as they hustle into the shops along the street. It's a different scene than what he's gotten used to waking up to. No vagrants asking for money. No streetwalkers pitching every guy walking by. No junkies loitering. The motel he's staying at now isn't as bad as some places he's stayed before but it doesn't compare to this.

More testament to remind him that he and Frankie are like night and day.

"It's just a drizzle now. Do you wanna go for a walk?" she asks as her arms encircle his waist. "Well, at least just to get my car."

"Sure," he says.

"Let me grab a jacket." She heads off into her bedroom again.

He walks over to the chair where his own jacket is lying. He checks the phone in the pocket to see if he's missed any calls.

Nothing. Good. He doesn't want to deal with Nick right now anyway.

He puts the phone back and shrugs the jacket on before sitting down and putting on his boots. As he is tying them, he notices a framed photo of a man standing with Frankie sitting by her TV and walks over to take a closer look.

His eyes move to the turning doorknob. He can hear the sound of keys jingling from the other side and stands up. Before he can reach the knob, the door swings open and he's looking a couple of inches down at...Sam.

And before he knows it, the guy grabs him by his shirt and is shoving him back a few steps.

"Where is she? What the fuck did you do to her?" Sam hollers out. Sam takes a swing and connects fist to jaw. His jaw.

"Sam!" Frankie screams from the bedroom doorway. "Stop it! Let him go!" She runs over to pry Sam's grip off of his shirt as he rubs his jaw.

"Are you okay?" she asks, standing in between the two of them.

He stands up tall, eyes glaring intensely at the guy who just sucker-punched him. He takes a step forward only to feel Frankie in front of him. He doesn't say a word, both of his hands tightening into fists.

Sam looks down at Frankie and he sees the guy's eyes widen.

"Did he fucking do this to you?" Sam asks and pulls her out of the way.

"No," he answers, not breaking eye contact and not backing down.

"Frankie! Did he hurt you?" Sam asks louder, shaking her arm in his grip.

He doesn't have to look away to see that Sam's grip on her arm is too firm. "Let her go," he says, his voice deathly low.

"Sam, you're hurting me," Frankie says, trying to free her arm.

She shuffles to stand between them again and Sam finally lets go of her arm and looks down at her.

He's still glaring at the guy, still contemplating whether to pay back that punch he just took, but he feels Frankie back up into him, her small hand moving to cover his fist.

"Sam, this is Cole," she says. "Cole, this is my friend Sam."

"Sam. We've met," he says icily.

Dismissing his presence, Sam touches the cut on Frankie's face.

His fists tighten even more as Frankie holds on to it.

"What happened?" Sam asks. "I tried calling you and it went straight to voicemail. Alice called and said she couldn't reach you either. I come in and..." Sam looks up at him with a side-eye.

"I'm okay. My phone died and I forgot to turn it back on when I plugged it in. I just had a little accident. I was crossing the street and some car almost ran me over. He probably didn't see me. Cole saved me," she explains.

"He followed you?" Sam asks her, referring to him as if he weren't standing right there.

"No!" she exclaims. "He was just walking me home."

"Did you not think to take her to a hospital to get her checked out? What if she has a concussion?" Sam loudly asks.

"She said she's fine," he answers, not caring what Sam thinks about that.

He pulls his hand free from Frankie's and walks past them toward the open door. "I'll wait outside, Frankie."

Cole is angry. She can tell.

The rain has died down to just a few drizzles now yet she still speed-walks to keep up with his long strides.

It took a quick explanation to Sam and practically shoving him out the door for him to leave, only for him to stoke the embers when he walked too close by Cole, shoulder checking him.

Cole hasn't said a word since they left her place.

"Hey," she finally speaks, pulling his arm to a halt. She stands facing him. She reaches up and touches his jaw. "I'm sorry," she apologizes sincerely. And she is. He didn't deserve that. He did nothing wrong.

"Didn't even hurt."

His mumbling cracks a smile on her lips as they tighten to hold in her laugh.

"Aww, is my oak tree pouting," she says playfully, caressing his jawline.

His own lips turn into a smile before his mouth opens and the wonderful sound of his laugh breaks through. He pulls her to him, holding her to his side as they begin walking again.

"I really am sorry. Sam's usually so...passive. I don't know what got into him."

"I do. I probably would have thought and done the same thing if I walked in and saw you looking like that," he answers. "No one's fault."

They continue walking down the street, hand in hand, pointing at shops and looking through windows. It's been a very long time since she's done this with anyone. She didn't realize how much she missed it until Cole showed up. Of course, Cole has shown her how much she's missed a lot of things. Like the refresher he gave her on the couch that morning.

She shivers at the thought of the thrill it brought her.

They walk hand in hand down the alley in silence.

"He has a key to your place," Cole states.

"Yes," she replies to his non-question. "I gave it to him last week."

The twitch in his hand as their steps slow down. He doesn't look at her but she can feel him withdrawing.

"It's not what you think." She looks up at him.

"Sam's two aunts are leasing the shop downstairs. He and his crew are renovating the place. I asked him for help when I wanted to change mine. Last week, I had a busy schedule so I gave him a key so that his helpers can move my furniture in and out for painting."

They get to her car and he still hasn't said anything. She can't read his expression and can't even guess at what he might be thinking.

"Can I take you to your place so you can change?" she asks.

"Okay. I hate driving. But it bothers me more to have a five-foot-tall woman driving me around," he says before silencing her objection with a kiss and taking the keys from her hand. He clicks the unlock button and shuffles her to the passenger's side of the car. Opening the door for her, he bows and says, "Your carriage awaits, ma'am."

Her eyes follow his every move after he shuts the door and walks back over to the driver's side. She can't hold in her laughter after he opens the door and feigns exasperation at the seat being positioned as far up and as high as it can go.

Her hands come up to stifle another bout of laughter as he pretends his impatience at waiting for the seat to be moved all the way back and all the way down to accommodate him.

"Good thing you don't drive a Beetle," he says as he gets in.

Five minutes after letting the car window defog, they are driving east. She isn't sure where he is staying but they don't take the highway as she expected. Actually, she isn't sure what to expect, just like everything else that involves Cole.

The things that he told her last night about his life were probably the last explanation she expected to hear. She doesn't condone what he is doing...what they are doing...but he is a different person from a different path than her. And different people might have had different and limited choices. People often have to choose between the lesser of two evils and she wants to believe this of Cole as well.

As she rethinks their conversation from last night, even Nick has a few things she'd normally commend. She hates having to admit that but at least she doesn't have to admit it to anyone else.

Dusty, on the other hand, has no redeeming qualities whatsoever as far as she can tell. The thought of him repulses her and she crosses her arms over her chest, shaking off the feeling of his hands on her skin. He's one person she never wants to cross paths with again.

This brings her to another matter. If things continue to go well with Cole, will she have to eventually face both Nick and Dusty again?

She looks out the window as they wait for the light to turn green. She ponders where things *are* going with Cole. Why the hell would she even think this is going to go anywhere? He's told her he doesn't stay in one place long.

How long does she have with him? One more night, one day, a week? She doesn't know and it seems neither does Cole. It's been close to a month since the first night they unofficially met and who knows how long he was in town before that night.

She can't deny the chemistry between the two of them. Physical chemistry like that doesn't come unless there is also an underlying emotional connection too. She just can't comprehend how a foundation of this kind was established given the fact of how they met and the very impossibly short amount of time they've spent together.

With Cole, she felt safe that first night. And now she feels comfortable and at ease like she can be herself at all times without thinking twice. Like old souls reunited after a long time apart. She imagines it's the feeling a home buyer has when they walk into a house for the first time and realizes, this is...*home.*

"We're here," he says, snapping her out of her thoughts and worries as he pulls the car to park next to a blue truck.

The Oasis Inn Motel, she reads the sign.

She opens the door and steps out without waiting for him. She isn't sure where she thought someone in his *line of work* would be staying, but this is tons better than the picture she'd painted. It's even better than the shady motel she'd spent the night in when she first arrived in Portland.

She looks around the lot to see many other cars parked in front of rooms with blue doors. Two blue doors to each single-story building, she notices. No one wandering outside either except for a couple and their two kids walking from their car to their door.

"I'm this way," he says.

She turns to see him waiting for her.

"This is a lot better than the one I stayed in when I moved here," she says, smiling up at him as she follows him to the door just past the truck.

The rain is starting to pick up again.

She twists his wrist to check his watch for the time as he unlocks the door. It's almost two o'clock. "Fancy watch there," she says as he lets her in through the door first.

"A man's gotta have something nice to look at sometimes," he says, following her inside and shutting the door before shaking the raindrops out of his gorgeous blond hair.

The room is clean and smells fresh. A small fridge with a microwave on top to one side of the room along with a flat-screen TV and dresser. One big duffel bag sitting on a chair, a smaller backpack on the bed, and a laptop along with other knickknacks sprawled across the table. Double beds, she notices. Instantly, her mouth opens to ask the question her mind hasn't even had time to finish thinking.

"Do your brother and Dusty stay here too?" she asks, whipping her head back at him.

"No, Frankie," he says reassuringly, as he cradles her face with one hand. "No. I'm alone here. I wouldn't bring you here if I wasn't."

"Okay," she says, nodding her head.

"Do you wanna sit down while I change?"

She sits down on the bed next to the backpack as he disappears into the bathroom with the bigger duffel bag.

Her curiosity gets the best of her and she peeks into the open bag. Inside are various toiletries, a bunch of envelopes, and other types of paperwork. She reaches for the folded piece of paper lying beside the backpack and opens it.

Cole Howard. It's a receipt for the room dated over a month ago.

Howard. That's his last name? Is it his real last name?

Startled by the buzzing in her back pocket, she pulls out her phone to check it. She goes through her texts to make sure there aren't any emergencies. Most of the texts are from friends sending the usual "Happy Birthday" texts and memes.

Her dad called twice. She makes a mental note to call him back when she gets the chance later in the day.

A message with an attachment from Karmen is last on the list. She taps the message.

No need to wish u a happy birthday. I know u had a very happy one!

Beneath the message is a picture of her and Cole from last night, dancing. Him looking down at her and her looking up at him. *Wow*. It's a beautiful picture. The perfect lighting, the perfect ambiance, the perfect moment.

- 21 -

cole

He soaks up the sight of her for a moment when he exits the john. She's fucking beautiful and it doesn't surprise him to see the eyes on her sitting alone at the table. He can't help but take a picture of his own with her looking out of the window. The overcast only enhancing her shine.

They leave the café after their lunch and walk to his truck, one of her arms wrapped around his waist. He enjoys this public display of affection from her more than he's willing to admit to anyone. It gives him a sense of belonging somewhere.

He's met many women in his travels. Though *met* probably isn't the correct term. They're one-night stands, no strings attached, no names necessary. That appeased him all these years. And now? He isn't sure if that will be enough anymore.

"Can we go inside?" Frankie asks.

He looks at the sign of the shop. *Jessa's Antiques*. He opens the door for her to step through first.

They are greeted by an older woman and the scent of incense. It feels like they walked into a psychic reading shop rather than an antique store.

He looks around the place as Frankie browses the displays.

His phone buzzes in his pocket and he checks to see where Frankie stands before walking to a corner to answer the call.

"Hey," he says quietly.

"We have a job," Nick immediately says.

Fuck! They've been in Portland for a month, it shouldn't be a surprise, but he doesn't like it and he doesn't want it to be this soon.

More time. Just a little more time.

"Where to and when?" he asks.

"Denver. We'll have to leave tomorrow. Dusty is coming along. I already made arrangements with him. We'll talk with him on the way. Maybe he'll decide to stay there. I don't know." Nick sounds grumpier than usual. He wonders if his brother is back in the bottle already.

Tomorrow? He looks over at Frankie and she is still talking animatedly with the shopkeeper.

"What time do we need to meet?"

"One should work," Nick answers.

They both hang up as usual, without saying bye.

He sees Frankie heading his way. His little enchantress. He doesn't know how he's going to do this. To tell her that he is leaving tomorrow. And then to actually leave her. *Fuck!* Nick didn't say how long they'll be gone, which most likely means they won't be coming back.

"Everything okay?" she asks as her arms close around his waist again.

"Didn't find anything you liked?"

"No," she says with disappointment. "So, you have a phone and I don't have your number?"

He chuckles, trying to conceal what's running through his head. He can give her his number. Most likely it's not going to be working much longer after they get to Denver anyway. He doesn't like what he's feeling. This feeling in the pit of his stomach, his instincts telling him that he is going to hurt her.

The rain starts to pick up again as they walk to his truck. He hurries her along to keep them both dry, both walking in silence. Once they are inside with the engine running, he turns to Frankie and asks for her phone.

She hands it to him with brows furrowed and watches as his fingers move around on the screen. He hands it back to her with the "Contacts" list still open and nods for her to check it out.

He sees her smile grow. He saved his name and number. He doesn't know what will happen tomorrow. He doesn't know what will happen *tonight* when he tells her. And he has to tell her. She deserves that. So if having his current number is going to make her happy for the time being, then it's the least he can do.

Her fingers move around on the screen and a few seconds later, his phone buzzes. He opens the message.

Thank you.

Below the message is the picture of the two of them, dancing.

"Now you have *my* number so you can reach me. Anytime," she says, leaning closer to him to bless him with a kiss. Quick but effective.

She sits back down in her seat and buckles up. The rain is pouring down now so they sit there quietly watching it cascade over the cars parked and driving by.

"Cole?" Her voice breaks into his thoughts. "I went into that shop looking for something specific."

"They didn't have it? We have time to look around if you want to find it. What is it?"

"A necklace with an Irish Claddagh charm. Vintage." She looks at him. "It was my mom's. My grandma gave it to her and neither women are *with* me anymore. It went missing that night."

He knows exactly what night she is referring to.

Fuck! Can this get any worse?

"Do you think you can ask your brother or Dusty...I'll buy it back if need be. It can't be worth much to either of them."

He wanted to sink his six-foot-five self into the seat and disappear.

His hands come up to try and wipe the frustration from his face before he reaches out to hold her hand.

"I'm sorry. I'll see if I can get it back," he says.

He doesn't even sound hopeful to his own ears. If Nick took it, he might have a chance. But that's not Nick's style. His bet is on Dusty. The fucking slimy rat.

"Okay," she says as she gives his hand an encouraging squeeze.

As they move into downtown Portland's traffic, driving aimlessly in the heavy rain, Frankie points at random places and cheerily tells him stories. They drive past the bistro where she works, which looks to be bustling for happy hour. She has a great sense of humor, with the perfect mixture of jokes and sarcasm.

Spending time with her like this is going to make leaving her that much harder.

After about an hour of driving, she suggests they make their way back to his place. The rain doesn't seem like it's going to let up anytime soon. She suggests take-out and a movie there until the rain lets up for her to drive safely home.

He couldn't believe it when he saw where she's been as he stares at the dot blinking on the laptop. So much so that he drove through the rain to see it for himself.

It's true. Her fucking car is parked outside this cheap and trashy motel room.

Is she fucking someone inside right now?

The curtains are closed. He has to know. He walks up to the door and tries to listen, but the sound of the rain is drowning out all sounds except for the sound of his own anger rising.

FUCKING SLUT! he screams inside. *How could you do this to me?*

He walks over to her car and kicks the side of it, leaving a dent. The sound of the metal bending is covered by the drumming of the heavy rain.

His anger doesn't subside.

He pulls out his pocketknife and bends down. Unfolding it, he smiles at the sharp blade gleaming and glistening under the rain. He pushes it into her front tire and smiles at the hissing sound, the sliding of the blade into the rubber giving him the satisfaction he needs.

Just one more, he tells himself as he slides it back out and heads to the back tire.

"You're freezing," he says as he closes the door behind them. The rain is coming down harder than it has all day.

"I should be okay after drying off," Frankie says, peeling her soaked jacket off.

He takes off his own jacket and swiftly walks over to the thermostat to adjust it before heading to the bathroom for a couple of towels. He walks back to see Frankie's face paler than her normal tone, her teeth chattering. He quickly takes the jacket from her hand and wraps a towel over her shoulders.

"Do you want to change out of your clothes? They're soaked through," he asks her.

She nods her head. "You should probably change too," she tells him.

"Change in the bathroom. There are a few clean shirts in my bag in there."

He takes off his own shoes and soaked jeans and throws them on the back of the chair before sliding his shirt over his head. He turns around to see an even more beautiful Frankie walking out from the bathroom wearing one of his shirts. She's taken down her long, raven-colored hair and is attempting to dry it with the towel. What a beautiful sight, standing there smiling at him with his much too big shirt covering her sweet skin.

"Wasn't it just sunny yesterday?" she asks.

He continues drying his own hair as he walks to her. She reaches for his hand as he nears and puts his palm up against her cheek.

"How do you stay so warm?" she asks, closing her eyes.

"How do you stay so beautiful?" he teases. "Get under the covers before you catch a cold," he says as he leads her to the bed.

After helping her in, he leaves for the bathroom.

He walks out five minutes later with a dry shirt on and his only pair of lounge pants. Frankie holds a finger up to her lips to signal for him to remain quiet and points to her phone. It looks like she is on a call and on speaker during a conversation.

"Well, Alice had to work so we had to reschedule. But I did try a new Mediterranean place downtown. Probably the best birthday lunch I've ever had," she says into the phone.

She gives his hand a squeeze before putting his palm to her cool cheek again. It's fucking adorable as all hell. This woman just keeps chipping away at the wall he didn't know he had built around himself.

"Well, if you would visit once in a blue moon, there are many new places around town that we can try out, Francine. I can buy you a ticket for whenever."

"I know, Dad. I'll think about it and check my schedule okay? I better let an old man like you get some rest now. I'll talk to you soon?"

Her dad sighs audibly. *"Okay, I get the hint. You have better things to do. Happy birthday, Frankie. Give Nic and Nat hugs for me. Halloween next week, right?"*

"I will. I love you. Bye, Dad." And she hangs up.

She settles down on the pillow and checks her other messages. She puts her phone down and turns to face him. Her smile draws him into her net a little more each time. It's beguiling and alluring. He wonders if it affects other men the same way. *Probably*.

She slides over his arm to rest her head on his chest. He loves the feeling of her being there by his side. His arms may be physically pulling her closer, but it's her energy drawing him into her.

"Nic and Nat?" he asks, looking up into the ceiling as the rain continues to pour above.

"They're my godchildren," she says cheerfully. "Three-year-old twins. They're Karmen's babies."

"The waitress at the bar? I didn't know you two were that close."

She laughs. "Nicolai and Natalia, Nic and Nat. One boy, one girl." She sits her chin on his chest and looks at him. "How about you? Any kids I should know about?"

"Nope," he says.

"Not even back in Montana?"

"Not even in Montana."

"What about...women? Am I one of...*many?*" she asks softly.

"I wasn't a virgin when we met," he answers.

"Jerk!" she says as she playfully gives him a pinch to his side. "I mean...do you have someone waiting for you in just about every place you go?" she asks.

"No," he simply says. It's the truth after all.

"Hmm," she says as she rests her head back down. "So next Saturday, there's this Halloween party at Vince's. We have a charity party there every year. Maybe we can go together? Matching costumes and the whole nine yards?"

She draws circles over his shirt.

Meanwhile, he doesn't know what to say. He's normally pretty capable of being blunt and telling a woman she isn't needed anymore. This is different. Frankie is different. *She isn't someone he doesn't need.* He just can't stay.

"And Sunday is Halloween, I promised to take Nic and Nat trick-or-treating so Karmen can work," she continues. "Maybe you can come with us?"

He can't answer her so he tries to prolong the inevitable.

"Are you hungry? Maybe we should order something before it gets too late," he says, trying to change the subject.

"No...not really." She moves to look up at him and he can see the question in her eyes before she even asks. "What's going on?"

Unable to look at her any longer, he reverts to looking at the ceiling before answering. "I have to leave, Frankie."

"Leave?" she asks quietly.

"For a job. Tomorrow."

She sits up and he doesn't have any choice but to face her. "For how long?" she asks. "For good?"

"Most likely," he tells her.

Fuck! This is even harder than he thought it would be. *How?*

The way she is looking at him, the sound of her questions are all like little razors that won't stop slicing away. *You'll get over it*, the devil on his shoulder tells him.

She sits, staring at him silently, lips tight. He finally sits up to face her, feeling defeated.

"Don't, baby," he says with regret. "Don't ask me to stay. You know I can't."

"But you can come back, right?" she asks.

"Frankie, I'm not gonna ask you to wait around for me. It's not fair to you. You're not just someone I want to call up whenever I'm in town." He pulls her into his arms. She's cold and shivering.

"But...I can be," she whispers.

"No. You can't be. Not for me. You fucking deserve a shit ton more than that," he says softly, kissing the top of her head. "I'm so sorry, Frankie."

"So, we only have tonight then." It's more of a statement rather than a question.

He's afraid to look at her. If he sees her crying, he'll probably throw reason out the window, call Nick and cancel everything, and fuck all their plans up.

Dammit. Why now?

Fucking timing.

- 22 -

Frankie

She puts her clothes on as quietly as possible. This is going to be rough but she doesn't have to wait for him to wake up and make it harder to say goodbye.

The sound of thunder crackles above as she writes him a quick note. Maybe it will help mask the sound of her opening the door.

She steps out of the bathroom and listens before walking toward the door. Before reaching for the knob, she looks back at Cole in the dark one last time and twists. She waits for the right moment, anticipating thunder, or anything to cover the sound of her exit.

When the moment comes, she quickly cracks the door and slips through, out into the rain.

She quickly runs to her car and before she can get in, she sees its condition. She looks up to the sky.

"Really?" she says beneath a breath when all she wants to do is scream.

The front tire is flat. She looks back and sees the back tire flat as well. And there's a huge dent on the side. Her insurance company is going to love this.

She looks back to the door.

No. She's come this far. She isn't going to go back inside and ask for help.

She makes a run to the office to get out of the rain. Of course, it's locked this early. She looks around and sees the lights of the gas station across the street with people inside and at the pumps.

She crosses the street with no other misfortunes and into the station. She looks out the window to see if she will find Cole trailing after her. No one.

She turns on her phone and taps the ride-sharing app to request a car. The dots on the screen blink, notifying her that a ride is right outside, at one of the pumps.

"Yes!" she says too loud as she requests the car.

Once the request is accepted, she runs out to the driver.

10:22 a.m.

He can't believe he slept in. *Maybe because that was the most satisfied you've ever been in your entire existence.*

The flood of sunlight shines on his face through the slit in the curtain. He takes a second to himself before realizing it's way too quiet. *Frankie.* Where is she? He thinks she might be in the bathroom, but there isn't any sound coming from there.

He sits up and looks around him. Her jacket isn't on the chair anymore and her phone isn't on the night table either.

He stumbles out of bed and into the empty, dark bathroom. Looking back to the table, he sees a note lying on top of his laptop and rushes over to it.

Cole,

We weren't meant for goodbyes.

- F

She's gone.

He scrambles for his clothes and then pauses. *No.* He can't go after her. This is why she left. She's trying to save them both from making this harder than it has to be. What would he have to say to her if he goes after her? Nothing's changed. He is still going to leave in a few hours.

He shoves the note in the pocket of his backpack and heads to the bathroom.

He turns on the hot water in the shower and numbly steps into it.

An hour later, he's packed and ready. Nick sent him the details of the job location and he keeps himself distracted by the research until it's time for the meetup. It's an eighteen-hour drive with Nick and Dusty. His head slumps at the thought.

He shuts his laptop down, no longer able to concentrate. He might as well head out now. He packs his laptop in his bag and heads for the door.

The sunlight scorches his eyes once he steps outside.

Frankie's car is still there. *What the fuck?* How did she get home?

He drops his bags by his truck and sees the reason. Both her driver's side tires are flat and there's a large dent on the driver's door.

He bends down to check the tires. They aren't just flat. It looks like they've been slashed. And the dent has no paint scuffs. If a car had hit it, there would have been scuff marks or paint residue.

His instincts are telling him that something is wrong. First, the car that nearly plows her over, and now this?

He checks his watch. Shit! Not much time. But he has to know if she's okay.

He jogs over to the office after throwing his bags into the back seat of his truck. The lady inside says she hasn't seen anyone matching Frankie's description. Depending on how early Frankie left, the office might have been locked and the lady might not have heard the knocking.

As he walks back to his truck, a guy stops him.

"Did you get your wife's car fixed?"

He recognizes the man as someone staying there with his family. "Pardon?" he asks the man.

"Her car," the man says again, pointing to Frankie's car. "I saw ya in the rain last night trying to fix it. No hope of that through the downpour though. Is it out of gas? I saw your wife running to the gas station at the crack of daylight."

He looks across the street at the gas station, putting the pieces of what this man is saying into a coherent picture.

Someone was here last night. Someone intentionally did this to her car. *Why?* This is not good.

He quickly thanks the man for his concern and declines his offer to help change the tires before he goes back to his truck. His next stop has to be the gas station.

The gas station attendant confirms that Frankie was in there at about six a.m. The woman isn't sure who she left with, but it looked like one of those rideshare vehicles.

As he contemplates whether to make the short drive to her place or not, he sees a tow truck rolling into the motel lot. He watches as the truck stops behind her car and begins the task of hooking it up.

Fighting the urge to turn toward her place, he makes the shitty decision to go in the opposite direction. In the direction leading away from her and soon after, he'll be taking the road even farther away from where he wants to be.

"Why is this motherfucker always late?" Nick complains from the passenger's seat.

He looks down at his watch. 1:15. He looks out the windows for any sign of Dusty and catches nothing.

They're parked behind a dilapidated building in an old industrial part of Portland. It being Sunday, there aren't any cars driving by or around.

He looks over and observes Nick fidgeting with his phone. Although grumpier than usual, his brother looks good. Even better than the last time he's seen him. He glances into the back seat at his brother's *one* travel bag.

"Packing light," he says to Nick.

"Don't need much," his brother grunts.

"What's going on with you, man?" he asks Nick.

"Nothing," Nick barks.

"Are you waiting for a call or something?"

"Dipshit's finally here," Nick growls and juts his chin out, ignoring his question.

He sees Dusty walking toward them. While Nick is looking better, Dusty looks like a walking zombie. He hasn't seen the kid in three weeks and he barely recognizes him. That's saying a fuck ton.

"Shit," Nick says out loud.

"Too late for second thoughts now," he tells his brother before he unlocks the door for Dusty to climb in the backseat.

At least Dusty had the decency to bathe, he thinks to himself before looking back at Nick and putting the truck into gear.

"About fucking time," Nick grunts.

- 23 -

cole

He's been driving for eleven hours straight. With every passing hour, he remembers telling Frankie how he hates driving. They are filling up the tank at a busy gas station. The drive this time is void of conversation, everyone seemingly lost in their own thoughts. Dusty slept through most of the trip except for the last hour. After finally leaving his phone alone in the cupholder, Nick fell asleep as well.

That stoked his curiosity. Something is going on with Nick and he isn't sure if it's good or bad. There's been no bantering, no lame jokes, or lewd remarks at the women they've come across on this trip.

He hears a phone ringing and feels movement in the truck. Nick is talking to someone but he can't make out the conversation.

He pulls his own phone out of his pocket and checks it. No new messages. Not that he is expecting any. He opens the last message on the list. Frankie's message. With their picture inside.

Ah hell, how he misses her already.

"Almost done?" Dusty asks from behind him. He'd gone to *use* the restroom as soon as they pulled up to the pump.

"Hey, Dusty." He glances through the tint of the truck to make sure Nick is still on the phone. "You remember that shop we went into a few nights after we got into Portland?"

"Yeah," Dusty answers. "Nick ripped me a new one for that night."

"Remember the apartment upstairs?"

"Oh yeah." Dusty's eyes gleam. "And that bitch inside. Sorry I didn't stay to give her what she wanted. You fucked her good though, right?"

He closes his eyes and his free hand tightens into a fist.

"What about it?" Dusty asks.

"Did you take anything from there?" he asks as coolly as possible.

"Yup," Dusty says, laughing. "Nothing much though. Some jewelry and a laptop."

"What did you do with the stuff?"

"Sold it, of course. Got me a few hundos for it," Dusty says, sounding proud of himself.

Shit! He's always tried his best to give the kid a break. This time, however, he's about ready to break the kid.

He remains silent as he puts the pump back on its hook and gets in the truck, Dusty sliding in the back again.

"How far do we have left?" Nick asks in a much better mood.

"About seven hours," he answers. "Everything okay?" he asks, curious about his brother's change.

Nick reclines his seat, hands behind his head, and a smile on his face. "Wake me when you need a break," Nick says, knowing he's staring at him.

He looks back at Dusty, who shrugs, not knowing why the change in Nick either.

Their point of contact, Victor, doesn't walk into the bar until 7:30 and heads to Nick and Dusty, who are playing a round of pool.

He's sitting at the bar with a beer and watches the men greet each other. He nods to Victor once the guy sees him.

Dusty quickly makes his exit and heads over to sit next to him at the bar. "You should go over there," Dusty says.

"Yeah," he answers curtly and gets up with his beer.

He hated standing around because he's usually the tallest guy in the group. One of Victor's guys is actually almost as tall tonight though. Thinner and leaner too.

"Cole," Victor says as he reaches the circle.

He reaches out to shake the guy's outstretched hand. He nods to the tall guy.

"Everything good?" he asks Nick.

"Yeah. Just a little change of plan," Nick replies.

He's not a fan of change of plans.

"Paul there," Nick nods to the tall guy, "will be coming along too. And the open window is midnight tomorrow."

"Not much time to see what we have to work with," he tells his brother.

"Sorry, man," Paul speaks for the first time. "The pickup for the location changed so we have to adapt. If we pass up tomorrow night, we'll have to wait another two weeks or find new buyers."

He's okay with that. Waiting two weeks to get the job done right is better than rushing in blind. He thought Nick was going to agree as well until he hears his brother saying, "Tomorrow night works fine."

He looks at Nick, silently warning his brother.

"Paul, you stay and show the boys around. I have some calls to make. I'll be in touch, Nick," Victor says as he waves to them and takes his leave.

Paul heads over to the bar to order some drinks, leaving them alone.

"What's the rush, Nick? Take the two weeks and do this right."

"Trust me. It'll work out like always. We have the whole day tomorrow to check things out. You can be ready," Nick tells him with a slap on the back.

12:12 a.m.

"Dusty, don't you fucking touch that."

He turns around to see Nick pointing at the small display case in the center of the shop. He shakes his head no at Dusty also. The enclosure has an alarm of its own. It doesn't take a genius to see that.

Dusty backs away from it and continues on.

"Safe is open," he tells Paul when he pulls the door open.

Inside are a couple bands of cash, some yellow envelopes, and more than twenty-five red velvet cases. Those are what they came for.

Paul quickly grabs a handful of the cases and shoves them into his bag along with the cash. He does the same.

"Two minutes," Nick warns everyone.

They all work fast, quietly, and efficiently. Even Dusty does his part this time, except he caught the kid stuffing a few pieces into his pocket too. He isn't going to make a big deal out of it at the moment. He knows Dusty. The kid is looking for cheap stuff to grab. Those are the ones that he can sell off quickly and without question at just about any pawn shop in any town.

He stops Paul from taking the small black bag in the safe when he sees the guy reaching for it.

"We're not here for loose diamonds. Brings too much heat," he tells Paul.

Paul nods and tosses the bag back.

"Time," Nick calls it and they all head to the same back exit they entered. Quickly and quietly.

Once they are outside and the door closes, they all separate and retrace their paths in silent agreement. They each have an hour to get to their next rendezvous. It's too late to be taking the bus this time so he decides to walk, careful to stay within the shadows. There's a bar that he already scouted out earlier in the day. He can take a cab once he gets there.

Walking in the shadows, he's reminded of another night. The night he met Frankie.

Not wanting to allow himself that distraction, he checks his watch and changes course to Plan B. He heads toward LoDo instead. Even at this time of night, LoDo should still be bustling and it won't be out of the ordinary for him to grab a cab from there.

He gets to the spot five minutes before Paul and Nick. Of course, the only one not there yet is Dusty. He has five minutes or they are leaving him.

He shakes his head. He gave Dusty specific instructions and gave him what he felt was the easiest and quickest route here and still, he's holding everyone up.

Just as Nick signals that time is up, Dusty pops out of the dark and heads to the car.

2:45 a.m.

"It's done," Nick says into the phone and waits as Victor gives him the rest of the details. He hangs up a minute after and turns to the group. "Nice job, boys. Paul, Vic is expecting you," Nick says as they shake hands.

"That was smooth," Paul said. "Anytime you boys in town, look me up." Paul shakes Dusty's hand briefly and walks over to shake his.

"No loose diamonds huh?" Paul asks.

"Nah. Too hard to unload without drawing attention unless there are specific instructions to grab them. Gold is easier to work with," he replies.

"I'll keep that in mind," Paul says, giving him a pat on the back. He watches Paul slip out of the building and into the night.

He's jostled awake by Nick, unsure how long he's been sleeping. He opens his eyes, yawns, and sees Nick telling him to be quiet. He looks in the back seat to see Dusty passed out, headphones on as usual.

The clock on the dashboard says it's exactly 8 a.m. He looks around the gas station that they are stopped at for any signs to tell him where they are.

"Where are we?" he asks Nick.

"Outside," Nick says quietly.

They both step out of the truck and he comes around the back to see Nick already starting the gas pump. He stretches and sees Nick checking his phone with a smile.

"Something change?" he asks his brother.

"No," Nick answers and puts his phone away.

As Nick opens his mouth to speak, the back door opens and Dusty steps out, yawning and stretching. "I'm going inside. You guys need anything?" Dusty asks them.

"No," Nick says.

He intended on going into the store with Dusty but Nick holds him back. They wait and watch Dusty go inside before Nick starts speaking again.

"We need to talk to him now. See what he wants to do. After this meet in Lincoln, I can make my last payment to Ralph. We won't have to do as many jobs anymore so maybe he'll want to stay in Lincoln or something," Nick says, eyes following Dusty around in the store.

"Okay," he replies. "How much longer until we get to Lincoln?"

"A couple more hours, but we don't meet with them till later tonight. I don't plan on staying in Lincoln, Cole. Once the deal is done, we head immediately to Casper to make the payment. Ralph will have someone waiting."

"The truck needs an oil change. I can get that done while we wait. I can talk to Dusty," he offers.

Nick nods, accepting the offer, as Dusty walks back to them.

Three hours later, they drop Nick and their bags off at the cheapest motel they can find. He didn't even have to ask Dusty if he wanted to come along. When he said he was heading into town to find a shop, Dusty jumped at the opportunity.

It takes him almost an hour to find a shop that doesn't have a two-hour wait for a simple oil change. Dusty sits impatiently in the passenger's seat, complaining the whole time. They opted to sit in the truck while they wait their turn rather than wait in the crowded waiting room. It gives him the opportunity to talk to Dusty anyway.

"Dusty, we need to talk," he starts.

"What's up, bro?" Dusty asks, not looking at him.

"Nick and me, we're going to be slowing down with the jobs after this one. Think maybe it might be time for you to figure out where you wanna go, man."

"Did I piss him off again? He's always had it out for me," Dusty whines.

"Nah. You did good this last job. No complaints, man. But Nick is getting tired. He's just ready to slow down."

"Then how 'bout you and me let him slow down and we do our own thing? You know all of his contacts."

"No, man," he replies with absolute certainty. "Just think about what you want to do. After this meeting, we're heading to Casper for some final business. If you want a ride there so you can figure things out, I'm okay with that. If you want to stay here and see what's around, that's fine too."

Dusty remains silent.

"Look, once this deal is done, I'll give you something extra to help you. And if you want the ride to Casper, I'll ask whoever we are meeting there to see if they can find something for you, all right?"

Now that it's out, he feels relieved.

The awkward silence that follows doesn't last but a few minutes before the attendant waves for him to pull the truck into the bay.

- 24 -

cole

Casper, WY

Ever since Nick said they're slowing down, why does it seem like they are going in overdrive? They arrived in Casper and waited to meet Ralph's guy as planned and handed their final payment off without a hitch.

He took part of the day to pay bills online and make a deposit at the bank. He hated this part. The part of having to make several deposits in various ways so as not to draw attention.

Cryptocurrency. Yeah, if only the people he works with would jump on that boat, things would be a lot easier.

Dusty declined his offer to introduce him to Ralph and instead asked for a ride to the airport. He gave the kid an extra two grand from his own cut to help him. Hopefully, the money doesn't pass through a needle into his arm within one night.

He went back to the motel where they're spending the night. Nick had been locked away in his own room.

He managed to get cleaned up and catch some sleep before Nick came knocking on his door twenty minutes ago. And now? They're standing at a gas station, filling the truck up again, at 4:30 a.m.

"Another job already?" he asks as his brother hands him a cup of gas station coffee.

"Sort of," Nick answers. "I'll drive."

"Be my guest," he says, waiting for the tank to fill. "I thought you said we were slowing down."

"We are," and Nick left it at that.

They each get into their side of the truck, and he pulls out the tablet and fires up the map.

"Where to?" he asks Nick, who's already shifted into gear and rolling out of the gas station.

"Portland," Nick replies.

What. The. Fuck? He'd been good at hiding his emotions and reactions from Nick, otherwise, his brother might have caught him flinching.

"Portland?" he asks. "Again? There a job this time?"

"Unfinished business," Nick simply says.

His thoughts are racing with a ton of questions and Nick obviously isn't going to answer.

What unfinished business could he have there? A deal? A job? They haven't worked any jobs in Portland itself, but they'd done a job in Monmouth and that's how they ended up in Portland. Did this have to do with that job?

The only eventful thing that happened in Portland that he knows of is the night at Frankie's. *Shit.* Does this have to do with her?

"You can put that away. I don't need it," Nick says, nodding to the tablet.

He keeps his cool. If he wants to figure out what Nick is doing, he has to outsmart him. Asking him bluntly isn't going to get him anywhere.

He should be excited that they are going back. He can see Frankie again.

And tell her what? Things still haven't changed. They probably won't be staying long and just like before, they'll have to say goodbye again.

We weren't meant for goodbyes. That's what her note said.

Unfinished business? He can't shake the feeling that Nick is definitely keeping something big from him. Is it Frankie? What fucking business would he have with her? Does Nick still want her? Is that it?

He suddenly recollects the night the car almost hit her and then her car tires being slashed the following night. Could Nick have done those things? What reason would he have?

"Relax, baby brother," Nick says. "Go to sleep or something. It's a long drive."

Sleep? That's the last thing he wants to do. "You wanna tell me what's going on, Nick? Why are we headed back there so soon?"

"Like I said. Unfinished business. Nothing for you to worry about." Nick reaches over to tousle his hair, something he hasn't done since they were kids. Whatever kind of mood he's in, it's clear that Nick isn't going to make a peep about what he has in mind.

They stopped to fill up the tank three times before breaking Portland in record time. Nick drove the whole way, without stopping to switch off and without slowing down. Once in town, Nick seems to know exactly where he's going.

His stomach tightens in knots when Nick hops on the 205 heading south instead of driving into downtown.

They're heading in her direction but was Frankie really his brother's unfinished business?

"Are we meeting someone?" he finally asks.

"Not you. Just me," Nick answers nonchalantly.

Approximately twenty minutes later, they pull into a shopping plaza.

He hops into the driver's seat that Nick's just vacated.

"Did you ditch that number you were using when we were here?" Nick asks as he picks up his bags from the backseat.

"No. I still have it."

"Good. I'll be in touch to see where you're at in a few days, Coley." And just like that, Nick shuts the door and he watches his brother running to the grocery store in the plaza.

He quickly pulls the map up on the truck's navigation screen. They are past Frankie's place but they aren't far enough. He doesn't like this shit at all. Something isn't sitting right.

He puts the truck in gear and gets on the road as fast as he can to head back up north. It's almost ten p.m. He checks his watch. Oct. 30 again. He remembers now that Frankie told him about Vinny's Place having a Halloween party of some sort and immediately heads that way.

- 25 -

cole

What the fuck would Nick want with her? He doesn't know. Does Nick know about her and him? He doesn't think so. He hasn't mentioned it to anyone. And even if he did, why would Nick give a shit? On the other hand, maybe Nick isn't here for her at all.

He reaches the opening to the alley next to Vinny's Place. Loud music is blaring inside. The door is propped open and people are either piling in and out. The place looks like it's packed to capacity. Talk and laughter are coming from behind the building so he turns into the alley and heads toward the noise. The place probably has a back entrance being used with this many people here tonight.

"Thanks, man! Keep the change!"

His head snaps back at the voice. He steps into the dark shadow of the building and watches as Nick hops out of a cab and enters the establishment.

Fuck! He needs to get inside and he has to move fast. He rounds the building and nearly plows over a couple making out.

"Sorry," he says before passing them and turns back to ask, "Is there another way in the place?"

"Yeah, man. On the other side," the guy points.

He runs without even thanking the guy. The back door isn't propped open but people are spilling in and out. Someone in a cowboy costume opens the door and tosses a bag of trash into the adjacent dumpster. The guy holds the door open for him to step in.

He's immediately assaulted with the temperature inside. A packed house full of bodies dancing, drinking, and mingling can turn up the heat a few notches.

He spots Vince behind the bar along with a couple bartenders. All three are too busy to notice when he walks past the side of the bar. He heads for the corner he sat at before.

Standing in the dark, he scans the room for Frankie or Nick. He can't tell who is who with everyone in costume. *Damn it!* But Nick isn't in costume. He's sure of that so that's who he searches for.

He spots Nick talking to someone. He can't tell who it is through the throng of people or the costume. *Luke Duke.* The guy Nick is talking to is dressed as Luke Duke from *The Dukes of Hazzard.* Can't be Frankie even if she were in that costume. The person is too tall.

He scours the crowd again to see if he can find Frankie. At the door, he sees Sam walking in alone wearing a Superman T-shirt. If he didn't come with Frankie then he must be here to see her. She has to be here somewhere.

He looks back at the bar and now Nick is gone. Luke Duke is still there but Nick isn't standing there anymore.

He catches Nick pushing a few people out of the way in a hurry, heading to the back exit. Keeping his eye trained on his brother's back, he tries to close the gap between them. He moves as quickly as possible through the crowd. And it looks like Nick is following someone. His sense of urgency kicks into overdrive but he gets stuck behind a group of people dancing and blocking the hallway at the side of the bar.

Fuck!

One of the guys dancing finally sees him and makes way for him to hurry through. He opens the door and hears Nick calling after someone in the alley.

"Dusty!" *Why's he calling for Dusty?*

"Nick, what the fuck are you doing here?! What the fuck is going on?" his voice booms over the music blaring from the bar.

Nick turns around, looking just as surprised to see him standing there. "Cole? What the fuck are *you* doing here?" Nick asks incredulously.

He closes the distance between them and Nick takes a few steps back.

"Why don't you tell me what the fuck is going on? Why are you here, Nick?"

"I thought I saw Dusty and followed him out here."

"You know it can't be Dusty. And you know what I mean. Why are you here...in Portland...at this bar in particular?" he roars louder.

"Woah! Back the hell off, Cole! What the fuck has gotten into you?"

A sudden blast of music fills the alley and Nick looks behind him.

Within a second, someone brushes past him to Nick, who is instantly met with a hug and kiss from...Luke Duke? Wait, *what?*

He stands in place, speechless and confused. Is this what this is all about? *Nick is...gay?*

He clears his throat to interrupt the duo.

Nick immediately smiles at him. Probably the biggest smile he's ever seen on his brother's face. Luke Duke spins around as well and it takes a second for him to recognize her face.

"Karmen?!" he all but screams.

"You two know each other?" Nick asks. "How?"

"Is she why you were in such a rush to get back here?" he asks back.

"We've met," Karmen answers Nick.

"Can you give us a minute to clear a few things up, sweetheart? I'll catch you inside," Nick asks Karmen.

"Okay," she says, giving Nick another quick kiss and leaving them. "Frankie know you're here?" she asks from behind them right before the alley is blasted with music again.

"Cole, I'm sorry, man. I didn't know how things were going to work out. Karmen and I met a few weeks ago. And I kinda really like her, man. I just wanted to see where things would go before I told you."

"Did you tell her about us?" he asks his brother.

"Yeah."

"How much does she know?"

"Just about everything and that I have a brother. Except she doesn't know he's you apparently.

"Christ, Nick. You could have just told me."

"So how *does* she know you, Cole? And who the hell is Frankie?"

Nick barely finishes his question before the sound of the music blasts through the alley again. Nick moves his head to look behind him for the second time tonight.

"Cole?"

Frankie.

He turns around to see the most beautiful cowgirl...*no*...the most beautiful Miss Daisy Duke running at him. He lifts her up just as she jumps at him and her legs wrap around his torso.

"Hi, baby," he whispers.

For a moment, forgetting where they are and who's presently standing behind him, he brushes a kiss against her soft lips and lets the scent of her engulf him. Damn, he's missed her.

"You're here," she whispers back breathlessly.

"Ahem," Nick clears his throat from behind them after some time.

He turns around and lets Frankie slide down. *Shit.*

"Keeping secrets of our own, huh? You must be Frankie," Nick says.

He freezes knowing that this can be catastrophic.

Frankie turns around to see who's just spoken.

Recognition crosses over Nick's face as his brother looks from her and up to him then down back to her. Their height difference probably makes things obvious. There's no way around that.

"Wait," Nick says. "Cole, is this...*Francine Hoang*?"

Frankie takes a step back, her back touching him.

He still hadn't figured what to say or do as he stands there, watching the shit hit the fan and flying every which way in that alley.

"Nick," Frankie hisses.

"What's he doing here?" "She knows who I am?" the two ask simultaneously.

"An answer today would be nice, Cole," she prompts with a scary-ass tone.

"I...I didn't...I don't...Apparently, he's here to see Karmen," he stutters out because she's fucking scary as shit right now.

"And you've been seeing *her*?" Nick exclaims, palms out at Frankie.

"That asshole is seeing Karmen? She has kids, Cole. Beautiful kids! You can't let him hurt them!"

"I would never hurt them!" Nick yells back. "I know I must seem like an asshole to you because of how...you know," he stammers.

"How you wanted to rape me?" she finishes for him.

Nick winces at her tone and choice of words. "I'm sorry. I really am. It wasn't my best moment," he says, sounding sincerely apologetic, which he's shocked to hear coming from his normally-crass brother. "But I would never hurt Nic and Nat."

"Frankie, can you please give me a few minutes to talk with him?" he asks, trying to defuse the situation. "Please?"

"You and I...we *definitely* need to talk," she says before she pulls her hand from his.

"As for you," she says and walks straight over to Nick, who looks down innocently at her, with his hand held out as an apology and peace offering. A hand that she quickly shoves out of her way before she lifts her leg and swings it quickly upward, right into his crotch.

He watches in disbelief as his brother topples to the ground like a fucking sack of potatoes in what must be agonizing pain.

"Apology *not* accepted, but I do feel a little better now," Frankie says before she stomps past him.

Unable to watch the pathetic sight of his brother crouched over on his knees any longer, he goes to help him stand up and Nick shoves him off.

"You're a whole fucking semi-truck taller than her! You couldn't have stopped her?" Nick hisses at him.

"You really think I could have?"

"Fuck!" Nick growls through clenched jaws. "Ahh...yeah. I might have deserved that," Nick says through his pain, still trying to stand straight.

"Can you walk, man?" he asks.

"So how much does *she* know?" Nick asks, his face still red from the pain.

"Everything," he answers.

"What happened to all that...*you-could-have-just-told-me* bullshit?" Nick glares at him. "Fuck!" he says, bending over again. "Have you been with her the whole time since that night?"

"No. Never even thought I'd see her again. Happened to run into her at this bar the day before we left town. I was with her when you called me."

"She why you're brooding this fucking trip?"

"Karmen why you were so dandy the whole time?" he fires back.

- 26 -

cole

He spots Frankie chatting with a group of people across the room. He's missed her more than he can ever admit. Even with the *job* keeping him focused, she's never left his thoughts. If anything, he thought about her more.

The music goes from a dance number to a Journey song. People are coupling up as others start to make their way off the dance floor toward the bar. Frankie's just taken a few steps before Sam stops her and bows an invite for the dance. *Good ol' Sam* and of course it had to be a Journey ballad playing.

Frankie accepts and takes Sam's hand as they step closer to each other.

Six feet, five inches of pure jealousy, the devil speaks again.

"He wasn't the only one watching her out there," Nick says, patting his shoulder. "Good luck with that one, baby brother."

He doesn't say anything. He watches the two of them out there. Given any other circumstance, he probably would have liked Sam. The man is probably the better choice for her too if he really wants to be brutally honest with himself.

He continues watching, finishing his beer quicker than usual. He grabs two shots off a tray from a waitress walking by and throws a $20 on, waving off the change, not wanting to take his eyes off of Frankie, who is now laughing at whatever Sam said. They're even closer than before if that were possible.

The song *finally* comes to an end and he sees Sam bending down to say something in her ear. Frankie doesn't seem too happy with what was said. He can tell by how she's looking up at Sam and shaking her head. She walks off the floor, leaving Sam looking frustrated.

The night is winding down. The place has maybe a fifth left of the crowd from when he first arrived. The band is beginning to pack their equipment as well. There are a few couples still dancing and laughing. Some people are too drunk to move. Some are still trying to get drunk with last-call.

Karmen and Frankie walk hand in hand toward the counter after all the pictures are taken. However, Frankie is stopped by the lead singer of the band midway. He stares as she turns and sees the guy handing her a rose. Unable to watch the rest, he turns around in his seat to face the bar.

"Didn't think you were the jealous type," Nick teases from the seat next to his.

"I'm not!" *Very convincing, Cole.*

He finishes his beer and asks for another from Donnie, who slides one over.

"You're gonna have to get used to that," Karmen says as she slides in between him and Nick.

"Hey, sweetheart," Nick says, turning his seat so they're face to face and then pulling the wig off to let her hair fall down above her shoulders.

He watches and listens to the two chatter and laugh. It's good seeing Nick like this. Polite and respectful of a woman versus the lewdness he's seen in the past few years. Whatever Karmen is doing with Nick, he can only appreciate. Nick looks healthy, sober, and happy. The last time he's seen Nick like this was probably the day their mom left him and took his brother with her.

"So how did this happen?" he asks, waving at them.

"I had a hangover and was looking for some aspirin at the pharmacy," Nick answers.

"I had a sick kid and was picking up a prescription at the same pharmacy," Karmen says.

"I was in the checkout line behind her. She's carrying Nat, who had a fever and trying to hold on to Nic, who was full of energy," Nick follows up.

Shit. They're co-storytelling already? He keeps the thought to himself and lets them continue.

"Well, I needed my insurance card. I couldn't dig in my purse while holding one kid up and one kid down," Karmen continues.

"So, I offered. My head was pounding and I just wanted them to be quiet," Nick says jokingly. "Plus, I thought she would just let me get the boy to calm down."

"I hand Nat over to him."

"And she pukes all over the front of my shirt," Nick finishes.

An extremely loud laugh escapes him. Just the mental picture of a kid vomiting all over his brother like in *The Exorcist* is damn hilarious, but to know that it actually happened is priceless.

"I handed the kid back to her and said fuck the aspirin," Nick says with a grin.

"Well, when I finally get outside, I see him arguing with a cab driver who wasn't letting him in," Karmen says, laughing. "I offered to give him a ride. It was the least I could do."

"Well, as she's driving the car, the stink of the puke on me kept building up and building up. Next thing we know, Nic is puking in the back seat too. Kid probably filled up his car seat with everything that was in his stomach," Nick says with a sour face. "She stops and hops out of the car grossed out by all the puke and the stench. My headache is tenfold by now."

"So, he gets in the driver seat," Karmen takes over. "And I get back into the car and tell him that I wasn't going to make it five more minutes. I told him we were three minutes from my place and asked if we could stop there instead."

"So now we get to her place and she jumps out of the car before I even stopped and she's bent over upchucking everything she's got in her. She's throwing up. The twins are throwing up. And I'm just covered in throw up," Nick says with a smile.

If this were a different Nick, the Nick he'd gotten used to being around the past few years, Karmen and those kids would probably have heard a few choice words.

"Since I was already covered in it, I got the vomit-covered brats out of the backseat and got them inside when she finally manages to get the door open for us."

"And he's been there ever since. Right, babe?" Karmen asks, wrapping her arms around Nick.

"Wait. So, you're staying with her?" he asks slowly.

"Yeah," Nick says and takes a drink of water.

"He's our hostage now, Cole." Karmen gives him a wink.

"So, you and Francine...I mean Frankie?" Nick asks with an arched eyebrow.

"I saw that happening," Karmen says and pulls her phone out of her back pocket. She flips through a few screens and shows Nick, who looks back up at him.

"Yeah. I can see what you mean," Nick says to Karmen.

"See what?" Frankie asks from the other side of the counter.

Surprising the trio as she slides one large platter in front of him and another between Karmen and Nick.

"You look like you could use some food," she tells him before swiping away his fresh bottle of beer and handing him a bottle of water in its place before disappearing.

Frankie surprises them again by walking over and sliding another plate in front of them and again...heads off to wherever she was needed. This plate is filled with what looks to be salami and pepperoni wrapped around mozzarella and basil leaves. Karmen picks one up immediately and feeds it to Nick.

"You know she saved my life," Karmen says in between bites. He turns back around to see Nick just finishing his last bite of the sandwich.

"How so?" Nick asks.

"I was seven months pregnant, hormonal, and must have walked in and out of about four bars in the area looking for my dirtbag of a boyfriend," she says while wiping her hands with a napkin. "Found him sitting over there with some skinny, fake blonde bimbo."

Both men give her their undivided attention. The music isn't too loud to hear her details and he's always thirsty to know more about Frankie.

"The place was empty except for the two of them locking lips and Vince and Frankie. Being the hot-headed Italian I was, I walked over and yanked the bitch off her seat by the hair. Roger, that scumbag at six feet and two hundred fifty pounds, nearly knocked the lights out of me. He didn't give a shit that I was pregnant with his kids."

"Piece of shit," Nick says quietly.

"Frankie called the cops?" he asks Karmen.

"She and Vince came running to get him off of me. That kid over there," and she points to where Frankie is standing, "covered my body with hers. Vince didn't stand a chance. Roger must have knocked him out. I see him flat on the floor."

"Well?" Nick urges.

"Frankie is laying over me taking kick after kick from Roger, plus his bimbo is pulling on her hair to get her off of me, and seconds later Roger lifts her little body up and throws her over the bar counter. Right over there." She points to the area in front of the double doors.

"Holy shit! I thought you said she saved your life," Nick says.

"I wouldn't be standing here if she hadn't, babe," Karmen says.

"Did someone eventually call the cops?" he asks, reaching for his bottle of water.

It disturbs him to hear her getting what sounds like a really brutal beating from people who definitely didn't need to exert that much force to stop her.

"Eh, maybe. Bimbo and Roger are still going at me. I'm thinking I'm dead for sure. Me and my babies." She pauses, her eyes growing sad. "But I hear Frankie screaming at them to stop, and just like that—" She snaps her fingers. "They did. So I manage to turn my head and through my one still good eye, I see her standing as tall as she possibly could. Her clothes and hair were a mess. She had cuts and blood coming from all over her face."

"The sight of her scared them?" Nick asks, laughing.

Karmen smacks his arm for the joke.

"No, but the shotgun she was carrying sure did," Karmen says with admiration.

"No fucking way," Nick says in disbelief.

"Yup. Vince had one under the counter. Bimbo goes running out the door screaming. Frankie walks right up to Roger and pumps that shotgun, pointing it at his head. Told him to get out. He ran for the door like a mutt." Karmen laughs.

He believes every word. His girl has fire and fight in her.

His girl?

"Fucking coward," Nick says. "And I don't mean about him running but for doing that to his own flesh and blood."

"So, the cops and ambulance show up minutes after. Cops go and pick up Roger, of course. Paramedics check out Vince and the ambulance rushes me to the hospital for an emergency C-section. Frankie rode with me. This little tiny bit of a girl that I had never seen before holds my hand while she's black and blue. A few hours later, Nicolai and Natalia were crying their heads off.

"I heard she'd been waiting in the waiting room the whole time. Vince came to pick her up but she insisted on staying. When the nurse went and told her that me and the babies were going to be just fine, kid over there," she points again at Frankie, "tells the nurse, 'I think my arm's broken.'"

"Get the fuck out of here!" Nick says, shaking his head in disbelief. "You're telling me she had a broken arm, stood up and pumped a shotgun at your ex, and *then* sat and waited for hours without telling anyone? No way in hell. I've seen bigger guys fall with less than that."

"It's true. Two fractured ribs and a fractured wrist she took for someone she didn't know. She didn't even know my name."

"No fucking way," Nick says again. Nick reaches into his pocket for his wallet and pulls a credit card from it and slides it open. "Cole, you go buy that woman a ring right now, baby brother!"

"You can't afford what she deserves," he says quietly, tossing the card back to Nick.

Fucking amazing. If it were about anyone else, he might have thought it to be an overexaggerated story. But he definitely can believe it knowing Frankie.

"You boys wanna hear the rest or what?" Karmen asks after she finishes her laughing.

"There's more?" Nick asks.

"So, I have my two babies now. Roger made bail and I didn't have a place to go. Frankie came to the rescue again. She was waiting in her cast outside my room the day they discharged me, and then brought me to her place. The babies were too small to go home at the time. And check this out." She looks at Nick and then at him.

"She tells me that since she's going to be off work and Vince was going to need help, she wasn't going to let me sit around on my ass, and she hands me a schedule. That doll over there gave me a job to come to that worked with the visiting schedule I had with the twins till they could come home. And when they did, I worked here full time and she took care of them for four months straight even with a cast."

He turns around to find Frankie. She's helping some of the waitresses clean tables and talking to some of the last few patrons.

"When she fully recovered, instead of coming back to work, she found another job so I could keep this one. She'd never admit that but Vince and I, we know the truth. She would have left altogether but Vince wouldn't have that. He loves her too much. Donnie and I actually have a bet that this place goes to Frankie when he's done."

"Are they related?" Nick asks.

"No. He has no kids. She's the closest he's probably got." Karmen waves over at Frankie. "I'm gonna go give her a hand."

He continues watching the ladies chat and clean as they go.

"I can see why you're falling hard for her," Nick says.

He whips his head around to look at his brother, who is still picking off his platter. *What did he just say?*

"Cole, I see the way you've been watching her. I've seen you with a shit ton of women, some even prettier than her, but I've never seen you look at any of them *that* way before."

"Maybe it's because I didn't get to spend real time with any of them."

"All right, if you want to keep lying to yourself. How much *real-time* have you spent with her then?" Nick shrugs. "I'm just saying, I know why you would be...you know...if you wanted to be in love with her. The girl is short and small, but she's got balls bigger than a lot of guys we associate with."

"Not gonna argue with that," he says nonchalantly.

"I know I'm on her shitlist. That's on me to make amends. So if you are in...I mean, if you really like her, I'll do what I can to get back on her good side."

Nick looks over to Karmen. "Karm and I are crossing bridges as we come to 'em. Her kids are amazing though. And who knows, maybe they'll end up at the farm with me. So, if you don't want to go back there, I'm okay with that."

He contemplates what Nick is saying. *Lying to himself? Is that what he's doing?* He never processed his feelings. Maybe because under the circumstances of how they met and the fact that they have really spent very little time with each other. Time. Isn't that something that's needed for there to be *love*?

"Hey, Cole," an overly silky voice calls from behind him.

Just as he turns around, someone slides underneath his arm and stands between his legs, her back against the bar counter. It takes him a moment to recognize the face with the makeup and the typical sexy nurse costume on.

Fucking Melissa.

Nick clears his throat and he sees his brother shoving what has to be a cold french fry into his mouth before turning to face the bar.

"How'd you know I'd be here? I saw you earlier but couldn't get to you," Melissa says, the smell of alcohol filling the space between them.

He removes his arms from the bar and tries to back his chair up. Melissa quickly leans forward and places her hands on both of his knees.

"I love this song. Dance with me," she says.

"I don't dance," he says, trying to get her hands off of him.

"Maybe we can find a place to do other things then? Like my place? Or yours?" she suggests with a shrug.

These are the kind of women and advances he's used to dealing with. Before, he'd be game if he were bored. But right now, all he wants is to get her off of him without making a scene. The last thing he needs is another misunderstanding between him and Frankie.

"I'm actually waiting for someone," he says, pushing her hands off.

Melissa takes the opportunity to dramatically fall right into his lap, her arms wrapping around his neck. *Shit!*

"Well, I'm here. Wait no longer," she says.

His eyes dart over to Nick, pleading for help even as he tries to wrench her death grip from around his neck. It's a huge fucking turn-off when women don't get the hint.

"Vince still has that same shotgun under the counter," Karmen says when she walks by.

Nick chokes on the cold fries he was shoveling in his mouth and Karmen gives his brother a good whack on the back to help him before she rounds the other end of the bar counter.

"Oh, it's you again. Melissa, right?" Frankie asks from behind the counter.

He looks back and forth from Karmen to Nick for help while Melissa sinks herself lower onto him, putting her leg under the chair arm so that he can't move her. He looks up at Frankie and she's got a twinkle in her eyes. It's more like burning fury.

Karmen is behind the counter pretending to wash glasses and his dear brother just scooted his chair over in the opposite direction.

Oh shit. Oh shit. He gives Nick that "thanks" look.

"Hey," Melissa purrs at Frankie.

I'm gonna die. She's standing right there by where Karmen just pointed!

"Can I get you some water to sober up?" Frankie asks politely.

"No thanks," Melissa says before she turns back and looks at him seductively. "Do you need water to help get me *wet*...so I can cool down?" she asks. She presses her ass onto him suggestively.

Oh god. She's gonna kill me. That's right. I'm dying tonight.

"Can I call you a cab?" Frankie asks with a hint of impatience now.

It seems like the whole place has gone quiet, listening, and watching the events happening in that corner of the counter.

"I...I was...she's drunk," he stutters for the second time tonight as he pries Melissa's arms from around his neck.

"No thanks. Cole just offered to take me out for some fresh air," Melissa says.

Nick scoots his chair the other way a little more. Karmen moves over too.

Please don't shoot me, Frankie.

"The fuck I did," he yelps out.

"Oh, no need to bother him, *Melissa*," Frankie says, looking right at Melissa. "I can walk you out. I was just going to take out the *trash*."

Nick snickers and Karmen's lips tighten, stifling a laugh.

Frankie comes around the bar counter and Melissa stands up quickly when she comprehends what she's just been called.

He immediately shoves his chair back and stands up just as Frankie comes to a stop in front of Melissa.

"Do you need help walking to the door?" Frankie asks her, looking fearlessly at the much taller woman.

Dramatically, she ignores Frankie and wraps her hand around his arm, and leans in. "No, he's got me," Melissa purrs.

"Melissa, I'm here for Frankie," he says, prying her fingers off.

Before he can say another word, Frankie walks in between him and Melissa, wraps her arm around the taller woman's waist, and practically shoves her toward the door.

"Actually, he's got *me*. So let me help you out."

Frankie gets to the door and shoves Melissa out into the cold before closing it without saying anything else.

Mouth opened with no excuses, he watches as Frankie picks up a few empty bottles from a table she passes before walking back behind the counter and dumping them into the trash.

"Frankie, I..." he starts to say.

"No worries, big guy, I got *you*," she says before shoving through the double doors so loud it sounded like thunder cracked above.

The few people left in the bar burst into laughter, Nick and Karmen included.

He, in defeat and embarrassment, slumps over the counter as if he's died.

- 27 -

Frankie

"Frankie," he calls from the other side of the shower curtain, "do you know what happened to your car that morning?"

Her car? She isn't sure what he is talking about. She turns the water off and grabs the towel and wraps it around her before pulling the curtains back.

"What do you mean?"

"The morning that you left. I came out and saw its condition." He turns to face her. Freshly shaven. *Gorgeous.* He looks amazing standing in her bathroom, with just a towel covering his lower half.

"Someone must have hit it in the rain," she says, shrugging and drying herself.

He spins her around so her back is facing him.

"You're still bruised. Does it still hurt?" He touches her back softly.

"Not really. I've forgotten all about it."

He slides his hands around her waist and guides her out of the bathroom. They reach the bed and he spins her around to face him.

She reaches for his towel to help it slip to the floor and traces her fingers across the ridges of his abs. The room is cool but Cole is warm like a human furnace.

He pulls the clip from her hair to let it fall down her back before he assists her towel to the floor too.

"I missed you," she says.

"You have no idea how much I missed you," he says with that so amazingly smooth, deep voice of his. The hint of his drawl creates moisture between her legs already and her knees inch closer together.

He backs her into the bed, his hand cradling the back of her head, his fingers threading through her hair. His other hand reaches behind her to pull the covers back before he gives her a kiss. A quick kiss. Soft and promising.

Last night with Cole was indescribable. He's still sound asleep in bed, where she should have stayed.

She switches pose effortlessly along with the instructor on the app as she replays the events. Not necessarily trying to make sense of it but to make sure it's really happening.

There are still so many unanswered questions. The first and the one she hates most is how long he will be staying. Then there's the other one. Karmen and Nick? It doesn't sit well with her at all. Nick is a savage. She's witnessed it firsthand. She can't grasp what Karmen would see in him and why she would bring him around Nic and Nat.

She switches pose again only to be surprised by Cole leaning on the bedroom door frame in his briefs, arms crossed, watching her. She pulls her earbuds out and switches to a Siddhasana pose.

"Morning, handsome," she greets him. "How was your first night at home?" she teases.

"Can't complain," he answers with his beautiful dimpled smile and gift of gab. "You've gotta wear yoga pants more often."

She rolls her eyes at him before standing up and walking over to give him a kiss. Warm. His body is always so warm.

"Why didn't you stay in bed?" he asks.

"I don't know. I woke up and my headache kept me up," she shrugs it off. "I thought some meditation and stretches would help."

"Hangover?" he asks before bending down and kissing the top of her head. She'll never get tired of that.

"Maybe. Want some coffee?" she asks.

"Sure. Do you run? The sun's bright outside, maybe some fresh air and adrenaline will help with the headache? I need to get a few laps in if you wanna join me."

"Sounds good. Go get dressed and I'll get your coffee."

They were ready and outside in under half an hour.

The bright sun outside aids in keeping the inside of his truck nice and warm. He seems to know where he wants to go so she doesn't ask to drive. In fact, she is relieved she doesn't have to. Her headache is still bothering her and she still feels tired. Maybe it's from their bedtime activities. She smiles to herself at the memory of the previous night.

"There's a park I normally jog when I was here last. It's not too far from here," he says. "It's the only park I know with a nice trail around. Is it okay if we go there?"

"Sure."

"Lunch after?" he asks.

"Sounds good," she replies. "Oh, I have to be at Karmen's at three-ish to take the twins out trick-or-treating? Wanna come and meet them?"

She sees him hesitate to answer. *Oh no.* At the memory of the last time she asked him this same question, her heart sinks. He's going to leave again, isn't he?

"Frankie, there's something you should know," he starts.

"You're leaving again, aren't you?" she deadpans.

He looks at her with confusion. "No."

No? No! Yes!

"Okay?" she asks now.

"Nick. He's staying with Karmen and the kids at her place."

"WHAT!" That has to be the last thing she expected to hear. "Since when? How long have you known about them?"

"I just found out about them last night. I really didn't know before that."

"Cole, I know he's your brother, but I've seen who he is. I can't just stand by and wait for him to hurt Karmen and those kids."

"I understand why you'd be concerned. Believe me, I do. But Nick's changed. And Karmen and those kids are probably why."

"He's changed until when? Until he's had one too many shots?"

"He's quit drinking. I know my brother and he's different now. He looks happy and he looks a shit ton healthier."

She sits quietly, mulling over this news. To say she is worried would be an understatement.

Nick repeatedly made clear his intention to rape her that night once it was *his* turn. He humiliated her when he ripped her panties off in the shower. He'd seen her body and put her in the most vulnerable position she'd ever been in. He's capable of hurting women without a second thought. And *that* was only a month ago. For her to believe he's changed? No way in fucking hell. And now? He's living with Karmen and the twins.

She tries to rub her headache away. *Fucking headache.*

"Frankie, I'm not gonna try to make excuses for him. I'm not even going to ask you to give him a chance. I just wanted to give you a heads-up." He reaches for her hand and brings it to his lips.

She loves the feel of his lips on her skin, but she's still not assured.

"And of course I'll go with you."

"Does Karmen know about what you do? Does she know about what happened to me?"

"Nick didn't say if he told her about you. But she does know about what we do. I don't know to what extent."

She stares at the group of jack-o'-lanterns on the top step of Karmen's house. She wonders if the sound of the doorbell even made it through all the commotion she can hear coming from inside.

She peers over to the side of the house and sees Karmen's car still parked where it should be. Karmen still has an hour to get to work.

The door suddenly opens and she's face to face with Nick. The one person she didn't want to answer the door.

"Hey, Nick," Cole says, immediately standing behind her.

She isn't sure if the move is for encouragement or for fear of her kicking his brother in the nuts again. She's definitely tempted.

"Hey," Nick says and steps aside for them to walk in.

The house is warm and *clean*. The twins can be a handful at their age and normally there are toys sprawled out every which way. She is surprised to see everything put away as it should be.

"Karmen is still putting on their costumes. Can I get you guys a drink?" Nick offers.

She shakes her head.

"I'm good," Cole replies.

"Make yourselves at home," Nick says before disappearing into the kitchen.

You sure as hell did. She's walked in and out of this place as if it were her second home since Karmen and the twins moved in here. And now *he* is telling *her* to make herself at home. *What the fuck?*

I'm not asking you to forgive him or give him a chance. I'm just saying maybe we can watch and see how things are first. That's what Cole said to her on their drive here.

Watch. Yeah. She'll watch, all right. With a fucking magnifying glass.

She walks over to the TV stand and picks up a canister. She reads the label on the other side and turns it to show Cole.

Nick's Swear Jar.

"*What the hell?*" she silently mouths to Cole.

He walks over and takes it from her hand. "Impossible. There's no more than ten dollars in here," he says.

She gives him a shove and he puts it back down with a big smile.

"Fwankie!" "Frankie!" come two little voices down the hallway as they run at full speed her way.

"Oh. My. God! Thing 1 and Thing 2!" She crouches to give them hugs and kisses and they topple her over, both hanging on to her. One around the neck and one around the waist.

"Come on, guys. Let her breathe!" Karmen says. "Hi, Cole."

"Nick! Is that your bwofer?!" Nat asks extremely too loud.

Nick reappears from the kitchen. "Yes, he is. That's my baby brother, Cole. Why don't you introduce yourselves?"

They quickly release her to stand in front of Cole.

"I'm Nicolai and I'm three," Nic says and extends his hand for a proper shake. One that Cole takes with a manly grip.

"I'm Natalia and I'm also thwee," Nat says, extending her hand as well.

Wow! Manners! When did that happen?

"Nice to meet you both," Cole answers.

"How come you're taller than Nick?" Nic asks.

"He eats his veggies," Nick retorts.

"Nick, can I have double veggies with dinner tonight?" the little boy asks in all seriousness.

"Nick and Mama say you're Fwankie's boyfwend," Nat remarks.

"Well, if they told you that, it must be true, right?" Cole answers with a chuckle.

Is it? She isn't really sure what they are yet. They've technically spent less than a week together.

"She's never had one of those before," Nic informs everyone like it should be public news. *Great kid. Just great.*

"Why would I need one? I have you two to hug and to kiss and to love and to tickle," she says as she tugs Nat into her lap for a tickle fest.

"So, what did you have planned, Frankie?" Karmen asks while Nick helps her slip into her jacket. "By the way, Nick wants to tag along to help."

"There's already two of us, we don't need help." She meant to sound neutral and that definitely wasn't neutral sounding. She isn't sure if Karmen knows about their history or not. She doesn't know how to ask or how to approach the subject either.

"Cole and I haven't had the chance to do anything like this before, so..." Nick trails off.

"Fine," she cuts him off quickly.

Karmen gives her a questioning look. She has to give Nick credit for using Cole as an excuse. *Well played.*

"We can go around the neighborhood here for a little bit. There's a little pumpkin patch carnival at the schoolyard a few blocks from here too," Nick suggests. "If you guys have time, we should catch dinner together. My treat," he says.

"That sounds like a plan," Karmen answers before she can object. "Kids, go get your bags." Karmen turns and gives Nick a quick kiss. "Why don't you go grab the car seats from my car. I have to leave," Karmen tells the slimeball.

"Come on, Cole. Give me a hand," Nick says, shoving Cole to the door. "From strippers in the backseat of your truck to car seats. Can you believe that?"

She immediately snaps up at Cole and sees him rolling his eyes.

"I heard that!" Karmen yells after Nick, who's already halfway out the door.

"He's kidding," Cole says as he rushes after his brother.

"When were you going to tell me about him?" she immediately asks once she and Karmen get the moment alone.

"Things happened so fast. We kinda just slipped into this routine and..." Karmen trails off.

"And he's living here."

"We fit well, Frankie. The kids love him. And I'm pretty sure he isn't short of feeling the same way about them. You should see how they are together."

"I can't tell you what to do, Karmen. But I'm not going to lie. I'm scared for you and for Nic and Nat." She pauses. "Cole said you know about what they...*do*. Did he tell you about how Cole and I really met?"

"What do you mean?"

He didn't. Karmen doesn't know about that night. Should she be the one to tell her and *then* let her decide if they still *fit*?

"How do you deal with his...*line of work*? The kids will ask, Karm."

"Nick and I just deal with things as we come to them. How about you and Cole?"

"He and I...well...we haven't spent much time together. The time we have spent together has been amazing, but I never know when that will end because he has another *job* to get to," she says in all honesty.

"I know what you mean. Nick says he'll always try to come back to us. Since he can slow down now, any jobs they take will be close by. It's a little reassuring and it might be enough...for now."

Nic and Nat come running into the living room at the same time Cole and Nick come back inside. She watches the interaction between Nick and Karmen as she leaves for work.

"Bye, babies." Karmen gives each of the kids kisses. "Oh wait! I gotta take a picture of everyone!" Karmen excitedly pulls out her phone.

Too many pictures later, Karmen finally departs for work, leaving three awkward adults with two much too excited kids.

"Thing 1, Thing 2! Whatever *shall* we do?" Nick chants, leading everyone out of the house.

No! No! No!

"That's supposed to be me in the picture with you, Frankie! Not him! Not them!"

- 28 -

Knock. Knock.

Cole offered to run out to pick up something for her headache. She forgot that he doesn't have a key yet. She wipes her hands on a kitchen towel and heads over to the door. Without looking in the peephole, she opens the door, expecting to see Cole.

"Hey, Frankie," Sam greets her.

"Sam!" she exclaims. "Come in."

"Is it a bad time?" he asks, looking over to the kitchen.

"No, no. I was just making some lunch." She walks back to the kitchen. "What's up?"

"I'm downstairs working and I felt like...I had to come up here and apologize to you," he starts.

She turns off the stove and walks back to him, not sure what he's talking about.

"About the other night. At the Halloween party," he reminds her.

Oh. That.

"I just thought that you and I...that we could have something special. Or at least that we were heading in that direction."

"Sam, you're a great guy. Any woman would be lucky to have you. It's just that I wasn't expecting that kind of relationship with you." She pauses and looks at him, hoping he can see how sincere she really is.

"You're a great friend to me and in the short time since we've met, I've come to think of you as family. I'm sorry I reacted the way I did. That was childish on my part."

"Oh, you mean stomping off and leaving me on a crowded dance floor? Yeah, definitely childish," he says with a smile. A smile that she appreciates. "But I guess I might have deserved it."

"So, we're okay?" she asks.

"You're always gonna be the one that got away, Frankie. But I'd rather have you around as a friend than not around at all."

He pulls her in for a hug. "Besides, it'll be awkward having to work downstairs for a few more months and not be able to talk to you," he says with a chuckle.

"Thanks, Sam. I would have hated that too," she says before wrapping her arms around him for a bear hug.

"So, you're serious with Cole?" he asks when she releases him and heads to a chair.

Sam chooses to sit on the couch.

"We're just figuring things out as we go."

"Where's he from?"

"Montana." She pauses and decides she has to tell him. "Oh, Sam. Just to give you a heads-up. He's kinda staying here. I mean...with me, here."

Sam's eyes widen. "What? Don't you think that's too soon? You've just met him and he's already moved in?"

"It's temporary, Sam. I know it doesn't make sense to you but it works for us. At least, it does for the time being. I just want to let you know because you're both important to me. You don't have to like each other, but I don't want to be caught in the middle every time you bump into each other either."

Sam sits quietly, seeming to think over what she said.

Her headache is starting to grow again. Feeling parched, she stands up, intending to get something to drink, but nausea takes over suddenly and her legs quickly rush her to her bathroom. She barely makes it to the toilet before she spews out everything she has in her. Then it just turns into dry heaves.

"Frankie!" Sam had followed her in. "Are you sick?" He rushes to help her hold her hair back and out of the way. "Here, hold this."

Her hand wraps around her hair and then she feels him leave her side. She hears the faucet turn on and off. Sam returns to her side moments later with a cold, wet cloth pressed to the back of her neck.

"Is that better?" he asks.

She nods her head in response. Her headache is pounding again. *What the hell is wrong with me?* Other than the headache, she hasn't felt sick. Suddenly, she's heaving into the bowl again.

"Frankie?" Cole's asks from the bathroom doorway.

Sam must have left the front door unlocked.

She can't answer or look at him, too busy trying to pump out whatever is making her sick from her stomach.

"She just *got* sick out of nowhere," Sam answers.

She hears Cole put something down on the counter before he reaches her side.

Sam moves out of the way but leaves the wet cloth still on the back of her neck. Cole removes the cloth to rewet it with cold water and replaces it.

"Thanks, Sam," she hears Cole say.

"Has she seen a doctor? How long has she been sick?" She can hear that *tone* in Sam's voice.

She doesn't have the physical strength to make them play nice at the moment so she has to just let the two men work it out on their own. And well, if one ends up killing the other, then so be it.

- 29 -

He pulls his phone from his pocket at the insistent ringing. Only three people know this number. He's just dropped Frankie off at work and he shouldn't be hearing from Dusty. He looks at the screen. It's Nick.

"Hello," he answers.

"Are you close to Vinny's Place?" Nick asks without a greeting.

"Yeah. I'm at Frankie's."

"Wanna join me for the game and have some dinner here? We should talk."

"Sure. Be there in ten," he says before hanging up the phone.

He turns the TV off without another thought and grabs *his* set of keys off the table. He looks down at the keyring with not one but three keys now. *You're such a sap*, the devil taunts him.

Monday night football brings in a good number of patrons at the bar. With perfect timing, he finds a parking spot almost directly in front of the bar thanks to someone who just pulled out of the spot.

He walks inside and heads to the bar, where Nick is sitting and talking to Donnie. The TV in front of him has on the news station rather than the game.

"Hey," he greets his brother and slides into a seat.

"Hi," Karmen says, appearing from behind the double doors with a plate that she puts in front of Nick. "What can I get for you?" she asks.

"Whatever he's having is fine. Thank you," he says politely. "Can I get a bottle of water?" He waves over to Donnie, who nods.

"You're staying at Frankie's?" Nick asks before picking up half of his sandwich.

"Yeah," he answers coolly. "How long can I tell her I'm staying?"

"Isn't that up to you?"

"You know what I mean." He lowers his voice. "What happens when we have another job?"

"We get it done and we come back. Not that hard," Nick says. He pauses and takes a bigger bite of his food. After taking a drink of his water, Nick continues. "Maybe we can take jobs near by so we can always make it back quick."

"You know we can't do that. Someone's bound to see a pattern that way," he reminds Nick.

"Then like I said, we get the job done and get back."

"And Frankie is supposed to just wait around for weeks or months each time? She's not a booty call. Karmen and the kids too," he says quietly.

"I told Karm that until things change, I'll come back after every job. She can change that arrangement anytime she feels she can't handle it anymore. I want it to work with her. And if you want it to work with Frankie, then talk to her. It's only a booty call if you make it out to be one."

Did Nick just give sound advice?

The news replays a segment he's seen earlier about the pawnshop robbery gone wrong. Nick is watching and reading the caption too. Once the segment is done, Nick looks over to him, asking his question silently.

He only shakes his head at his brother.

Karmen comes through the double doors and puts a plate with all the fixings in front of him similar to the one Frankie made him.

"I'm warning you. It probably isn't as good as Frankie's," she says with a smile.

"Thank you," he says before digging in.

"How's Frankie? The twins said they had a lot of fun last night. Thank you guys for taking the time to be with them."

"They're great kids, Karmen. Frankie might've had too much fun. She got sick this morning," he says before eating a pickle.

"Is she okay? Wait...you mean like morning sickness kind of sick or like fever and chills kind of sick?" Karmen asks suspiciously.

"She didn't have a fever. She had a headache the past few days and this morning, she just threw up everything she had in her. Still insisted on going into work tonight."

Karmen stops leaning on the counter and stands up. Nick has stopped eating and is now staring at him.

"What?" he asks, confused at their reactions.

"Oh my god. Oh my god," Karmen chants and looks over at Nick, who clears his throat. "Morning sickness," she repeats loudly, fanning her face.

What the hell is their problem? Donnie looks over in their direction and shrugs. Karmen reaches out and shakes Nick's forearm resting on the counter.

"Nick, do you think..."

"I don't know. Maybe?" Nick answers.

The two of them and their fucking secret language.

A phone rings to break the awkward silence and Karmen pulls her phone out of her back pocket. "Speak of the devil," she says before showing them Frankie's name and picture on the call screen. She answers with a huge smile.

"Frankie! When were you going to tell me?" Karmen says into the phone.

Tell you what? he wonders.

He watches as her smile turns into concern.

"Alice? Wait. Just slow down. Vince! Vince!" Karmen calls across the bar in a panic and waves Vince over.

"Alice. What's going on? Why are you calling on Frankie's phone?" Karmen asks into the phone. "I have to put you on speaker."

"Karm, it's Frankie. One minute she was talking to Katrina and Oscar and the next second, she's on the ground. Oscar barely caught her. She's passed out cold and the ammonia didn't wake her. We're getting in the ambulance heading to University now. Can you or Vince meet us in the ER?"

He stands up immediately after hearing the panic in Alice's voice. He should have never let Frankie go to work today.

"We'll be there in ten minutes," Karmen says before she hangs up.

"Go!" Vince says to her. "You call me and you keep me updated, all right?"

"I'm parked right out front," he tells her.

"I'll drive," Nick says, pushing out of his seat.

Karmen grabs her belongings from the back and heads to the front door. "Which way?" she asks in a panic.

"There." He points to his truck.

Karmen rushes to get the back door open, both Nick and him not far behind her.

He pulls the navigation up and hits the hospital icon as Nick pulls into traffic.

"Nick, can you—" he starts to ask.

"Imagine how much longer it'll take us to get there if I get busted for speeding," Nick cuts him off.

"Babe, take the third exit from now. It'll take us around to the ER entrance," Karmen says from the back seat.

He's been on road trips that have lasted four days straight. Why did this feel like the longest ten-minute drive of his life?

The hospital finally comes into view just when he thinks his fucking soul is going to hop out of his body.

"There, Nick. The ambulance bay," Karmen points. "You can let us out there."

Nick follows her instructions and they both jump out.

"I'll park and catch up," Nick hollers from the window.

Karmen runs from ambulance to ambulance until the doors of the third one she comes to swing open, nearly hitting her. He catches up to her just in time to see a familiar brunette hop down.

"Oh my god, Alice!" The two women hug each other and look behind them.

The paramedics lower the gurney from the back. He's seen blood and guts before but the sight of her pale, still, and unconscious makes him light-headed as if he's been punched in the gut.

"Is she okay? What happened?" Karmen asks the paramedic, who tries to calm her down so they can push Frankie to the entrance.

He picks up his girl's hand as they push her by him. It's cold to the touch and burns him at the same time. They go through the doors where a doctor and two nurses meet them.

"She came to on the ride. Disoriented but passed out again," one of the paramedics says.

"Francine Hoang. Twenty-nine years of age," the other one rattles of her stats.

"Francine! Francine! Can you hear me?" The doctor flashes his light into her eyes and rubs his knuckles between her chest.

She moves her head and he can feel her hand squeeze his own.

"Baby, I'm right here," he says, returning her squeeze.

"Are you guys family?" the doctor asks.

"Yes," the women say in unison. "We're her best friends."

He feels a hand on his shoulder, turns around, and sees Nick standing behind him.

"Do you know if she's taken anything? Over the counter or street drugs?"

"No. No drugs," Alice says.

"She took some ibuprofen for a headache," he answers. He sees one of the nurses adding notes onto her tablet.

"Has she been sick recently?" doc asks again, pushing the gurney along.

"She's complained of having bad headaches," Alice answers again.

"And...and she threw up this morning," Karmen says.

"Is it possible she can be pregnant?" The doctor looks to him for an answer.

"No? I...I don't know," he answers.

Pregnant? What! She would have said something. What if she didn't know? What if she's pregnant? Woah! What if she's pregnant! It's been over a month since their first time. It's possible. And he had thrown caution out the fucking window like never before that night. Oh, fuck!

"Yes, there's a chance," Karmen answers and Alice turns to look at her in shock. Suddenly *he* feels like he should be on a gurney too.

"Any major trauma, accidents, or surgeries recently?" He faintly hears the doctor speaking.

Pregnant? He feels her hand slipping out of his while his insides feel like they've just been tossed into a blender.

"She's coming to," the doctor seems to be telling the nurse. "Let's get her a pregnancy test and an ultrasound before we order the X-rays. Put a rush on it."

"Got it," one of the nurses says before she walks away.

"You all can wait right over there. We'll let you know as soon as she's in a triage unit," the other nurse says before disappearing behind the doors.

- 30 -

cole

He looks up at the clock on the wall again for the thousandth fucking time. Almost an hour has passed. It seems like way too much time for him to simply know if she is pregnant or not. How long can a pregnancy test take for fuck's sake?

He can hear Karmen speaking on the phone with Vince. Alice is pacing back and forth on the phone as well. She looks right at him when she hangs up and heads over.

"We haven't officially met. I'm Alice," she introduces herself.

"Cole. Thank you for coming with her," he says politely.

"Is there something that you guys aren't telling me? You and Frankie met a little over a week ago. Why does Karmen think there's a chance she can be pregnant?" Alice shoots right off.

He looks over at Karmen and then at Nick, who's sitting beside him.

"Cole and Frankie went out on their first date over a month ago. I invited him to the surprise party," Karmen lies.

"Frankie didn't say anything about that. She would have told me if she went on a date with someone, especially if it got *that* far on a first date. What's really going on, Karm?"

"It's true. She and I used a dating app and went on a double together. This is Nick. He's Cole's brother," Karmen introduces. "He's also my boyfriend now."

Alice looks at Nick and doesn't seem like she is going to buy the lie for one second.

The double doors swing open and the nurse motions for them to follow her. Thank fucking god!

All four of them quickly sweep through the doors with the nurse holding them open with a button.

"She's awake and has her bearings back. The doctor is waiting for her blood test results and X-rays to get back. Shouldn't be much longer," the nurse says. They follow closely behind the nurse as she makes a turn. "There." She points to a corner room with the door closed. "Just keep it down okay?"

Karmen and Alice open the door and walk in together. He watches as the ladies hover over Frankie.

She looks at him with patient eyes, waiting for her friends to step aside. When it's his turn, he reaches for her hand and sits on the bed next to her.

Are you pregnant? Are we having a baby? That's the first thing he wants to blurt out but it probably isn't the right thing to ask.

"Hey," he says instead.

"Sorry for the scare," she says with concern on her face. "Please don't say 'I told you so.'"

"Are we—" Just then the doctor bursts through the door.

"Well," doc says, taking a deep breath and looking through her digital chart. "Let's see what's going on with you."

He steps back to lean against the wall.

Nick steps outside and her friends sit down in the only two seats in the unit. The doctor motions for Frankie to sit up and does the normal routine of listening to her chest and lungs.

"How long have you been getting the headaches?" doc asks.

"About a week," she replies.

"Did you get them often before that?"

"No, not really."

"Does nausea come and go often?"

"Just this morning. It kinda came out of nowhere."

"Any fatigue, shortness of breath?"

"I think so. I've been feeling really tired lately."

"And when did that start?"

"About the same time as the headaches."

For crying out loud! Just tell me what's wrong already, doc. Is she pregnant? His hands tighten into fists at this anxiety. Not knowing what to do, he shoves them into his jacket pockets.

"Do you remember what happened before you passed out?"

"I...I think I was talking to my boss about a banquet. Then I felt...vertigo and this funny taste in my mouth. Like copper, I think."

"Hmm...do you remember being in the ambulance?"

Frankie shakes her head.

"These bruises here," doc says while he pushes on various spots on her back. "What happened there?"

"Oh. The weekend before last, I was crossing the street and some guy didn't see me. He nearly ran me over but Cole got me out of the way. I took a tumble and my back hit the curb," she explains.

Nick reappears in the doorway.

"You said it was just a little incident," Alice says from her seat.

"I really didn't think anything of it. Other than the bruises and little cuts, I was fine."

The doctor pulls the back of her gown together and picks up his tablet. He enters in some information and a *ping* comes through. He reads through it as everyone silently waits to hear what he has to say.

"Well, your blood tests are back. First news is, you're not pregnant."

She's not pregnant! Did she want to be? Did he want her to be? Is this good news or not? What the fuck? God fucking damn it!

"I don't know if you were trying or not but I can confirm that you're not," doc continues. "Your X-rays look good. From what you just told me along with vertigo, fatigue, headaches, and nausea...these are all symptoms of post-concussion syndrome." The doctor picks up his tablet again and adds more stuff. "It's the lingering symptoms that can occur following a concussion. Did you get checked out after the incident?"

"No, I didn't," she answers quietly.

He wanted to kick his own ass all up and down these sterile halls. He should have had her checked out.

"You're very lucky," the doctor continues. "This could have been a lot worse. Concussions are common but people don't realize how dangerous they can be, even for adults."

"But I'll be okay, right?"

"You need to give yourself some time to heal. Unfortunately, there isn't an overnight cure. We can only treat the symptoms. I'll give you a script for the headaches. Take them as needed and accordingly. I'll also give you something for the vertigo. I'd like to suggest you take some time to recuperate if you can afford to. I can write you a note for light-duty work if you need but I would prefer that you not stand on your feet more than a few hours at a time.

"If you absolutely have to, be sure you sit down and catch your breath in between. The bruising on your back looks like it's already healing but it doesn't hurt to ice it. Switch between ice packs and hot cloth. That should help with the stiffness of the muscles around. Follow up with your primary in two weeks," the doctor says. "Do you have any questions?"

"So, I can go home soon?" Frankie asks.

"As soon as the nurses can get your discharge instructions and scripts ready for you," he says. He shakes everyone's hands and leaves.

"I have to call Vince," Karmen says.

"I've gotta let Katrina and Oscar know too," Alice says.

Both ladies step out of the room with Nick following.

He sits back down on the bed next to her. He picks up her hand and gives it a kiss.

"I should have brought you in," he says regretfully.

"You couldn't have made me. It's okay," she says forgivingly. "I bet Karmen thought I was pregnant, didn't she?" Frankie asks teasingly.

"Yeah...she might have hinted at that a little." *A little?*

"Sorry," she says. "I mean sorry for her thinking that. Not the part where I'm not pregnant. I mean...you know what I mean," she stammers, blushing.

"I know what you mean," he says, giving her an out.

"You would be the first to know if I were, babe," she says. "Unless you decide to skip town on me and I can't get a hold of you," she teases him.

Unsure of how to react to that along with everything else from thinking she was pregnant to find out she wasn't pregnant, he opts to remain quiet.

"And we would discuss it before there would even be anything I'd need to tell you, okay?"

He's happy with that and nods his head.

"So, I met Alice..." he says and Frankie laughs quietly.

"She calls you *the gorgeous god*, you know."

He rolls his damn eyes and shakes his head.

"Can't blame her," Frankie says with a wink. She throws the sheets off. "Where are my clothes?"

He finds her bag and then leaves her to get dress. The ladies step back inside the room to help her and he's outside in the hallway with Nick.

"Karmen know how Frankie and I really met?" he asks his brother, keeping an eye on the door.

"I told her the truth. Yes."

"And she's okay with it?"

"Not at first. She nearly threw me out of the house. But we're trying to work through it. And she and Frankie will have to eventually cross that bridge too. I wouldn't want Karmen to have to choose."

- 31 -

Frankie

She wakes with her vision blurred. A glance at the night table and she finds it's almost noon. Cole isn't in bed. The bathroom door is open so he isn't in there either. The bedroom door is shut all the way though.

Where did he go?

But she remembers him saying he would be picking up her prescriptions from the pharmacy. That's probably what he's out doing.

The curtains are slightly parted and light is coming in. A glass of water and a note sit on her side of the night table. It's a note from Cole telling her to drink the water and that he'll be back soon.

She thought she heard a noise coming from the other side of the bedroom door. It's probably Sam and his workers working downstairs though. She sits up, picks up her glass of water, and picks up her phone with the other hand. Lunch service would have well started by now and she hasn't even called Katrina. *Shit.* She walks to the door and opens it.

Surprised to see Nick sitting on her couch, she drops the glass of water and takes a step back into the room. She looks down to see what she's wearing before looking back at him. She's fully clothed, thank god.

"Woah," he says to her, standing up. "I didn't mean to scare you."

"What the fuck are you doing here?"

"Karmen, the kids, and I just stopped by to see how you're doing. Cole wasn't here but that Sam guy let us in. Karmen and the kids are talking with him downstairs right now." He holds both hands up to show her he means no harm.

This is the first time they have been alone since that night. And to find him sitting on her couch by himself shocked her. The flood of emotions come rushing back. The feeling of his hand on her leg, trying to go higher up her thighs. The humiliation she felt when he ripped her panties off.

She takes another step back into the room

"Frankie, stop. Your foot's bleeding. I think you stepped on some broken glass." He takes a step around the coffee table.

"NO!" she yells at him.

"All right," he says calmly. Hands back up again. "All right."

She stares at him, wanting to scream at him to get the fuck out of her home. But her brain and mouth don't cooperate. Instead, she stands...frozen.

"I know what you must be thinking," he says. "I'm sorry. I didn't think me sitting here would remind you of *that*. I really didn't want to do that."

She feels a whoosh of cold air sweep through the room. The door just opened and closed. She isn't sure who just came in. She can't move and can't turn her head to look. All she wants to do is scream at the asshole standing in her living room and shoot him dead at the same time.

"No. You don't know." Her voice shakes, barely able to control her anger. "You have no fucking idea what I'm thinking. Because *you* weren't the one that had their head bashed against a wall. That was *me*. *You* weren't the one that almost got finger-fucked by some drunk asshole or raped by some repulsive scumbag. That was *me*! And *you*? *You* weren't the one that was humiliated and had their dignity ripped from them, asshole. *That was me!*"

For a moment, she doesn't care who it is that just walked through that door. She's furious. Burning within from the fury. Furious that Nick is sitting here. Furious that he's living his life with Karmen and the twins as if he's God's gift to them when indeed, he's the fucking devil incarnate.

"Frankie." She hears Cole's voice close to her. She can't look at him though. Too filled with rage and fury.

"Did you know I couldn't sleep for four days straight after that? No. You had no fucking idea. Did you know how many fucking times I would have to check my locks each and every single night? Does it make you hard knowing you can have that kind of control over someone's life even after you left? *Does it?*"

"Frankie," she hears Cole calling her again. Closer. Softer.

She feels his finger wiping something from her cheek. A tear.

"I'm sorry," Nick says. "There's nothing I can do to take any of that back. And I'm incredibly sorry about that."

She finally turns to look up into Cole's face. She sees his pain and his turmoil. But instead of calming, she hurts even more.

She realizes he can't give her the strength she needs to deal with this. That strength has to come from within.

She pulls her face out of Cole's reach and turns, hands in fists, in the direction of the bathroom, where she quietly shuts the door and cries for the first time for everything that happened that night.

"What happened?" he asks Nick.

"I was just sitting here, waiting for Karmen and the kids to get up here. She opened the door and saw me...alone."

He understands now. He knew things would eventually come to this even though he would have much preferred it happened later. He doesn't know what to do. He saw the hurt and anger in her eyes before she turned away from him. She hadn't needed him.

Watching Nick standing there, he can see his brother's changes too. He actually feels sympathy for him. The guy had come pretty far from who he was a month ago. Regardless of how things are between him and Frankie, he can't ask her to give Nick a chance. He has no right to. And from what he just witnessed, she's been traumatized more than she ever let him know.

He steps over the broken glass and sees blood.

"She stepped on it and cut herself," Nick says. "Go. I'll get this cleaned up before the kids get up here. I'll get lost after."

He slowly opens the bathroom door, not sure what to expect, but the sight of her tears at his inner being.

She's sitting on top of the counter. Her face red and wet from crying. Her head slumped with her feet in the sink, bleeding.

They never talked about what happened that night or about how she dealt with it in the aftermath. She's always seemed so strong, everyone's go-to person to fix their problems. He knows she is capable of sympathizing with the ability to forgive like no one he's ever known in his life. He's a testament to that ability. Admittedly, he did hope that she could give his brother that same forgiveness with time. He'd never push for it though. Seeing her like this diminished that hope. Nick had...*they*...had hurt her more than he thought.

She looks up at him. Her beautiful green eyes are red. Her long midnight lashes are soaked.

"I'm sorry," he says as he walks in and shuts the door behind him. He isn't sure if he should approach her or give her space. Just minutes earlier she pulled away from him.

"I should have been here," he says regretfully.

She shakes her head. "It's not your job to save me from him, Cole."

Whether she knows it or not, he would step in between them any day though.

"We should clean that up," he says, reaching for her feet in the sink. Needing an excuse to touch her.

"Yeah," she says as she lets him lift her feet out of the sink. She wraps her arm around him and leans on him. "Thank you."

He kisses the top of her head, wishing there is more he could actually do.

"Karmen and the twins are gonna be coming up those stairs soon. I can tell them you're not up for company right now if you need. Nick is leaving," he adds.

"The twins can stay. I'd like the distraction. Maybe we can babysit and Karmen can spend the day with...him."

Who wouldn't love her? She hates the guy yet she's still willing to do something that benefits him. Amazing.

Wait...did he just think...love?

"You sure you're up for *that* many distractions? They're kinda...energetic," he says, pushing the other thought to the back of his mind.

"There's two of them versus two of us. I think we can deal. Besides, we can load them up with sugar before they go home."

"Ooh...ulterior motives...I like the sound of that."

They both laugh together as he finishes cleaning her cut.

- 32 -

Frankie

"Sam's already with the tables," Alice says when she looks up from her phone.

"You invited Sam?" she asks and looks in the mirror at Alice, who is standing behind her, curling her hair as they get ready for a night out on the town. It's been a while and Alice had talked her into this.

"Uh yeah! He's the person that got us in. He's like VIP there. The firm he works at helped design the place or something."

Ping. Ping.

"Here. Hold this." Alice hands the curling iron over so she can check her phone again. "Karm and company are there too. I just told them to meet Sam inside."

"Cole too?"

"Yes, your gorgeous god is there too. He better look the part tonight or I'm gonna be disappointed."

She rolls her eyes at Alice. She isn't worried about how he'll look. He can look just as amazing in flannel and jeans as he does with nothing on. She's more worried about him and Sam having to sit together.

"There. Hair and makeup are done. Go change," Alice says before they both rush into the stalls to change.

They are the last two to get ready. The other coworkers whom Alice invited are either already waiting for them outside or chatting with Katrina, who has patiently waited for everyone.

She quickly squeezes into her skin-tight, short, black dress. The fabric feels amazing, soft and smooth. She touches the sheer fabric on the sleeves and brushes over the silver sequin motifs that cover the fabric over the deep V-neck portion of the dress and then throughout various other places down the body. The dress is probably a little too short for the weather outside, falling at about midway down her thighs, but Alice let her borrow a black hooded long-coat to go over it. Alice always knows how to make a girl look *and feel* sexy.

"Alice, we gotta go. Katrina's closing up," she says.

She straps on her black heels and gives herself another look in the mirror before slipping into her coat.

The stall door opens and Alice steps out looking amazing, as usual. Tight red dress, black stilettos, and the sass to use everything she's got to get what she wants.

"Damn!" she hisses at her best friend.

"Ready for a good time?" Alice teases as they grab the makeup and hair products and shove them back into Alice's kit.

They rush by Katrina and Oscar. "Bye, Chef," they both say simultaneously.

"Have fun, ladies," Oscar says from behind.

They step outside into the alley, where everyone starts to pile into cars. She rides with Alice since Cole dropped her off at work earlier. He still won't let her drive anywhere yet even though it's been over a week since her hospital trip.

It takes everyone over half an hour to get to the place and find parking. The Martini Lab, it's called. Apparently, even their valet parking is full tonight. She believes it as she spots the line to get in.

She puts on the hood of the coat and waits for Alice to round up the other seven people joining them before they make their way to the front of the line as people groan and complain.

"Alice. We're on Sam Greenberg's guest list," she tells the bouncer.

"He's already inside, miss," the guy says as he unhooks the velvet rope.

The place is a lot bigger than she expected. The ambiance inside is lighter than that of a nightclub. Accent lights in various shades of blue and purple are spread around. Each of the four corners of the place is sectioned off by floor to ceiling glass with seating. Probably for their special guests or VIPs. Tables and seating line each side of the wall fashionably. The darkest spot in the club is the dance floor in the middle, where hip tunes cater to the number of people dancing.

"There," Alice yells and points to where they are heading.

It's the far back glass section in the corner. She sees Sam waving and Alice waves back. Karmen and Nick are laughing at something Sam is saying. Cole, however, is nowhere in sight.

"You guys made it!" Sam exclaims as everyone ushers into the section.

"You helped do this?" Alice asks. "It's amazing!"

The music isn't loud at all in their section. It's perfect for conversation. The glass does an amazing job keeping out all the background noise.

Drink in hand, Karmen comes over to her. "This place is so *ultra*, isn't it? Here, taste this drink. I don't even know what it's called but it tastes amazing!"

Karmen pushes the glass to her lips for a sip before she even has time to object.

"Oh yeah! That's good!" she says, surprised. "Karm, you looking freaking amazing!"

She turns her friend around to get a better look.

With the kids, Karmen doesn't get out much but when she does, the woman knows how to look her best. Tonight, she's wearing a pink velvet wrap dress that ties at the waist for accent. The low-cut back and plunging neckline accentuate Karmen's figure and assets in just the right way.

She looks over at Nick and sees him with a bottle of Perrier. Joe, one of her coworkers, is talking to him. She admits that he cleans up well for such a slime ball. His hair is slicked back tonight. He's wearing a black sweater with a white collared shirt underneath and black jeans, looking very much like the everyday hipster even without a beard.

She can see how Karmen would be attracted to him. Tall, broad muscular shoulders, that aura of mystery, brooding hazel eyes. She's suddenly curious about his age. Cole is thirty-six. How old would that make Nick?

She takes off the hood of her jacket and looks around for Cole. It shouldn't have been hard to spot him in a crowd but she can't seem to find him.

"He's in the men's room," Karmen informs her all knowingly.

"Champagne for the little lady," Sam says, handing her a tall glass before swooping in for a hug.

"This place...I dig it," she says, nodding her head in approval.

"Teamwork. I can't take all the credit," Sam says, leading her to a seat.

"Hey, let's get to the bar," Maxine, a coworker, says.

"Oh, no need," Sam stops them. "You can place your order right on the tablet there," he points to the middle of the table.

"No way!" "That's too cool!"

"Someone will bring it over, no need to fight the crowd at the bar," Sam informs everyone.

"I'm impressed!" she tells him.

He breathes on his knuckles and polishes the imaginary lapel of his imaginary jacket and they laugh together hysterically.

She's gotten used to seeing Sam in his basic jeans and long-sleeve shirts. With the exception of the night of her surprise party, she hasn't seen him dressed up before. Tonight, he looks great. Dressed almost as if he and Nick coordinated except Sam is wearing a light blue sweater. She wonders if Cole got the memo about the matching outfits too.

"Having second thoughts about us?" Sam asks her jokingly. "Not too late," he says with a wink.

She smiles warmly at him and takes a sip from her glass.

"Oh shit, oh shit. He's coming this way!" Annie, another coworker, gasps and fans herself.

"I know who I'm going home with tonight," Maxine says.

She turns to see who the fussing is over. She should have guessed even before seeing him.

Cole is trying to make his way past her coworkers who are crowding the opening into their section. He definitely didn't get the memo about the outfit. *Thank God!* And he definitely looks fucking hot as a July sun, every delicious bit the part of the gorgeous god.

He shakes hands and tries to ignore the ladies batting their full lashes at him. His hair is styled sideways as usual. He's wearing a white-collared button-up with blue stripes tucked into dark dress pants the same shade of blue as the stripes. His cuffs are rolled up to his elbows and the top two buttons unbuttoned. *SEXY!* Like a fucking *GQ* model.

cole

He stands to help his girl take off her coat. The moment she shrugs out of it, he hears the sound of Sam choking on his drink.

"Better put that jacket back on, baby brother," Nick says at the exact same time.

He looks down at Frankie and is completely fucking speechless.

She's stunning. Her hair and makeup make her eyes smolder and luminous. Add the dress on to that, and she's the sexiest and alluring woman he's set eyes on. *Hot fucking damn!*

"Alice and I had to go shopping. Do you like it?" she asks him.

"You look amazing, baby. So beautiful. How did I get so lucky?" he says quietly. "*Fucking sexy,*" he whispers into her ear.

"Kids, turn around and let me take a picture," Karmen says to them excitedly. "O. M. G., Frankie, you look so effing hot!"

"Karm, you're making me feel like it's prom night all over again," Frankie says right before she smiles and poses with his arm behind her for the snaps.

"Wait, babe! Nick! Let me get a picture with you and your brother."

He looks over at Nick and shrugs. He can't remember the last time he took a picture with just him and Nick. He's sure there might be one or two hanging in the house at the farm. Those might be the only pictures ever though.

The next two hours go by quick and he's actually enjoying the scene. He's never been in a setting like this before. Not just the ultra lounge but a setting where he's having fun, making conversation about random things, having a few drinks with a group of decent people.

Frankie is dragged on and off the dance floor by one person or another. His girl has moves and is having a good time. Karmen dragged Nick out there a few times too. After seeing the mess that is Nick dancing, he's glad Frankie hasn't pressured him to do the same.

A cocktail waitress stops by with another tray full of colorful drinks and hands him one of two long necks on her tray. She looks at him suggestively, her cleavage on display.

Nick clears his throat from the seat next to his. "Can I get another bottle?" Nick asks her, trying to pull her attention away.

She hands another Perrier to Nick before going to Sam and handing him the other bottle of beer left on her tray. She bends over to say something to Sam, giving him a pretty *nice* view as well.

"I must be getting old if I can't appreciate the looks of that anymore," Nick says.

"Or you're scared Karmen will pull a Lorena Bobbitt on you," he answers.

"She could and would too, that one."

"You're really happy, aren't you?"

"I think so, Cole."

"Do you love her?"

"Bro...I probably loved that woman and her kids the moment I got into their car with vomit all over me."

He laughs remembering that story. "Is that even possible?" he asks.

"Why not? Because we just met? That's bullshit." Nick opens his bottle of water and leans back without taking a drink. "The very second she hopped out of that car, throwing up and telling me she can't do puke...I knew her. Saw who she was...who she is. People can't hide who they are in moments like that."

"Yeah. That's some deep shit, Nick." It's a completely deeper explanation than he expected to come out of his brother.

"You'll get it soon," Nick says with a big slap on his back.

"Ow," he says jokingly.

Frankie and Karmen are back from dancing with some of the other ladies. She slides next to him while Karmen walks over to Nick.

"Feeling okay?" he asks her.

"Yup. No headache," she answers before leaning over to sear his lips with hers.

Her kiss pulls him into her like it always does, his hand unconsciously sliding behind her head, cradling and guiding it so her lips can mold into his. For a second, he forgets that they're in a crowded lounge. It's just the two of them.

"Well, the night is almost over and I think we owe Sam a dance for getting us into this posh place," Annie says before she and Alice drag Sam to the crowded dance floor as a hip song sampling a '90s hit begins playing.

"Last dance, Frankie. You know I don't get to do this often," Karmen says. She's already pulling Frankie into the crowd.

"I think she was trying to tell you something," he says to Nick.

"Yeah. That one's a social butterfly except she doesn't want to go anywhere without me and I don't like leaving the kids with Granny Jane."

"Every kid hates their old babysitter."

"Not that. I'm afraid they're going to give her a heart attack one day. Imagine coming home to that!"

He shoves his brother playfully. It feels...surreal to be joking with Nick like this.

He looks out to see where his girl is. She's dancing with Karmen and Sam.

"See the way he looks at her?" Nick asks, his head nodding in Sam's direction.

He nods his head. But he's known and seen it on more than one occasion.

"He's in love with her," he tells Nick. "Can you blame him?"

"You look at her that same way, Coley."

"I'm sure," he replies.

His attention focuses on Frankie. Sam turns to dance with Karmen and Alice, taking his eyes off of her. He sees a guy taller than Sam move behind her. The scum dances and moves closer and closer to her then puts his hands on her hips and begins grinding on her crudely while his hand slides down until his finger reaches the hem of her dress.

He immediately stands up when she tries to stop the guy from rolling up her dress.

Sam turns around and shoves the scum off of her.

In scumbag fashion, the guy steps back and tries to pull the dress up anyway while Frankie tries to keep the top of her dress from exposing too much.

He takes huge strides to get to her as quickly as he can but not before he sees Sam pulling back his elbow and landing a solid one square on the guy's jawline, sending him a few steps back and releasing his hold on her dress.

He reaches for Frankie and places himself in between her and the asshole. Sam steps up and stands right next to him, ready for a fight if one comes.

"Cole! Sam! Let it go," Frankie hollers, tugging on their arms. "He's just drunk."

Some of the people dancing around them stopped dancing and are now watching.

"Why you mad at me when the bitch wanted it?" The idiot dares to take a step up to them.

"Cole! Don't," Frankie pleads, hanging on to his arm. "Sam! Stop it!"

Nick steps in front of him and Sam. "Hey, everything's cool now. Let's just all enjoy the rest of our night, all right?" Nick says, trying to cool everyone down. That's a first. He's usually starting a fight and has no problem finishing one either.

"Nah. I'm not cool. That motherfucker sucker-punched me, mad he can't control his bitch," the buffoon says.

It takes him two steps and three seconds to get around Nick to land a hard solid one on the other side of the moron's jaw, making the scumbag stagger and fall down to one knee. He looks up to see the bouncers finally doing their jobs and arriving. Nick and Sam stand next to him as the ladies usher Frankie off the floor to their section.

"Way to make a scene, bro," Nick hisses at him.

"Asshole deserved it," Sam says in support.

"We're gonna have to ask you to leave sir," one of the bouncers says to the guy while they help him stand up.

"Why the fuck I gotta be the one to leave? They jumped me!" the scum protests.

"We saw what happened on camera," the other bouncer says as he points to a camera.

"I was just dancing with the girl!" he tries to defend himself.

"Would the lady like for us to call the police to charge him with harassment, sir?" one of the bouncers, who is dressed more like a manager, asks them.

"Fine. I'll go. Fuck this place!" The scumbag tries to stand on his own but it doesn't look like his legs are cooperating.

- 33 -

"That's right, you trashy piece of shit! Beg!" he yells with satisfaction at the bastard lying next to his feet.

"I don't know you, man. We ain't got no beef. I'm sorry, man. I'm sorry. Please, just please..."

"You 'ain't got no beef' with me but you put your hands on the wrong girl tonight, you dumb fuck! You put your hands on MY girl, motherfucker!"

"What girl, man? I'm sorry. Please..."

So annoying and pathetic, the sound of this grown bastard begging for his life.

It took him almost an hour of trailing this bastard and finding the right moment for this. The sound of his metal bat connecting with the back of the bastard's skull was satisfying.

He looks down at the guy now with disgust. Fucking Sam and her "boyfriend" weren't men enough to handle the situation properly. They let this asshole get her dirty. And now look at the bastard.

He grabs the guy by the collar of his shirt and sits him up.

"Let me look into your eyes, you garbage. Correction, your eye." The other is useless already.

He pulls out his trusted blade. The cold metal comes to life in his hand. He needs more than just beating this guy. He needs for his blade to taste that hot red liquid. He needs for his ears to hear the last hiss of breath that leaves his body.

Ah...yes. That's what he needs.

He drives the blade into the guy's stomach, ever so slowly. Savoring every second and every reaction. Relishing the movement of the guy's eye as he realizes what is happening.

For you, my love...

- 34 -

Frankie sits in silence on the drive home after dropping Karmen and Nick off. She's been quiet even before that. He thought Karmen's chattering was giving her a headache. But since they've been alone in the truck, she hasn't even looked in his direction. He has the feeling that she's mad about something.

Particularly at him.

He pulls into his parking spot and she unlocks the door to let herself out even before he shuts off the engine. *What the hell?* He gets out of the truck and she's already through the first set of doors.

He enters the apartment and she's walking from the kitchen to the bedroom, her jacket now on the chair. He follows her into the bedroom and sits on the bed within the frame of light coming from the bathroom.

"Frankie, what's going on?" he treads lightly.

He starts removing his shoes, expecting her to answer. He looks up only to find both of her hands planted on the counter, her head slumped between her shoulders.

"Do you have a headache?" he asks.

She shakes her head.

He gets off the bed, walks over to her, and just before he's able to wrap his arms around her, she pushes him away.

"Hey, wait." He holds on to her hand and gently pulls her back. "What's going on?" he asks again.

She finally looks at him and he can see that she is absolutely livid. At what? He looks sternly into her eyes, demanding an answer.

"You didn't have to do that," she finally speaks. "You didn't have to hit him. I told you to let it go."

"The guy nearly stripped you naked in front of a crowd and I'm supposed to fucking let it go?! Are you serious right now?" *Unbelievable!*

"Sam had him already. You didn't need to step in, Cole!"

"So, is this what it's really about? You wanted Sam to rescue you tonight?"

She pulls her hand out of his and walks away.

"So what? You made up with Sam and now you don't need me anymore? Is that it?"

"I told you before, it's not your job to *save* me."

"So you're mad that I didn't let Sam *save* you."

"Cole! Stop *saving* me! Stop making me feel like you're here because I need saving! Like you're just here because you feel shitty that I needed to be saved from your brother, to begin with."

What?

"What if the police had gotten involved, Cole? What would have happened then? Did you stop to think about that?"

It takes a moment for it to all come together.

Fucking beautiful. Beautiful and amazing.

This woman standing angrily in front of him thought that he would get into a mess with the cops. She would rather suffer through the embarrassment and humiliation rather than let him have to deal with the police. No words can describe the feeling churning in his chest.

Actually, there is a word.

He sits down on the bed and reaches out to pull her over to stand in front of him. They're nearly eye level and he can see her anger simmering.

"Sweetheart, I'm sorry. That's not something you need to worry about," he says before pulling her head closer until their foreheads touch. "I'm not here to save you. I'm not here because I feel guilty or any of that. I'm just here because...I love you, Frankie. I fell for you hard and I don't know how it happened so fast."

He moves his head off of hers so she can see he means exactly what he's saying.

"I love you. Plain and simple," he says.

It's the truth. Still. Saying it guts him in a way. A good way. He thinks. Yeah. Definitely a good way.

She searches for what she needs to see in him. Her eyes sparkle, the light from the bathroom forming a halo around her. She leans down with her lips and seals his feelings for her with a kiss. The kind of kiss he's least expected from his angel. It isn't soft and sensual but long, deep, lustful, and hungry.

Her fingers quickly unbutton his shirt and before he knows it, she's unbuckled his belt too. Her lips never leaving his, her hands quickly find their way into his pants and grabs hold. His arousal creates a smile he feels on his lips.

He takes his shirt off while she finishes unzipping his pants. He stands up to slide those off too, causing their lips to part.

He steps behind her, swipes her hair over one shoulder, and kisses the bare one.

"I think you might be a little overdressed for this," he says.

He slips one hand into the opening of her deep V-neck and fills it with her soft, plump flesh. His other hand places his already throbbing hard-on under her dress, in between her upper thighs so she can feel him.

He tries to peel away the skin-tight dress unsuccessfully. "I've been wanting to take this fucking dress off of you all night and now I can't figure out how," he growls, frustrated.

"You're clever. You'll figure it out," she challenges him.

One of her hands wraps around the back of his neck, splayed in his hair. Her other hand causes wildfire across his sensitive cock as she holds it in place for him to feel her own heat through the very thin fabric of her panties.

"You're driving me crazy."

Unable to contain his frustration any longer, his hands grip the seams of the V-neck and he rips it easily off of her.

"Fuck the dress. I'll buy you a new one."

She laughs. A sexy and alluring laugh. Teasing and inviting him.

He leans her over the bed, sliding off the last piece of garment she has on. Kissing her naked back now, with both hands on her hips, he holds her in place as he slides himself into her. Like butter. She's smooth and tight.

When he pulls out, he throbs at the sight of her cream on his shaft. Her soft moan is like music to his ears. A siren's luring melody. He grinds his teeth, barely clinging on when he retreats, and then enters again, deeper. His eyes drinking the image of her bent over the bed, marveling at how sexy she looks.

She places one knee on the bed, allowing him to move even deeper with each thrust. He swears he can feel himself hitting the center of her stomach. Her hips move to meet him each time, taking what he's giving.

Her moans grow louder. She's close already. He can feel it. He wants to feel her cover him with her heat.

He leans down to kiss her shoulder and nibble on her ear. His hands grip each side of her hips firmly now, holding her in place as he rides her faster and deeper.

"I'm gonna fuck away every memory of any other cock that's been inside you," he promises, trying to hold on to his own excitement.

"Swear it," she gasps in between thrusts.

Fucking hell. This woman is going to kill him where he stands.

He hammers into her a few times and then slows it down. Repeating the rhythm over and over again until she drops to her elbows. It only lets him go at her deeper. Maddening his senses.

"Fuck!" he hisses.

"So deep," she whispers in almost a plea. Softer than the sound of their skin on skin impact.

He feels her erupt all over and around him only seconds before he explodes and fills her. Letting her take every last drop of him. Letting his soul flow in to mingle with hers.

His head is spinning. He can feel the sweat on his head and beads rolling down his back. His heart is racing as if he'd run a marathon.

He helps her climb onto the bed and moves to lie behind her as they float slowly down from their high, the sound of their heavy breathing now filling the room.

"Wow," she says. "We just had our first fight, you know."

"Then makeup sex is fucking amazing!"

She pulls his hand from her hip up to her lips and places a kiss on his palm before placing it under her face.

"I love you, Cole."

Fuck!

She has him. Nice and neat, this tiny raven-haired, green-eyed goddess has him.

"I know, baby," he says before kissing the back of her head and pulling her closer to him.

And it's true. He does know, without question. Call him a sappy sop but he can feel it. Can feel the weight of the words coming from her.

He pulls the covers out from under them and covers both of their satiated, naked bodies before Frankie falls asleep tucked safely next to him.

He finds the remote and turns the TV on before pushing the coffee table out of the way for space to do his push-ups. *Local News at Noon* is playing. *Perfect.*

Fifteen minutes into his routine, there's a knock on the door.

Frankie probably forgot something. She's really going to be late. He opens the door and Sam is standing on the other side.

"She's already left for work," he grunts without a greeting.

"Yeah, I didn't see her car outside. Actually, here to see you," Sam retorts.

"Come in," he says. *What does he want...other than his girl?*

"Have you seen the news?" Sam asks.

He points at the TV and Sam makes himself right at home on the couch. *What the fuck?* He walks to the kitchen for a bottle of water, not bothering to offer Sam anything.

"You wanna tell me what this is about?"

"There," Sam says and picks the remote up to adjust the volume. "Watch."

"Early this morning, a couple out for their morning jog came across the gruesome sight of the body of a white male in an alley behind their building located in Northeast Portland. The victim has now been identified as thirty-two-year-old Mickey Cornell.

"It is reported that the victim was beaten by a blunt object and was stabbed multiple times. The medical examiner has not yet the cause of death at this time. Friends and family of Cornell claim that the victim was last seen alive leaving The Martini Lab, a new lounge located in the downtown area, at about one-thirty a.m.

"An initial statement from the Police Bureau suggests that there are currently no suspects in the case, which is currently ruled as a homicide. The number to the crime tip hotline should be on display there on your screen. The Bureau asks that if you have any information about the case, please do not hesitate to call."

The screen shows a picture of Mickey Cornell along with the crime tip hotline number. He immediately recognizes the guy from the lounge last night.

Coincidence?

"You know who that is, right?" Sam asks.

"He was an asshole. Probably got what he deserved pissing someone else off." He looks over to Sam, waiting for him to say something.

"Tell me you didn't have anything to do with this," Sam retorts.

"Why would I?" he asks calmly through the accusation.

"Coincidences like this don't just happen. And if you had anything to do with it, you're dragging Frankie into something she didn't ask for."

"He left the place alive. Not my problem what happens to him after that," he barks at Sam.

Sam stands up and heads for the door. *Finally.* "I don't care who you are but someone like you...you don't deserve her. She deserves better. She can *do* better."

He watches Sam's jaw twitch, wanting to say more. He sits down on the couch and leans back. His arms cross lazily behind his head. "I agree. But Frankie and I *do* just fine."

He doesn't have to look at Sam's face to see the man's reaction. The sound of the door slamming is reaction enough.

Coincidences don't happen but the guy was a scumbag who preyed on women. Who knows how many others he inappropriately put his hands on that night or any other night. Frankly, it doesn't bother him that he is dead, cold as it may sound. He isn't too worried about it. The police would have pulled footage from the security cameras and would have found that they all stayed there as a group for a long time well after the guy was escorted out.

- 35 -

Frankie

"Frankie."

"Hmm…" she replies groggily, her head on his chest after their lovemaking.

"Do you think you can take some time off from work? Can Vince find someone to help out?" Cole asks.

"I guess I could. I don't really take time off so I don't really know, but I don't see it being an issue. Why?" She looks up at him curiously. "Am I not spending enough time with you? I know you're probably bored at home." She frowns.

He kisses her head. "I enjoy being lazy and getting fat around here."

She pinches his side which probably has zero percent fat on it. If anything, he looks like he is getting the opposite of fat. Not to mention his stamina. *Yeah, don't go there, Frankie.* He looks amazing. He feels amazing.

"So why are you asking?"

"It's getting close to Thanksgiving. We normally get back to the farm when we can. It's a twelve-hour drive from here. Nick wants to bring Karmen and the twins there. Maybe you'd like to come with me?"

"Really?" She feels herself smiling like a little girl. "You wanna bring me home?"

"Home is wherever you are, baby. But yeah. We'd only stay a few days."

"When do we leave?!"

"It's been too long since I've touched your soft skin, baby girl."

His finger brushes the picture of her on the screen, imagining her reaction. He tries to remember her smell.

Ping. The sound of her calendar notification on the laptop.

Doctor's appointment? He clicks on the reminder. 9 a.m. with Dr. Eubank. He knows that's her primary doctor just like he knows everything else about her.

They roll into Karmen's driveway right on time. Cole seems to have a thing for punctuality.

She steps out of his truck and is immediately assaulted by all the commotion coming from the inside of the house.

A black Nissan passenger van is parked out front, with the top rack loaded to what she is sure is beyond maximum weight. She looks over at Cole.

"Holy. Shit," he whispers. "Are they moving there?"

She gives him an elbow. "Give her a break. She's never taken the kids on vacation before."

The door opens and Nick walks out with two *more* suitcases.

"Holy shit," Cole whispers again.

"Hey, you guys are here. Can you do us one and grab the car seats from Karmen's car?" Nick asks as he drops a bag and throws the keys to Cole.

"Is there going to be enough room for our three bags and the two of us?" Cole asks.

Nick rolls his eyes before briskly answering, "It's a twelve-seater. Plenty of space."

They grab the car seats and walk them to the van; Cole looks over at her and shakes his head in disbelief.

"Maybe we can drive on our own?" she asks.

"No!" Nick barks from the back of the van. "This is a family trip so we stick this out *together*." It sounded more like a plea from a hostage.

"Bathrooms going once! Going twice!" Karmen screams from the porch.

The twins race down the steps, Nic jumping onto Cole just as his car seat gets strapped in. She drops the one she is holding in time to catch Nat.

"You guys ready? Are you excited?" she asks.

"Yes." "Yeah." "I want to see all the puppies." "No! The horses."

"Well, I don't know if it's puppy season, Nat. But there'll be a pony or two for sure!" Nick tells her as he rearranges some bags.

"Really?" she asks Cole, who nods his head and buckles Nic in.

The other Nick shuts the back of the van and comes to finish the car seat install job she failed at doing for Nat. He's moving fast and working quickly without even a complaint.

"Frankie! Catch!" She barely catches the phone that Karmen tosses at her. "Your dad's on a video call," Karmen says.

What? She looks around to see where Cole is standing so she can position herself without him in the frame. "Oh shit!" she whispers before turning the front of the phone over.

"Hi, Dad." She waves into the screen nervously.

"Five minutes until takeoff, okay, David?" Nick says from behind her.

"Gotcha. Thanks, Nick," her dad replies. *"The man runs a tight ship,"* her dad says.

"Daaddd...how are you?"

"Better now that you can remember me," he pouts. *"Karmen and Nick call me more than you do."*

"I can see that!"

"A road trip, huh? How long's it been since you had a vacation? It's good you're taking the time, my love."

"Yeah. I promise to show you lots of pictures and tell you all about it. If I have a good connection, I'll video chat for you to see too."

"You better." He smiles at her. *"Now that tall guy in the back there. Is he going to make a proper introduction being that he's courting my only child?"*

Courting? Oh god.

Her eyes dart to Karmen, who isn't paying her any attention at all.

Cole clears his throat and stands behind her. He helps her hold the phone so that both of them are in the frame.

"Hi, Mr. Hoang. I'm Cole. I'm sorry to meet you like this, sir." Does his swag come naturally for him when he meets a girl's dad?

"Cole. Strong, confident voice. I like that."

Was that some kind of manly approval?

"Call me David. And one last thing, Cole. My heart stands there in front of you. You take care of her. Have a safe trip, kids!"

"Yes, sir. I'll keep that in mind, David. And thank you." Cole waves to him before handing the phone back to her.

"Bye, Dad. I love you!" She blows him a kiss and waves to him.

"Ditto, my love." And he waves bye as they hang up.

Guilt settles upon her. She's off having the best few months of her life and has forgotten how lonely he must be back home. She looks at Karmen and her family, which now happens to include Nick.

She hugs her best friend from behind before handing the phone back. "Thanks, Karm," she says.

"David isn't getting any younger, Frank. You gotta do what you can to make him feel included."

Karmen steps into the third row and she follows. The kids are each buckled into the middle row. Nick gets in the driver's side and Cole closes their door before he climbs into the passenger's seat.

"He knows Nick and you guys told him about Cole?"

"He likes talking to Nick about guy stuff. Lawn mowing, sports, that kind of stuff."

"My dad doesn't have a lawn to mow."

Karmen laughs at her. "He knows that Cole is Nick's brother and that you and he are seeing each other. Actually, he kinda guessed when he saw a couple of your pictures from the night we went to Martini Lab and Halloween."

She completely forgot that Karmen and her dad follow each other on social media. She's actually shocked that her dad didn't call her about Cole sooner, or at all.

"Nick, will it be next week when we get to your farm?" Nat asks. They are already on Interstate 84 going east.

"No, baby. It's only a twelve-hour drive. We'll get there just in time to see the sunrise tomorrow morning," Nick replies.

"Tomorrow morning? That's Tuesday, right?" Nic asks.

"That's right, buddy!" Nick exclaims from the driver's seat.

"Good job!" Karmen gives Nic a high five before turning to tell her they are currently working on learning the days of the week.

"Oh hey. You should turn your location off of your phone to help save battery life. I don't think there are charging ports back here," Karmen says before she fidgets with her phone.

"Good idea," she says.

- 36 -

Frankie

She joins Karmen and Nat on the sidewalk and they all head to the entrance of the store. Their first stop was immediately made for sustenance once they get into town.

People around town must be early risers. The market already has many customers roaming the various aisles. The place is exceptionally clean and never having been in a small town's market before, she's pleasantly surprised at the selections of various produces and amazing cuts of meat.

As their cart easily fills up, she can feel eyes on them, can hear whispers as they walk by. She isn't surprised. She isn't sure how big the town is in size and population, but it definitely seems like the kind of place where everyone knows everyone.

They're in the wine and beer section and she chooses a couple selections but stops to look at Karmen. Can Nick even have these in the house?

"It's okay, you know. He's not an alcoholic. He chooses not to drink. He can handle a bottle of beer at home when we're just relaxing," Karmen answers her silent question.

Maybe this will be a good time to see how he really is with them at home. And if he has a drink and gets out of line, she'll be there to see it firsthand. Karmen won't be able to argue her concerns about him then.

"I think we should be good. The van isn't going to have much room for more anyway," she says as they move toward the checkout line.

Karmen begins chatting with the friendly cashier while she and Nat unload their cart onto the belt.

The cashier is a stunningly elegant, tall, and blonde beauty. She checks her name tag. *Madison. Customer Service Manager.*

"How long are you ladies staying in town?" Madison asks.

"I don't know if 'in town' is actually where we'll be staying. My boyfriend has a farm around here and we're visiting," Karmen answers.

"Oh yeah? Which farm? I was born and raised here. I might know him but I'm not aware of any of our local available bachelors seeing anyone outside of Colt Springs," Madison says.

"Howard Acres. My friend and I are from Portland and we've never been here before. My boyfriend's name is Nick. Nick Howard."

The cashier falters and knocks over the bottle of wine she just scanned.

"Nicky's in town, huh? Did he bring his brother too?" Madison asks.

She studies the cashier silently.

Madison's smile never leaves her face but her body language has changed. Do people around here know what Cole and Nick do for money? Are they the black sheep of the town?

That saddens her. To know that they do what they do to be able to buy their family property back in a town where people treat them as outcasts has to be tough.

"Yeah. Cole's here too," Karmen answers. "Do you know them and where their farm is?"

"It's not too far from here at all. But it's actually not their farm anymore. Hasn't been for a long time now," Madison speaks politely.

"Oh yes. You're right!" Karmen says.

She slides her debit card through the machine while Karmen grabs most of the bags. Madison hands Nat a few stickers and the kid is overjoyed.

"Well, I hope to see you ladies back in here," Madison says as they're leaving.

It takes them fifteen minutes to be able to strategically place their grocery bags into the van thanks to Karmen's overpacking. They walk around the corner and find the bakery, their rendezvous point with Cole and Nick.

Stepping inside, she's awakened by the pleasant aroma of coffee. The shop has ample lighting coming in through the wide windows and the place is buzzing with patrons merrily chatting or on their devices, but there are no signs of Cole or Nick inside.

The small round tables only seat four each. Luckily, Karmen found two that are next to each other. She takes her coat off and hangs it behind one of the chairs and then unzips Nat's jacket.

Nic skips through the door, followed by Nick and then Cole. She waves at them from her seat, watching as they wipe the snow off of their feet.

"Hey, folks! Look what the cat dragged in! If it isn't the Howard boys!" one of the older gentlemen standing in line announces.

The men head over to shake hands and greet a couple of the other people inside. Cole looks over at her and smiles. There's something different about him. *He's home.* Home, where he wants to be. She can't but get mixed feelings about that thought.

"What do you feel like having?" Karmen asks her. "I got it this time since you paid for the groceries. Ready to go order?"

They walk to the counter but Nick waves them over to the small group of men.

"Karmen, this is Mr. Elliott and Mr. Parson. They're our neighbors," Nick makes the proper introductions. "These twins here are Nicolai and Natalia. Nic and Nat, sir," he introduces the twins proudly.

Mr. Elliott. That name sounds familiar.

"Nicky! You're finally a dad! That's great, son." A round of congratulations and handshakes pass.

Impressive. He doesn't mention that they aren't his kids like she expected.

"Cole, how 'bout you, son? You have a few of your own to show off too?" Mr. Parson asks.

"I'm working on that, sir," he says and pulls her from behind Karmen. "My girlfriend, Frankie, sirs. Frankie, this is Mr. Elliott and Mr. Parson," he introduces.

Wait...we're working on it?

"It's great to meet you both." She extends her hand to which they take turns to greet her.

"The pleasure definitely belongs to this old heart of mine. I might need to have my pacemaker checked. You are stunning, young lady," Mr. Parson says, causing her to blush.

"Your grandparents would be proud of you boys. Hey, Linda, whatever they're having put it on my tab, all right," Mr. Elliott tells the cashier.

"Oh no, no," Nick tries to object.

"Don't worry about it. Just be sure to bring everyone over to the house for dinner before you boys head out, all right?" Mr. Elliott says sternly.

"Yes, sir," Nick and Cole reply simultaneously.

"Thank you, Mr.—" Frankie starts to reply but Mr. Elliott cuts her off by holding her face in between his hands and planting a big kiss on her cheek.

"Call me Liam," he says as the small group laughs except for Cole, who clears his throat loudly from behind her.

- 37 -

Frankie

They drive past a big building which Nick explains to the twins is where the tractors, lawnmowers, snowplows, and other machinery are kept. Sort of like a garage, he tells them.

About a quarter-mile up the slightly inclined road, a group of three brown buildings come into view. Two of the buildings are smaller log cabins. The large building located in the far back at a higher elevation has to be the farmhouse. She's completely dazzled by the size of the estate and its backdrop.

Cole turns into the driveway and she sees smoke coming from the chimney of the main house as well as the other log cabins.

"Is someone already here?" she asks.

"The caretakers that work for Mr. Elliott live in the two cabins we just passed," Cole answers. "We called and told them we'd be coming in today so they probably warmed the place up."

"Mr. Elliott? The one we just met?" Karmen asks.

That's why his name sounded familiar. He's the one that bought the place from their uncle.

"Yeah," Nick answers.

"The barn, Mama! Look at the barn!" Nat yells and points excitedly to a barn about a quarter of a mile east of the main house.

"Can we go? Pwease, Nick! Pwease!" Nat pleads.

"Let's get unpacked and dressed in warmer clothes first, okay? Then we can ask your mama if we can go," Nick answers their pleas.

They stop in the driveway in front of the detached three-car garage and a couple with a teen girl come out through a side door of the main house to greet them.

Cole gets out of the car and stretches. She steps out and immediately shivers in the cold. It's even colder than when they were in town.

"Cole," the man says before coming in for a handshake. The woman and teenager each give him a hug.

"This is my girlfriend, Frankie," Cole says.

She extends her hand to shake all of theirs.

"This is Nelson and his wife, Belinda. That's their daughter, Liz. Nelson takes care of the animals and Belinda takes care of the house with Liz's help. They live in that cabin there too." He points to the cabin closer to the house. "There are two other guys that live in the other cabin as well but they're probably out at the barn right now."

"It's nice to meet you all. I hope it wasn't too much trouble to get the place ready for us," she says.

"Oh, it's no trouble at all. We don't get much company here so we're all so excited that these boys are finally bringing a houseful," Belinda says.

"I can babysit!" Liz chimes in.

Belinda leads the ladies and children into the house while the men begin the task of unloading all of their luggage.

The house is just beautiful. Large windows line the front, which also has two bay windows protruding. The dark wood exterior is accented by the light-colored stones that frame about two feet off of the base around the building.

Using the side entrance, they step into an immaculate beautiful farmhouse kitchen. Wood beams along the white ceiling, cabinets a matte shade of pastel teal, double stainless-steel range with a light-colored stone hood overhead, and a huge island in the center to provide ample workspace. A fireplace is already lit and blazing from the corner of the kitchen.

"It's beautiful! This kitchen is amazing!" Frankie says out loud. "Cole's been slumming it at my place compared to this."

"Don't worry. The kitchen is probably the only thing that's been updated in this place," Belinda laughs.

"Nat, you and your brother do NOT touch anything!" Karmen says, in awe of the place.

"Don't be ridiculous. Make yourselves at home. Treat it like you want and touch whatever you can," Belinda tells the kids.

"Oh *please*, don't give them that kind of permission," Karmen jokes.

Belinda informs them that the house has five bedrooms and three bathrooms. The two smaller bedrooms are located downstairs just past the foyer, a bathroom in between. Nick and Karmen will be using the master bedroom upstairs that has a shared bathroom leading to an adjoining room that's been prepped for the twins. She and Cole will be staying in his room, which has its own bathroom.

The kitchen leads into an open dining area with the long traditional rustic farmhouse-style dining table that sits in front of one of the bay windows. The curtains match the color of the kitchen cabinets and are drawn back to make use of the sunlight spilling in from outside. A couple chairs sit in front of the fireplace, providing extra seating.

They follow Belinda past the dining area into a cozy foyer, where yet another fireplace is burning brightly. The room has simple decor with two sitting chairs and a table in front of the fireplace. Not far behind are a set of wooden stairs leading up to the next level. Two closed doors are off to each side of the stairs.

The men start piling in with the bags and she sees Cole hauling way too much. He shakes his head at her with a certain exasperated look. They packed three bags and he's carrying at least six. She laughs at him when he comes to join her in the foyer and drops all the bags.

"This place is amazing! I was just telling Belinda how you're slumming it with me compared to this," she says.

"Don't be too impressed. The kitchen is just about the only thing that's been updated."

"Belinda just said that same exact thing."

"Nick! Your shit's over here," he yells back to wherever Nick is.

"Swear jar! Swear jar!" The twins chant, and everyone laughs loudly.

"Kids! Shoes off! You're gonna get the place all muddy!" Karmen yells after them as they wander around what must be like a huge playground for them.

"Come on. I'll show you where we're staying," Cole says.

He picks up only their *three* bags.

She follows him up the stairs, which brings them first into what looks like a very large family room. Two matching leather couches are set facing the TV. The whole floor is carpeted, unlike the wood flooring downstairs. A fireplace sits a distance behind one of the couches. A long window that spans almost the full length of the room lets in all the lighting ever needed during the day.

The view out the window is immaculate. The stretched land is currently blanketed in untouched mounds of pure white snow. She can picture how beautiful the landscape would look in the spring when the grass is green. Bench seating is placed right next to the window with tons of throw pillows. A small round table with four chairs and a small bar sits against the other side of the room.

Cole points to the doors and bathroom at the opposite end of where they're facing and tells her that's the master bedroom where Karmen, Nick, and the kids will be sleeping. He points behind them, around the corner of the staircase landing next.

"We're staying this way," he says, allowing her to walk to the double doors.

She opens the door and is wowed yet again.

Cole's room is a completely different style from the rest of the house. The walls are painted a dark blue-gray with one light gray accent wall above a huge California king-size bed which sits in the middle of the room. The bed sits on a platform frame with a wooden headboard matching the color scheme of the room.

Opposite the bed is a window that spans about the same length as the one in the family room. Its dark curtains are drawn to each side. The view is spectacular and breathtaking. To the right is a doorway that leads to what she assumes to be the closet area and bathroom. In the corner closest to the door is another lit fireplace unit. Last, but not least, are the double doors along the far wall that lead out to a small balcony.

"Cole, are you kidding me right now?"

"Do you like it?" he asks with a smirk. One sexy ass smirk.

"It's freaking amazing! It really puts my place to shame!"

He leaves the bags on the floor and takes his jacket off and tosses it onto the chair in front of the fireplace. He stalks over and pulls her into his arms. It feels like it's been forever since she's been engulfed by his warmth. She feels him kiss the top of her head. She tilts her head to look at him and pulls his head down to hers for a real kiss.

He backs her up into the bed and she smiles against his lips. "Not a good idea, my love," she says regretfully. "I'm not going to want to leave the room otherwise."

"That doesn't sound bad at all," he says, smiling mischievously while his hands are already unzipping her jacket.

"Karmen and the kids will come looking for me," she says, laughing as he peels her jacket off and drops it onto the floor.

"The door's locked," he says boyishly. "How did I get so lucky?" he asks.

"Do you believe in fate?"

"Not until I met you," he says with another kiss to her head, his fingers thrumming through her hair.

"I didn't until I met you too."

"Yeah?"

"I thought I was living my best life before you came into it, Cole. I had my jobs. My friends. My dad. Even Karmen and Alice have become family. I was happy when they were happy. And I always thought it was enough. I kept so busy that I didn't know my life was missing you."

"I love you, Frankie. I do. And I know it's fucking crazy how fast we've moved. But don't say things like that," he says. He sounds almost angry.

She takes a sharp inhale at the pain that's just exploded in her chest. He squeezes her shoulder and pulls her closer.

"It's just...I don't deserve a girl like you," he says quietly. "I know what I do puts me on the outside of your social circle, the outside of any normal circle actually. I'm aware of that. I just...I just want to be a man you can be proud to have. That's all."

"You are, Cole. You are." And then his lips sear hers, making any obstacle outside or inside or her circle irrelevant.

- 38 -

"Hey, Karm, can you check the bread?" she asks as she tends to the rest of tonight's dinner.

"Got it."

There's a knock coming from the side door. Belinda wipes her hands and heads to answer it.

A couple of deep male voices can be heard before Belinda invites them inside. Both she and Karmen focus their attention on the doorway, waiting to see who walks in. And hot damn does their eyes get a good fill of the two men who are now standing in the kitchen.

"This is Jake St. James and that one's Lucas Barton," Belinda introduces. "They're the boys that live in the other cabin and work here with us."

This has to be where all the gorgeous gods live!

Jake, though he isn't as tall as Cole, can pass as a brother with his blond hair and deep, round blue eyes. He's a lot tanner than Cole but even under his jacket, she can tell his physique can probably give Cole a run for his money.

Jake steps forward first and shakes their hands.

"Hi. I'm Frankie," she says.

"I can be whatever you want me to be," Karmen spills out.

Jake smiles and if swooning is a thing, then both she and Karmen have definitely swooned. *Holy shit.*

"Lucas, miss. Pleasure." He extends his hand to her first and then Karmen.

Lucas is almost as tall as Jake. Brown hair and brown eyes with a tan also. His voice is deep, rich, and damn sexy. *His* physique? Let's not go there either. He's just as gorgeous as Jake in his own way. Where Jake looks like a pretty boy, Lucas is rugged and has the complete badass cowboy look going for him.

"Smells great in here," Lucas notes.

"Stay!" both she and Karmen yelp at the same time.

"We have plenty for everyone," she tells them.

"There's plenty of me you can ea—"

"Karmen, wipe the drool off, babe." Nick cuts Karmen off before she can finish when he walks in to greet the *gods*...the men. To greet the men.

She blushes what must be a bright shade of scarlet. The same blushing that Karmen is doing right next to her.

Nick gives the guys bear hugs and pats on the back, which surprises her. She can't recall ever witnessing anything like that with him and Cole. He must have convinced them to stay because they are now stripping...*taking* off their jackets. Yeah. That's what they are doing.

"Cole! MY man!" Jake says to the guy standing behind her. *You mean your boyfriend, right?*

Cole is leaning against the fridge, arms crossed before Jake gets over and gives him a punch to the stomach. Seeing the two of them standing together makes her feel like she's died and gone to Chippendale heaven. She never knew she had a thing for blonds until just now.

"Nothing like watching my girlfriend gawking over another man," Cole teases.

If she wasn't red before, she is definitely red now. Her hand comes up to hide her face and her smile. She walks over to Cole and slides an arm around him.

"Girlfriend? Damn! I knew it was too good to be true for a pretty little lady like that to be waiting in a kitchen here just for me," Jake says back at Cole.

He looks at her in all seriousness. "You are one beautiful one," he says before shaking Cole's hand.

"Frankie, I promise you whatever Cole can do, I can do better. Or at least, we'd have fun trying." He puts on an extra charming smile and she's puddle on the ground.

Cole shoves his shoulder and then they're both laughing and bear-hugging.

"Come sit at the table," Cole says.

Cole gives Lucas a pat on the back also. He gives her a quick kiss before he heads over to the table with everyone.

She finally remembers the pasta, which she hopes is still warm and begins plating. Belinda grabs a couple more plates and salad bowls for their additional dinner guests.

"They're all ready," she tells Belinda and Karmen five minutes later. She stacks two plates on an arm and grabs one in her other hand. Karmen stacks three as well and Belinda takes the remaining two and they all head over to the table.

Even seated, she is barely eye level with the tall bunch. She places a plate in front of Cole at the head of the table, another on his left side where Jake is sitting, and then the other on the empty spot where she assumes she'll be sitting to the right of him.

"This smells amazing!" Lucas says from next to Jake. "You ladies did a great job!"

"That's because we have a great chef in the house." Karmen points over to her.

"This is you?" Jake asks.

"Yep. From the bread baking to the made-from-scratch-sauce, the homemade pasta, and even the house salad dressing," Belinda says. "I couldn't keep up with her."

"Oh my god. This is too good," Jake says with a mouthful of pasta. "Cole. I'm officially jealous. You get to eat like this all the time?"

"Yup! I also have to work out that much harder because she feeds me too well."

"Try these deli meat rolls before Karmen and I hoard them to ourselves," Nick says, passing the platter.

It feels like a real holiday, except it isn't an actual holiday. She wonders why they didn't just wait until Thanksgiving next week to make the trip out here. She looks around the table and everyone is enjoying their meals. Laughing and smiling.

It's picture-perfect.

"Hey, Frankie," Jake hollers out. "Let's just cut to the chase, all right."

"Umm...okay?"

"Marry me. Be adventurous, live a little. Just marry me. A friend of mine is ordained and he can have us married by midnight." He's giving her the puppy dog eyes. *Irresistible puppy dog eyes.*

Cole shakes his head at Jake. "Bring a girl home and the vultures swoop in."

"Hey, I don't see a ring so it's all fair game, bro," Jake says.

"We're a little too early in the game for a ring," she replies with a smile.

"That means you can still change your mind," Jake says with a wink.

"So how long are you guys staying?" Lucas asks.

"We leave Sunday morning," Nick says.

She begins to clear hers and Cole's plates from the table but he pulls her over to him. She wraps her arms around his shoulders and leans in for a kiss.

"Thanks, baby," he says quietly.

"Dessert?" she asks just as quietly.

"Maybe later," he says *softly*.

No way can she have missed that double entendre. He pulls her down for a quick kiss. *I love you,* he mouths to her silently.

"Cole," Nelson says. They turn their heads to find everyone watching them. "Man, you are so done."

- 39 -

cole

Frankie walks to the kitchen window and looks out into the day.

It's perfect seeing her standing there, with her hot morning cup of tea, dressed comfortably in sweats, and enjoying the view he's loved for most of his life.

She was perfect...is perfect. It makes him feel some type of way. Not unmanly for him to admit that either.

He watches her wave out the window at someone. Probably Nelson.

He hasn't had the chance to speak to Nelson, Jake, or Lucas yet about the farm and what needs to be done at the moment. He checks his watch for the time and then heads to the fridge to dig out the fruits he needs for his breakfast.

He quickly chops the bananas and strawberries and puts them in three separate bowls, topping them with blueberries, granola, acai, and honey. He hands a bowl to Nick, who eyes it suspiciously. Little Nic is more open to the idea and takes it right away to the dining table. Frankie takes hers to join him.

"Damn! This IS good. I can do this. You'll have to show me what's in it," Nick tells him.

"Sure. Hey, have you talked to the boys to see if they need help while we're here?" he asks his brother.

"Not yet. I'll call Nelson to have them stop in before their day really starts."

Fifteen minutes later, all three men are knocking on the door.

"Morning, guys," Nick says, letting them in.

"Morning," he greets them after.

"Didn't expect you up this early," Jake says to him. "Since, you know, there's that magnificent, gorgeous, hot, and oh-so-sexy little lady you got keeping your bed warm."

"Give him a break," Lucas says. "The guy only had one other girlfriend in his life. He wouldn't know how to handle someone like that marvelous piece of woman sitting over there." Lucas winks at him.

"If only you knew the dream I was having about her last night," Jake says.

He rolls his eyes and shakes his head while he considers beating the crap out of these two assholes.

"You all make me feel like I brought home a potato sack," Nick says, putting his bowl in the sink.

"Nah, man. Karmen's freaking gorgeous," Lucas says.

"But you'll kick our asses if we say anything," Jake finishes.

"We want to check with you guys to see if you all need any help around the farm. Since we're both here, we can pitch in wherever you guys need us," he says once everyone quiets down.

"Actually, the next few days might be light. We won't have any new snow so we won't have to plow," Jake says.

"I was just heading out to check on the animals but nothing is going on there. No one's sick and needing extra attention. The barn is in top shape. No repairs are needed at the moment," Nelson tells them.

"I'll take a drive around the fence. I'll give Nelson a hand with the horses after but our supply order won't be ready until tomorrow for pickup."

"The place and the house look good. Thanks, boys. You know we can't do this without you," he says sincerely.

"Well, if it's that light of a day, why don't you guys join us? I was going to suggest we all go into Bozeman so the ladies can pick up anything they might need. We can all grab lunch out," Nick says. "Belinda and Liz are welcome to come too. We have a twelve-seater van out there."

"I'll pass on the shopping stuff," Nelson declines. "But I'm positive Belinda and Liz would love to go if there's room."

"I'm in," Jake says.

"I'll have to pass, but if I can take off into town to check on my mom, that would be cool," Lucas says.

"Of course, man. Take all the time you need. Take one of the trucks and be sure to plow her whole street for her too, man." He gives Lucas a hearty pat.

There's a loud knock at the front door. The men look at each other and watch as Frankie walks over to answer it. He can hear her greeting someone but he can't tell who she's talking to. But she opens the door all the way and lets their guest in.

Fucking Jimmy. The bastard is here, striding in as if he owns the place. His level of arrogance knows no bounds. He feels Nick standing next to him, watching silently. This isn't going to go well.

"He's been coming around a lot lately," Jake says quietly.

"What the fuck does he want?" Nick asks through clenched teeth.

"I don't know, but he brought a couple people in suits with him last time. That was two months ago," Jake answers.

"Hey, Cole, this man says he's here to see you and Nick." Frankie follows Jimmy into the kitchen.

She eyes him warily before she walks back over to Nic, who is still at the table. She says something to the kid and he gets out of the chair and runs toward the stairs.

"What are you doing here?" Nick barks out.

"Heard you boys were in town," Jimmy speaks, still sounding as arrogant as he remembers. They haven't seen Jimmy in almost ten years and now he's here. *Inside the house.*

"And?" Nick asks coldly.

Jimmy steps into the kitchen. Even in his sixties, Jimmy is tall. Almost as tall as he is. And the man loves using his height to intimidate who he can. He remembers that part very well about his uncle.

"Maybe we can talk shop in private," Jimmy suggests, eyes referring to the other three men in the room.

"They're fine," he retorts.

"Fine by me," Jimmy says.

"Get to the point, Jimmy. Why are you here?" Nick growls at him.

"I'll cut to the chase. Some of our land that was sold off is now available for investment. I did my research and had my people work the numbers over the equity of this place. I need you to convince Elliott to borrow against that equity so we can get in on this deal first."

"*We?*" Nick asks incredulously. "There is no *we*!"

"Don't be stupid, boy!" Jimmy's baritone booms into the room. "This is our chance to get our land back and help seal our family's name into this community. Just like my dad wanted! You play your parts and I'll make the deal!"

"No," he says with absolute finality.

"Don't tell me you're as dumb as your brother, Cole. You're supposed to be the smarter one."

"Don't call them that," Frankie says from behind Jimmy.

He recognizes the tone. It's that scary tone again.

"Excuse me?" Jimmy says without the courtesy to even turn around to look at her.

"I said don't call them that. YOU have no right coming in here and demanding anything of them," she says coldly, coming to stand in front of Jimmy, staring up at him as if she isn't over a foot shorter and smaller than the man.

"The kind of investment you're talking about requires a lot more than what equity this place has unless that investment is to fill your own pockets," she says.

How did she figure that out so quickly? The other five men, he included, are stone silent, not quite understanding what is going on with this scene.

"Maybe you need to leave the room. This is a family discussion," Jimmy speaks down his nose at her.

"She's family," Nick says.

He steps past his brother to get to his girl but she steps further into the center of the circle, putting the island between him and her.

"You have some balls coming in here demanding they take another *loan* for you after what you did to them!" Her scary tone gets even angrier.

"Who are you? What is your stake in this?" Jimmy pounces back.

"I said she's family," Nick says louder.

"Get out," he says even louder, barely controlling his own anger.

Jimmy is a piece of shit he's been wanting to knock out. But Gramps might roll over in his grave for disrespecting his elder if he actually went through with it.

"I'm not going to tell you boys again what we need to do," Jimmy continues to push the subject.

"They don't need you to tell them anything. They've been doing what's needed to be done this whole time." Frankie isn't backing off either.

"So, you two brainless bastards are gonna let some city hussy come in and destroy our family's legacy? You do have shits for brains then. My father, *your grandfather*, would be turning in his grave if he knew," Jimmy's voice booms and vibrates in the kitchen.

Before he knows what's even happening, Frankie swiftly steps to Jimmy. She draws back her hand and reaches as high as she can, giving his uncle the slap of all slaps right across the face.

A wide-eyed Jimmy stumbles a couple of steps back, his hand coming to his jaw in disbelief. Frankie is standing there, fuming, hands balled into tiny fists now.

"*Brainless bastards?!* What the fuck do you think your father did when you sold his fucking house before his grave was even warm, you asshole. Now take your fucking bullshit and GET THE FUCK OUT!" she screams at Jimmy with a murderous tone.

After collecting his wits, Jimmy steps up.

He immediately stands in front of Frankie. The man's face is red, from anger or shame, he isn't really sure. But wisely, he makes his way to the front door and exits, slamming the door loudly, vibrating even the windows.

"Why did it just take a tiny bit of a woman like that to stand up and give Jimmy what he's deserved for a very long time now?" he hears Nelson asking.

"Holy shit! That was intense!" Jake says.

He turns and faces Frankie. He's never seen her pissed off like this before. Not even in the alley with Nick that night. He should be feeling emasculated but he's so fucking proud that she would stand up for him...and for Nick. She didn't have to. They didn't need her to but she was fearless and protective and...fucking incredible.

"I'm sorry. I didn't mean to butt in like that. He really pissed me off," she says.

"You scare me and amaze me at the same time, Frankie." It's true. She does.

"You should ice your hand," Nick says calmly from behind them.

"Does it hurt?" he asks her.

"Not anymore." She places a small kiss on the inside of his hand.

"Holy shit, Frankie. I swear I will be your humble servant till my last breath. I'll follow you into battle any day, I'll take a bullet for you, and love you like no other," Jake professes.

Jake, give it a rest, man! He shakes his head at the guy in disbelief.

"What happened?" Karmen asks, surprising everyone.

"Frankie beat up an old man!" Jake yells out, and everyone erupts into laughter except for Karmen.

- 40 -

cole

Frankie is sitting on the bench in front of the window. She has the TV on but she isn't paying any attention to it, busy on her phone.

God, she's beautiful. Full of life, fire, and passion for the people around her. It's no wonder so many are drawn to her.

She pulls her legs up onto the bench, resting her head on her bended knees, staring out of the window. He turns his laptop camera in her direction and takes a quick picture. Before he can strike up a conversation, Karmen walks over to join her.

"Everything okay?" Karmen asks her. She sits behind Frankie and starts to play with her hair.

"I was just texting dad a few pictures. Makes me miss home sometimes. Makes me miss *her* more. At least, what I can actually remember about her."

"It was a long time ago. Better to keep the good memories and miss her, than the bad memories and be angry," Karmen tells her before she leans her own head onto Frankie's back.

Frankie's phone rings, breaking the peaceful moment. She picks it up and answers lazily.

"Hey, Sam."

Good ol' Sam.

"Yeah. Everything is beautiful here! I think we should be home by Sunday night."

Does the guy think she was brought here to be slaughtered? Christ, Sam. It's only been a day.

"What?" He hears the concern in her voice and looks up at her.

Karmen sits up too.

"No. I wasn't. I'll ask Cole but I don't think he was either. Okay. Thanks, Sam. Bye," and she hangs up.

"Everything okay?" he asks her.

"Yeah. Well, kind of. Sam said before he left the shop last night, there was a guy he hasn't seen before inside the building. Sam wasn't sure how he got in but he asked for me by Francine. He said the guy didn't look like someone I'd associate with, whatever that means." She looks at him, her brows furrowed. "Were you expecting someone?"

He shakes his head.

"Maybe it's just a guy delivering something," she says, brushing it off.

"Could be," Karmen agrees.

"Look, they're coming back to the house." Frankie points out the window. "I better go get ready." She saunters off to the bedroom with a smile back on her pretty face.

He shuts his laptop and gives Karmen attention.

"Hey, Cole, you should tell her as soon as you can," Karmen says to him quietly. "You know...about your *job* next week. Give her as much time as possible to process it."

Shit. Nick already told her.

"There's never going to be a right time for it if that's what you're waiting for," she says to him before she walks to the stairs.

She's right. He's put it off, waiting for the right time.

The holidays are usually their busiest and easiest jobs. People leave town, businesses close for days.

Nick hasn't given him the details yet but he knows it's coming. It's the reason he chose to bring Karmen and the kids here. Because he isn't going to be around for Thanksgiving. And he's put off telling Frankie because she's going to ask questions that he isn't going to have answers to. This can be one job, or it can be three jobs back to back, running over a couple of weeks.

"You told Karmen about next week," he says to his brother once they have a moment alone. They are sitting on a bench inside the mall, waiting for the ladies, who are browsing inside the department store.

"Yeah. I'm guessing you haven't told Frankie."

"I don't even know where to start. Things have been going too well. It's like we're a normal couple in a normal relationship now. I'm supposed to just drop it on her that I'm leaving and don't know when I'll be back?"

"It's *like* you're a real couple? That's your problem right there. One day she's your girlfriend and then the next day you don't know if you're even in a real relationship? You either are or you're not because *she* is one hundred percent in one with you.

"Discuss things with her and try to work through them together. And if you're *not* looking at long term with her, just drop the bomb and let her know you're leaving the day you leave. You either want to come back to her or you don't. Ain't rocket science, baby brother."

"That fucking actually makes sense," he says to Nick. "How did Karmen take it?"

"She was mad as all hell. And she has the right to be. Since I gave her enough notice, my job now is to reassure her that I'm coming back to her. And I intend to."

"So how many are we doing this time?"

"Two. Santa Fe then Shreveport."

"Fuck! Two weeks?"

"Yeah. Maybe even more."

Shit. He remembers how rough it was the first time he had to tell her he was leaving and how she had handled it. That was only after a day together. This time, they've had more time together, more memories, a stronger connection.

"Ready?" Frankie says from behind everyone.

"Holy smokes!" Jake of course has to be the first to say anything.

How she makes flannel and jeans look that good, he doesn't know. She looks beautiful in just about everything and anything. It's a miracle she hasn't been snatched up by some guy by now.

"Beautiful as always, baby," he tells her.

"You look great as always too. How do you make a shirt and jeans look so hot?"

Not giving a damn who's watching, he turns her to have her back facing him. He brushes her hair aside and kisses her cheek softly.

"Is that bandana the one I think it is?" he whispers quietly into her ears.

She nods her head. She has kept it this whole time?!

"Everyone's waiting," she says and tries to take a step.

He holds her by the hips to stop her from moving. "Wait."

She attempts to face him but he shakes his head and holds her still before reaching into the inside of his jacket pocket. He pulls out the light blue Tiffany's & Co. box from inside and holds it in front of her at eye level.

"Cole?" she asks.

"Open it."

She looks back at him and he gives her a quick kiss. "Open it," he repeats with a smile.

He holds the box for her while her fingers pull the white bow off and she lifts up the top of the case to see the white-gold necklace with the key-shaped diamond pendant inside. He'd picked it up just before they left Portland. Tonight is the perfect night for her to wear it.

"Oh. My. God! You did NOT just do this!" she exclaims. "I'm afraid to touch it! It's gorgeous!"

"Second to you. You gave me a key once. I thought I'd return the favor."

He places the box into her hand and takes the chain out. He unclasps it and wraps it around her neck. She brushes her beautiful hair out of the way for him to clasp it in place, kissing her cheek once he is done.

She turns around and looks up at him. "I love you," she whispers as her fingers lightly brush over the pendant that falls just below her neckline as everyone piles out of the house and into the waiting van.

"Nick, have you been to this place before?" Karmen asks once they hit the road.

"No actually. It's pretty new. Opened a couple of years ago."

"Cole, have you?" Karmen asks him.

"No. Really not my scene."

"Yeah. Having to fight with guys whose girls are hanging all over him isn't his scene," Jake adds. *Thanks a lot, you dick.*

"Well, let's hope there isn't any of that tonight," Frankie says.

"Don't worry. Stick with me and you won't have to deal with any of that," Jake says. "I'll only have eyes for you."

"Why do you give him so much crap?" he hears Frankie ask.

"He's a cool guy. I like pushing his buttons because he's always so calm and cool about everything. Even back in high school."

"You guys went to high school together?"

"Of course, I was a freshman. Lucas a sophomore and Cole a senior. He never knew us underlings though. But we sure knew of him. Most of the guys in town didn't have girlfriends in high school because the girls were all pining for him!"

"I can see that happening," she says. "So, he had a lot of girlfriends?"

"Nope. Just one."

"Just one?" He hears her incredulous tone.

Jake needs to shut his mouth up right quick about this subject.

"Hard to believe, huh? Didn't mean he didn't mess around with half the girls though. How about you? I bet you had all the guys pining over you, didn't you? Lucas and I have a bet on who gets to kiss you first."

"Good luck with that!" Karmen says. "Did you not see those diamonds he put around her neck?"

"Nah. Frankie ain't about the material stuff."

"You're gonna have to get in line. And Frankie's got a very long line," Karmen adds.

"No I don't!" Frankie's sweet laugh fills the van.

"That's because Cole line hopped and knocked everyone out of the way," Karmen says.

"Stop telling stories, Karm. You need to come out to Portland. I'll introduce you to my friend Alice," Frankie says to Jake.

"Is she as pretty as you?"

"Prettier!"

"No way!" Jake exclaims.

"It's true!" Frankie insists.

"So are we singing tonight or what!" Karmen sounds overly excited.

"I'm gonna pass," Frankie says.

"Definitely," Jake says. "I'm gonna serenade the panties off of you ladies."

"Coming real close to that line, Jake," Nick says.

He chuckles at his brother.

"And THAT'S why I can't joke around with you, Karmen. Nick's too old for a sense of humor and he'll beat the shit out of me." He pauses. "But old men sleep early, so me and you...we can rendezvous afterward."

The ladies laugh loudly at Jake's antics.

- 41 -

cole

Once they finally arrive, he checks the place out. The building looks like an oversized beige farm shed with green doors instead of an actual lodge. The parking lot looks nearly full like the whole town came out tonight. This is a lot more crowd than he expected to be around. Music can be heard through the closed windows of the van as they circle around the lot again.

"Lucas is inside. He said he grabbed us some seats by the pool tables. Twenty bucks a game, Nick?" Jake asks from the back seat.

"You bet!"

"There! Nelson's waving over there. I think he found us a parking spot." He points to the left of them.

Nick sees where he is standing and steers the van in that direction and pulls into the open spot.

"Thanks, man," he tells Nelson as they step out of the car. He opens the door for the ladies to step out. Jake being last. "Lead the way, Jake."

"Lots of people here tonight," Belinda states.

They make their way to the end of the line at the door. He pulls Frankie to his side to make way for outcoming traffic and he can feel her shivering.

"ID, miss?" the security guy at the door asks Frankie.

He looks at the guy who he's quite familiar with.

"Oh shit! Cole!" the guy yelps.

"Todd! How are you, man?" He reaches out and grabs his old high school buddy's hand for a good shake.

"I'm good. You back in town?" Todd asks.

"For a few days."

"Oh, is this your girl, man? Cole and I went to high school together," Todd says to Frankie and hands back her driver's license. "Get inside and out of the cold, guys. They got a touring band in here last minute. I'll catch up with you inside a little later, all right?"

The place is definitely full tonight. Jake leads them to the right once they are inside. Four pool tables and some pub-style seating come into view. Lucas waves over at them. There are two bars to accommodate patrons. One near the pool tables and another closer to the open floor where people are standing in front of the band and dancing. The music is loud enough to fill the whole place and he can see people straining to hear each other.

Nick helps Karmen out of her jacket and they grab a seat with Nelson and Belinda at one of the tables. He helps his girl slip out of hers and puts it on the back of a chair. Before she can sit in it, Lucas sidesteps him and swoops her up in a spin.

"Can I borrow her a second?" Lucas yells back, already halfway to the bar.

"What do you guys wanna drink?" Jake points at everyone.

"Amaretto sour for me," Karmen tells him.

"I'll have one of those too," Belinda says.

"Pitcher for the guys then," Jake says.

Jake joins Lucas and Frankie at the bar. Lucas seems to be introducing her to a group of people who are all shaking her hand and trying to talk to her through the music.

Five minutes later, the trio walks back to their table. Lucas has a tray of glasses and a pitcher. Frankie has a drink in hand and Jake has a tray as well.

"Sorry, Karmen, doesn't seem like there's gonna be any karaoke tonight," Lucas says to her.

"Oh, it's fine! The band is really good anyway!"

Frankie reaches him and slides her arm around his back, snuggling in. His jacket is still on. He can feel her hand sliding underneath his shirt, feeling his back. Scratching with her nails softly, giving him goosebumps. She watches him with a mischievous smile.

"Watch it before we end back up in the van," he warns her with a whisper next to her ear.

She flashes him an enticing, cock-hardening smile and he almost makes good on his threat.

He clears his throat instead. "What are you drinking?" he asks.

"Taste." She holds the cup up to him. "Montana Mule," she says as he takes a sip.

"Not bad," he says, taking the glass of beer that Lucas hands him. "This is more my thing."

"Come on, everyone. Let's get the night started!" Jake says excitingly.

Everyone takes their glasses to salute. "Cheers!" "Cheers!"

Soon after, a couple of guys approach their area with outstretched hands.

"Jesse," he greets the first guy.

"Hey! Saw you and Nicky walking in and had to come say hi! Nicky!" Jesse yells over to his brother.

"Holy shit! Jesse!" Nick gets out of his corner chair and walks over to greet the guy. "Good seeing ya, man. Adam. Ricky," Nick says, greeting the other two.

He sits down and plays catch-up with their old friends. Lucas, Jake, Frankie, and Karmen are at the pool table discussing the rules of the game. He takes his eyes off of her and checks his watch. Just past nine p.m. He gets pulled into the conversation in front of him for a long while.

"Hey, there's my boy!" Todd gives him a good smack on the back. He shakes hands with the other guys before taking a seat next to him.

"How are things with you? How's the wife and kid?" he asks his long-time buddy.

"Divorced now. She's moved on out to Bozeman. My son's great though. Plays basketball."

"I'm sorry. I didn't know."

"Nah. It's all right. Long time ago and everyone's happy now."

He offers Todd a glass but he declines and points to his security shirt. "What about you? Is that little one the missus?" Todd asks.

"Not yet," he answers. "We're not that far along yet." Though it feels like they've been together a lot longer than it really has been.

"Better hurry up. Those two boys over there got eyes on that one!" he laughs.

"Tell me about it. They haven't left her alone since we got here. Fucking vultures."

"Well, it's good seeing you, man. I gotta scour the place, make sure no one's dying," Todd jokes before he gets out of the chair. "I'll check on you all later, man. Keep an eye on Barton for me, would ya?" Todd pats him a good one on the back before leaving.

"Having fun?" he asks Frankie once she returns to his side and takes a seat.

"I know it's not your thing. Thanks for bringing me," she says.

She pulls his hand to her cheek and he is puddle in his seat again. Puddle until Jake fucking pulls her out of his grasp and onto the dance floor. She laughs and waves at him before Jake distracts her.

"Cole, I've never seen you look at anyone that way before. Not even M—" Nelson starts to say before Belinda elbows him.

"It's good to see both of you so happy and grounded," Belinda says, looking back and forth between him and Nick.

"You okay? You had a couple of drinks there," he asks Nick.

"Yeah. Just looking at my gorgeous woman dancing with that idiot out there," Nick says. "I think I'm gonna marry her." Nick's remark surprises everyone at the table.

"It's about time," Nelson says.

"Oh, Nick. That's awesome," Belinda says. "The house has been empty for too long."

"Did you have too much to drink?" Jesse asks Nick before they all burst into laughter.

"Coley, how about a game?" Nick asks.

It doesn't seem like he has a choice. Nick is already out of his seat and heading to an open table. He grabs his glass and joins his brother.

'How long has it been since we've had a night like this?" Nick asks.

"We played pool in Denver."

"Shut up! You know what I mean, shithead!"

He laughs at his brother's scowl. "Were you serious about marrying Karmen? Don't you think it's too soon? Always thought you'd end up with some blonde stripper from some small town, getting drunk and partying through the night till you're at least fifty," he teases his brother."

"Asshole. Dead serious. Never met anyone like her. And those kids. Man, I wish I can tell you what it's like to fall asleep watching some Disney movie with them and waking up with their arms and legs all over me."

Nick takes another shot, pocketing the ball easily.

"And I'm not getting any younger. It's not gonna be today or tomorrow, but I know she's the one."

He sees his brother's face brighten when he talks about the kids. It's weird and cool to see at the same time.

Nick never really had a home life. Other than himself, his brother didn't really have many friends as a kid either. Then once their mom left the farm with him in tow, he can't be sure if Nick ever had any real friends his age bouncing around from place to place. It's amazing how good is really is with the twins though.

"Feels like a hole you didn't know you had inside of you gets filled in," he says to Nick.

"Yeah," Nick agrees. "I'm guessing that's how Frankie makes you feel."

He doesn't answer. He doesn't want to have to describe to his brother how exactly she makes him feel. He doesn't want to say out loud how she makes him look forward to their end game, not just because he hates what they do but because it means he can be the better man she deserves.

Sometime later, Belinda and Nelson come over to them. They are heading back to the farm so the kids aren't left alone too long. He checks his watch and sees it's close to midnight already.

A hand slides up his back and he quickly turns around.

A tall, good-looking blonde steps up to him, her hand resting on his hip, looking up at him. "Haven't seen you in here before," she says to him, her eyes not subtle at all.

"Sorry," he says, removing her hand from his person. "I'm here with someone."

"You sure?" she purrs at him, reaching toward his face and he dodges her touch.

"I'm sure," he says with disinterest.

She pouts a second before making her way over to some other schmuck at the next table.

"I saw that! She was hot!" Jake yells out to him as he saunters over. "I can take Frankie home if you wanna party with that one."

"Fat fucking chance," he tells Jake.

He turns around and Jake is pointing toward the stage, where the band members are getting back on. He sees Frankie stepping on as well, leaving Lucas and Karmen off to the side of the stage.

"Does she play or is she completely hammered?" Jesse asks.

"A little guitar," he answers lacking some confidence. Not that he's ever heard her play. But he knows she does from pictures he's seen of her.

They all move away from the pool table and head to the edge of the dance floor separated by a partition.

Her necklace is glistening under the spotlight. She looks even smaller up there. People are starting to pile onto the floor again.

"Listen up, guys! My name is Gary. Some of y'all know me and some of y'all don't. But I'm the road manager for this great band playing for you guys tonight." Some hooting and whistling go off in the crowd. "Well tonight, we have something extra. We don't normally do this but we think it's a great idea to be spontaneous."

The crowd gets quieter, waiting to hear more.

Frankie puts her hands to her face. She looks over to the side of the stage at Karmen, who shakes her head. Lucas gives her a thumbs-up.

"Frankie has been convinced to join the band for a few songs. Think you can rock the house, Frankie?" Gary asks.

"I don't know. Seems like a very tough crowd," she says with a smile that has him wondering if she's more than a bit tipsy. But she looks to be having a good time when one of the band members brings over an electric guitar and helps her adjust the straps around her shoulder.

She takes the mic confidently from Gary. "So, my friend Lucas here, he's gonna help me sing this one. I hope you guys don't mind."

"Ready?" the drummer asks her.

She steps over to Lucas's mic and speaks into it. "Yeah! I'm ready." She nods her head at Lucas and turns around to high-five the bass player and the other guitarist.

"On your lead, Frankie," the guitarist says into the mic.

She counts off loudly. Seconds later, she plays the intro to "You Shook Me All Night Long," and the crowd explodes into screams.

Guys are pushing at each other out of excitement. Everyone is pushing forward closer to the stage. The first verse comes around, Lucas is singing, and just about everyone in the crowd is too.

"HOLY FUCKING SHIT!" Nick and Jesse are yelling beside him.

Nick is jumping up and down next to him like a kid in a candy store, singing like he's at a real concert.

He can't believe his eyes and ears. His hands come up to his head and even he's shouting out the chorus with everyone else when it comes around. It's like they are teenagers all over again.

The solo approaches and Nick hangs on to his arm in anticipation, Jesse is hanging on to Nick. And just like that...his girl shreds into it hard, sending the crowd louder than the place has been all night. Lucas finishes the final verse in dramatic rock fashion and Frankie just absolutely kills the ending.

- 42 -

Frankie

The wind really starts coming hard as Karmen make the turn off the main road after their grocery store run. The van sways heavily. Todd's truck in front of them has dropped its plow, paving the way for them once they round the bend on the road leading to the house. It makes the drive quicker. At this speed, they should be there in less than ten minutes.

"Frankie," Karmen says.

"Hmm…" she answers, feeling relaxed, her eyes looking out of the passenger window.

"Can we talk?"

"About?" she asks cautiously because Karmen asking anyone for permission is already a bad sign.

"I'm not sure how to bring this up so I'm just going with it."

"Uh, okay?"

"It's about you and Cole…and Nick."

She snaps her head, giving Karmen her full attention, just as they pass the first building. "What do you mean?"

"I know what happened the night you all *met*," Karmen says quietly, her eyes never leaving the road.

"You mean you know *his* version," she hisses with contempt in her voice.

"Frank, I know there will never be any excuse for what he did. And that he can apologize until his last breath and it would still be unforgivable. I would never ask that of you."

"Then why are we having this conversation?"

"Because I need you to be okay with me being with him. You're important to me. You know that," Karmen says softly.

"How long have you known?"

"Since the Halloween party."

"So, you've known for almost a month and you didn't say one word. Just like you didn't say a word about bringing someone home to the twins and having him live there?"

"I wanted you to see how well we work together. He loves the kids. He loves me. I know you know how I feel about him."

"This whole time I haven't said anything to you about him because I didn't want to be the one to break the news about how much of a scumbag he is, Karm. I didn't want to be the bad guy. I was fucking sure that when you found out what he did to me, and god knows how many other women, that you would get rid of him on your own. But no! You knew and you're still keeping him around?"

They're now pulling up in front of the garage next to the house. She sees the four, maybe five, men congregating by the side door.

"Frankie—" Karmen starts to say.

"You have a daughter, for Christ's sake! What if...what if he...?" She can't finish her thought out loud.

Instead, she swings the door open and hops out as soon as Karmen stops the car. She's livid and the source of her anger is standing right in front of her, laughing and smiling like he owns the fucking world.

She takes two steps toward him before Karmen cuts her off, her hands in front of her and pushing back.

"He wouldn't do that. You've seen him with them," Karmen whispers.

"How do you know that? You've known him like a month!" she screams before turning and walking the other way, not knowing where she is even going. She can hear the sound of the snow crunching as Karmen tries to catch up to her.

"Frankie!" Karmen grabs her arm and spins her around. "I'm not asking for your blessing."

"Good. You're not gonna get it."

"I'm not even asking you to be friends with him! I'm just giving you a heads-up. I plan on having him around a very, very long time."

She shoves Karmen's hand off of her arm. "You're making a fucking mistake, Karmen." She turns around again. She can't look at her best friend.

"Frankie! Stop!" *Nick.* He's yelling at her.

She can't look at him either. He came into her life, humiliated her, and robbed her of her peace of mind. And now? He's taking away her best friend and the twins too.

Oof!

She stumbles forward. Something hit her in the back, hard. She turns around just in time to see another snowball flying straight into her chest. She looks up at Karmen, who is already packing another one.

"You're being childish and stubborn!" Karmen yells at her. "You know you are!"

How can Karmen be mad?! The thought infuriates her. Before she knows it, she's running full speed and tackling Karmen right into the pile of snow behind her, knocking the wind out of both of them. Then she's trying to shove Karmen deeper into the snow over and over again. Pouncing and pushing. Annd Karmen is laughing her head off of the whole time!

"Stop it! Frankie! Stop!" Karmen screams in between laughs. "You know you're not even really mad at me!"

"Ugh! Yes! I am!"

She feels an arm wrapping around her and pulling her off of Karmen, her two feet dangling well off the ground.

Nick hurries to help her friend stand up. *Nick. That asshole!*

"Frankie!" Cole hollers sternly from behind her.

"Let me go!" she yells, fighting and squirming in his arms with adrenaline and anger.

As soon as he sets her down, she quickly steps to Nick and connects her foot to his shin as hard as she can before she is pulled back by the hood of her jacket.

"Shit!" Nick says, only looking slightly affected by her kick.

That pisses her off even more.

Karmen is laughing hysterically at how she must look right now. Like a child throwing a tantrum and then having the teacher step in. Karmen steps up to her tenderly.

"I'm sorry, Frankie," her friends says in that special way about her. Karmen hugs her tightly. Sincerely. Hopeful.

She sighs. She doesn't have to forgive Nick. She doesn't even have to like or get along with him. But she doesn't have the right to tell Karmen who to love either. If she wants a future with Cole, she's going to have to deal with Nick anyway.

Karmen, probably feeling the tension leaving her body, holds her hand and leads her back to the house. She isn't even sure where Cole and Nick are anymore. Jake, Todd, Lucas, and someone she doesn't recognize watches her like scared bunnies ready to scatter at any moment.

"You hit me with a freaking snowball," she pouts at her friend.

"Yeah. Well, I'm telling your dad you fucking tackled me!"

They walk hand in hand past the group of men and then turn back simultaneously to yell, "Unload the bags!"

- 43 -

cole

"Is this a bad time?" Todd asks from the back of the van as they unload the groceries as instructed.

"No, man. Frankie beats up like a person a day or something," Jake answers. "Yesterday, she slapped Jimmy Howard into next week."

Todd whips his head around and looks at him wide-eyed.

He shrugs in response.

"Gotta admit that was an awesome fight though," Jake keeps going. "I used to think Nick was the scary one."

"You all right?" he asks Nick.

"She gave a mean kick but I'm fine," Nick answers. "At least it wasn't higher up this time."

He checks the men in his presence. Unable to contain it any longer, he laughs so hard his sides hurt. The other men follow suit. It takes several minutes before they get it out of their systems and head inside. Belinda is already waiting at the door to help them put away everything.

"They're upstairs," Belinda tells both him and Nick.

"You guys make yourselves at home. Sit down. Have a drink," Nick says to the men.

He follows his brother quickly upstairs. Nick rounds the corner and slowly opens the door. Frankie is lying in bed, over the covers, next to Karmen. He isn't sure what they are talking about, but Karmen looks at them standing in the doorway.

"Nick, why doesn't your room look this nice?" Karmen asks from the bed.

"Because Cole has taste," Frankie answers bluntly.

He chuckles and Karmen smacks her stomach for it.

His tiny ferocious girlfriend sits up in bed and stretches like a lioness waking from slumber. "I guess I should apologize to your buddies for that awkward show," she says.

"I don't think they cared. Weren't even paying attention," Nick tells her.

"Yeah. Sure." Frankie brushes it off. She stands up and walks to the door. Instead of moving out of the way, Nick steps in front of her.

"Frankie, I—" Nick starts to say something but she holds her hand up to his face.

"Nope! Not today, Satan," she says as she sidesteps Nick.

She takes his hand on her way out of the room with Karmen laughing hysterically behind them.

"A bit tough on the guy, aren't you?" he asks.

She gives him the glare down. "Never mind," he quickly says and they head down the stairs. "Are you and Karmen okay?"

"We'll work it out," she says just as they reach the bottom of the stairs.

Nick and Karmen join them a few minutes later and the ladies breakaway into the kitchen with Karmen's arms around Frankie's waist.

"Aren't there knives in the kitchen?" Lucas asks.

"Don't even start, man," Nick warns. "Cole's girl scares the shit out of me."

An hour later, Frankie walks into the room with a yellow Labrador puppy in her arms. She cradles it like a child as Jesse struts in behind her with a couple of bouquets and a case of beer.

Frankie looks at him with her own puppy dog eyes. She walks over to him with the puppy. "He's soooo cute!"

"We're not getting a dog, baby." And everyone laughs at them.

"Hope it's okay. I had to bring him along. I just picked him up on the way over here and didn't want to leave him alone for the first night," Jesse tells Nick.

"The kids are gonna go crazy!" Karmen says. "Is it okay if they play with him?" Karmen asks Jesse.

"Sure!" he tells her.

Karmen and Nick pry the puppy from Frankie's arms and take it upstairs. Everyone listens to Nat's scream of delight.

It's been too long. He locks the door and walks into the dark corner of the alley to light up another cigarette.

How long before she comes home? It's been too fucking long.

- 44 -

"Dig in, everyone!" Nick announces dinner.

"Where do I start though? It's so fancy looking," Lucas says.

"Cole, man. You get this all the time?" someone asks from somewhere at the table.

"Right? I just asked him that the other night too" Jake comments.

He takes a look at the cup of soup for the first time. He's never seen anything like it before. Clear broth with a couple of pieces of some sort of vegetable in the middle and a shrimp on top.

"It's a winter melon soup with shrimp," Frankie tells him. "It's a Vietnamese recipe that my dad taught me."

She takes his cup and spoons some for him to taste. He sips the broth and it soothes him. "Baby. That's good!" Then he takes the winter melon off the spoon she holds.

"So how did your dad learn to make this?" Todd asks her politely.

"He's part Vietnamese and it's been passed down. His grandfather was Vietnamese and his grandmother was French-Canadian. Then *his* father, my grandpa, married an American woman, my grandmother. They relocated to the States where my dad was born and met my mother during college. She was an exchange student. They got married when he was thirty-two and she was twenty-seven."

How interesting. Why didn't he ask her about this before?

"Wow. Was she from Vietnam?" Todd asks again.

"Nope. She was an exchange student from Ireland. She's one hundred percent Irish."

"That makes so much sense now," Nick says. "THAT, folks, is why she's so scary."

Karmen gives Nick an elbow.

"She must be a very beautiful woman. Look at how gorgeous you turned out," Lucas says.

She reaches for her wine glass and takes a long sip. "She was. She passed when I was ten," she says softly.

"I'm sorry to hear that," Todd sympathizes.

He reaches for her hand and peers into her eyes. He didn't know that either. And it's something he should have known.

She squeezes his hand before forking a piece of steak and feeding it to him with a smile, clearly changing the subject and the somber mood.

"This steak after that soup. You have to teach me how to make this," Jesse says from the other end of the table. "Seriously, Frankie. Tell me something you CAN'T do! Cole. Brother. There has to be something that she's not good at."

"Sure, there is. Growing. Apparently, she failed at that," Jake says with a laugh.

Frankie lets loose her sweet laughter. And the table joins in.

Frankie

She's quiet and content. Drifting off to sleep before she hears him take a deep breath.

"Frankie."

"Hmm..."

"We need to talk."

We do? "This is the second time today someone's said that exact same thing to me. Do I need to remind you how it went the first time?"

"I have to leave again," he blurts out.

She immediately sits up. This isn't the kind of news she's expecting after all they've done together in the past few days. "Leave?" she gasps.

He sits up next to her, taking her chin with the pad of his fingers. "Nick and I have a couple things we have to do."

"Things as in *jobs*," she says removing herself from his touch.

"Yes."

"When?" she asks quietly.

"Tuesday. After we take you guys back to Portland."

After they take them back? What does that mean?

"How long will you be gone? Are you coming back? Is that why I'm here? Like this is some kind of farewell retreat?"

"Two, maybe three weeks, and I do plan on coming back to you, if you'll have me, Frankie. I didn't bring you here for that. We just knew we won't be around for the holidays and this is the best we could do."

She's speechless. She should have been expecting this to happen. They never talk about his *jobs*. He avoids the subject like it's the plague. But it's been a month since his unexpected return to Portland and she should have seen it coming.

"Baby. Say something."

"I don't know what I'm supposed to say. You know how I feel about *that*. You know how I feel about you. And you know how I feel about *you and that*."

"I love you, Frankie. I can't change the way things are right now. I can't possibly ask you to sit around and wait for me. But I want you to know that home is wherever you are. And I *will* keep coming home to you until you say no more."

After a moment of silence, he pulls her to him and she exhales loudly out of frustration. She rests her head on his chest. He kisses the top of her head again, comforting her.

"Do the people around here know about you and Nick? Do they know what you guys have been doing to keep this place?"

"I think a few people know. The rest either don't care or assume we work construction."

"Does Karmen know about this?"

"Yeah. Probably before we even left Portland."

"Seems Nick communicates better with her." She punches his stomach softly and he falls back on the bed, pulling her with him.

"Are you and her going to be okay? Seemed really serious earlier."

"We'll work it out. You knew that she knew everything, didn't you?"

"She wanted to be the one to talk to you about it."

"Am I wrong for not being able to see him the way everyone's been seeing him?"

"No, baby. You just got to see a side of him that no one should have had to. Unfortunately, it's a side that's hard to forget."

"She says she's not asking me to forgive him. But I know she wants me to."

"I think she wants that more for you than for him."

Cole sets up his laptop for her downstairs so she can work in peace while he's out on the farm with the other men. Three hours later, it feels like she hasn't accomplished anything with Vince's books. She generated report after report and just can't piece the puzzle together. Something is going on. She normally keeps the books in top shape because it's so important for them to be able to stay a step ahead.

She picks up the phone and calls Cynthia, one of her vendors.

"Hey, Frankie!"

"Hi, Cynthia! How are you?"

"I'm good. It's been a while since we last spoke."

"Yes, it has. But hey, I have a couple questions. First, is it possible for you to email me all our invoices for the past three, maybe four months? And second, there's a check payment here that I had sent to you against one of the invoices. It was deposited but it wasn't deposited into your normal account. I want to double-check and make sure that's right."

"Sure. I can email you the invoices up until October third."

"Are you behind on your accounting like I am?" she asks.

"Uh no, doll. October third was when you emailed saying that you had a more competitive deal that you couldn't pass up. Remember?"

"I emailed you that?" That can't be right.

"Yes! I responded to your email with new quotes but I never heard back. As for the check...let me see. The last payment we received from you was a couple of days after that. We haven't seen a payment since then. And your account with us currently has two outstanding invoices. I just thought you guys were behind on the paperwork and wanted to give you a little time. Is everything okay?" Cynthia asks her.

"There must be some kind of misunderstanding. Can you give me a week to straighten this out with Vince? I'll be sure to get you guys paid up. In the meantime, can you please send what you can over? Can you be sure to CC, actually BCC, my private email as well? I think you have that on file. Oh, that email that you said I sent, could you forward that back to my private email too?"

"Sure thing. It might take me till after the holiday if we get too jammed so bear with me, all right?"

"No problem. Thanks, Cynthia. In case I don't hear from you before then, Happy Thanksgiving."

She hangs up the phone and stares at the laptop screen. Her head slumps to her hands above the table. She isn't sure if it's just about the situation at the bar or if it's about Cole. She sits up and takes a deep breath, tilting her head back, drying her eyes.

"Something smells good in here!" Nick yells out from the kitchen entrance.

Of course, he has to be the first voice she hears.

Her head slumps back into her hands, on top of the table. She closes her eyes for a few more seconds listening to Karmen chatting with everyone in the kitchen.

A part of her wants to tell Karmen they need to pack up and get back to Portland right now but it wouldn't be fair to her or the kids. Besides, there's nothing more she can do at the moment until Cynthia sends over the information that she needs.

"Everything okay?"

She finds Cole standing across the table from her and gives him a pouty face.

"Rough day?" he asks.

She nods her head. She pulls his laptop forward and begins logging out of the various windows and closing them out.

His hand rubs the tension from the back of her neck. It feels amazing and her head slumps forward again. He stops the massaging and kisses her head after a few minutes and then sits down. She turns in her seat and pulls her legs up over his lap and leans on him.

"Anything I can do to help?"

She looks at him and shakes her head. "How was your day?" she asks, changing the subject.

"It's getting better now," he replies.

The reflection of the flames from the fireplace dancing in his beautiful blue eyes. She tilts her head slightly and closes her eyes when his lips greet hers. Her hand coming up to cradle his jaw. *Mmm...*

"Hungry?" she asks him once they get their sweet fill of each other's lips.

"I can eat," he says.

"Me too."

Instead of letting her swing her legs off of him, he picks her up and carries her to the kitchen. Cole sets her down on the counter and gives her a quick kiss.

"Lucas, pack some for yourself and Jake too. There's plenty," she tells the man.

"Hey, we're supposed to have dinner at Liam's tonight. The kids too," Nick informs her. "Nothing formal."

Cole brings over a bowl of chili for her and a spoon.

"If he's your neighbor, how come we can't see his place from here?" she asks.

"He's the neighboring farm. We used to own the many, many acres in between his place and ours. He's on the other side of the hill. About a half-hour away," Cole tells her.

"What time are we expected?" Karmen asks.

"Seven," Nick answers her before he leaves the kitchen.

"Everything you make is so good," Lucas tells her. He stands closely next to her now, distracting her from her own bowl. He tries to feed her with his spoon.

"Lucas!" Cole yells, startling her and making Lucas chuckle.

"Didn't hurt to try," Lucas whispers to her and she laughs with him.

- 45 -

Frankie

Liam Elliott's farm is lavish and massive. She isn't sure how many barns and buildings they passed before reaching the main house, which Cole explains sits in the middle of the man's property. That can only mean that there is a ton of land and property that they haven't seen.

They park on the gravel right out front of the log-sided, lodge-style home, which has to be at least ten thousand square feet in size. The grand door opens and a woman welcomes them in. Stepping inside, she looks into a foyer that's bigger than the size of her whole apartment. Cathedral ceilings loom overhead with a nice chandelier hanging above them. There are leather chairs for seating on both sides of the walls.

The lady leads them into a room with a beautiful view through the floor-to-ceiling windows. The landscape is spectacular with the white of the snow smoothly blanketing everything.

"Beautiful," she tells Cole, who's standing with his hand around hers. "But a bit much for me," she whispers to him.

"I always did think this was too much house for the old guy," he tells her with a smile.

"There they are!" Liam shouts as he enters. Probably because it's the only way to be able to communicate in this big house.

Liam comes over to shake the men's hands. "More beautiful than the last time I saw you," Liam kindy tells her. "You remind me of Jannie. Jan Howard. That's these boys' grandmother. She was so lively."

"Thank you, Liam. Your home is beautiful. It looks very...*cozy*," she says.

The sound of Liam's cackle immediately echoes through the large room. "She hates it!" Liam says to the group.

She looks sheepishly at Cole.

"You can be honest, Frankie. I don't like it much myself. Way too much house for me. But my wife, she was into all of this. Come here," he says. "Let me introduce you." He puts his hand on her shoulder. "This is my oldest son, Junior. That's his wife, Rosie, and their baby, Abigail."

Frankie introduces herself and shakes the couple's hands. "Your baby is adorable."

Liam moves her on. "This is my youngest son, Jason."

She shakes his hand and Liam moves her on to the stunning beauty standing next to Jason. "This is my niece Madison." *The beautiful cashier they met their first day in town.*

"Madison," she says. "We've met! Well, sort of."

Madison smiles at her and shakes her hand briefly. Tall, blonde, beautiful, *and* rich, she thinks to herself, suddenly feeling insufficient.

Madison reaches out and touches the key pendant on her necklace. "Very beautiful," she says with a sweet smile.

"Oh, thank you. It was a gift." She takes the pendant from Madison's fingers and lets it hang again.

Madison takes her eyes off of the piece and looks over her head. She spins to see Cole shaking hands and greeting the men with familiarity. Of course, he would know them. They probably grew up together.

Madison leaves her side and joins the group, standing next to Cole, who greets her warmly. Feeling awkward, standing there alone, she walks over to Karmen, who's talking to Rosie by the windows. She reaches them and realizes they are talking about babies. Of course. She smiles at Karmen and turns to face the window, taking in the view alone.

"That feeling sinks in quick doesn't it?" Jason says from next to her.

"Excuse me?" she asks, not comprehending.

"That feeling that you're just a speck of dust in this place."

She looks at him again. *What did he just say?*

"Oh no! I mean, not just *you* in particular. I mean in general. I get that feeling all the time when I'm here."

"Oh! I get it," she says to him. "You don't live here?"

"God, no. Way too gaudy for me. This place is the definition of ostentatious. I like to be where the sun's at. I live in Phoenix. Just up here for the holidays."

"No way. I'm originally from Tucson. I moved to Portland five years ago."

"I traded all of this for the desert and you traded the desert for rain," he laughs.

"Phoenix is a lot different than here," she says to him.

"Yeah. And a lot further away from the family. They're not too approving of my kind."

She looks at him, confused again.

He motions for her to step closer to him and then he pulls the collar of his sweater forward so she can see his white shirt underneath with the phrase "Daddy's Boy" imprinted.

"Not referring to that 'Daddy' over there." He points to Liam.

Understanding settles. She laughs with him and gives him a thumbs-up and a high five. She genuinely likes him.

"Hey, everyone, let's move into the dining room," Liam announces.

She looks around and sees Cole, Liam, Madison, and Junior are already out of the room. Karmen, Nat, Rosie, and Abigail are walking ahead of them. Jason hangs back with her and Nick, who is carrying little Nic as they walk next to her as they enter the dining room.

"Gaudy ass hell, right?" Jason whispers to her as they enter yet another massive room. "And this is supposed to be the informal dining room."

"You mean there's one bigger than this inside the house?"

"Yeah. With a table for twenty. I can't remember the last time it was even used," he says.

Everyone takes their seat at the table.

She, Jason, and Nick are the last to walk in so they have to take what's left of the open seats. She waves at Cole, who is sitting next to Liam at the head of the table. Madison is seated next to him, Nat and Karmen next to her. Nick takes the other end of the table and puts Nic next to his sister. He pulls a chair out for her next to his side, opposite the little boy, while Jason takes the only seat remaining to her left.

Nick is awfully quiet tonight, making his presence next to her more tolerable.

"Let's have a toast before we eat," Liam's voice booms across the table. He begins talking before all their glasses are even filled.

"I want to welcome Karmen, those beautiful babies, and gorgeous Frankie over there. Many, many years ago I had high hopes I'd be making a toast like this one at Cole's and Madison's wedding. The wedding that would have bridged our two fine families, immortalizing the friendship between myself and your grandpa."

She looks over at Cole, who is still talking to Madison. *What did Liam just say? Cole and Madison? Wedding?*

"But since that didn't happen, I want everyone to know that our friendship is still solid. My house is your house."

Cole shakes hands with Liam. Madison right there, next to him. Hand on his shoulder. Close and familiar.

She should have seen it before. He let go of her hand the moment Madison walked into the room. He hasn't said one single word to her since then. Hasn't even looked in her direction.

"Frankie," Nick whispers, his hand patting hers under the table.

She looks up at him, seeing the concern in his eyes as Liam's words sink in deeper. She numbly looks at Karmen, who's watching her with concern written all over her face too.

She looks back down at her salad, appetite gone.

Nick rubs and pats her hand underneath the table again. She takes a deep breath, sucks it up, and takes a small sip of her wine, forcing it down past the hard knot lodged in her throat.

She survives through dinner quietly, barely even touching her food, and thanks to Jason, who continues to comment on everything in whispers to her, making her bend her head to hear him and giving the impression that they are conversing. In reality, she hasn't heard anything he said. She's said less than one coherent sentence to him.

I need to get out of here.

But there is no way she wants to make a scene. So she keeps to herself. Jason keeps close and Nick hovers.

She feels confused and alone in the room. Every single time she builds up the courage to look at Cole, he's busy with Madison, Liam, or Junior. She willed him to look her way many times and he never did. She should have had the guts to walk over to him and demand an explanation but for some reason, she doesn't.

After dinner, they all retreat back to the room they were in before. Cole leaves her behind again, as he walks with Junior this time, Madison still hanging by his side. Another lady passes out drinks to anyone wanting one. She declines the glass of wine she's offered.

Karmen and Nick finally make their way to her. "Frankie, just hang on. We'll get out of here soon." Karmen says, holding her hand.

"That's in the past," Nick says to her quietly. "He loves you...now."

She looks at him like she's never seen him before. Her thoughts and emotions a whirlwind inside of her head, inside of her hurting heart.

"Yeah," she says, nodding her head even though Nick didn't ask her anything.

"You look really cold. Let's go stand by the fireplace," he tells her quietly.

She nods her head again. It's all she can do.

Why didn't Cole tell her about Madison? Did he know she was going to be here? And the market where she works at...he sent them in there. There are so many questions.

Cole plans to live here when he's done doing what he's doing. Does that mean he intended on coming back to her? To Madison? Where does that leave her?

In Portland, where he comes and goes. Where's he's leaving you next week and coming back to you when he can. Fucking inner voice.

"Jason, where's the restroom?" she asks. The words didn't sound like they were even coming from her mouth.

"Go down that hallway," he points behind her. "Make a left at the corner and it's the last door past the study. It's dark that way."

She thanks him and follows his direction without looking at anyone. She doesn't know where Cole is standing and doesn't want to see him and Madison in the room together anymore. Her feet walk as quickly and quietly as they can carry her. She rounds the corner quietly and sees the open door to the restroom at the end of the hallway. She walks to it and passes the cracked study door.

She stops when she hears voices.

"I waited to see if you'd come to see me," a silky voice says. "You never tell me when you'll be in town."

"There's a reason for that."

Cole? She stands in the dark hallway, frozen. Her heart beating slowly, every thud feeling like it will burst through her chest.

"I told you I'd wait for you here. Our home. I could have had the farmhouse finished by now just the way we would have liked."

"And I told you not to."

"I don't care what goes on outside of this town. Or how many *others* there are. You can have one in every city you set foot in. I don't care. I've loved you since high school. I loved you the day you left. And I still love you now. You didn't have to leave. My uncle would have given it all back to us on our wedding day."

"And I'm supposed to be okay with that?" he asks.

"What we had between us is still there. I know you feel it too and I've really missed you. We can pick up where we left off."

Her hands come to her mouth to suppress the sound of her breathing when Madison moves in closer to him. Air is passing right through her. Like she's physically disappearing and all that's left is...hurt.

Cole doesn't move to stop Madison, doesn't push her off of him.

The sound of his belt unbuckling seems amplified in her ears even while she sees his hands gripping Madison's. The hand covering her mouth is covered by tears she didn't know are flowing.

Footsteps. Footsteps are coming down the hallway.

Thud. Thud.

She quickly and as quietly as she can take a couple of steps to retreat into the dark bathroom and closes the door. Not turning on the light, both hands now covering her own mouth, suppressing whatever noise trying to escape. Her tears come in silent streams as she backs up into the sink, wanting to disappear into the walls.

The sound of a man clearing his throat is heard from the other side of the door.

"Nicky," she hears Madison saying, not politely either.

"Madison."

"Just chatting with Cole," Madison purrs.

"Well, people are asking for you," Nick barks out.

She hears a set of footsteps moving in the other direction. A moment passes.

"Straighten yourself up," Nick says right before the sounds of a belt buckling. *Cole's belt.*

She hears another set of footsteps going down the hall in the other direction, back into the room where everyone is congregating. Back into the room that she can't return to.

The doorknob twists and she's frozen in place. It opens slowly and the person on the other side of it is...Nick.

"Shit. Frankie."

Unsure what possesses her to do so, she steps right into him. He catches her and holds her up with his arms as her legs give out. She presses her face into his shirt, trying hard to muffle the sounds of her cry unsuccessfully as she shakes with quiet sobs.

"I need to get out of here," she whispers to him.

She feels him patting her head. "Okay."

"I don't want to make a scene. I can't go back in there." She shakes her head vehemently.

"Here. This way. I can take you." It's Jason. She isn't sure how long he's been standing there. But she's thankful for his help. "We can go out the back."

"I'll try to get Karmen out of here as soon as I can." She nods her head, not wanting to look at him. Or anyone.

"Come on," Jason says. He takes her hand and leads her far away from the room, from the crowd, from the noise, but not far enough from what she just saw in that study.

- 46 -

cole

"Cole, can I talk to you for a second?" Karmen practically yanks him over to the fireplace, pulling him into the present and away from what he was thinking about.

"I've waited long enough. Nick and I are leaving with the kids. Find your own ride home if you even give a shit about going back there." She sounds pissed.

Karmen looks at him, her eyes scalding. "Look around, Cole. Where's Frankie? Remember? Your girlfriend?"

"I just saw her talking to Jason," he says.

"No. While you've been entertaining your ex for the past half-hour, Frankie's been gone. She left."

Karmen stalks off to where Liam is talking to Nick.

What? She's gone? He scans the room. Jason is gone too. *"While you've been entertaining your ex."*

Shit! He's fucked up.

The drive home is silent as shit. Even the kids probably feel the tension in the air. Nick is driving faster than he should and Karmen won't even look at him.

They pull into the driveway and Nick stops him from opening his door. His brother helps Karmen get the kids out of their seats and she rushes them inside and out of the cold.

"You fucked up big time," Nick says when he steps back into the driver seat. And he sounds exactly like the Nick he'd hated. The ruthless, asshole, not-giving-a-shit Nick. Except he is giving a shit.

"I know," he replies.

"You'll be lucky if she's still even here."

"I know!" he retorts louder.

"No, you don't fucking know!" Nick roars at him.

He whips his head around at his brother with his own anger. It's been a long time since he and Nick have gotten into anything like this.

"She fucking saw you! She sat at that table watching you and Madison *reconnecting*. You never even checked on her ONCE after that fucking speech about your preplanned wedding and I'm assuming you didn't bother to tell her about Madison either. And she watched you, for god knows how long, while your ex and her hand were trying to get down your fucking pants!"

"Shit," he whispers. *What did he just fucking do?*

"You don't know shit! Since the day I met her, that girl's been a fighter. But she fucking ran tonight. So you straighten what you think you *know* out before you even walk into that house."

Nick gets out of the van and slams the door.

Oh fuck! *What did he just let happen?*

Madison, that's what happened. All these years, he avoided seeing her. He didn't expect to run into her tonight. He didn't even think she still lived in town.

He's been over her since a long, long time ago, even before he made his choice to leave. She might have not gotten the closure she deserved or needed when he told her he was leaving ten years ago, but he'd closed that chapter of his life without regret.

And tonight, when she tried to kiss him, there was nothing. He'd dodged it. His being unresponsive to her only made her try harder to get a reaction and he should have expected that coming from her. But he hadn't.

Nick was right. He'll be lucky if Frankie is even here.

He gets out of the van and makes his way into the house. The fireplace by the dining room is still going warmly. Yet the energy in the house is different now. He quickly climbs the stairs and rounds the corner, pausing before he turns the doorknob. He isn't sure what he's going to say or how to start, he just wants her to be inside. He takes a deep breath and opens the door.

The room is dark. Cold, even with the fireplace still burning. The bed is empty. The guitar given to her by the band still sits on the chair by the fireplace. He walks over to the bathroom. It's dark and empty, like the rest of his room.

He searches the family room and doesn't find her in there either. He goes back downstairs, hand raking through his hair. He checks both of the extra rooms downstairs and strikes out too.

Where did she go? Did she come back here? Did she leave?

He takes the flight of stairs two at a time, hurriedly walking back into his room. He slides the closet door open. Her bag is still inside.

He pulls his phone out and calls her. It goes straight to voicemail.

Jason! He has to get Jason's number.

He hears movement in the family room and goes to check it out, finding Nick in the dark, sitting on the couch.

"Is she here?" Nick asks.

"No. Can you get me Jason's number?" he asks urgently.

After a minute of his brother being unresponsive, he pushes harder.

"Her phone is going straight to voicemail. She doesn't know anyone here and I don't even know if she's got her wallet on her."

"Karmen can't reach her either," Nick says. "Jason's number is going to voicemail too."

"Shit." He's really starting to panic now.

"I guess the only thing you can do now is to wait. If she comes back here, she comes back. And if she turns up in Portland, someone will call Karmen." His brother stands and heads back to his room.

He checks the time. It's almost eleven p.m. He can drive around aimlessly and see if she's at a bar somewhere or checked into a place. There aren't many hotels in town. There are probably less than a handful of places open at this time of night so he can check those out too.

He heads back to his room, stepping inside, and stares into the emptiness. *What the fuck did he just do?* How stupid he had been even going anywhere alone with Madison in the first place.

He moves over to the window and looks down into the driveway and then over to the two cabins. Nelson's cabin is dark. But Jake's and Lucas's lights are still on. If Jason brought her back, they would have seen or heard the car.

He leaves his room and heads downstairs, leaving through the front door of the house and running to the cabin. He stops himself from banging on the door and instead knocks.

Lucas answers the door a minute later. "Hey," Lucas says flatly.

"Have you seen Frankie? Did you happen to see or hear someone dropping her off?"

Lucas steps out onto the porch, moving him back before he shuts the door. "She's inside. But...she doesn't want to see you and she doesn't want to talk to you right now. She said if you can't give her the space she needs, then she's catching the next flight out, man."

"She's here?" he asks Lucas.

"Yeah, man. Showed up over an hour ago and she didn't want to go inside the main house."

"I have to see her," he says.

"I don't know what happened but she won't see you. She's not in the best condition either. Maybe you really should give her some space."

"Lucas, this isn't the time to be fucking with me," he growls. He tries to reach for the door but Lucas blocks him.

"Stay out of my way and keep out of my business," he says icily to Lucas.

Right before he can turn the knob, Jake opens the door. "Cole. You need to leave or she's leaving," Jake tells him without a hint of a joke.

He looks from Lucas to Jake before shoving Jake out of the way and steps inside the cabin. One of them tries to pull on his arm and he pulls it out of their grip, turning around to show them that he isn't fucking around with them.

He looks around the living room and finds it empty. He checks Jake's room first. Empty. The bathroom door is wide open and dark. Lucas's room. She has to be in there. He heads in that direction and swings the door open.

She's sitting in the recliner chair by the window and instantly spins her head around at the sound of the door crashing into the wall.

Tears cover her face, her nose and eyes red.

"Frankie," he's able to say before she stands and stares at him.

"Get out," she says. "I know I'm at the mercy of being at your place right now but if you can't give me the space I need, I'll find my own way home and away from here."

"I'm not leaving you. Not like this."

"Why? You left me the moment you saw her. Is this what you want? Do you want to see me like this?"

"Can we talk? Let's go back to the house and talk, okay?"

"GET! OUT!" she yells at him.

Jake and Lucas are standing behind him now. "Come on, man. She'll be okay here," Lucas tries to convince him.

He ignores them. "I'm not leaving without you."

"Fine. Then I'll go!" she all but screams at him.

She tries to barge right through him at the doorway and he takes a hold of her by the shoulder. He can feel her trembling in his hold as if she were in pain. In reality, her pain is burning him alive.

She looks up at him, both hurt and fury in her eyes, tears covering her cheeks.

"Frankie…"

"Don't touch me!" She tries to pry his hands off of her. "You don't get it, do you? I can't talk to you right now. All I see when I look at you is the image of you and her making up. All I hear when you speak is the sound of her unbuckling your fucking belt! And you did NOTHING to stop her!"

"Oh shit," he hears Jake whisper from behind him.

"It's not what you think," he tries to tell her.

"I saw what I saw, Cole. Firsthand. And I think you could have easily fucked her and then came home and slept in bed right next to me."

"No," he shakes his head. "Nothing happened."

"I trusted you." She looks down at his hands on her arms. "Let me go, Cole. I'm not going back to that house with you. And I sure as hell am not going to sleep in your bed next to you."

He lets his hands slip off of her. "All right. Just promise you won't leave until we talk."

"I don't owe you anything."

And she's right.

He fucked up. And she doesn't owe him a damn thing. Defeated, he steps out into the hallway as she shuts the door in his face.

"Make sure she doesn't leave."

"I'm not gonna hold her hostage," Lucas says before he walks away. He, too, seems pissed off now.

"If she *needs* to leave, I can't stop her. Sorry, man." Jake pats him on the back.

He makes his way back to the house and steps inside. How is he going to fix this? He can't even be sure she's going to give him the chance to fix it. Not that he deserves one. If he'd walked into Lucas's room and saw the same thing she had seen, he is one hundred percent sure she wouldn't be getting a second chance from him.

Unsure when he fell asleep in the chair, he wakes up to the sound of water trickling. The shower is running. The door is closed but it's definitely the shower running. It has to be Frankie.

It's still dark outside. Large snowflakes are falling. He checks his watch. It's just past six a.m. She never gets up this early. She probably didn't get any sleep.

He reaches for a log and places it into the fireplace and waits for her. He isn't even sure what he's going to say to her. He just knows he doesn't want to lose her.

He can't lose her.

The shower shuts off and he's back in the chair, anxiously waiting.

Almost twenty minutes later, he can hear the twisting of the doorknob before she opens the door and walks out with a towel in her hands trying to dry her hair. She's dressed in her usual sweatpants and sweater. Something he's become accustomed to waking up to almost every morning now.

Their eyes meet for a brief moment before she looks away and walks past him to the window while she continues to dry her hair.

"Frankie...I fucked up."

"Tell me something I don't already know."

"There's nothing I...there's no excuse for what happened last night. I'm sorry. I never meant to hurt you."

"Why didn't you tell me about her?"

"It was a long time ago."

"I meant when you saw her again last night. Why didn't you tell me who she was...or is...or whatever...to you?"

"Was. She isn't anything to me now. It was the first time I've seen her since I left. And I didn't think she was still living here."

"Really? You look pretty fucking familiar or at least well on your way to getting reacquainted. I was in the same house and you did it anyway."

He let that sink in. The pain in her voice quakes him down to his soul.

"You had plenty of chances to pull me aside and tell me. But you didn't. You let go of my hand the moment you saw her. You left me, Cole, and you never gave me a second thought."

"I didn't mean for it to be like that."

"What's that supposed to mean? You just got lost in the moment?" she says sarcastically.

"No. She and I are over. It *has* been for a decade. I'll admit that I feel...that I felt guilty for the way I left but she knew long before that, what she wanted with me wasn't going to happen. Last night, I was an idiot thinking that we could remain friends on some level."

"Well, I don't think she got that memo." She pauses. "What is it that you think she wants with you and why would it be any different than what I might want with you? And if you're saying you couldn't give that to her, what makes it any different with me or any of the others you probably have spread across the country?"

"Frankie. You *know* there's only you. Everything I want, I want with you."

"I heard *her* tell you that she still loves you and she's waiting for you. Did you originally have plans on coming back here to patch things up with her?"

"No! God no! That will never happen. You know where I want to be, Frankie."

Her hand comes up to rub her head. "I thought I did, Cole. But seeing you last night...She was practically undressing you and you didn't even try to stop her. Maybe you do belong here with her. She's definitely your *type*."

"Baby, I'm sorry. But nothing happened. I stopped her. I did. I know it will never happen again. I don't owe her anything. I made my decision the day I left and I can't carry the burden of what she did with that decision. I know that now. And whatever it takes, Frankie, I'll show you where I want to be."

She walks over to the double doors and watches the falling snow. Light is coming in now, the sun getting ready to rise. She looked tired and fragile, one hand throwing the towel on the bed while the other rubs her temple. He really can't tell what she's thinking and her stillness is making him anxious.

She moves away from the window and he watches as she lifts the corner of the covers off of the bed and slides in. Her back still facing him, she pulls the covers over herself.

Five minutes go by, maybe even more, before he gathers up the nerve to walk over to her side of the bed, ready to grovel.

Once there, he sees the shape of her body curled up underneath the comforter, her eyes closed. She's fallen asleep and looked like she needed the rest.

Fuck it. If she's going to wake up and leave him, then he's going to take this opportunity to lie next to her one more time. He'll deal with whatever she dishes out to him when she wakes.

As quietly as he can, he walks back over to the closet and changes into his own usual sleepwear before coming back to bed and climbing in next to her.

Again, unsure when he actually fell asleep, he wakes with the light coming in through the double doors. The bed seems warmer than usual.

Frankie is asleep nestled in between his arms, her face against his chest where his heart beats. He pulls her in just a little closer, not wanting to wake her. Her arm wraps around his waist tighter. He knows she's going to wake up soon and this moment will be lost.

He starts racking his brain for the right thing to say and comes up empty. There are no right things to say. There are no right things to do. He'd completely and utterly fucked up. The ball is completely in her court right now.

He kisses the top of her head softly, afraid to wake her. She stirs but he's relieved that she stays asleep. He studies the gray skies and the snow falling for some time, wanting to hold on to her as long as he possibly can.

"We can't talk if you're smothering me like this," he hears her strained voice after a long time has passed.

He loosens his hold from around her, not letting go. But she moves all the way out of his arm anyway, never making eye contact with him.

She turns away from him toward the doors and winces at the light coming in.

Knock. Knock.

"Cole, Nick needs you downstairs like now." It's Karmen.

"Stay in bed. I'll ask Karmen to bring you some tea and aspirin. I'll be right back."

He opens the door and Karmen is glaring at him, still fuming from last night probably. She is holding a hot cup in one hand and a bottle of Advil in the other.

"Thank you," he tells her.

"I didn't do it for you," she says. "You need to get your ass downstairs and deal with that bullshit down there," she whispers to him.

What now?

- 47 -

cole

"The answer is still no," Nick says to Jimmy. "And why are you even here, Madison?"

"I told you. She wants to help us get that loan from her uncle. If Cole and her went to speak to him together, we can have the paperwork signed and done before the end of the year."

"No," he immediately replies. "We're not doing it. You can find your own way."

"Cole, be reasonable. If you had just let me handle things in the beginning, we wouldn't have had to be apart all these years," Madison says with not an ounce of sincerity.

He looks at her and can't remember how he found her attractive in the first place.

That's because you have a short, dark-haired, green-eyed, fierce woman upstairs who will definitely walk out on you if she comes down and sees this.

"The farm wasn't the reason why we broke up, Madison. You know that. I think you both need to leave. This discussion is over," he says more sternly.

Madison completely ignores him and walks to the dining table to pick up the vase full of Jesse's bouquets from the other night. She brings them back into the kitchen, humming as she plucks the dead leaves and petals off into the kitchen sink as if he hadn't spoken. He'd always hated that about her. She always had a way of making him feel like his opinions didn't matter.

"I always loved being in this house. The kitchen could have been done better though," she says.

"Leave! Now!" Nick growls.

"This kitchen is perfect and practical. I love this kitchen. A perfect touch of class and style. Not too uppity and with just the right amount of warmth for *our* family. Maybe someday I can see how *your* kitchen compares."

He and Nick snap their heads in the direction of the voice. Karmen and Frankie are walking into the kitchen like they're taking a stroll in the park.

He makes eye contact with Frankie. She's just simmering with anger right beneath the surface. They haven't even worked out what happened last night yet and now she walks into this shitstorm. He can't take his eyes off of her, silently pleading to her for her to not lose her shit.

"Morning, Madison," Karmen says. "We weren't expecting you so early."

"Early? We keep early hours around these parts. Lunch should already be prepped by now," Madison replies snobbishly.

"Sorry I couldn't come down sooner. Cole and I had a long night," Frankie says.

She walks over and slides her arm behind his waist then reaches up for a kiss.

He doesn't pass the chance and kisses her. He's missed her lips but he can still feel her holding back.

"Jimmy, you're back. Madison, nice seeing you again so soon," she says, eyes flaming.

"Pleasure's mine," Madison replies with the sweetest fake smile.

He hated that about her too.

"What did I miss? Everyone seems so tense," Frankie says with a smile. "Thank you for taking care of those flowers for me, Madison. You seem to be good at taking care of things for me when I'm not paying attention."

He definitely caught that one.

"Same shit, different day," Nick answers her question.

"Cole, sweetie, I think this is a private conversation. Frankie, maybe you can go wait upstairs so we can finish talking."

He glares at Madison, who continues to meddle with the flowers.

"Madison has offered to speak with her uncle about that loan we talked about before. Cole and Nick can stay here permanently and help build the family back to its good graces again," Jimmy says, much too polite.

Frankie leaves his side and walks over to Jimmy. He sees his uncle taking a step back.

"Good graces?" she asks. "Last I checked, Joseph falling ill and passing didn't mean the family name fell too. You, as head of the family, just didn't have the balls or tenacity to upkeep his legacy. You should have been helping him keep the place together when he couldn't anymore, yet you squandered everything he had in bad investments."

"You need to watch your mouth before you speak. You don't know what you're talking about. This is none of your business," Jimmy retorts. His face is red with fury.

"I know enough, Jimmy. I know that you had at least twelve LLCs incorporated and defaulted in the state of Montana alone since the early nineties. None of them having anything to do with Howard Acres, which I'm betting means that Joseph didn't know about them.

"And Liam has an eye for business or he wouldn't have what he has so if you ever approached him with a solid investment plan, you wouldn't need Nick and Cole to vouch for you."

He didn't know anything about the LLCs. He never thought to look into anything like that. This was all news to him and he's betting it's news to Nick too.

"So the answer is still going to be no, Jimmy. Just like it was the last time you were here. Remember?" she asks.

"But this loan can mean that Cole and Nick get to stay here and work with the development team, right, Madison?" Jimmy asks, sounding like a plea.

"Yes. So we can all move on with *our* lives," Madison answers. She finishes toying with the flowers and then sets them in the middle of the island.

"Jimmy, I think it's time for you to leave so Cole and I can discuss this. Don't hold your breath though. WE won't be changing our minds. Nick, do you need time to discuss it with Karmen too?" She doesn't take her eyes off of Jimmy.

"No," Nick immediately replies.

"Did you come in through the front door again? Nick, be a good host and open it for Jimmy. He looks ready to leave now."

Jimmy stammers and sputters, looking back at Madison when Nick grabs him by the elbow and leads him to the front door.

There's a certain amount of satisfaction in watching Nick dragging Jimmy out. It's not completely them disrespecting their elder so Gramps shouldn't have too much of a fit.

Frankie walks over to the island and spins the flower vase around slowly. She walks over to the sink, gathers up the dead petals, and rounds Madison to dispose of them in the trash. He watches as she wipes her hands with the kitchen towel that is lying in front of Madison.

"Madison." She turns to face her now.

He looks from one woman to the other. The contrast between the two is like night and day. Madison looms over Frankie by eight inches. Frankie stands unfazed by Madison's posture and coolness.

He reaches for Frankie's hand but both Nick and Karmen hold him back by the back of his shirt, shaking their heads when he turns to them.

"Let's drop the pretenses, shall we? We're all adults here and it's too early for me to be playing this game with you. As I said, Cole and I had a long night," Frankie says.

"Cole and I have things *we* need to discuss. Things that have nothing to do with you," Madison says politely with her perfect manners.

"Everything that has to do with him, has to do with me. Otherwise, I wouldn't be here. And the discussion about the farm won't happen without Nick and Karmen either. They have a say just as much as Cole and I do," Frankie answers, unintimidated.

"Cole and you?" Madison scoffs. "Cole, maybe we can go out for coffee. Our favorite place should be open by now."

"I don't know how ladies out here behave, but where I'm from, we don't hang all over a man who's clearly moved on and we sure as hell don't do it shamelessly in front of an audience including his new girlfriend. So you can stop speaking to him like I don't exist or I can stop speaking to you like a lady really quick."

He can hear how pissed off she is but he can feel she needs this. To stand her ground.

"Madison, I don't make decisions without Frankie. If I didn't make that clear before, I am now. I'm not going to change my mind about this. Neither is Nick," he says, stepping in anyway.

"Fine, sweetie. But we have other things to discuss."

"No. We don't," he tells her, looking directly into her eyes.

"This is a chance for us to start building what we've always wanted together. We should talk about our future, get us back on track. She doesn't know you like I do. She doesn't understand you like I do. This town, our home, a city girl like her would never fit in here."

"Then I won't set foot in this town again without her. You don't know anything about her or about us. *My home* is with her. Wherever she's at is where I'll build."

"You've been away for a long time. You just need time to get back into things. Like last night. How perfect was that? I think we need to finish that *discussion.*"

"Last night was a mistake I won't make again. I think you should go now. We have things to do."

"I'm sure you were used to getting your way when you were with him. But things have changed. He's moved on. A smart woman like you should understand that," Frankie tells her.

Frankie hasn't looked at him but he knows she's listening. The comment Madison had made about last night hurt her.

She walks to him, surprising him when she slides her small hand into his, interlocking her fingers tightly.

"Madison, I know we're bound to run into each other from time to time when we're in town. This is a small town. I don't mind if you want to say hi to Cole in passing but do me a favor."

Madison looks down at Frankie as if she were a nuisance. "What's that?" she asks.

"I may be a lot smaller than you, a lot younger. I might not have the money to buy the class that seeps through your pores, but I can still school you on a thing or two about Cole. If you know him as well as you say you do, you'd know he isn't a sellout. Don't ever try to buy his pride and dignity again."

Frankie removes her hand and walks over to the back door.

"I hope it's okay if I let you out this way. As he said, we have things to do before we head *home.* If you need extra help getting off the property, I'm sure I can get Jake to step in to help."

Madison snaps her head around and faces Frankie, who's staring up defiantly, holding the door open. Madison picks her purse off of the counter, looking at him. She starts to reach in for a hug but he opts to extend his hand for a shake instead. She ignores it and turns around, heading out of the open door.

Frankie closes it and walks back to them, her arms crossed over her chest.

"Is there anyone else I need to kick out today?" she asks, looking right at him. "Because my head is fucking killing me."

She heads for the stairs and Karmen is right behind her.

"You have some major groveling to do," Nick tells him once the ladies are out of earshot.

"No shit!"

"She's fucking insane! Even on her off day. I think she even scares Jimmy. Damn, I just want to give him a good one. Just one! Right to the mouth. But Gramps would definitely be beating my ass, even from the grave. And what's with that thing she was saying about Jimmy and some LLCs? Do you think he was swindling Gramps's final dollars?"

"I don't know but would you put it past him?"

He walks over to the coffeemaker and finds a tea pod. The battle down here is done, but the one upstairs? He isn't sure how that's going to go. That thing between him and Madison is settled but he has to be sure that *she* knows it's over been the two of them. On top of that, he has to make up for what happened last night too.

"Coley, if you don't fix this. *I'm* going to be pissed at you too," Nick says next to him.

"I remember a time when you and I barely spoke. I miss those times." *Asshole.*

He walks into the bedroom expecting to see Karmen, but Frankie is walking out of the bathroom alone.

"Hey," he says to her, watching as she walks over and climbs into bed. "I brought you another hot tea." He sets it on the night table and sits on the bed next to her. "Bad headache?"

"Headache. Heartache. It's all bad."

"I know saying I'm sorry isn't going to fix what I did. But I really am...sorry."

She finally looks up at him. Her eyes aren't full of fury anymore. They are full of sadness now. He touches her cheek and she holds his hand there and closes her eyes.

"I don't know how long it'll be before I can look at you and *not* see what I saw. How long will it be before I stop wondering who you're with every time you leave?"

Her honesty hurts and the tear sliding down burns his hand. She isn't trying to take jabs at him. She's hurt. He'd hurt her.

"Give me a chance." His thumb caresses her cheek softly, trying to wipe her tear away. "I love you. If it takes me never setting foot in this town again or whatever town she's in to show you, that's what I'll do."

"She wasn't the only one in the wrong, Cole."

"I know."

He leans in slowly and feels her slightly hesitate but he takes a chance and goes the distance to kiss her anyway. It takes her a second but she responds, kissing him back and it's like he's a schoolboy getting his first kiss.

Don't fuck this up, dipshit!

Why did his subconscious always have to talk like Nick?

- 48 -

He watches the spinning rainbow ball on the laptop screen and waits for it to disappear so he can see what is syncing.

He clicks on the notification quickly. Cole 406-555-8582 has been updated to her Contacts.

He stares at the picture associated with the number. It's a picture of her and Cole.

Cole, the fucking thorn in his side.

***

Frankie

"Expecting more visitors?" she asks Cole when they pull up into the driveway.

A white Ford SUV is parked in front of one of the garage doors.

"No," he answers before he gets out of the truck and heads over to her side, the bag from the phone store in one hand. They also stopped at a couple stores where she picked up a couple of souvenirs for Alice and Vince. He's carrying those bags too.

She steps out of the car and walks to the house. Shaking off the light snow and taking off her boots, she walks into the kitchen. No one is in the kitchen but she can hear voices chattering away from the dining area.

"Jason!" she exclaims.

"There's MY girl!" Jason says, standing up from one of the chairs.

She places her jacket on the staircase banister before rushing over to him for a giant hug. Karmen is sitting in the chair opposite him.

"He's been waiting for almost an hour now," Karmen tells her.

"Everything okay?" she asks him.

"Just wanna check on you and make sure you're okay. That's all," he says. "I had to get out of that house anyway. Too stuffy. So I came here to party with you!"

"Ahem...Please don't try to steal my BFF. I'll fight you to my last breath for her," Karmen tells him jokingly.

"Shit! All right. All right. Calm down, bitch!" Jason says with his hands up and they all laugh.

"Hey, Cole," Jason greets him.

"Hey," Cole says. "Make yourself at home." He nods to Jason and then heads up the stairs with the bags.

"Everything okay with you two?" Jason asks with genuine concern.

"We're trying," she says.

He sits back down in the chair and she pulls a chair from the dining table to sit between him and Karmen.

"Hey, Frankie," he says quietly, leaning out of his seat. "That thing with him and Madison last night? Don't let it get to you so much. I mean, don't let that come between you and him. It was her grasping for straws."

"She was definitely grasping at something," Karmen says.

Jason stands up to try and check over the staircase before sitting back down. "It's just Madison being Madison. This is a small town and she used to be the town beauty queen. Back in high school, maybe even a little after that. Cole was one of only a few that would have been well suited, whether it be by looks or family money. So she clung on."

She and Karmen are paying close attention now.

"It's all about appearances to her. I don't think she's ever loved anyone more than herself. Everything always has to be perfect with her," Jason continues.

"I can see that," Karmen says.

"But what you don't know is that life stood still for her here. Underneath all that posh, and blonde, she's afraid to leave the town. Rather be an old beauty queen here than a nobody somewhere else. I'm sure when she saw Cole last night, she jumped at the chance to try and make herself relevant again."

"She waited for him. And you probably saw what happened last night. He didn't exactly discourage her either," she points out.

"Frankie. Girl," he sighs loudly. "Karmen, can I step in the BFF shoes for a few minutes?"

"Go right ahead," Karmen invites him.

"One. If you decided that you're gonna give the man a chance to right his wrongs, then you can't bring his wrongs up at every chance and every battle. You have to do your part in letting that go too. And two..."

He looks up at the staircase again before motioning them to gather around closer.

"She didn't exactly *wait* for him. About a month after Cole told her he was thinking about leaving, she was looking for a way to hold him back. Cole had things going on and was barely spending time with her, so she found someone else to do the job."

"Not following you...so she cheated on him?" Karmen asks, astonished.

"Worse. She tried to get pregnant. What else would keep a man like Cole glued somewhere?" Jason suggests.

"How do you know this?" Karmen asks just above a whisper.

"I saw them," he says nonchalantly. "And being a kid at that time, I dug around and found her calendar, where she was definitely keeping track and she had stopped taking her pill."

"You saw them? Who!" Karmen asks.

"Who else looks like Cole and can pass for a sibling?" Jason asks, giving them that come-on-you-should-know-this look.

"Jake," she answers quietly.

"No fucking way!" Karmen straight out screams.

Jason is nodding his head vehemently.

"Jake told me last night as a last effort to get me to talk to Cole. I guess he's well versed in the ways of Madison's manipulation skills," she tells the two.

"But they're really good friends," Karmen says.

"They are now. Back then, they barely knew each other. Probably never even spoke until he moved into the cabin. Madison was the most popular girl in town. Jake being in his very early horny twenties, of course, would jump at the chance to shag the town beauty."

"Does Cole know about this?" Karmen asks.

"I don't know. I don't know if Jake ever told him. Madison definitely wasn't going to. Especially since she never got pregnant anyway."

"Jake's never brought it up," she answers. "Letting sleeping dogs lie or some shit."

She couldn't believe a woman like Madison would stoop to that level when Jake told her last night. How much easier and less lonely would her life be if she only dared to leave town if there is absolutely no one else here for her to love?

The trio is startled out of their conversation when they hear the sounds of people coming through the back entrance.

Nick, Nelson, and Lucas are discussing something. Jake is the last to enter the house, shaking the snow out of his hair as he wipes his boots off on the mat. A minute later, Cole comes down the stairs and heads to her. He places a gentle kiss on top of her head.

"Can I grab those envelopes from you?" he asks. She's totally forgotten about them since putting them in her purse.

"Yeah. Over there on the stairs." She points to her purse.

He fumbles to get it open and pulls out the envelopes. He heads to the kitchen and she hears the men greeting each other.

"It's their holiday bonuses," Karmen tells her.

"That's nice of them," Jason says.

"They work hard to take care of the place. Nick and Cole don't get to come back here often enough," Karmen says out loud.

"They'd come back more often if you ladies moved out here," Jason teases them.

"So how long are you here for?" she asks Jason.

"For another dreadful week. I'm out of here the moment that turkey's cut. I miss my man!"

"He didn't want to come along?"

"Hell no. I won't subject him to this kind of torture. Plus, Dad wouldn't exactly roll out the red carpet for him."

"Well, you're both welcome to visit us in Portland anytime," Karmen says.

"You bet your asses I'll be taking you up on that offer."

"Do you wanna stay for dinner?" she asks him.

"No. I can't. Dad requests my presence at the dinner table. I should be getting back there anyway. I have to check on things back home."

Jason stands up. She and Karmen stand up with him. Karmen gives him a hug and a kiss on the cheek. She gives him the hug of all hugs and he leaves his arm around her shoulders as they walk to the kitchen together.

"Cole," he greets him again once they are in the kitchen. "You take good care of this one. There's something about her that just draws people in. Some people can get addicted to that kind of energy."

"Truer words were never spoken," Cole says.

"Hey, Nick," Jason says. "Karmen is awesome! Too bad she ended up with you."

"Yeah. Thanks a lot, asshole!" Nick grunts.

Jason laughs loudly as they walk him to the door, helping him get into his jacket before waving him goodbye. She really hopes to stay in touch with him. They exchanged phone numbers last night already and began following each other on social media just this morning.

- 49 -

cole

He picked Nick up at five a.m. from Karmen's place. He thought he was miserable leaving Frankie but Nick is a complete fucking grouch this morning. And to think his brother was the one who gave him all sorts of decent advice prior to going on this job.

They've been driving for almost ten hours, stopping only once to fill up the tank. Nick was asleep most of the drive until now.

"I'm starving. Let's grab something in the next town," Nick says.

"Sure. Anything from Victor?" he asks.

"Not yet. He should be calling me soon. I'll drive once we pull in somewhere."

He nods his head and watches Nick check his new *personal* phone. One similar to the new personal one burning a hole in his own pocket. Their burner phones sit in the cupholder in between them. He's avoided checking his phone thus far, not wanting to make it harder on himself wondering how Frankie is doing. He knows this is her first day back at work and she's pulling a double.

Nick points at a road sign, telling him there's a town approaching.

"After a week of Frankie's cooking, everything is gonna taste like shit," Nick complains.

"Don't remind me."

The burner cell in the cupholder rings and he tunes out the conversation Nick is having with who he assumes is Victor. The conversation lasts about five minutes before he hangs up and then a text message follows.

"Everything good?" he asks Nick.

"Yeah. Just a little change of plan. Victor wants Paul in on this deal too. We're gonna have to take the longer route and pick him up in Avon, Colorado."

"Cutting things really close, aren't we?"

"I guess this job is Paul's deal to begin with. Fine with me. I don't have a problem with the guy. He's bringing the final payout for the last job we did too."

He takes the next exit and looks around for a quick and decent place to grab a bite. He spots a sign for a sandwich shop and pulls into the plaza. After rounding the parking lot twice, he finally finds a parking spot and pulls in.

"Sandwiches works for me," Nick says as they begin cutting through the lot. "Everything good with you and Frankie now?"

"Gettin' there," he says. *Except she still thinks about Madison when she thinks he isn't looking.*

"Good. I like the kid. Too bad the feeling isn't mutual, but I probably deserve it."

"She tolerates you."

The place doesn't have a line and they go straight to the counter to order. Five minutes later they are both sitting in a booth, taking bites out of some very bland sandwiches.

He checks his watch before pulling out his phone. He taps on the icon for the security alarm and wipes his hands while it opens.

"What's that?" Nick asks.

"It's the app for the new alarm system in her place. It's good to know about these things," he tells Nick.

Which is true for their line of work. Technology can work for them or against them. He shows his brother the ins and outs of the app and what it can do.

"It's a lot fancier than what she had before," Nick points out.

"Yeah. Don't remind me," he says bluntly.

She didn't have much of anything in the form of security before. She was practically a sitting target for the likes of Dusty...well, for the likes of all three of them, alone in that building all by herself, night after night.

They reach Avon earlier than expected. Nick called Victor and they are currently waiting to hear back about where to pick Paul up.

Nick is driving and so he's in the passenger's seat with it reclined back. His phone pings and he pulls it out of his pocket. He turns the screen on and taps the message notification. It's a message from Frankie.

Thank you for the flowers, my love. I miss you more than you'll ever know.

A picture of her smelling the bouquet he sent follows the message. She looks fucking beautiful. Her hair is down and she looks like she's home, where he wants to be.

He sends a quick reply.

I love you.

He'd never said those words and meant it as deeply as he did for Frankie. There isn't a fucking second that goes by that he didn't want her to hear it and know that he meant it.

"Yeah. That smile isn't subtle at all, baby brother," Nick says.

"Shut up!" he barks back but he can't stop smiling.

"If you need some alone time in here, I can take a walk. What do you need? Like two minutes or something?"

"Shut. Up!" he growls at Nick.

His phone pings again and he turns the screen back on and opens the new message. It's a picture of her holding a cup of tea with a pouty face. He can see her new laptop open in the picture *and* she's wearing the T-shirt he wore the day before.

Hot fucking damn. Maybe two minutes alone isn't such a bad thing.

I love you too. Late night for me hence the pouty face.

God help me! The sight of her with his shirt on definitely tugs at something. Saved by the ringing phone. The call they've been waiting for comes in on the burner phone, distracting him from her.

"Mikaela Way and Benchmark," Nick repeats into the phone before hanging up.

He immediately sits up and reaches for the tablet, tapping on the screen to find the intersection.

Nick looks at the screen before he drops the phone back into the cupholder and moves the truck in the direction they need to go. Fifteen minutes later, Paul is climbing into the backseat with his two bags.

"Hey, guys. Nice seeing you two again," Paul greets them.

He acknowledges Paul with a nod. Nick is already setting the tablet to reroute them to Santa Fe.

Paul hands a small bag in between the seats over to him. "From Victor," Paul says. "You should count it to make sure."

"Everything went smooth?" Nick asks.

"Yeah. Owner didn't overestimate his losses. Made the claim go by a lot quicker," Paul informs them.

"And this job?" he asks Paul.

Paul pulls out his own tablet from his other bag. He sees that it still has the plastic on the screen. Paul taps the window and shows them the location.

"This one is a two for one," Paul starts. "The building has two places we need to visit at opposite ends of each other with three other shops in between. Same owner, same inside man. One shop's a high-end consignment store. The other is a jewelry dealer. Both locations, same security set-up. It's a lot more modern and a lot more work than what I'm used to."

"Is this another inside job?" he asks Paul.

"Yeah. The guy is covered. Victor says he'll take his cut down to twenty-five. There's paperwork in that consignment shop worth a lot more than the jewelry. That's what he's really after. Everything else is left for us. He can make the connection for a buyer after we find out what we have in hand."

"So the jewelry is a diversion," he speaks his thought.

"Basically," Paul confirms.

"We should get there by six," Nick informs them. "Cole, find places for us to stay outside of the area. I don't think we should be driving around the area until about nine a.m. The holiday crowd should be out and about around that time. The job won't be until Thursday."

"Yeah. Happy Thanksgiving, right. Best way to spend it. Making money," Paul says.

He can think of better ways to spend it.

"Do you know more about the security system?" he asks.

"Here." Paul hands him the tablet and he scrolls through the screen before finding the model.

"Just curious, Paul, how are you coming across all these connects?" Nick asks.

"You really wanna know?" Paul pauses. "I'm their insurance broker."

"No fucking shit!" Nick says and laughs.

He turns back and looks at Paul to make sure he isn't joking. Paul's dead serious.

"So you're milking these guys. You get a commission off the policy sale. They somehow come back and *pay* you for the job *and* you get the cut from the sale." Nick says out loud exactly what he is thinking.

"In a nutshell...yeah. Sometimes I even help them file the claim. That part, I do straight by the book though."

"Why do these people do it?" he asks out of curiosity.

"You mean set themselves up?"

"Yeah."

"For some, they're in too much debt hanging onto the place. They're just looking for a way out of the debt even if it means they walk away with zero. Walking away with zero is better than standing in the negative."

"Makes sense," Nick says.

"And then for some, it's not just about the money. Like this one we're doing? The paperwork we're looking for is actually a last will and testament."

"And that's worth more than the jewelry itself?" he asks incredulously.

"To some, yeah. I mean, why would they care about a couple hundred thousand in jewelry that they don't even own when they can find out who will inherit an empire worth a couple million or more? Gives them time to either protect what they're getting or make changes to ensure they're getting something."

Makes sense, actually.

It takes them over three hours to drive around the location to his satisfaction. The holiday traffic doesn't help speed things up either. They managed to find a place open for a quick bite to eat before splitting up, each man finding their own way back to their lodgings.

He's currently on an obnoxiously uncomfortable bed with his laptop open to an aerial view of the location. His tablet is also open to more information about the security system.

The timing has to be exact for this one. There is absolutely no room for error. Holiday or not, they can't bank their chances on a response time other than the normal and that isn't much time at all. Their best bet is to split up and get into both locations at the same time. He'll have to ask Nick which he prefers to do. The jewelry or the documents.

The job is set for 7:30 p.m. on Thanksgiving. Dinner time for most families.

During the holidays, it's usually around the time when things are the most chaotic with friends and family either heading somewhere or just arriving. It's also the time that on-duty patrol for the security monitoring services and on-duty police officers tend to make pit stops to their family gatherings for a little taste of the festivities.

At this time of year, the sun will have set a while providing the dark cover they need.

- 50 -

Frankie

She flips on her computer monitor, surprised that the desktop is actually on.

Taking a deep breath, she focuses on the task at hand. First things first, she checks her work emails. After clearing out all of the junk mail and replying to the others, she stares at the screen, trying to figure out what she should do next. Where does she even start to figure this thing out? She hasn't received any emails or invoices from Cynthia since they've last spoken. And at this point, she's unsure where to even place the order for the weekend crowd.

That's right! Since October third, she was still placing orders with Mad Hatter Distribution. Even though Cynthia said she never received any orders or communication since then, the purchase order that she emailed in weekly had to go somewhere because they never bounced back to her.

She opens the accounting software and scrolls through the vendor's list. Finding Mad Hatter, she double clicks to open up the vendor's details. She grabs a folder from her drawer and digs through, looking for an older invoice.

Comparing the old invoice from the beginning of September to what she sees on screen now. *Bam!* The addresses are different and so is the email address. Someone edited the information.

She opens the web browser and quickly types in the address from the screen and waits for the map to populate. The address seems to be going to a post office box in Lake Oswego. How is that possible? She tries to google the email address with no luck in finding any social media or any other information linked to it.

Next, she generates a report to see if she can find when the details to this vendor were changed and by whom. The report will also show her if there were any other edits made.

Reading line by line, she sees the vendor edit was made under her own login on October first. *What the hell?* That can't be right. She's a hundred percent positive she did not make that change.

She pulls up the desktop calendar to check what day October first had fallen on. Friday. She would have been at work at Katrina's at the time the edit was made. But this bar would have been open and in full swing.

Did Vince do this? Could he have? He's the only other person that knows her password and a change like that would have required it.

Password! Change your password! She immediately goes to her settings and changes her passwords and sits back in her chair. She isn't sure what's going on but at least now she has a starting point and trail to follow.

She glances at the time at the corner of her screen before she logs out of everything. It's already well past midnight.

"Everything okay? You look tense," Karmen asks her when she walks into the office.

"Yeah...I mean no. Just trying to figure something out," she says with absolutely no enthusiasm whatsoever.

"Any luck?"

"I found a starting point. That's some luck, I guess." She looks at Karmen and sees her friend looking tired. "Are you okay?"

"Yeah. Just tired. I feel like we've been running a marathon between the vacation and coming back to work almost immediately. All my bags haven't even been unpacked yet."

"It's not too late to cancel tomorrow." They are having a small Thanksgiving dinner. Vince, Alice, and a few other people are supposed to be joining them.

"No way! Besides, you and Vince do all the heavy lifting anyway." Karmen walks over to the desk and sits down in the chair opposite her.

"Something on your mind?" she asks.

"So..." Karmen begins and she waits to hear what's on her mind. "I...I'm kinda late."

"You need me to stay and close for you?"

Karmen stares at her blankly. "No, Frankie. I'm late. Like *late*, late. Like a week late."

"Oh my god." Her hands come up to cover the surprised grin on her face once comprehension settles. "Wait. Is this good news or bad news?"

"I don't know if I am or not yet. And I don't know, Frankie. I don't know how Nick will take this. It's not exactly planned and we are pretty careful but I wasn't on the pill. And I know you and him aren't the best of buddies right now, so even if it's good news for us, maybe it won't be for you? And then the thing with his *job*...I just don't know how I'm supposed to be feeling. Everything is moving so fast."

"I see your dilemma."

cole

Unable to sleep and done with the tossing and turning, he flips the TV on and scrolls through the channels. He picks up his phone from the nightstand and checks for any messages from her. It's almost one a.m. in Portland and Frankie is probably still at the bar.

He taps on the security app and sits up in bed.

It's disabled. When he'd last checked, he was pretty sure it had been set. Maybe she was home already and forgot to set it. He taps the screen to enable the alarm, puts the phone back on the nightstand, and stares at the tablet.

Doesn't hurt to look again. He's not sleeping anyway. He pulls his tablet from the nightstand and goes over the security system for the job one more time. It's amazing the amount of information readily available via the internet. He's read and gone over diagrams all night.

The phone on the nightstand pings twice, a few seconds after the other. He picks it up and checks the notification.

The apartment door was just opened and the alarm was disabled again. Is Frankie going somewhere this late at night?

The phone pings and a message comes through. He taps on the message icon and opens it.

Home now. I miss my cowboy.

Home now? Then why and how was the alarm disabled earlier?

He opens the app and checks through the notifications. The front door was opened at 10:37 p.m. and the alarm was disabled shortly after that using the correct code. The door wasn't opened again until exactly 11 p.m. And then again just now when the app notified him. Is someone in the apartment? Or did she come home and then leave again?

Fuck it. He taps on the phone icon and calls her.

"Hi, babe," she answers. *"I didn't wake you, did I?"*

"Sleep doesn't come easy without you," he tells her honestly. "Long day?"

"Yeah. It was a slow night at the restaurant so it dragged out a bit. I went straight to the bar after that. Stayed longer than I wanted to," she says, sounding tired even to his ears.

"Everything okay at home?" he asks. He doesn't want to scare her.

"Yeah. Everything's fine." She pauses. *"Are you okay?"*

"I'm okay, baby."

"We're having a little turkey dinner at Karmen's tomorrow. Vince, Alice, and a few other people will be joining us. I'll have to Uber there in the afternoon."

"Where's your car?"

"I let Karmen take it home tonight. Hers is in the shop. She's probably going to need to run to an open grocery store in the morning for something last minute anyway."

"How'd you get home from the bar tonight? Did you walk?"

"Yeah. Short, quick walk. Nothing exciting. No tall, gorgeous god walking with his hand holding mine," she says with a giggle. *"I did plow into someone coming out from the alley though."*

"I doubt you made a dent, baby."

She laughs at him. *"Actually, kinda odd, he apologized to me and called me Francine. I don't think I know him but I apologized and ran across the street."*

He swings his leg off the side of the bed because that red-flagged him. "Did you lock the door behind you? Set the alarm?" he asks as calm as he can even though the cyclone of anxiety is growing inside.

"I locked the door and texted you as soon as I got in. I won't need to arm the system until I go to bed, right?" He hears the sound of her yawn. *"If I didn't need to shower, I would ask you to switch this to video just so I can sleep next to you."*

A smile forms across his face. "Go. Shower and get to bed, baby. I'll call you when I can."

"I love you."

- 51 -

cole

He and Nick are in the truck waiting for Paul now. They're parked in the parking lot of a Walmart Supercenter. It's almost ten p.m. and the lot is nearly full of people who are here to camp out for the Black Friday sale. It's the perfect place for them to blend in. Paul has fifteen minutes to get here or he'll be finding his own way home.

"Victor says Paul can join us for Shreveport if he wants," Nick tells him. "I'll ask him. Maybe the guy wants to go back to his kid though."

"I need a favor," he says, completely ignoring what Nick just said.

"What is it?"

"Can you ask Karmen to get me Sam's number? I don't want Frankie to know about this."

"Yeah," Nick says, turning to look at him now. "What's going on?"

"Nothing," he says. "I need it as soon as she can get it."

Nick points up ahead and they see Paul moving in between cars, heading their way. They wait for him patiently and he starts the engine up as soon as he gets in.

"Everything all good?" he asks the guy from the driver's seat.

"Yeah. Better. The lot was unattended so I just put the keys in the drop-off," Paul answers.

"We're heading to Shreveport. Victor says you can come along if you want. Otherwise, we can drop you at the nearest major city for you to catch a flight or find a way home. It's a twelve-hour straight drive there," Nick tells him.

"Victor mentioned it. Shreveport isn't one of my clients but if you boys don't mind, I'd like to tag along to see how things work outside of Victor."

"You're more than welcome. As for the job itself, same deal, just a different middleman. That's all." Nick adds their destination on the tablet. "You can sleep if you want. We're trying to go straight through. Tomorrow is Black Friday. The traffic and crowds give good cover."

He hits the freeway on-ramp and anxiously makes way out of Santa Fe. The freeways are predictably free of traffic, allowing them to move along nicely at a good pace. About two hundred miles and they should be across the state line into Texas.

"Hey, I'll forward you the number," Nick tells him.

They've just pulled into a gas station just outside of Dallas city limits to fill up. He drove for the past eight hours. Nick slept up until the last hour. Paul stayed up with him the whole drive, trying to keep him company with various stories. The guy was filled with random information and tales.

He pulls next to a pump and shuts the engine off. He hops out of the truck and starts the pump. Nick and Paul both get out to stretch their legs.

"I'm getting coffee," Paul says. "You guys want anything?"

"I'll go in and grab some when I'm done here," he answers.

His phone pings and he pulls it out of his pocket. It's the text from Nick with Sam's number. It's too early to call Sam though.

"What's going on, Cole?" Nick asks.

"I don't know yet. I'll tell you when there's something to tell," he replies curtly. "Did Mitch send over the details yet?"

"Yeah. Just saw them when I woke up. I'll drive the rest of the way and you can find where we'll be staying the next couple of days. Job won't be till Sunday."

Four hours later they pull into another gas station just outside of Shreveport to fill up the tank. Just past ten a.m. While Nick pumps, he takes the opportunity to see if he can catch Sam on the phone.

He lets the phone ring five times, almost disconnecting the call before the sound of Sam's voice answers.

"Sam. It's Cole."

"*Yeah? What do you want?*" Sam practically barks out at him.

"I need to ask you to check something for me about the security system. You have the app and access, right?"

"Of course I do. What's this about?"

"The night before Thanksgiving, can you check and see if anyone was in the building at about ten-thirty p.m.? Or see if anyone came in around that time?"

"Why? Are you trying to keep tabs on Frankie?"

"Look, man. I'll get to the point. Someone was in *our* place around that time and it wasn't Frankie. I need to know when they got in the building. Where they got in and how. And I DON'T want Frankie to know about this to scare her."

Sam doesn't answer. For a moment, he thinks the man hung up but he can still hear noises in the background. A minute passes and he can hear Sam cursing.

"Someone used the code to get in through the side door at ten twenty-five. Maybe it was Karmen. Did you ask Frankie about this?"

"Maybe you're right. Do me one and don't mention this to her. As I said, I don't want to scare her. I'll be back soon anyway."

He already knows it can't be Karmen. Karmen was at work at that time too. He just didn't want to stir Mr. Knight-In-Shining-Armor to jump into action and scare the fuck out of Frankie.

Whoever was there was in the building for ten minutes before getting inside the apartment.

"Thanks, man."

"Yeah." And Sam hangs up on him.

Fucking asshole.

- 52 -

Frankie

Karmen swings the door open, her eyes sparkling, a huge grin across her face. "I got a 'plus' on one and two blue lines on the other! I'm having a baby!" Karmen screams.

She joins in on the screaming and hugs her friend closely. "Oh my god! Oh my god! Yay! Wait...why am I happy?"

Karmen shoves her off playfully. "I don't care how Nick will take the news but right here, right now...I couldn't be any happier. I'm glad you're here to share it with me, Frankie."

"And if he doesn't take it well, you'll still have me," she teases.

They both flop onto the bed silently focused on the ceiling. She is truly happy for Karmen. She doesn't mind helping out with the twins and she can do the same for the new one when he or she comes along.

"When are you going to tell him?" she asks Karmen.

"I'll wait till he gets back. I don't want him rushing anything and messing up. Sounds wrong even saying that."

"I know what you mean. Do you know where they are?"

"In a different time zone is all I know," Karmen says. "Have you talked to Cole?"

"Yeah. Only brief conversations and short texts. He won't tell me where they're at either." She looks at the clock on the nightstand. "Hate to cut the moment short but we have to get to work. I'll drop you off at Vince's and I'll see you at about eleven tonight. DO NOT lift anything you shouldn't be lifting. Let Donnie and Vince do it," she says sternly.

"I've been down this road before, Frankie. I think I know what not to do," Karmen says, smacking her leg before sitting up and putting her jacket back on.

He stares at the laptop again, closing out all the useless crap, his anger near a boiling point. An opportunity for him to do what he needs to do has to open up soon. He's tired of waiting around.

"Love." She said that to Cole.

And then there's still Sam. Always hovering. Always around. Fucking cockblocker.

The email that she was waiting for finally comes through to her personal email address. She checks the email and sees that Cynthia had indeed cc'd her company email address as well; however, she had never received anything there.

She opens her company email and quickly navigates to the Settings tab. She isn't sure what exactly she is looking for. Just anything that may stand out.

After scrolling back and forth, up and down for ten minutes, and then staring at the screen, something catches her eye.

There are two subfolders within her Inbox with the same name. One spelled "Invoices" and the other "Invo1ces." At first glance, it can easily be missed.

She double clicks the one spelled differently and discovers all the missing purchase orders she's sent along with all communications to and from Cynthia at Mad Hatter. There are close to fifty emails.

She can feel a headache coming on. Someone had to have done this. Was it Vince? First things first, she immediately changes the password to her company email. Not taking any chances, she changes the password to her personal email address too.

She goes through the bank statement next. Checks sent after October third have been deposited. A copy of the check was included on their bank statement. She strains her eyes to make out the name of the bank and the account number to which they were deposited and scribbles it down on a Post-it. She is going to have to file a claim against the checks with the bank in the morning. She sticks the Post-it onto the bottom of her monitor before searching online on how to remove the email filter.

Now that this one issue is taken care of, there are plenty more questions that she needs to be answered. The question burning at the top of her list is *who* would have done this, followed by *why*.

It's now Saturday and they are waiting for Victor to show up.

"Victor's bringing us to meet the buyers somewhere else? We're just meeting him here, right?" Nick asks.

"Yeah. He says he's got the payment ready for that paperwork too. I'll be catching a ride back with him. Big payout this time around, huh?" Paul asks.

The truck is quiet again for a short period. They're sitting in the truck just outside of a crowded bar.

"Mitch's buyers are pretty particular and meticulous in what they're looking for. Are they usually like that?" Paul asks.

"Yeah. I don't know much about them. They're probably all designers too so they have specifics that they want," he answers.

"Makes sense. I like that they don't haggle. Here's what we want, take it or leave it," Paul says.

"We've all worked through Mitch for a long time. Everyone knows what's expected of the others involved. Makes the deal smoother and quicker."

"I wish all of Victor's buyers were like that," Paul chuckles.

"Mitch works with quality. Victor works with quantity. He thinks more buyers make more money."

"That theory's just been proven wrong. I made more with Mitch's buyers who came prepared with the amount they wanted to spend. If this was one of Victor's buyers, we'd be haggling way into the night, down to the last dime." They all laugh at Paul's statement. "Thank you for letting me come along, even though it means having to break me off a chunk."

"Hey. You worked it, you earned it. We didn't break off anything for you. Right, Cole?"

He nods his agreement. He's tempted to ask Nick if they'll immediately be heading home after this meeting but doesn't want to discuss the topic of where home is in front of Paul, so he keeps his mouth shut.

Home.

He's also been diligently checking the alarm system and making sure she's arming it at night after that one incident. Something about that still bothers him but his hands are tied at the moment. So far, nothing like that has happened again.

"By the way, I meant to ask this before but it slipped my mind until now," Paul says, starting up another conversation. "Did Dusty ever smooth things out with Victor?"

He whips his head around to look at the guy. He can see Nick looking in the rearview mirror too.

"You know, with that job he fucked up?" Paul asks, looking back and forth between him and Nick.

"Which one are you referring to?" Nick asks nonchalantly.

"That small one where the shop owner got shot. Just outside of Portland, I think it was. I didn't even think you guys deal with guns."

He stares blankly at Paul. What is he talking about? Dusty was in Portland?

"Why do I get the feeling you don't know what I'm talking about?"

"Because we don't. At least I don't," Nick admits.

"Last month, not long after you boys left. Dusty reached out to me asking for Victor's contact. Said he needed a small job in the Portland area. Victor found a small one for him. Not sure what happened but the owner ended up getting shot and the job was a debacle. Cost Vic some out-of-pocket money. He didn't find out until later that Dusty wasn't with you boys anymore."

Something heavy settles inside of him. The news segment he and Nick saw on TV at the bar flashes through his mind. That had to be it. Dusty was in Portland the whole time and they didn't even know it. Except, Dusty probably didn't know they'd headed back there either.

- 53 -

Frankie

The bar closes right on the dot thanks to the lackluster crowd still trying to recover from the holidays. Sam and some of his crew members arrived late for a kind of company gathering of some sort. She and Karmen were both more than happy to see the extra faces. It helped pass the time.

After closing, Sam offers to walk her home. His car is parked across the street from her place anyway.

"You know Karmen could have dropped us both off, right?" she asks Sam.

"Yeah, but it's not that far." They continue to walk in silence for a couple of blocks. "So, Cole and you, you guys are still good? Are you okay with him being gone for who knows how long and who knows who he's with?"

"I trust him, Sam. I wouldn't be with him if I didn't." She pauses. "Besides, his being away doesn't have to be a bad thing. I know you think everything is moving fast but him being away gives us the time to slow down too."

"And you think you love him?"

"I know I do." She looks up at him. "There are things between us that no one can know or feel. I don't expect you to understand."

"Kind of like what I feel for you," he mumbles but she still heard him.

The only thing she could do was ignore it. "We're here," she says instead, stopping next to his car.

"Don't be ridiculous! I have to walk you to the door at least. It's dark behind the building. Remind me to add some solar lights back there or something."

She laughs and waves him to lead the way across the street.

The snow crunches beneath their feet as they make their way to the back. Sam was right. It is dark behind the building. Her car is gone and so is Cole's, leaving the lot empty.

She pulls her key out of her jacket, unlocks the back door, and steps inside, activating the sensor lights. Sam punches the code into the keypad.

"Thanks, Sam. Do you want to come up for coffee or something?" she asks, already heading up the stairs.

"No. It's getting late. I should get home. I'll leave once you get inside and lock your doors," he says with a smile.

She opens her door, steps inside, and turns to wave at him.

He waves back at her with a smile.

Once inside with the alarm set, she takes off her beanie and unwraps her scarf, leaving both on the chair along with her jacket. She pulls her purse off and takes her phone out. After checking it quickly and seeing there are no messages from Cole, she heads over to her night table to charge it. The bedroom curtains are still open so she heads over to close them.

She looks down into the street in time to see Sam just crossing with his key fob pointed to unlock his car. She taps on the window hoping to catch his attention for a wave.

Instead of looking up at her, he stops and turns his head quickly to his right, into the dark street.

Following his line of sight to see what caught his attention, she bangs on her window as she sees a quick glare off the windshield of a car heading right toward him.

"Sam! Sam!" she screams for what seems like forever.

But he doesn't hear her.

In a matter of seconds, her hands are covering her scream as the dark car, with no headlights on, plows right into Sam, sending him rolling over the hood of the car and tumbling over the whole vehicle itself before falling onto the street.

She watches in horror as Sam lies still as death on the dark pavement. The car never even stops.

She runs to the door, swings it wide open, and rushes down the flight of stairs. The cold stings her face when she gets the second door open. She hits the ground running and rounding the building, screaming for help as loud as she can before reaching Sam and sliding down beside him.

"Oh my god! Sam! Sam! Hang on. Please hang on!"

He isn't moving and she's afraid to touch him or move him.

"God, someone help! HELP!"

A car comes out of the alley and turns in their direction. She jumps up and flags the car down. The driver rolls down the window and she tells him to please call 911 and points to Sam. His passenger hops out of the car while the guy is dialing. The passenger runs over to Sam with her.

"I'm a nurse," the woman says. "What's his name? Can you tell me what happened?"

"Sam...his name is Sam. And some car plowed right into him while he was crossing the street."

"He has a pulse. It's weak but it's better than nothing. There's a blanket in the back of our car. Can you go get it for me?"

She makes a run back to the car. The driver is getting out, his phone to his ear, and he's talking to someone. He runs over to Sam and his friend while she opens the back door and grabs the little blanket in the back.

When she returns to his side, the woman was just starting CPR.

"Oh god. No. Please. No."

- 54 -

cole

Ring. Ring. Ring. Ring.

The ringing phone wakes him up. He looks at the clock on the night table in his motel room. 4:34 a.m. It isn't the burner phone either, it's his personal phone.

He picks up the phone and checks the screen. It is an unfamiliar number but less than a handful of people have his number so he swipes to answer it.

"Hello."

"This is Armando calling from First Response Home Monitoring Service. Is this Mr. Cole Howard?"

"Yes," he answers briskly.

"Can you provide me with your code word, sir?"

"Pygmy. What is this about?"

"Thank you, sir. Our system indicates that as of six minutes ago your front door opened while the alarm was engaged and it currently remains open. We were unable to reach the primary contact. Is everything okay, sir?"

He immediately bolts straight up in bed. "I'm not at home right now. But my girlfriend should have been."

"Can you give me her name, sir?"

"Frankie. I mean Francine Hoang."

"We were unable to reach her, sir. I'm going to send a dispatch unit out immediately."

"There's a second alarm system on the lower floor. Has that one been tripped too?"

There is a long pause before Armando answers. *"Sir, I've notified our dispatch unit in the area. I'll also notify the closest police station."*

"What does that mean? Has the alarm on the first floor been set off too or not?"

Armando remains quiet for what seems like another eternity. *"Yes, sir. One of those doors remains open as well."*

Fuck!

"Would you like me to remain on the line with you, sir?"

"No. I have to try and get a hold of her." He hangs up without another word.

His panic and anxiety level builds as he rushes around the room stuffing his belongings into his bag before heading out the door and down the hall. His fingers are continuously hitting the redial button to Frankie's number.

A minute later, he bangs on Nick's door, not giving a damn who else he wakes up.

"What the fuck?" Nick answers the door. He's still fully dressed except for his boots.

"We're leaving. You have two minutes to get your stuff or I'm leaving you," he growls before he heads back down the hallway to the exit.

He half runs to the truck, throwing his bags in the backseat before jumping in behind the wheel and starting the engine, throwing it into reverse.

Nick comes out the door just as he puts the truck into gear.

He opens the app on his phone and checks it as Nick rushes over. It's been close to ten minutes since the call and the door is still open.

"What the fuck is going on?" Nick asks him as soon as he is inside. "Did we get made?"

"Can you get Karmen on the phone? Right now," he says as the truck lurches on to the road.

His hand fumbles on the navigation screen. He taps for directions, not bothering to use the tablet. "Put her on speaker," he demands when he hears Nick dialing.

"Hey, babe," Karmen answers.

"Karm, you're on speaker. Cole needs to talk to you."

"Karmen, is Frankie with you?"

"Frankie? No. I just got home. Sam walked her home from the bar. She should be there right now."

His hands are dialing Sam's number already.

"What's going on?" Both Karmen and Nick ask at the same time.

"The alarm at our place was tripped ten minutes ago. The service can't reach her and neither can I. Both the door to the building and the door to the apartment have stayed open. They're still open now."

"What?!" Karmen screams into the phone.

"Karm, can you go over there right now?" Nick asks. "Just check the place out and wait for someone to get there. Do NOT go inside by yourself."

"Yes. Granny is still here. I'll let her know. I can be there in fifteen minutes."

"Haul ass, Karmen. Please?" he pleads.

"Call us back as soon as you find out." Nick hangs up the phone.

Sam's number continues to ring until it goes to voicemail. He hits the fucking redial button getting the same result.

"It's a twenty-hour drive. You're gonna need to keep your shit together, baby brother, or we're not going to make it back at all."

"The dispatch from the alarm service should have gotten there by now and called me with an update."

"Yeah, and we know how well *they* work, don't we?"

He just can't stop laughing with satisfaction. He couldn't help himself.

The sound of broken bones and Sam's body tumbling over the hood of the car still lingers in his ear, causing him to laugh uncontrollably again.

Oh, the satisfaction. The joy. What a fucking high.

One down. One to go.

"Nick, I'm here. I don't know what's going on but there are cops out front of the building. Sam's car is still parked across the street. They let me into the apartment and all her stuff is here. Her purse, her keys, her phone, and the jacket she was wearing tonight. I can't even tell if she's got shoes on or not at this point."

Oh god. He can feel his feet getting heavier on the gas pedal and his hand tightening around the steering wheel.

"I'll call you back as soon as I find out something."

"Okay, babe." Nick hangs up.

"If it were a crime scene, they wouldn't have let her in there," Nick says.

He has a point.

"You need to keep calm. We have two bags filled with enough cash to look like we robbed a small bank in here," Nick warns him.

It's been over half an hour. The security company hasn't called him back yet and there is still no word from her. Twenty-hour drive and he isn't even an hour in yet.

"Maybe I should drive," Nick suggests.

"No."

Not knowing what to do, he dials Sam's number again. He counts the three rings, waiting for the voicemail greeting to come on after the fifth like it has the other ten times he's called.

"Hello?" a voice answers. *Her* voice.

He slams on the brakes to slow down and pulls over on the side of the road. He throws it in park and jumps out of the truck immediately, leaving the door open and the engine running.

"Frankie!"

"Cole?"

"OH, thank god! Where the fuck are you? Are you okay?"

"I'm okay," she says.

Something is wrong though. He can hear it in her voice.

"The alarm service called me. They couldn't reach you and the door was left open," he says more gently.

"Cole...It's Sam." She pauses. *"He walked me home. When I got inside, I went to the window to wave at him. I watched as some car just came out of nowhere and hit him."* She's completely shaken up, he can

hear it in her quaking voice. *"Didn't stop or even turn on their lights. I...I got to him as fast as I could and some people, they stopped to help and called 911. I rode in the ambulance with him."*

'What? In front of your building?" he asks.

"Yes! He wasn't breathing and...and...they were doing CPR in the ambulance. They're working on him now. They gave me his personal items and I need to call his aunts."

"Okay. I'll have Nick call Karmen to go be with you, okay? I'll see you soon."

"You're coming back?" she asks.

"Frankie...of course. Hang in there."

"I love you," she says barely above a whisper.

"I love you too." He hangs up feeling like he can breathe again.

His hand rakes through his hair as the panic begins to subside. He spins around and walks back to the truck. Nick is already climbing into the driver's seat.

He reaches the passenger's side and takes a deep breath to compose himself before opening the door and getting in for the long ride.

"Karmen is already on her way to the hospital," Nick tells him as he pulls back onto the highway. "What happened? She said Sam was in an accident and Frankie went to the hospital with him."

It's too much of a coincidence that Sam gets run over by a car in front of her building. A car that speeds off with no lights on. Something is going on. Something that has to do with Frankie whether she knows it or not.

"The snow coming down isn't helping us," Nick mumbles.

They ride in silence hour after hour. He stares out the window, for the most part, watching the snowflakes hitting the windshield. The sound of Nick's phone ringing breaks through the silence. Nick puts it on speaker.

"Karmen, how is it?" Nick asks.

"He's out of surgery and in ICU. His family is here too. There's nothing more we can do here. I'm taking Frankie home."

"How is she?" he asks.

"She's shaken up. The police were talking to her when I got here. She feels shitty that she can't give them much. It was too dark out. She just knows it was a dark car. The headlights weren't on and the driver didn't

stop. Probably some drunk prick. He was pretty lucky the people that stopped to help were nurses."

"We'll be there as soon as we can, babe. The weather isn't cooperating much though."

"You're heading back?"

"Yeah," Nick answers.

"Please drive carefully, Nick."

"Gotcha. I'll see you soon."

Nick hangs up the phone and glances at him. "You're not thinking about Sam and Frankie having a thing, are you?"

"What?"

"I don't know. Just never seen you lose your shit like that."

"Something is going on around Frankie. I just don't know what it is. Too many coincidences."

"What are you talking about?"

"The second time I met Frankie, I walked her home and the same shit happened. A car with no lights nearly plows her over if I hadn't been there to shove her out of the way. How often does something like that happen twice in the same place?"

"That's how she got that concussion, right?"

"Yeah." He recollects the events. "Then the night after, she spent the night with me at the motel. The next morning, I find her car with the tires slashed and a dent that looked like someone kicked it."

"What did she say about that?"

"I don't even think she knew they were slashed. She thought someone hit it because it was raining so hard the night before."

"You think someone's stalking her or something?"

If he hadn't thought that before, he sure as hell thinks about it now.

"Shit."

"What?" Nick asks.

"Do you remember that asshole from the lounge we were at with Sam? I don't know if you know this but they found him dead in an alley the next morning."

"What the fuck? No. I didn't know that."

"And when we were at the farm, Sam called and told her that some guy got into the building and was asking for her by name. Called her Francine. She thought it was just a delivery guy."

"Why didn't you tell me about all of this before?"

"Didn't seem like one thing was connected with the other before." He suddenly remembers something else. "That first night, at her place...I remember you saying something to Dusty about him knowing the area. How did he know to specifically go there?"

He can tell Nick is trying to think back to that night.

"Did he say he's been there before?"

"He didn't say to that particular building but he said he knew the area."

Dusty. Is he behind all of this? Why?

"That night we got back to Portland for Halloween when I followed you out into that alley. You said you thought you saw him. How sure were you?"

"I was sure enough to run out there after him. Didn't think about it much after that."

"Nick, I dropped Dusty off at an airport. I didn't ask where he was going. And Paul just told us that he was in Portland."

"You think he's got something to do with all of this? Why? What would he have to gain? You know Dusty only gives a shit about his next high."

"Why would he have gone to that particular bar *if* it was him that you saw? Frankie would be the only link. Wouldn't it make sense if he were asking around about her, he'd be asking for Francine? That was the name you read off of her ID that night. He doesn't know she goes by Frankie."

Nick turns his head to look him dead in the eye. "Shit."

- 55 -

cole

He climbs into bed carefully next to her, not wanting to wake her. If she needs sleep then he can wait until morning to greet her properly. Tonight, he's right next to her where he wanted to be since the day he left and that is enough.

With the worry about the events gone and the burnout from the long drive, he teeters at the brink of sleep anyhow.

Moments later, she moves. Her hand slides over to his side of the bed, touching him. He feels her freeze when her fingers glide against his side. She jolts her hand back and sits up.

"Cole?" she whispers.

"Shh...I didn't mean to wake you," he says quietly.

She moves quickly to the side. With a soft click, soft light from the lamp on the table lights the room, allowing him to see her beautiful face.

"You're here," she says with a smile before throwing herself into his arms.

He welcomes her happily, holding her tightly against him. Kissing the top of her head, smelling her intoxicating fragrance.

"Why didn't you wake me? I didn't think you'd be back yet."

"I wasn't the quietest coming in and you slept through it. Seemed like you needed the sleep."

She pulls away to look at him. Her hand touches his scruff. "I missed you," she says before reacquainting his lips with hers.

Her kiss is soft and sweet, like nectar for his soul. He pulls her closer to him, his tongue asking for an invitation. Her lips part and he's in, trying his best to quench his thirst for her. It'll never happen. He'll always crave more.

"Mmm..." she hums once they break for air.

"I missed you too," he says. "How do you get more beautiful every time I set eyes on you?"

"I was going to ask you the same thing." He watches her as she's watching him. "How long have you been here?"

"Not long. Half an hour maybe."

"I can't believe I didn't hear you come in."

"Long day?"

"Yeah. The whole thing with Sam and then some things at Vince's." Her brows furrow and his fingers automatically try to smooth over the creases, wanting to swipe her worries away.

"How is he?"

"He's still in ICU. A broken arm, a broken leg, and a broken rib that punctured his lung. But at least he's not listed as critical anymore."

"That's good. It could have been worse." *It could have been you.*

"I just can't help but feel responsible. If I hadn't let him walk me to the back, he wouldn't have been out there in the first place. He was standing at his car already."

"Hey. Don't do that. It's not your fault. Accidents happen." *Except this probably wasn't an accident.*

She's back in his arms, her head tucked under his chin, holding onto him tightly. "I'm just glad you're home."

"Yeah, let's try not to scare me to death like that again. Okay?" he says, squeezing her.

"I'm sorry. I didn't mean to. I should have grabbed my phone first thing. The service would have called me and I could have gotten help sooner."

"You did the best you could. You got him help. He'll recover," he tries to reassure her.

She kisses his bare chest, trailing up to his chin, and then she finds his lips again. This time with more intensity. Deeper. Sweeter. She nestles her whole body alongside his, molding herself into him. Completing him. Her hand plays in his hair. His own hand exploring her body before settling on her bare legs.

"You're wanting to take everything I have left in me, aren't you?" he teases her once he breaks free of their kiss, gasping for breath.

"Only what you're willing to give," she says with a smile.

Her face is smugly glowing with allure and seduction, exciting him beyond control. In a swift move, he pulls her shirt all the way up, over her head, and off of her. She giggles at his haste and he surprises her by moving to settle himself between her legs. Her soft skin and perfect breasts press up against his own bare skin.

"Glad you think it's funny to drive a man crazy," he says.

Before she can say any more, he closes her mouth with his. She meets his kisses with her own fervor. Without even bothering to completely remove his briefs, he pulls the top of them down just enough to free himself. She arches underneath him, pressing herself into him, exciting him beyond belief.

It takes him two seconds to push her incredibly silky panties to the side and push his throbbing tip through her entrance. Impaling her in the second it takes to breathe. The amazing feel of her causes him to break free of her enchanting kiss and hiss into her neck. He hears her panting beside his ear and smiles.

Her nails glide over his back, thrilling him. "I want you," she says. "I don't want to feel scared anymore."

He lets out a low-barely-in-control grunt as her tightness stops him from sliding deep into her.

Thank god.

Her legs tighten around his hips with each one of his thrusts as he fucks her with his aching cock and his whole being. Her nails dig into him just enough to send his senses wild while he pounds her deeper and deeper until he hears her soft screams turning into pleas.

He gives her all of him, to the hilt, and holds himself there, allowing himself to take a much-needed breath before he retreats and pushes back into her all the way again.

She rewards him by showering him with the hot liquid of her satisfaction, her moan music to his ears. Pleasing her drives him over the edge too.

He unloads his own string of heat into her, filling her, intermingling with hers, emptying everything he has in him, and loving every second of it. He's lost track of how many times he's come in her since the first time. But every single time gets him more addicted to her.

Depleted, he rests his head on the pillow beside her head, not wanting to move just yet. Not knowing if he even has the strength to move if he wanted to.

- 56 -

frankie

"Holy cow! You look incredible!" she exclaims.

She steps out of the bathroom and is surprised by how he's even more gorgeous than his usual self. He's wearing a knitted pullover sweater that fits him perfectly over a pair of camel-colored pants. How does he know exactly what to wear to look so *delicious*? His hair is slicked back tonight. She hasn't seen him style it that way before but she likes it just as much as any other way he's had it.

"Look who's talking." He whistles.

She's chosen to wear a simple fitted black dress with her knee-high green boots. Her thick, oversized knitted green cardigan should give her plenty of warmth for the winter night. And if that wasn't enough, there's always Cole and his natural body heat.

She walks over to where he's sitting on the bed and he pulls her to him.

"So beautiful," he says before giving her a delicious kiss.

"We should get going or I'm going to have my dessert right now," she says to him.

He laughs at her and lets her go. Standing up, towering over her, he places another quick kiss on her head. She loves the way that feels. Like his most cherished of jewels.

"Do you know where this place is?" he asks.

"Yeah. It's a steakhouse downtown. Not too far from Katrina's."

She makes the round of turning off the unnecessary lights, leaving only the one in the kitchen on. Cole is already waiting for her at the door.

"After you," he says.

It takes them several drives around the block for them to find parking but they end up finding a spot a block away.

Cole has his arms around her as best as he can to keep her warm during their walk to the restaurant doors. Once inside, she is pleasantly surprised by the warmth inside.

Karmen and Nick are still sitting by the hostess booth.

"Look at you two," Nick says. "You guys are like a beautiful couple from the magazines."

"Hey, Nick," she says flatly.

"Is everyone here?" the hostess politely asks.

"We're all here," Karmen quickly answers.

The hostess leads the way and seats them at an incredibly gorgeous booth in a corner, right under a dim crystal chandelier. It's a gorgeous ambiance. Perfect for tonight.

They all place their order, which arrives amazingly quick. She and Karmen are having a great time talking and laughing like they always do. Nick seems more quiet than usual, which doesn't really bother her.

She and Cole have their own moments as well, feeding each other, talking, laughing, and kissing like they are the only ones in the room. She loves being with him, next to him. No matter where they are, it's always still just the two of them. Their own universe. He makes it easy to have a good time.

After their meal is cleared away, the waiter returns with the dessert menu. Nick excuses himself to the men's room and Karmen slides over to sit next to her.

They look at the menu together. "Crème brûlée," they squeal at the same time.

"Babe, do you want some dessert?" she asks Cole.

"No thanks. I'm stuffed. Maybe some champagne though."

She looks at him questioningly. Champagne? Uh, okay. The waiter takes their orders and leaves just as Nick comes back to his seat.

"Everything okay?" Karmen asks him, rubbing his back. "Still tired?"

"I'm okay. I think I'm going into a food coma."

Karmen laughs at him loudly and plants a kiss on his cheek, wiping the lipstick off afterward.

Their waiter is back already with their desserts and four glasses of champagne. She eyes Karmen, who looks back at her. Before the waiter leaves, Karmen asks him to take a picture of the four of them.

"Baby, can you come and sit next to me? Bring your glass and have a toast with me," Cole says to her.

"Sure." She slides closer to him with her glass and gives him a kiss on his delectable lips. He reaches into his pocket and pulls his phone out, opening the camera app. He's never one for taking pictures, let alone selfies. He flips the camera, hits record, and she stares into the screen.

Oh. My. God. What's happening?

She spins around to watch Karmen, who is staring in disbelief at the box on the little black box on the table.

"Karmen, will you do me the honor and marry me?" Nick proposes.

Karmen's hands come up to her mouth in complete surprise. "Nick! Oh my god. What? Are you serious?" Karmen looks at Nick.

"Open it," Nick says nervously.

Karmen picks up the box and flips the lid open. She sees Karmen's eyes getting watery with joy. "It's beautiful," she says brushing her fingers over it.

"You've brought meaning to my life. A life that I want to spend my remaining days catering to you. Loving you has pulled me out of the bottom of bottles and the pits of misery. Only whiskey I need is you, darlin'," Nick says. "Please say yes. Will you marry me?"

Wow! How did he come up with that?

Karmen close the lid on the box and put it back down on the table.
"Nick. I love you. You know I do. But I...I..." Karmen stutters. "I can't give you an answer until I tell you what I need to tell you."

"Whatever it is, I'm sure we can work through it," Nick says, going into panic mode.

"I hope so," Karmen tells him before she reaches into her purse and pulls out an envelope. She hands it to Nick, who eyes her warily. "Read it and let it sink in. Then ask me again when you're ready."

She feels the twitch in Cole's hand as they watch Nick open the envelope and pull out the letter inside. She squeezes his hand, telling him to be patient. They watch anxiously while Nick reads it over and then looks up at Karmen, who eyes him nervously now.

Cole still has his phone recording when Nick slides out of the booth and paces in front of them. His hands come up to his mouth and then covers his whole face. When he finally removes his hand, his eyes are red with tears. And he's looking right at Cole.

"Cole, baby brother."

Concern for Nick crosses over Cole's face in an instant.

"It's not just me and you anymore. I'm going to be a dad, man! She's pregnant!" Nick exclaims with excitement, whoops loudly, and jumps up and down.

Cole puts the phone down and gets out of the booth to give his brother a huge hug. The first time she's ever seen them hug.

"Oh, man! Congratulations! Holy shit!" He gives Nick a hard pat on the back before letting him go.

Nick helps Karmen slide out of the booth and Cole picks up his phone again.

This time, Nick actually gets down on one knee and asks Karmen with tears and all, "Karmen Meadow Chiarelli, will you marry me?"

"Yes! Yes!" Karmen screams.

- 57 -

frankie

Two weeks quickly fly by since Cole's return and Nick's proposal. She's enjoyed every second of the time he's spent with her but she can't help but worry about the approaching holiday. On top of that, she's seriously stressed about what's going on behind the scenes at Vinny's.

She worked tirelessly to get the books back on track. She discovered two more accounts that were changed like Mad Hatter's but she was able to smooth everything out with those vendors and filed the appropriate documentation with the banks.

The only thing she hasn't made any progress on is how these changes were made and by whom. Since then, she's changed all her passwords and things have been seemingly back to normal.

"Everything okay? Every time I see you look at the screen, I can see how stressed you get." Cole puts a hot cup of tea on the table for her.

She's been sitting at the dining table for the past hour, trying to figure things out. Cole was sitting across the table from her on his own laptop until he offered to make her tea.

"Yeah. Just work."

She takes a sip of the hot liquid and lets it warm her while Cole returns to his seat, beer in hand. She loves being at home with him like this. Their life has come together unexpectedly and meshing into something she is too happy to even put to words.

"You know I haven't forgotten about your birthday this Friday, right?" She looks at him with a smile.

"Don't remind me," he says, not looking at her.

"How about you and Nick come down to Vinny's that night since Karmen and I have to work anyway. We can have a little celebration. Alice might come along too."

He shrugs. "Sure."

She studies him for a moment and before she knows it, the question rolls off of her tongue. "Babe, are you leaving again? Christmas is a week away and..." She looks at him, choosing not to finish.

"I honestly don't know. Before all of this, I would have said yes. The holidays are big for us. Now with Nick, Karmen, and what they have going on. I honestly don't know what the plan is. Nick and I haven't talked about it."

"If Nick wants to stop right now because he's got a baby on the way, can you?"

He takes a deep breath, exhales, and leans back on the chair. When he finally looks at her, she knows she's probably not going to like what he's going to say.

"Frankie, I know this isn't the answer you want to hear. But if Nick needs to stop, I *have* to pick up the slack and continue on. There would be no way for us to meet the payment schedule otherwise and we're too close to let it go now. We're less than half a year's payment away and that's with us doubling up."

"But there can be...there has to be a way for you both to earn a good income," she tries to reason with him.

"Not enough for us to make the payment, keep up with the farm on a daily basis, and have something set aside for us to continue running the farm once it's paid for."

He looks at her and she realizes this is the first real conversation they've had in regards to anything financially related and it definitely isn't what she wanted to hear.

"I'm sorry," he says. "I don't mean to upset you."

She shakes her head. "I'm not upset. I just...it's just...I don't know what to do. I hate that you have to leave and do *that*. And I hate wondering when you're going to leave again."

"I know. I hate it as much as you do. Believe me." He reaches over the table for her hand. "There's nowhere on this planet I'd rather be than with you. I can't even begin to show you how thankful I am that you even gave me this chance."

She interlocks his fingers with hers and gives him her best pout. "Maybe if I got pregnant, you'd stay," she says playfully.

He shakes his head. "Babies don't come for nine months. We only need to make five more payments," he says with a huge grin. "I'll be ready when the kid comes. I've given Nick too much of a head start already."

He gives her a fucking smirk and a scoundrel's wink when her jaw drops on top of the table.

- 58 -

cole

After going to three different dealerships, Nick finally decides on one. An SUV that will accommodate his growing family. It's almost surreal watching his brother signing documents that'll put him into a family vehicle. Nick made some requests to the salesman so he won't be picking it up until the next day.

"Let's grab a bite," Nick says when they head out of the lot.

"Sure."

He picks an Applebee's that he saw earlier. They get inside and are promptly seated. After five minutes of browsing over the menu, they place their orders with the friendly waiter.

"So how are things?" he asks. They haven't really talked much since the night of Nick's proposal.

"Good. Karmen has her first doctor's appointment after Christmas. Can you believe it? I'm going to be a dad!" Nick still seems excited. "You need to stop slacking and catch up!"

"Frankie and I are fine the way we are for now."

"Speaking of, how is she? Anything else happen that I should know about?"

He ponders the past two weeks. "Nothing. It's been pretty quiet, which is good. She's always running around keeping busy."

"How did she make out with the issue at Vince's?"

"What issue?" He looks at Nick dumbfounded.

"She didn't tell you? Karmen mentioned something about Frankie finding out someone's been messing with the books. Making changes using her information and email or some shit like that."

"No. She never told me. She seemed a little stressed but she made it seem like it wasn't a big deal."

Nick shrugs. "Karm says it could be a pretty big deal. The way she explained it to me, it sounds like someone's been dipping in the till and pocketing the extra cash. Plus, it seems like someone was running a booze scam."

"What?"

"Yeah. When we were at the farm, Frankie spoke to a vendor that claims she canceled their contract. They haven't made deliveries to Vince's in months. But Frankie's been sending payments and orders to them like usual except it wasn't going to them. Was going to some postal box somewhere? Last I heard, Frankie still hasn't figured out how the shelves are kept stocked. And I guess they've had some complaints about the drinks being watered down or some shit."

"She never mentioned any of that."

"She filed a report and a claim with the bank and all that stuff too. She never said anything?"

"No."

"Did you ask her what's got her stressing?"

"Of course. She always says it was just work." Could this be related to everything else? "How much money are we talking about?" he asks Nick.

"Don't quote me but I think Karmen said it's in the range of ten thousand dollars."

The waiter comes back with their drinks, momentarily interrupting the conversation.

He sits back and thinks about everything. Ten grand isn't chump change. It's a lot of fucking money. He is definitely going to have to ask Frankie about this.

"If I were her, I'd just drive to the address of that postal box and see who shows up," Nick says.

"Not a bad idea, but don't encourage her to do that. If she filed a report, the police should be doing that anyway."

The waiter brings their food out and they eat mostly in silence.

"We should talk about next week," he says.

"Yeah. We should."

"Are we working?"

"Yeah. I don't want to but it's gotta be done. I'm waiting for Mitch to get back to me. Trying to stay close to home so I can make it back for that doctor's appointment."

"Nick, if you need to be with Karmen. I can do this run alone. I can hit up Paul and see if he'd be interested."

"Of course I want to be with her, but I'm not gonna let you do it alone."

"I'm just saying, if you need the time, take it," he offers.

"I can't. It won't be fair to your girl," Nick replies.

"Frankie and I already talked about the possibility of me doing things alone going forward. She doesn't like it. Not that she ever did but she's not the one carrying a Howard."

"I'll think about it." And Nick looks as if he is seriously thinking about it.

Nick pulls his wallet out the same time he digs for his from his back pocket and puts cash on the tray. "I got it. Consider it an early birthday gift," Nick says.

"Don't remind me. I didn't think you even knew. By the way, I'm going down to Vinny's Place tomorrow for a few drinks. Frankie says you should come too."

"Sure," Nick says, already putting on his jacket. "I can give Karmen a ride home after so Frankie can have her car back."

"Come on. I'll drop you off and head over to pick Frankie up from work. It's almost time anyway."

Half an hour later, he's sitting in the truck and waiting for Frankie, wondering why she never mentioned anything about the books to him. Frankie is good at carrying the weight and finding solutions. She's smart and resourceful but that doesn't mean she can't discuss things with him.

He pulls the truck around their building, into his spot, and puts it in park. He turns to look at her, tugging on her hand to look at him.

"I know this isn't the ideal relationship you deserve. But you know you have complete control over it. I love you, baby. If it's too much for you, too much unnecessary stress, you can change that. You can tell me and I'll never fight you on it. I'll let you go."

"Cole, our relationship is just fine. It makes me happy. It's your job that's not ideal." She squeezes his hand. "There's no such thing as a perfect relationship and I know that *both* you and I have a say." She pauses. "I told you I can wait for you the first time you left and I'll still be here when you get back this time."

"Have I ever told you I've never met anyone like you before?" He pulls her over the center console for a kiss. A kiss that ends too soon because her seat belt is still buckled, locking her in place, not allowing her to move any further. "Even the truck is trying to take you away from me now."

She laughs at him. "Can we get inside where it's warm now?" she asks, unbuckling herself.

She beelines straight to the shower once they get inside the apartment.

He hangs her jacket up in the closet and rids himself of his own boots and jacket before heading to the fridge. He reaches for her favorite soup that they picked up yesterday and gets to warming it up.

While he waits, he glances over to the dining table and sees their two laptops still there from the night before. Curious, he goes over to open hers and turns it on.

Of course she wouldn't require a password.

He glances to the bedroom door and hears the shower still running. He quickly flips through the various windows she's left open, not really knowing what he is looking for until he gets to the window logged in to her personal Gmail account. If she left this logged in, with luck, her Google account would be logged in too. He quickly navigates to the Google Account page and browses through for the link he is looking for. *Device activity & security events.*

He clicks on the link to review and reads through it quickly. According to the details, an unknown laptop has access to her Google Account, which would probably mean her emails and anything synced, up until three weeks ago. The last used location is simply listed as Portland, OR. He clicks on the "Lost This Device" link to see if he can get a better approximation of its current location and finds that her password is needed.

He isn't sure how long the shower has off but he quickly closes the window and closes the screen before walking back over to the stove to shut off the range. Frankie walks out of the bedroom towel drying her hair just as he reaches for a bowl from the cabinet.

"Smells good," she says.

"Have a seat and I'll bring it to you."

She chooses to sit on the couch and flips on the TV. The local news is playing and she watches while continuing to dry her hair.

"Frankie, why didn't you tell me you were having problems at Vince's?"

She spins around to face him. "Let me guess. Nick told you," she says, rolling her eyes. "It's nothing for you to worry about. I'll figure it out."

"I know it has to do with work but maybe I can help somehow," he says. "Do you wanna talk about it now?"

"What do you want to know?" she asks as she stirs the soup he just put down on the coffee table in front of her.

"How bad was or is it?"

"I think I caught it in enough time to recoup most of our losses. With the proper documentation, the banks should be able to credit our account bank."

"How much are we talking about?"

"Close to fifteen thousand dollars," she says uneasily.

"That's a lot of money within the span of what...two months?" Someone's bound to get pissed that she's eliminated their pocket change.

She takes a sip of the soup before she answers him. "It is. I haven't really talked to Vince about it. I've kinda been going behind his back and getting things fixed without him knowing."

"The banks would talk to you without his authorization?"

"Yes. I'm their primary contact."

"Can you explain to me how this was pulled off?"

She looks at him questioningly. "In our accounting software, someone changed the addresses to the vendors that receive check payments from us. Someone also used my work email address to email those vendors canceling our service contract with them even though I was sending purchase orders and payments per usual. Except a filter was created within my email so that any communication from these particular vendors would be rerouted into a hidden folder."

"Okay. So how have the shelves been getting stocked each week then?"

"That's the part I haven't figured out yet. Plus, I've had Karmen go through our reviews. We've had several complaints about our drinks tasting diluted. It's one of the reasons why I haven't talked to Vince about any of this yet."

"Meaning?" He waits but she doesn't answer. "You don't think he has something to do with this, right?"

"I don't want to think that, Cole. But who else would have access to my login with the passwords? I don't really know what to think."

"Nick says you filed a police report?"

"Yeah. It's the only way the banks would start their own investigation."

He sits back on the couch and remains quiet for some time going over what she just told him. His gut tells him that there would be no way Vince had anything to do with this.

"Baby, I remember you saying you lost your other laptop. Would that one have access to all the same things you do at the office?"

"Yes, it would." She turns to look back at him. "I changed my password to everything three weeks ago though. Plus, the person who has it would have to know how a bar runs for all of this to have worked, right?"

"Do you remember where you might have lost it?"

She looks at him, dumbfounded. "Babe, when I say lost...I actually meant it was stolen. *That night.*"

It's his turn to look dumbfounded now. Why didn't he remember this before? Dusty said he took some jewelry and a *laptop.*

Fuck! Did he really sell it or did he keep it? How does everything keep coming back to Dusty? And if he is involved with this, how did he know about the technicalities to pull this off? Dusty has a hard time using the map on the tablet, let alone figure out the logistics of a bar scam like this. It doesn't make sense.

- 59 -

"Hey, Cole! Happy birthday!" Karmen greets him at the door. She gives him a hug once he steps inside the house.

"Thank you," he says with a smile.

"Thanks for giving him a ride. I have to head to work and the dealership said it won't be ready for another hour."

"It's nothing. I just dropped Frankie off at work anyway."

"You guys have to take the car seats out from her car and put them in your truck though. He's gonna have to take the twins with him. Granny won't be here until seven tonight."

"Sure, I can do that now."

"Cool. Her keys are right there."

He grabs the keys off the hook and heads back outside to her car. He clicks the remote to unlock the car and opens the back door.

Funny how life works out. In four months, he knows how to safely secure car seats into just about any vehicle. And now, Nick is about to add another one.

Oddly, he finds himself jealous. No planning, no overthinking. Whatever happens, happens. That's how Nick approached this whole baby thing.

Sometimes he wishes he could shoot the shit like that. But even if he could, Frankie is too level-headed. He definitely enjoys all the practicing they're putting in, each time more intense than the previous time. But he'd be lying to himself if he didn't admit that he wouldn't mind if they had a little accident of their own.

He hears the front door of the house open and sees Nick trotting down the steps to him.

"Let me give you a hand," Nick says, going to the other side for the other car seat. "Hey, while we have a second to talk. Mitch got back to me. You're gonna have to leave in two days. Three at most."

"Me? So, you're gonna stay behind?"

"Yeah. But I'll still be the point of contact. We're just gonna have to be on the burners and keep close contact. Paul's in. You're picking him up in Reno. He's dropping his kid off there to be with her grandparents for Christmas."

"Where's the job?"

"San Francisco and San Diego. These are both Mitch's connects. The San Francisco batch rides with you to Diego. The Diego job has a buyer that's going to wait for you in Yuma. You'll be bringing something back from them to Mitch. He'll meet you at his place in Lake Tahoe on Friday. I'll get the information to you later today so you can have as much time as possible with it."

"Thanks."

"No, man. Thank you for letting me stay back. Don't worry too much about Frankie. We'll get her to stay with us as much as she can tolerate me."

He chuckles at that. "Yeah. That really makes me feel a lot better," he says sarcastically.

Nick chucks a cheese puff at him and he dodges it.

"So, how's it feel to be a year older?"

"Can't complain," he says, unable to hide his smile. At least the day started out amazing.

"Uh-huh," Nick says. "Good morning, I'm guessing."

He picks up the same cheese puff and throws it back at his brother, who catches it and puts it in his mouth only to spit it out a second later. "That shit's gross!"

"Swear jar!" he says, pointing at Nick.

"Come on already. Let's get this in your truck. Practice makes perfect."

He shakes his head and follows Nick, making sure to lock the car.

"I'm telling you. I don't know why you haven't knocked up Frankie yet. You're just waiting for some douche to come sweep her off her feet, aren't you?"

He gives Nick a hard shove to the shoulder. "Shut up! Not everyone wants to have a baby with someone a couple months after meeting."

Frankie

She's pleasantly surprised to see that the bar isn't busy at all when she and Alice step inside. It's enough to give her things to do but it isn't too loud or too busy for her not to be able to celebrate her *gorgeous god's* birthday with him. Vince even brought in some extra help.

"Oh my god! I can see that thing from a mile away!" Alice yells at Karmen. "Girl! You better let me get a closer look!" Karmen rounds the bar to give Alice a huge hug. "And the baby? This one's mine, right? Frankie already has the other two." Alice pouts and Karmen laughs. "Karm. For real. Let me see!"

She leaves her two chattering best friends and heads in through the double doors to put her bag down. Vince is on his hands and knees on the floor trying his best to wrap the gift for Cole which she had delivered to the bar.

"Need some help?" she asks him.

"I'm sorry, kid, I think this is as good as it's gonna get." He stands up, wiping sweat from his forehead. She can't help but laugh at him.

"Thank you, Vince. I didn't expect to get off so late at Katrina's." She puts her bag down in her chair and then gives him a hug. "Thanks for calling in Suzy to help Karmen tonight too."

"Of course! It'll give Suzy time to get used to our busy nights too once Karmen has to cut down on hours."

"I'll try to be here as much as I can."

"Don't worry about it, Frankie. There's no reason for you to stretch yourself thin. Enjoy your time with Cole. I like that one." He gives her a pat on the back. "Speaking of...I just want to make sure you and Karmen are happy. You girls are doing okay, right? I mean...she's moving really fast. Nothing against Nick. I just want to make sure she and the twins are going to be okay, you know. You two are about the closest thing I have to family."

"I know it seems fast but I think it works for Karmen. Cole and I, we're good. We're happy together. Don't worry about us so much. I can't run this place alone if you give yourself another heart attack," she teases him.

"Are you kidding me? You can run this place blindfolded." He spins her around and shoves her toward the double doors. "Come on. Let's see what kind of shenanigans we can get into tonight."

Karmen and Alice are still chatting excitedly about something. Donnie is attempting to flirt with a couple of blondes. Suzy is definitely going to be banking a lot of tips from the two different groups of college frat guys that she's talking to. Easygoing night.

"I gotta admit. Her ring is freaking gorgeous! Ugh!! When will it be my turn!" Alice feigns envy. "You get a diamond necklace. You, over here, get an engagement ring. I haven't even found my next victim...I mean friend for the night yet."

"Whore," she calls out her friend before she sips her drink.

Karmen bursts into laughter and Alice is trying to steal the drink out of her hand.

"Gimme that, you don't deserve something this good!" Alice demands.

She takes two big sips before letting Alice wrestle it away. "Great. Now you're gonna be a lush whore," she teases Alice. This time it's Alice who lets out a burst of laughter.

"Where's the birthday boy anyway?" Alice asks.

She checks her phone. It's almost 11:30. "He'll get here when he gets here," is all she can say.

"Karmen, go stand over there with the girls so I can get a picture of you three," Vince says when he returns from somewhere off the floor of the bar. "I don't get to see the three of you together enough."

"Good idea! Here, use my phone." Karmen is already handing it to Vince.

"You ladies are growing up so fast. Frankie's living with a guy. Karmen's getting married and having another baby. Then there's...well, there's Alice."

The four of them erupt into laughter at the same time and Vince finally snaps a couple of pictures.

"Oh. My. Effing gorgeous god!" Alice says, eyes peering above the rim of her glass.

She turns around to see who Alice is drooling over this time.

Cole. Of course.

He strides through the bar with Nick like the scene unfolds in slow motion. *Oh my effing gorgeous god indeed!* He's wearing the jogger outfit she gave him this morning and it looks like the two pieces of clothing are made just for him, fitting him in all the right places. His blond hair is slicked to the side tonight and she can't wait to get her hand caught up in it. He and Nick are laughing about something, oblivious to the heads they are turning.

"Frankie! You go home to *that* every night? You lucky bitch! Every time I see him, he's even more gorgeous than the last," Alice whispers to her.

"I tell myself that every time."

"And Karmen...You want to wait until the summer to marry *him*? You better get his ass down to the justice of the peace tomorrow!"

"He's hot, right?" Karmen asks Alice.

"Do they have any more brothers, cousins, or relatives in town?!" Alice asks playfully.

"Next time we go to the farm, you're coming too," she replies to her friend.

Cole finally gets to her, his hand reaching behind her neck, cradling it as he gives her a quick sweet kiss. "Hey, baby," he says, greeting her with his deep, smooth voice.

"You are sexy as hell! A lot of Exorcist head-turning across the bar while you were walking in just now," she teases because she knows he hates the attention.

He laughs at her. "Didn't see. Too busy watching the most beautiful woman in here."

"Ahem...Can I get some of that?" Alice asks shamelessly from behind them.

She blushes red and Cole straightens up, pulling her into his side. "Hi, Alice," he greets her friend.

"Happy birthday," Alice says. "I got you something, but Frankie's got it in her bag."

"You shouldn't have but thank you," he says, giving Alice a quick peck on her cheek.

"I think I might need a little more of that," Alice says jokingly. "You look freaking great!" She turns around to Nick. "And so do you! That's a beautiful ring, Nick. I couldn't be happier for Karm. And congratulations on the baby too!" Alice gives Nick a quick hug and pat on the back. The trio immediately is engrossed in a conversation about the wedding.

"Want a beer?" Vince asks Cole.

"Sure. Thanks, Vince."

Vince picks one up from behind the counter, opens it, and hands it to him. "Happy birthday!"

"Oh, thank you." He looks down at her and she slides her arm around him again. Nestling into his side comfortably. If only she can just fall asleep right here.

"I really don't know what to do with all these birthday wishes and gifts," he says. "It's usually just me and Nick."

"Well, your circle is growing," she tells him.

"All because you gave a stray like me a home." He kisses the top of her head.

- 60 -

Frankie

The next hour or so kept her pretty busy. She and Karmen took turns checking on Cole and Nick, who are now having a wagered game of darts with some of the frat boys. Alice is sitting at the bar with a tattooed-bearded guy. He introduced himself as Mick. She's stopped by and talked to both Mick and Alice a few times while refilling their drinks. She's pleasantly surprised at how genuinely nice he is. He makes conversation easy and has a great sense of humor. Best of all, he keeps up with Alice like it's a walk in the park.

The night is winding down. There are still three tables left though.

Alice and Mick are still sitting at the counter along with two of their regular couples grabbing a late-night bite when Vince announced the last call.

She returns to the counter with the platters of hot burgers and cold sandwiches just as Cole and Nick come to join Alice and Mick.

She waves to the frat boys, who are leaving. The ladies who were hanging around earlier must have already left.

"Hot! Hot!" Karmen says, bringing out the sides and the fixings. Vince follows behind with two more platters of food. Enough for their small party.

Moments later, she and Karmen walk through the double doors with the candles lit and singing the happy birthday song to Cole.

"Make a wish," she tells him excitedly.

"I'm not sure what else I'd need to wish for," he says.

He blows out the candles and takes the cake from her hand and sets it on the counter. She wraps her arms around him, face pressed against his chest and he places a tender kiss on top of her head as if on autopilot. She can hear his heart thud against his chest loudly. The same pitter-patter rhythm as her own. She's never known a love like this. A connection to someone like this.

"Thank you, baby. For everything." She pulls away and he immediately seeks her lips. "You are heaven sent, Frankie."

"Oh, I don't know about that," she laughs after their kiss. "But I do love you."

"Let me take a picture of everyone!" Karmen says.

"Actually, I'll take it for you, Karmen. You can get in the picture too," Mick offers.

It takes them a minute to gather around Cole so everyone is in the frame.

She stands in front of him, holding his cake.

"Cheese! Cheeesse!" The shutter is heard several times before Mick gives them a thumbs-up and she slides the cake back on the counter.

"Mick, hit that record button NOW!"

Startled by Karmen's excitement, she looks over to her friend. Nick is choking on the water he's drinking. When she faces Cole, he's...down on one knee...reaching for her hand.

"Babe, what's wrong?" she asks him.

He smiles nervously at her. "I've been waiting for the right time, the perfect moment, thinking that moment might be a while from now. I've been carrying this"—he unzips his sweater so he can reach inside somewhere and pulls out something—"around with me for what seems like forever because I was so worried about the short amount of time we've spent together."

Holy fucking shit!

"I'm not so good with words so bear with me, sweetheart." He actually gulps and breaks a sweat before he continues.

"From the moment we met, you've got me in knots. You unravel those knots and turn them into flutters every time I set eyes on you. You've loved me and given me a home even though I don't deserve an iota of any of that. But you did it anyway."

He holds a ring between his thumb and finger.

"Screw the timing, baby. I love you. That's not gonna change a week, a month, or a lifetime from now. Marry me, Frankie."

The room is absolutely still and quiet. She isn't sure if she's even breathing anymore. Everyone and everything fades away. She stares at him, this beautiful man on one knee holding an amazing emerald and diamond ring, proposing.

Her free hand covers her mouth, afraid that if she makes a peep, the moment will vanish. She nods her head in disbelief.

He grins and she sees a tear slide down over his cheek while he slides the ring onto her finger. *Perfect fit.* He stands up and she's already wrapping her arms around him, holding onto him tightly, wanting to hold onto him forever. Unable to believe that their forever began when he'd carried her into that bathroom all those months ago.

"OH MY GOD!" Alice screams.

She pulls away from Cole, unwrapping her arms and gazing up at this gorgeous god. *Her* gorgeous god. She wipes away his tear while he thumbs away at the streaks on her cheeks as well.

"A little warning would have been nice," she squeaks.

He bends down to kiss her. Their first official kiss as an engaged couple and they don't care who is or isn't watching.

"Everything about you has been a surprise to me. You were due a good one."

"I love you," she whispers.

"I'll never stop loving you," he says in return.

Walking alone down the hallway to the back door, she admires her beautiful engagement ring. She still can't quite wrap her head around it. And his proposal. It was just so perfect. So sweet and romantic. So unexpected coming from a guy who isn't much for words.

She pushes the door open and is assaulted by the cold night. She makes the walk, humming to herself, and quickly tosses the bag into the open side of the bin then heads back inside where her fiancee was waiting to take her home.

Right before she swings the door open, a guy rounds the corner of the building and slams right into her.

"Shit," she says, taking a few steps back.

"We meet again," the guy says.

She doesn't recognize his face but something about him is familiar. Something she doesn't like. She can't put a finger on it but her instincts are screaming for her to get the fuck out of there. Quick.

"Pretty little necklace," he says with a smirk.

Her hand immediately comes up to cover her pendant. "Excuse me," she says, trying to get him to move out of the door's way. She isn't sure if the goosebumps came because of the cold or because of him.

Suddenly the door swings open, nearly hitting him. It's Donnie with two bags of trash.

"Is everything okay?" Donnie asks, looking at her before looking at the other guy.

"Yeah," she answers. She holds the door open for him. "I'll wait for you," she says and watches him hurriedly walk and toss the bags into the dumpster. He trots over to hold the door for her to go in first.

"We're closing down here already," she hears Donnie tell the guy before the slamming of the door and the clicking of multiple locks echo down the hallway.

- 61 -

Frankie

"Hey, Frankie. Come inside." Nick opens the door for her and helps her with the three huge bags full of gifts she brought along.

She called ahead so that Karmen can take the kids to the store while she brings the gifts in. She isn't exactly comfortable being alone with Nick but she has to talk to him anyway.

"How long before they're back?" she asks him.

"' Bout an hour. She asked if you can help finish wrapping the rest of their gifts while she's out. I started on some already so there isn't much more to do."

She takes her jacket off and puts it on the couch. Her boots come off next and she sits by the blazing fireplace. There are seven more gifts to wrap and she picks one that she assumes will be for Nat and begins working.

"We ordered dinner too so you don't have to worry about cooking. Just relax."

"I'm not staying for dinner," she tells him without looking up.

"Thought Karmen said you were," he says with a hint of curiosity like he wanted to ask a follow-up question.

"I made other plans. Sorry. I'll be here for Christmas dinner tomorrow though."

"Okay? Can I ask what plans you have?"

"No," she replies, leaving it at that.

While Cole has been away, Nick has been more prominent in her business as it is. She didn't want to encourage that at the moment.

He comes to sit cross-legged opposite her and picks up a gift to start wrapping.

How odd it is to be sitting here, silently wrapping Christmas gifts with him. It isn't awkward but it isn't an enjoyable experience either.

"I know you're probably never going to forgive me or like me," he starts to say.

"Not gonna argue with that," she interrupts.

"You're starting to sound like my brother." He pauses. "But thanks for tolerating me."

She doesn't have a response to that and continues wrapping the next gift. It takes her wrapping another gift before she speaks to him again. "I need to ask you something."

"Sure."

"I need to know that this will stay between us. Cole and Karmen don't need to know."

"You know I can't promise you that," he answers. She's surprised by his honesty.

"Do you have a picture of Dusty?" she asks, still not looking at him. Her question seems to surprise him and he stops his wrapping.

"Why are you asking about him?"

She can see his hand tighten around the scissors.

"Cole said you all parted ways but he didn't say where and when," she replies as steadily as she can, still not looking at him.

"Frankie, you need to tell me why you're asking," he says calmer, with more patience.

"I'm not sure. I don't know what he looks like but I have the feeling that I ran into him recently," she answers. She finally looks at him and sees him staring at her.

His lips tighten.

"When?" he asks.

"That night at Vince's. Cole's birthday. Maybe even before that too."

"Did you tell Cole about this?"

"One, I can't be sure it was him. As I said, I don't know what he looks like. And two, I knew Cole was leaving. The last thing he needs is a distraction. If you're smart, you probably shouldn't be *distracting* him with this either." She can tell he's silently agreeing with her. "So, what does he look like?"

"He's not quite six feet tall, scrawny. Brown hair, dull brown eyes. Kinda looks like Shaggy from Scooby-Doo except weed probably won't cut it for him. He's into the harder stuff."

"The company you two keep," she says, shaking her head. "And did you guys bring him back here to Portland with you before parting ways?"

"No. We left him in Wyoming."

That makes her feel a smidge better actually.

"Frankie, if you even *think* you've run into someone close to being him, I need you to leave, go the other way, or into a crowd. Hop into a shop or something. If Cole's not around, call me. I'll drop everything to get to you as soon as I can. Got it?"

"But he's not here, so I don't have to worry, right?" She looks him in the eyes waiting to see his reaction.

"I'm just saying," he replies.

"Well, these are all done," she says, shoving the stack of wrapped gifts over to him.

He still has one more to go but seems capable without her help. She stands up and pulls her phone out of her back pocket to check the time. A few minutes past six p.m.

"Karmen will probably text me later anyway. I have to go. I'll see everyone tomorrow."

"You're really not gonna tell me where you're going?" he asks.

"Why would I need to?"

"Wait. Hold on a second." He stands up and reaches for his phone on the coffee table. A second later, her phone pings and she checks the message.

You have my number now.

"Use it anytime, Frankie. I'm serious," he tells her in all seriousness.

She has the feeling that there something he isn't saying. If Dusty isn't around, then why does he seem so concerned?

"How did you even get my number in the first place?"

"You're engaged to my baby brother, Frankie." He gives her that grin that makes her want to kick his teeth in.

"Well, I hope you like pizza and *Elf*!" she says from the hospital doorway.

"'*Elf*'? I haven't seen that in ages," Sam replies with a huge smile.

She's glad to see him looking almost normal again. Other than the two casts, his bumps, bruising, and swelling are nearly gone.

"You look so much better than the last time I saw you," she tells him.

She puts the pizza and her laptop bag down on the visitor's couch before going to his bedside. She gives him a tight squeeze and feels him flinch.

"Oh shit. Is this on the side of the broken ribs?"

"Yeah. Still stings a bit," he says. "I'm glad you're here though. It was a nice surprise to hear you were coming."

"Where are your parents? Should we wait for them?"

"No. They wanted to give us an unsupervised date night." She laughs at the waggling of his brows, shaking her head. "They'll be back later, or maybe in the morning. I don't really like them out so late. The nurses look after me around the clock here anyway."

He lowers the bed and she slides the reclining chair next to it. She pulls the food table over, making sure he has enough space between it and his broken leg before opening the box of pizza and taking a slice out for him first. Then she grabs her bag and pulls the laptop out from inside and sets it on the table, running through the task of setting it up for their movie.

"New ring?" Sam asks.

She doesn't answer and continues to set everything up with only her right hand.

"Well, I've already seen it, so kinda late on trying to hide it now."

"Sorry," she says.

"I'm guessing you said yes," he flatly responds.

"Yeah," she answers him.

"I guess that's what I get for trying to be the gentleman and beating around the bush about what I think of you."

"Sam, I—"

"Well, if it has to be someone...I guess he'll do."

She smiles at him, appreciating that he doesn't make this awkward. She gives him a soft kiss on the cheek.

"Thanks, Sam."

"Yeah. Yeah. Let's get this movie started before he sends a search party."

She keeps mum about Cole not being around for this or any other holiday. It's better this way. Besides, Sam will probably worry about her being alone in the apartment again. Look what had happened the last time he was worried.

She sends Cole a quick text telling him she's having dinner at the hospital with Sam. Nick might actually be dumb enough to tell him that she isn't with him and Karmen. The last thing she needs is for Cole to be worried and get himself into a mess too.

- 62 -

cole

They are currently just outside of Fresno at a gas station. Paul asked if they could make a bathroom stop but he thinks it's more for the guy to be able to call his daughter. It's now past midnight, making it Christmas.

He saw Frankie's message come in earlier about having dinner with Sam but didn't respond. He checks the security app and sees that she's back at the apartment just a little over two hours ago. He closes the app and taps the phone icon, calling her, hoping she's still awake.

"*Hi,*" a sleepy voice answers.

"Merry Christmas. I didn't mean to wake you."

"*Merry Christmas, my love. The one time I want Santa to bring me Cole for Christmas,*" she says.

He grins at her clever play on words.

"*I fell asleep on the couch so I'm glad you woke me up.*"

"How's Sam?"

"*A lot better than the last time we saw him. But still in casts. He might be able to go home to his parents' place next week. He's still gonna need a lot of help.*" She pauses. "*Are you okay?*"

"I'm okay, baby. I miss you but I'm okay." He really does miss her. "You sound tired."

"*Yeah. I'm not really feeling up to par the past few days.*"

"Do me a favor and take some Emergen-C. Please?"

"*How do you know if that stuff even helps?*"

"I know there's a lot of vitamins in it," he says with a chuckle.

"*I will,*" she says. "*Should I still expect you home this weekend?*"

"If all goes well, yes."

"I can't wait. It's quiet around here without you."

That makes him both smile and worry at the same time. She has to be the only one in the building for the next few days. The workers are most likely off to be with their families for the holidays.

"I'll be home as soon as I can. I love you, baby. But..."

"I know, I know. You have to go," she finishes for him.

Frankie

It was a great idea to not have to sit down at the dinner table together for dinner. Instead, everyone just got their own plate and sat down wherever. She sat in front of the fireplace and chatted with George, Gina, Alice, and Mick most of the night. Karmen and Nick are busy making googly eyes at each other, it being their first Christmas together.

Vince and his friend Maribel are now handing out the gifts from under the tree to the respective recipients. The kids are tearing away at their wrapping paper, screaming with excitement with each rip.

She is handed a box by Karmen, who also hands Nick a box. And why is she the one who always ends up sitting next to her archnemesis, Nick? She begins opening the box in her hand with lackluster speed and pulls out a white hooded sweater. She unfolds it and sees the same imprint on the front and back. *Bestie 01*, it reads.

"Bestie 02?" she hears Nick asking from next to her. "Are we into the matching clothes stage, sweetheart?"

"Oh my god," she exclaims, throwing the sweater at Karmen, who's laughing hysterically.

"Nope. Not us, babe," Karmen tells Nick.

"What is it with the two of you anyway?" Alice asks her. "I've never seen Frankie be openly hostile to anyone and still be nice to them at the same time."

"I wouldn't call it nice," she tells Alice. "We don't see eye to eye. On many levels."

"Because her levels a lot shorter than mine," Nick retorts.

She makes sure he sees her rolling her eyes before catching the sweater that Karmen throws back.

Karmen sets the few gifts to Cole off to the side so she can take them home with her. Her friend jumped for joy when she saw the Instant Pot from her and Cole. Add the air fryer from Vince, and the woman can definitely say she's having a great Christmas.

Nick hands two small boxes from under the tree to her. One is from Cole, the other from him.

She looks at him suspiciously and chooses to open the one from Cole first. It better not be another expensive piece of jewelry. She opens the lid and sees the cutest silver keychain inside. *"You Are My Home"* is engraved in perfect script lettering on it.

"What's in the other one?" Alice asks.

She puts the keychain back in the box and begins opening the box from Nick. She lifts the lid and sees a shiny key inside. She looks up at Nick, not understanding. Karmen, who's been sitting next to him, leans on him and smiles at her.

"It's a key to the farmhouse. Cole made the arrangements with our lawyers for the paperwork to add yours and Karmen's names to the deed when we...you know." He doesn't finish. "So I thought the key to the place would be a nice gift."

"Holy shit!" Alice exclaims.

She picks up the key and stares at it in shock. Oh. My. God.

"Are you kidding me right now?" she blurts out the first thing that she can think of.

This is such a huge gift, such a huge step. And Cole isn't even here for her to discuss it with him. It's too much. They haven't even talked about anything yet. Hell, she hasn't even gotten past the fact that he proposed four nights ago. And now she's about to own a farm too?

"I can't take this." She shakes her head. "It's way too much. I thought the necklace was extravagant. Then came the ring. And now? It's a whole farm plus like twenty acres! It's too much."

"It's actually fifty acres now, but who's counting," Nick says with a shrug.

"I can't accept this." She puts the key back in the box and gives it back to Nick.

"That's fine. Once you two get married, it'll become yours anyway." He shrugs, not fazed.

"He's right, you know," Vince says from his seat on the couch.

"And what if I don't want to live there?" she asks and looks over at Vince.

"No one said you have to," Nick answers. "But Karmen and I plan on being there."

"Bitch, stop fighting it already. You own a farm! Yee-haw!" Alice exclaims with way too much cheer.

If she knew what Cole was doing right now, she'd be calling him and giving him an earful. Didn't they already talk about not giving any more extravagant gifts? This is definitely beyond extravagant.

"If it makes you feel any better, it's really not that much divided between four people," Nick says nonchalantly.

"Yeah. That makes me feel a lot better," she answers sarcastically, wanting to smack the smirk off his face. "I suddenly feel like my gifts come up way too short. So I'll be taking those back."

She snatches the boxes that Karmen just handed to him. Or at least she tries to but he's too quick and already has a death grip on them.

"No way!" He's ripping them open even before she removes her fingers off. He opens the lid of the square box and she's surprised to see his eyes light up as much as the kids'.

"YES!! Karm, I finally got my own *Star Wars* box set! Holy smokes! Lightsabers! And not the flimsy kind too." He takes the two lightsabers out of the box and stands up.

"Dude! That's cool!" Mick says.

Nick tosses him one and the two men are going at it with the lights, sound effects, and saber action.

The old man did always used to say, if there isn't an opportunity, have the balls to create one. Merry Christmas!

Soon, Frankie. Soon we'll be having our own celebrations.

He opens another bag of sugar and begins pouring it into the mini-SUV. "Let's see how many opportunities I get now," he speaks to himself.

He wads up the bag of sugar into a tight ball with his gloved hands. He walks behind the car and just to make sure, he crouches down and stuffs the wad as far into the tailpipe as he can. Shouldn't cause too much damage but she won't know.

She finishes a good portion of her soup and orange juice before lying down on the couch. By the time she wakes up again, her place is dark except for the glare coming off of the TV. She picks her phone up from the coffee table. It's already past six? That was some nap but she does feel a lot better. Not so tired anymore. Her place also feels too warm now so she tosses the blanket off to the end of the couch.

She's hungry and in opening the fridge, realizes that she has to go get food and water. Some fresh air might be good for her too.

The cold fresh air indeed makes her feel good. She stands and stretches outside for a bit while her car warms up. Driving through the neighborhood to the market, she notices people are busy hustling around.

Wandering up and down the aisles, she realizes it's been a long time since she's done this alone. She's usually either with Cole or he does the shopping now. Feeling winded, she decides it's best to start making her way home. She grabs a couple of already made soups, salads, and fruit bowls in case she isn't up for cooking later.

She hurriedly gets back to her car, taking slow steady breaths, and starts it, giving it a minute to warm up and to defrost the windows. After a minute, the car stutters and stalls out.

"What the hell?" she says and tries to turn the ignition again and again. She checks the gas gauge. The tank is nearly full.

"Great." She pulls out her phone and unlocks it. 7:45 p.m. Karmen would be at work by now. Vince would be there too. So she decides to call Alice. The phone rings until the voicemail greeting comes on. She hangs up without leaving a message and dials again with the same result. She Googles for a tow service and finds that most of them are closed. The open ones have an unbelievable wait time. She finally settles on one that can be by to pick up her car in just over two hours.

Her phone rings just after she finishes the call. She looks down, hoping it will be Alice, but to her surprise, it's Cole. She answers it quickly.

"Hey," she says.

"Did you leave the apartment?" he asks, sounding concerned.

"Yeah. I feel a lot better and needed to get some food for the fridge. How did you know?"

"The alarm was turned on over an hour ago and you haven't turned it off again," he says. *So he's been keeping track? A bit excessive.*

"Yeah. Well, my car won't start now and the only tow company I can get to come out won't be by for another two hours."

"Baby, you can't sit and wait there the whole time. Give me their number, I'll deal with it. Call Nick and have him come get you. Please? If you don't, I'll call him anyway. You're sick, you shouldn't have gone out in the cold so soon."

"Okay," she says with resignation.

She feels bad that she worried him. It wasn't her intention. She didn't think he would check the app often enough to notice when she came and went.

After hanging up, she quickly copies the phone number off of her call log and texts it to him then searches for Nick's number and dials.

"Frankie?" He sounds a little too concerned. *"Are you okay?"*

"I'm at the market close to my place and my car won't start. The tow truck company won't be able to pick my car up for another two hours and Cole wants you to come get me."

"I'll be right there. Let me wrangle the twins into their shoes and jackets," he says with no questions asked.

"Thanks," she says before hanging up.

The cosmic universe just insists on shoving her and Nick together like some inside joke.

- 63 -

cole

He watches Paul retrieving his bags from the back seat and waves at the man. "Thanks for the help, man." He's dropping Paul off at the hotel he checked into before Christmas.

"Pleasure's mine. You make for good company and business but I have to admit, I'm ready to see my kid now. Thanks for the ride."

"Can you do me a favor? If you hear from Dusty again, let me know?"

"Yeah. No problem. Drive safe, man. Give my regards to Nick too." Paul gives him a quick wave and shuts the door.

He immediately pulls out of the lot and heads onto the road without looking back. He taps the phone icon on the screen, taps on Nick's number, and listens to the sound of the ringing coming through his speakers.

"I'm heading back early," he says before Nick even says a word.

"Everything okay?"

"Yeah. Mitch's guy came early. No reason to stay another day."

"Drive carefully," Nick says before hanging up.

He checks the time. It's probably still too early to call Frankie, especially if she needs sleep. Instead, he focuses on the road and the nine-hour drive ahead.

Over four hours into his drive, his phone rings and he taps the screen to answer the call. It's the number from the shop that her car was taken to.

"Hello," he answers.

"Hi. Cole? This is Tim from the auto shop about the Honda CR-V."

"How bad is it?" he asks.

"Well, it's pretty bad. Seems there's a bunch of sugar in the tank. It didn't get to the engine but the fuel injector is shot. We'll have to replace that and clean out everything associated including dropping the tank and cleaning that out. There's also the bag of sugar that was wadded and stuffed into the tailpipe. That damaged the ECU and that'll need to be replaced as well. Your wife might have parked in a bad area and some kids were probably messing around. Sad to say."

"What are we looking at with cost and time?" he asks.

"Our quote, including parts and labor, comes to eight hundred ninety dollars. We can have it ready in about four to five days."

"Okay. Go ahead and do it. I'll stop by and pay for everything tomorrow morning."

"No problem. We'll get the parts ordered right away. I'll be here tomorrow too."

"Thanks, Tim."

He hangs up.

What the hell is going on? If it happened over Christmas, Tim might be right. Some kids were probably walking around and thought it'd be a funny prank. But his instincts tell him that with everything else going on around her, this was deliberate. He just can't figure out why.

He checks the time on the dashboard. Four more hours of driving and it's going to get dark soon. He taps the screen and listens to the ringing sound from the speakers, waiting for Nick to answer again.

"Hey," Nick says. "Anxious to know about the baby, Uncle Cole?"

Their first doctor's appointment. He completely forgot about it. "How'd it go?" he asks.

"Coley, I wish you could have been there," Nick says quietly. "It's great, man. Got to see the heartbeat and hear it too, slightly. Our next visit, we should be able to hear a clearer and stronger beat. July twenty-third, man. You're officially going to be an uncle on or around July twenty-third."

He can't help but grin to himself. Nick is excited. He is ecstatic as well. It's not going to be just him and Nick anymore. Nick is adding another Howard into the family.

"I can't wait to meet the kid. Gramps would be happy."

"Gramps would already have Karmen moved out to the farm by now if he were still alive. No way is the kid going to be born anywhere else."

They are silent for a brief moment before Nick speaks again. *"Completely forgot to ask you why you called."*

"The shop called me back about Frankie's car."

"Bad?"

"Pretty bad. Someone put sugar in her tank and then tried to block the tailpipe."

"That sounds juvenile. Everyone knows the sugar in the tank thing is a myth and doesn't cause engine damage. Might be some kids showing off."

"It could be but with her history, what are the odds?"

Nick is uncomfortably quiet now. *"You think someone wants to get rid of her car? Why?"*

"I don't know for sure but I'm thinking it has something to do with the bar and that issue she's been having. Without a car, she walks home from there. And the couple of times that she's walked home since I've known her...shit happens. And that's only the shit that I know about."

"Fuck," Nick says under his breath. *"She asked me something the other night and told me she didn't want me talking to you about it. She was worried about distracting you while you're away."*

"And...I'm already on my way back, so what is it?"

"She asked me about Dusty. Wanted to know what he looked like and if we parted ways with him in Portland." Nick pauses and he can hear him taking a deep breath. *"She thinks she's run into him. Maybe more than once."*

"What the fuck? Did she say when or where?"

"The night at the bar for your birthday and maybe even before that. I didn't want to scare her so I kinda gave her the impression that we left him in Wyoming and she stopped talking about it."

"Something *that* important, you didn't think I should have known right away? I left her at home alone this whole week. All the workers at the shop are off for the week for Christmas, Nick."

Shit!

"I didn't know. I'm sorry, man."

"I'll be there in four hours. Maybe you can check up on her when it gets dark. Or at least check around outside and see if anyone shows up."

"Yeah. I can do that."

He hangs up and white knuckles the steering wheel.

Normally, if he has a bad feeling like the one he's having now, he would abort the job. Obviously, that isn't something he can do this time. Someone deliberately got rid of her car so she's either stuck at home most of the time or she has to walk home because whoever did this knows her well enough to know she would rather do that than hassle anyone else.

"Why?" he asks himself. It's a question he ponders the rest of his drive home.

"Why didn't you tell me about the farm and what you were doing? Isn't that something that we should have discussed first?"

"You don't like it?"

"It's not that, Cole. It's really, really *too* much. It doesn't feel right. I didn't earn it or deserve it. That's something that's a part of your family."

"And you're a part of my family now too, Frankie. Nick wanted to do that for Karmen and I figured once we got married, I'd have to make that change again anyway."

Frankie has her bottom lip in between her teeth. He can tell she's running things over in her mind.

"We don't have to live there if you don't want to. But it belongs to us and we can come and go however often you want. What's mine is yours, Frankie. Everything I have, everything I am. It's yours," he says, looking into her beautiful green eyes.

She cups his face, caressing it lightly. "I love you. But going forward, let's cut it out with all the expensive gifts, okay?"

He shrugs and she smacks him playfully as he gets up. He picks up his bags and heads to the bedroom closet. Leaving them on the closet floor, he reaches for the boxes on the top shelf on his side of the closet. He didn't even have to worry about her seeing them up there on account she's so damn adorably short.

He returns to the living room and sees all the gifts lying on the coffee table. He definitely didn't expect that many.

"They're not all from me," she says with a laugh.

He begins tearing into his gifts. Nick got him a pretty cool smoothie blender, one of the fancier ones that he's seen on the shelves. Karmen got them a gift certificate to some seafood restaurant he'll have to look up. Come to think of it, he's never taken Frankie out on an official date. He'd skipped over so many steps and jumped right into proposing, and yet...she still said yes.

He picks up the biggest box on the table and recognizes the wrapping paper as one of the ones they bought. He rips it open, peels away the lid, and sees a very heavy and warm-looking black jacket with a light-colored Sherpa lining. He pulls it out and slides into it.

"Very Montana, isn't it?" she asks from behind him.

"How do you always know what I need? It's awesome. Fits perfectly. Thank you, baby." He turns around and gives her a quick kiss before pulling her onto his lap and handing her a small box.

"If this is another piece of jewelry from you, I'm not keeping it," she says.

"Open it, woman!"

Her little fingers dig into the edge of the wrapping paper, tearing away ever so neatly at the wrapping until she pulls out the small box holding a smartwatch.

"Do you like it?" he asks.

"It's awesome! Is this your way of telling me to stop using your watch?" she asks with a fake pout.

"I've already set most of it up for you. You can check your emails, texts, and sync it to both your phone and laptop." *And it has a GPS.* He didn't need to tell her that though. "We can download the app on your phone a little later."

"Does it tell time though?" she asks him.

He shakes his head with a grin and allows her hand to guide his lips down to hers. Her sweet lips. Warm and soft.

It doesn't take long for her tongue to trace slowly over his bottom lip before taking a small nibble and then sucking on it lightly to soothe the bite. That causes a low growl to escape from his throat and his hand comes up to her nape, cradling it so she can open to him.

- 64 -

Frankie

It takes her half an hour longer than if she walked just to find a parking spot that she can get into with Cole's huge truck. She hurries across the street and walks the short distance into the bar.

It's a busy night and she looks around to make sure Karmen has sufficient help before heading back to the office. Vince was already sitting behind his desk, his eyeglasses perched on his nose.

"Hey," she says to him.

He gets up out of his chair and comes around to hug her. "You look a lot better than the last time I saw ya. I'm glad Cole's back too."

"Busy night. I see you called in extra hands for Karmen. Thanks."

"It's my job to take care of my girls," Vince says.

"So, what's up?"

He takes off his glasses and then hands a stack of letters over to her.

Shit. It's the dispute claims from the bank. She didn't count on him checking the mail because she usually does that. But with the holidays and her being out, the pile must have stacked up.

"Frankie, why didn't you tell me about these? Something is going on and you're not telling me. I know it. I can see it on your face when you're back here."

"Vince, I'm sorry. I know you have a right to know. I was just hoping that I'd be able to take care of things before telling you about it. I'm sorry if I overstepped my boundaries. This *is* your bar and I should have discussed it with you first."

He holds up his hands. "None of that talk. This bar and *I* wouldn't even be standing if it weren't for your hard work. But it's also not your job to carry all the burden. So sit down and tell me what's going on. We're not going to go under anytime soon but that's a lot of money to dispute with the banks and you know they're going to put up a fight."

With resignation, she begins to tell him everything. It takes over an hour of explaining and showing him how it had been done and then what she did to correct the matter.

"I'm sorry, Vince. I feel like there's a good chance that this could have been my fault. I should have changed my passwords as soon as I found out my laptop was stolen."

"This isn't your fault, kid. You didn't know. And from the sounds of everything, the banks shouldn't have a problem reimbursing us. That's what the insurance is for. Besides, you did the right thing in filing a report with the police. They'll give us the proper backup documentation." He gives her a small pat on the back. But she knows he's worried. She can feel his tension and worries by the way he squeezes her shoulder and kisses the top of her head.

"Get back home and get some rest before Cole sends the hounds looking for you," he says quietly.

"We'll be okay, Vince. We'll figure it out. Let the police do their job," she tells him. The last thing she needs is for Vince to go old-school gangster.

"Of course, Frankie. Get home before you're stuck helping out here," he says with a jolly chuckle. "Get better quick so you can come celebrate New Year's Eve with us. Maybe then we can start talking about that wedding. God knows Karmen hasn't shut up about hers."

- 65 -

cole

"Do you realize how much has happened here with us at this bar?" he asks his girl. They're sitting at the counter with the New Year's crowd going at full force.

"Lots of firsts," she says with a smile.

He looks down at her ring and touches it. "Yeah. And a couple of lasts too. I fell in love with you here, you know."

"Did you?"

"During your birthday party. I watched you all night. I couldn't move and didn't even want to blink. Didn't want to miss anything about you." He really needs to stop with this chick-flick level of sap he's got going for Frankie.

"How are you so romantic?" she teases him. "How long were you even here?"

"I came in at about eight that night, I think. You were the last person I expected to see walk through those doors for that party."

"I'm glad you stayed," she says.

She picks up his hand and brings it to her cheek. "I thought about you a hundred times after you left that morning. I didn't think I would see you again and even under the circumstances...I missed you."

He pulls her closer and places a soft kiss on top of her head.

"You two wanna save some of that for the honeymoon?" Alice asks from next to him. Frankie blushes and he pulls her closer. "Geez. Do you not get enough of that at home?"

He couldn't stop the grin from spreading on his face even if he wanted to.

"Stop playing hard to get and you can be on your own honeymoon," Frankie tells Alice.

Alice pulls her out of her seat and out of his arms. She drags Frankie to the dance floor before anyone can even say anything.

"Hey, man." Mick climbs into Frankie's empty seat. "Sorry she ruined your moment," he apologizes. "She's *spontaneous*," he says.

"I can see that," he replies.

Donnie comes over to them and asks if they want anything. They both order another beer just as Nick comes back and stands next to them with his own bottle of water.

"All the bars on the block are busy tonight," Nick tells him when he comes back from scouting.

"Ten! Nine! Eight…" the countdown begins.

"I love you," he can see her saying.

"Four! Three! Two! One!"

The bells start ringing above them and there is confetti flying all around. People are yelling and screaming while their group holds their glasses in toast together before drinking. Frankie leans down from her seat on top of the bar counter to kiss him, letting the champagne trickle from her mouth into his, surprising him. It's sexy as fuck too.

"To many more years together," she says into his ear after.

"Many, many more," he says to her before helping her down from the bar counter.

Vince turns the music back on but lowers the volume so people can continue talking to each other and order drinks.

"Hey, Cole, do you mind if I get in a dance with Frankie? Alice will be with us," Mick asks him.

"Be my guest," he says.

Alice pulls her out on the floor while Mick follows closely behind them. He watches the three of them together before feeling a hard whack on the back. He turns around to see Nick handing him a beer.

"You should take lessons before your wedding," Nick says.

"Yeah. No thanks."

Nick shoves him playfully. "Happy New Year's, baby brother." This is the first time he and Nick have ever celebrated the night together like this.

Last year, he ended up having to drag his brother out from a strip club while they were in Atlantic City. Nick had gotten into a brawl with the bouncers after one of the girls got upset at his inappropriate touching. Drunk and belligerent, it took three of the club's bigger bouncers to hold Nick back while another dealt him some really heavy blows to the gut and face. Once he was able to get them off of his brother, Nick went into a fit of rage and beat the crap out of two of the three before both he and Dusty were able to drag him out of there.

The stripper who started the whole thing came running outside after them. The fight turned her on somehow and she hopped in the backseat of the truck with Nick. They were having sex before he was even able to pull out of the parking lot.

How different life has become for both of them in 365 days.

"I think I'm growing on Frankie," Nick tells him.

"I wouldn't put money on it," he tells his brother, wiping the grin from Nick's face.

"Asshole!" Nick barks out.

They are standing around watching the crowd and enjoying the music when he feels a hard shoulder check from behind. He turns his head to see a guy walking by with a smirk.

"You got a problem!" the jerk says to him.

"Keep it moving, man!" Nick tells the guy and signals for him to keep going. "You don't want any problems here."

The asshole flips them off and continues through the crowd to join Melissa's group. Makes sense now. Why does she keep showing up here?

"That definitely was like high school again. Like the jocks picking on us outcasts," Nick comments. "Wait...except you were a jock in high school, weren't you?"

He gives his brother a hard smack on the back for being a prick. The music changes and Frankie heads back to him, holding Alice's hand with Mick talking along with them.

From his peripheral view, he sees Melissa's group pointing and laughing in the trio's direction. And before he knows it, the big guy that just shoulder-checked him walks up behind Frankie, puts his hands on each side of her arms, and picks her up, knocking Alice down in the process. Meathead then deliberately drops Frankie who falls completely to the ground.

He didn't even realize his feet have moved as quickly as they did and within a few seconds, he's standing over her and shoving the dirtbag as hard as he can.

Mick is trying to help both Alice and Frankie up from the ground.

"What's your fucking problem?" he roars at the guy.

Nick pulls Frankie up. She limps a bit when she tries to stand. "You okay?" Nick asks her.

"Fucking prick!" Alice yells at the guy once she gets back up.

"Cole, I'm okay." Frankie steps in front of him and tries to calm him down. She turns to face the guy. "I think you've had too much to drink. You should leave now," she says to the guy.

"It's all fun and games. Can't take a joke?" the guy says to her.

"I'm asking you to leave. You're not welcome here anymore," she says more firmly.

"We're paying customers just having a little fun and they're trying to kick us out!" one of the girls from Melissa's group yells out, trying to add fuel to the fire.

Melissa steps to Frankie. "Can take a joke?" she asks with a bitchy smirk.

"Get your friends and get the fuck out of here," he hollers at Melissa. He's had enough of her antics and this one definitely crosses the line.

"Who the fuck do you think you are, talking to her like that!" The guy lunges, knocking Frankie right into him, trapping her in between them. The asshole tries to take a swing at his face but can't connect because Frankie's hands are shoving up into his chin, pushing his head up as far as she can.

"Frankie!" Alice shrieks and can see her trying to pull her friend out from between him and the guy.

The guy releases his shirt, grabs Frankie by the hair, and shoves her out of the way.

Watching that happen in slow motion, he reaches his boiling point. His right hook connects to the guy's jaw, sending him a few steps back into Melissa. Once the asshole gets his footing, the guy launches himself, tackling him onto the ground as a group of people hurriedly step out of the way.

With the wind knocked out of him and on his back, the guy lands him a few solid hits to his ribs and one to his jaw.

Once he catches his breath and an opening though, he's able to land a solid uppercut, dazing the guy enough for him to flip him onto his back, reversing their positions.

The guy takes direct hit after hit to his mouth and jaw until he can't defend himself anymore. Blood starts to trickle out of his mouth.

It's Nick and Vince who try to pull him off of the douchebag.

"Cole, that's enough!" Nick growls at him. "Stop! He's done!" Nick holds his arm back and Vince pushes him off the guy.

Once he stands with Nick still holding on to him, Vince is on his knees next to the guy. "Do you want us to call you an ambulance?" Vince asks the guy loudly.

"Fuck you!" the guy yells at the old man. He gets up and shoves Vince out of his face.

"The wise choice would be for you to leave," Nick tells the guy with steel in his voice.

"Let's get out of this shitty place," Melissa says.

Her group of friends makes a scene while they head to the door without even waiting for this guy, who's still giving him the side-eye like he wants to go another round. The jerk spits on the ground before he walks away and out the door.

- 66 -

Frankie

His lips are back on hers, guiding her down on the couch. He sits down beside her and her hands are trying to pull his shirt off over his head. He pulls her sweater over her head before taking his shirt off.

She can feel the difference in his body language, the vibe and energy permeating off of him. It's intense, barely contained.

His eyes, dark with fiery desire, are pulling her into his web, daring her to join him. It's a new kind of intensity for her and for them. Their lovemaking has been growing in intensity but was always filled with passion and care. This new charge of electricity he's introducing to her is one of pure lust and promises of a new high.

He shoves the coffee table hard out of his way before sitting on the floor, pulling her leggings and panties off together. It takes him one second to pull her to the edge of the couch, his hand holding her legs up before assaulting her with his magnificent lips and tongue. The assault sends a shock wave of excitement through every cell of her being, her body arching, lips parting, letting a loud moan escape.

She loses track of the seconds and minutes that pass by as he tastes her and taunts her body, making her beg for more. And just when she thinks she can't hold on anymore, his lips leave her sensitive, now swollen, clit.

He swiftly flips her, putting her on her knees, her hands placed on the back of the couch now. His hand travels up her body, unhooking her bra. She can feel him leaning on her, can hear him unzip his jeans. Then his hand leaves her skin and fists her hair, his moist lips on her neck.

"Do you want me?" he asks into her ear while his fist pulls on her hair.

She nods her answer. *YES!*

"Tell me," he demands, pulling on her hair a little harder.

"I want you." The words escape as she surrenders to him.

His lips cover hers when she feels him line up at her slit, pushing deep into her in one stroke, stretching her. His lips leave hers and the sound of her moan follows when he withdraws from her.

"I need you," she whispers through a shiver. Her body needing his, her soul needing his warmth.

His hand now on her hip pulls her onto him. Not giving her time to adjust to him, he's already slamming his hips back and thrusting in again, plunging even deeper. His pace is fast and hard. Primal. *Fucking.* That's what he's doing. He is fucking her and driving her insane. The sound of each time their bodies meet mixed in with the gasps and screams she can't stop from escaping fills the whole apartment.

His hand travels from her hip to her lower back, pushing her down, arching her even more. She plants one hand against the wall, seeking anything cool to help her hold on. Crossing her ankles, hoping to enjoy the ride a little longer, only causes him to go even faster and deeper, his low guttural grunts growing louder with each thrust.

"I'm coming! Baby, I'm coming," she whimpers and screams. How that's possible, she can't be sure.

He pulls even harder on her hair and she explodes. She closes her eyes, tossing her head back as bright stars burst before her eyelids. An orgasm so magnificent her ears ring from the rush.

His arms come under hers, pulling her up against him while he continues to fuck her with even more vigor as she rides out the waves of ecstasy, sending her further and further out.

"We're not done yet," he says into her ear in a low, husky voice. B

efore she can collect half her thoughts, one arm wraps around her waist. He moves them, positioning them to where he now sits on the couch and she's on top of him, the hot liquids from her orgasm helping her slide all the way down on him.

"Ride me, Frankie," his low voice growls into her ear. "Fuck me with that beautiful pussy," he commands her.

So fucking sexy.

Both of his hands are on her hips, already holding her down onto him, moving her to grind on him, sending pure pleasure through her again. Her hips dance and twirl on him. Her hands travel up her own body, grabbing a hold of her breasts.

"Fuck," he whispers when she begins using her legs to lift herself off of him to come back down, again and again, taking all of him. His hands leave her hips. They travel up along her body to cover her hands, making her squeeze hard, causing her nipples to perk at the attention.

She tilts her head back at the exhilaration.

"That's it, baby," he says to her. "You fuck me too good. I got hooked on this pussy the moment my dick slid in."

The confession gets her soaring. The way he handles her, the directions he gives her. The raw sexiness of it is a form of torture all on its own. It's the perfect touch of dirty yet erotic in it's own way. This side of him can be addicting. Even more addicting than the way they made love every other time.

She picks up his finger and brings it to her lips, sucking on it before giving him a little bite.

"Oh fuck," he hisses.

His growl encourages her to grind deep down on him again and again. Lifting off and coming back down fast and hard on him until she nearly explodes all over him again.

Slowing down and trying to catch her breath, she leans back on him. Her head resting on his shoulder, eyes closed as she enjoys the feel of him completely encased by her. Her hips move, her body pleading for him. His hands hold her hips in place as he begins to thrust into her from beneath. Pounding relentlessly.

"Baby," she whispers.

"Say you're mine," he says into her ear as he thrusts in harder. "Tell me," he demands.

"Yours," she says breathlessly. She melts into him. "I'm. Coming. Again," she gasps, warning him before everything that follows are only moans and whimpers, her insides screaming in pure pleasure and turmoil.

She unravels and spirals into a sea of bright starbursts again.

She hears a low growl, can feel it coming from his chest right before he slams her down on him and fills her with his seed. His raging cock throbs and pumps fast into her, jet after jet after jet of him completely filling her, sending her further out into bliss than she's ever been with him or anyone else on the planet.

It takes more than a few moments for her to return back to her body again. She lies on top of him, spent. She can hear the sound of his breathing begin to slow down. The rate of his heartbeat a steady thud again.

- 67 -

Frankie

After they finally decide it's time to leave their apartment, they arrive at the farmers' market just past four o'clock, wandering from booth to booth, buying fruits and vegetables until Cole spots Nick holding Nat and walking to them. Karmen is looking at something at a table right behind.

"Hi," she says flatly to Nick. "Thanks for meeting us."

"Sure," he says nonchalantly.

"It's not as cold as I expected it to be," Karmen says, coming up to give her a hug. "So, what's all this about?"

"Let's find a warmer place for us to talk." She heads over to an area with sufficient seating and a heat lamp that is blasting.

Cole sits down next to her. Karmen and Nick take seats with the kids, who are playing with the new toys they just got.

"I know you plan on having the baby at the farm," she starts. "And I was kinda worried and brainstorming about what we can all do to make a living there. I came up with a couple ideas and wanted to run them by everyone. Plus, I wanted to introduce Nick and Cole to someone who might be able to help us implement that idea.

"Nick, I don't know if you had anything in mind for the farm but I'd like to know now if you do," she says to him.

"I haven't thought about it before but have been thinking about it more lately. But I came up empty."

"Well, what do you all think about possibly leasing out twenty acres for farming? Specifically hops farming," she says, looking at everyone, who stares back at her in silence.

"I've been doing some research and found that most of the breweries here get most of their hops from farms in Colorado and Montana. There's actually a niche for it with microbreweries popping up everywhere."

"And how does leasing the land actually work?" Nick asks.

"I'm not a hundred percent sure about the logistics of it, but I know someone who's meeting us here in a few minutes to discuss that. His name is Eric and he owns a brewery here in town. He's actually in the market to do exactly what I'm talking about. He's a master brewer and has a degree in agriculture too."

She looks at everyone around the table again.

"I think that if the two of you are interested in really learning about brewing as a business, he would be an excellent teacher and possible business partner. I've done the research on that and have found a couple breweries in the Colt Springs area. Bozeman has a couple of hops farms already and the numbers are growing."

Cole stares at her as if she's gone bonkers.

"I'm sorry if this sounds ape-shit crazy. As I said, I don't want to step on any boundaries and I was just brainstorming."

"It does sound ape-shit crazy *but* at the same time, it sounds like something we can actually do," Nick tells her.

Cole still hasn't said a word.

"Say something," she says to him.

"How does your little head come up with all these ideas? You never cease to amaze me," he says to her.

She smiles at him and sees Eric behind him. "Eric!" she yells and waves him to come join them. She gets out of her seat to greet him and he pulls her into a bear hug.

"Frankie! It's been way too long! You keep disappearing on me."

She smiles at him and turns around to introduce him to everyone. "Eric Powell, this is my...uh, fiancée, Cole Howard. Cole, this is Eric."

The two men shake hands.

"Fiancé? Congratulations!"

"Thank you," she tells him. "And this is his brother, Nick. That's his fiancée and my best friend, Karmen," she introduces everyone.

Eric takes a seat after shaking hands with both Nick and Karmen.

"I kinda filled them in on the idea but I'm sure they have questions for you."

"I'll try to clear everything up as best as I can," Eric says to the table. "I guess you want to know why I'm looking to do this in the first place."

He looks from Cole to Nick. "The obvious answer would be because I'm in the brewery business. The less obvious answer would be that because breweries are popping up left and right, we all end up getting our supplies from the same places and we basically end up with some of the same product just with different names."

"Makes sense," Cole says.

"So, for a brewer like myself, who *wants* to stay in the business long term and who enjoys doing what I do…I think naturally, I'd want to get in the business of farming my own hops and maybe even creating something better than what I've been using. Give me an edge. Of course, I wouldn't throw everything I have into experimenting on a strain right off the bat. I'll start with what I know for profitability, at least. My project plan is to grow what I know and allocate a portion of my rented land to try and develop something new."

"And how would this all work?" Cole asks.

"Well, we'd first have to discuss in detail what the expectations are as owner and tenant. We'll have to discuss and come to an agreement on what would be included in the lease. Things like building structures, farming equipment, farmhands, et cetera.

"We'll also have to discuss what's off-limits. That's usually like property lines and such. Fortunately, land leasing is pretty common and in Montana, you should be able to find amazing attorneys and agents who specialize in farm leasing. They'll be able to handle everything for you from checking the soil conditions and evaluating the property to get you the best lease rate possible.

"I'd want to start with at least a four-year lease. With hops, it can take anywhere from three to four years for a hundred percent production. Frankie mentioned to me that you might be interested in learning the brewing business. Crop share has been known to be written in leases and that's something I wouldn't mind discussing either. Sort of like bartering."

"How do you intend on marketing against the competition if you say there are many others in our state already growing?" Cole asks.

"That's a good question. Breweries are indeed growing in numbers, but we're still a small community. Just in the Portland area here, I have more than enough buyers who are already interested in finding something new to use AND they want to be the first to use it."

"What normally happens at the end of the lease?" Nick asks.

"That too would be discussed before anything is signed. Generally, we either continue with a new lease or if things don't work out, we end our agreement. Any equipment that I've put into the land will be removed unless we negotiate a sale. Things like irrigation systems that are installed are usually sold to the landowners since it really wouldn't do any good for someone leaving the farming business behind unless they're simply relocating."

She sees the two brothers look at each other. She can't really make out what they are thinking or silently communicating. But if she has to guess, they probably need time to let things sink in. Cole probably wants to do some research of his own.

"Hey, Eric. Thanks for all your time. I think we all have things to think about," she tells him.

"Of course! Here's my business card." He hands one each to Nick and Cole. "If emailing is easier for you, it works for me too. Shoot me any questions you have, any time of day."

"Thanks, Eric. We'll be in touch." Cole is first to stand and shake Eric's hand. Nick follows suit.

She waves at Eric as he walks away. She looks back at everyone sitting at the table. "Is it too much?" she asks nervously. "I mean, I don't expect an answer now but is it something you guys will consider?"

"It's definitely very enticing," Nick says.

"But it's something we don't want to jump into without knowing more details, baby."

"Of course not. I wouldn't expect anything less. I know you'll have to do your own research and stuff. But at least it's an *idea*?"

"It's a great idea," Nick says. "It gives us somewhere to start, at least."

"Karmen? What do you think?" She's been silent the whole time.

"I think I'll let you guys worry about this stuff. You guys just show me where to work and what to do and I'm there."

"But you have a say too. You'll always have a say. You know that, right?"

"And you know when I have something to say, no one's going to stop me from saying it, Frank. But in this case, I really don't have an opinion yet. I've been stressing and worried about how we're going to make a living out there and if this is an option, then I'm in."

"Well, there is something else that I've been working on. Mostly for me and Karmen. I can't show you anything right now. It's just that it might require an acre or two? Possibly as close to the main road as possible?" She looks from Cole to Nick.

"Give her an inch and she takes a mile," Nick mumbles.

- 68 -

"It's going to suck having to go back to work tomorrow after having so much time off," she says.

She's been watching TV on the couch while Cole is on his laptop, answering emails and doing research on various things, including the farm leasing idea. She's glad that he's taking a genuine interest in it.

"I'm gonna miss having you home all this time," he says, picking up her feet and massaging them.

"Mmm...that feels good," she says with a stretch.

"Sometimes I really wonder where I'd be if it weren't for you," he tells her.

"Some motel with some hot blonde, having amazing, growly hot sex, I would imagine."

He laughs at her. "Do you imagine stuff like that often?"

She rolls her eyes at him and shrugs.

"After you, I can't even imagine being with anyone else," he tells her.

Yeah. That just melted her.

"But before me, you must've had women lining up at your door. You're so freaking gorgeous!" She hums in pleasure at his foot massage. "After you, I didn't think about anyone else," she tells him. "There were days where I wondered where you were and nights where I racked my brain trying to imagine what you look liked." She pulls on his arm and he releases her feet to move closer. "I'll never regret being with you that night."

His hand touches her cheek tenderly. "Thank you, Frankie. You are just...amazing. The most amazing woman...the most amazing person, I've ever known. And I just want to be able to be a man that you're proud to stand next to."

"Cole, I would stand next to you any day, any time, and anywhere." She leans forward and kisses him again.

He returns her kiss with fervor, pulling her into him. The fire between the two of them is still undeniable. It's been undisputable from the very first time their lips touched. He brings a new zest to life for her, something she has been missing and didn't even realize it until she woke up that morning long ago and found her bed without him.

Now, she can't imagine returning to her old life sans Cole. She wonders if he knows that. Before she has time to dwell on that anymore, he scoops her up and they are on their way to the bedroom.

Hours later, she wakes to the sounds of sirens and commotion passing by the window. She can see the lights flashing even through the drawn curtains.

Something is going on because even with how busy their street is, it's never like this. She sits up in bed.

"What is it?" Cole asks from next to her.

"The sirens, they're too close."

She climbs out of bed and goes to the window. Looking right first, in the direction that a police cars are driving from. And then to the left where it heads.

Fire! There's a fire!

"Oh my god! Cole! I...I think there's a fire! I think it's the bar!" she screams, watching the blaze light up half the block. The smoke filling and the flames illuminating the night winter sky.

He's by her side in seconds and pulls the curtains apart to look for himself.

"Get on your phone and call Vince, Frankie. I'll run down there and see. Get dressed and meet me down there in the truck, okay?"

Her hand is already swiping at her phone. She looks down at the notification on the screen.

"Shit!" There are two missed calls from the alarm company for the bar. That means they already tried Vince and he hadn't answered. They would have reached Karmen by now, maybe even Donnie.

"Baby, stay calm." He kisses her head before he's out the bedroom door.

She can hear the sound of the beeping on the keypad before the door opens and closes.

She runs to her closet and grabs a pair of sweatpants from the top of her laundry basket. Her fingers are still trying to dial Vince's number. She didn't think Vince would be such a heavy sleeper unless his phone is on silent just as hers had been. She slips on the sweatpants and rummages through her closet for a sweater just as her phone buzzes.

She swipes to answer it. "Karmen! I think the bar is on fire and Vince isn't answering."

"I know! The security company called me. I can't get a hold of Vince either and Nick is already heading down there. I'll be there as soon as Granny gets here to stay with the twins," Karmen says, sounding very worried. "The bar's closed tonight. There shouldn't be anyone there, Frankie. Stay calm."

"Cole's already running down there. I'm getting dressed and heading over. I'll keep trying Vince."

They both hang up without saying another word. She puts her phone on the counter and slips her arms into her sweater, zipping it as she slips into the closest pair of sneakers available.

She hears the sound of the door opening and grabs her phone off the counter. Running out of the bathroom through the bedroom, she expected to see Cole but comes to a dead stop at the sight of the man standing in front of the door. A stranger yet familiar.

"How did you get in here?" she asks, backing up.

"The same way I got in the other night, I guess," he answers with a shrug and smirk.

She knows that voice. The stranger in the alley. The one she ran into on the walk home alone. She's heard it in her nightmares too. Then, it hits her like a freight train.

"*Dusty?*"

"You remember. I'm flattered."

She tries to make a run back into the bedroom, her fingers trying to dial 911.

Her hair is yanked hard and she stumbles backward. His hand grips the back of her neck and slams the side of her head into the frame of her doorway, creating a different kind of bright stars. It's déjà vu all over again.

"That's for all the trouble you've been giving me." He slams her head against it a second time.

"Do you know what it feels like to listen to you getting fucked by my buddy time and time again in the next room? I mean, I've heard Cole make bitches moan before but not the way you do."

He spins her around to face him and tries to kiss her. She turns her head quickly even through the throbbing pain.

"Fucking bitch!" he yells before connecting the palm of his hand to the side of her face.

The sound of the slap echoes through the room, drowning out everything else. The slap throws her off balance but he catches her by the front of her sweater, standing her up then landing a punch to her stomach followed by a second blow, toppling her over.

Her phone slides out of her hand and she can hear the sound of keys jingling before she slips into the dark.

- 69 -

cole

"Cole! Cole!"

He turns around to see Nick in his car on the street and runs over to it.

"It's Vince. I'm gonna ride with him in the ambulance to University. It's really bad. Can you go pick up Frankie at the apartment? She should have been here by now."

"Yeah. I'll call Karmen and have her meet you over there too." Nick grabs onto his arm before he turns away. "Is he going to make it?" Nick asks.

"Honestly. I don't know, man. It's really bad. The girls need to get down there as soon as they can."

Nick nods and drives off.

He runs back over to the ambulance and jumps in, thanking the paramedic for letting him ride along with the old man. He wouldn't feel right having Vince ride alone.

He was told that a passerby managed to help Vince get out before the flames got to him but he was beaten to a pulp.

The paramedic lifts his shirt up to get a better hearing through the stethoscope. "Shit!" the guy says.

Cole looks up at the guy's scrunched face.

"Bernie! Foot on the pedal, buddy. He's got multiple stab wounds to the abdomen here," the medic hollers.

What the fuck? Who would do this to Vince? He can't help but reach over and hold his hand.

"It's bad, isn't it?" he asks the paramedic, who nods at him in response as if his grim facial expression isn't an answer enough.

The guy calls a code into his radio unit and can feel the lurch of the ambulance when it picks up even more speed.

Almost ten minutes later, they are coming to a screeching halt at the ambulance bay of the emergency entrance.

He's been here before for Frankie.

Frankie. Where is she? In his haste, he forgot to grab his phone off of the night table before leaving. She should be here with him by now.

The ambulance doors pop open and two nurses with a doctor ready to help the paramedics bring the gurney down. The nurses push the gurney in, the paramedic who was in the back with him rattling off Vince's stats.

"Cole!"

He turns around and sees Karmen running to him.

"Karmen! Be careful."

He holds onto her elbow as she runs in after the gurney.

"What happened? Is that Vince? How is he?" she asks, in hysterics.

"The bar is gone, Karmen. I'm not sure what happened but by the time we woke up and I got there, it was already in flames. Someone walking by pulled him out."

"We were closed today. What was he even doing there at this time of night?"

"I don't know. But it's bad."

Her phone is ringing and ringing and she finally answers it. She looks up at him and hands him the phone. "It's Nick."

"Nick," he answers once he takes the phone from Karmen. "Hold on, man. Mick is here in the ER. Looks like he's on duty tonight. He's coming over."

"Cole! Wait! Let Eric talk to Karmen. Matter of fact, have him call Alice to go down there ASAP," Nick yells at him in a rush of words.

"Why? What's wrong?" He can feel something is wrong in the pit of his stomach.

"Look, I need you to keep your shit together," Nick says, pulling the trigger into his gut.

"What the fuck is wrong?" he barks.

"When I got to your place, your truck was already gone. I barely caught a glimpse of it heading down the street away from the bar. Frankie wasn't the one driving. She's not answering her phone either."

"WHAT!" he hollers. Both Karmen and Mick turn to look at him and he runs over to them.

"Mick, can you call Alice to come down here and stay with Karmen? Karmen, I need your car keys. I need to go now and I need to take your phone with me."

"Cole, what's going on? And where's Frankie? Why isn't she here?" Karmen hounds him.

"Karmen, please! I have to go now!"

She nods her head and shoves the keys into his hands while Mick is on his phone.

"Mick, thanks, man!"

He runs out of the ER doors, clicking the remote on the key fob in every direction trying to find where she parked. Luckily, he spots the flashing lights on the Camry quickly enough.

"Nick! Where am I going?" he asks, already running full speed to the car.

- 70 -

Frankie

She can feel herself floating. *NO! Not floating.* Just moving. She's lying in the back seat of a moving car. Her hands are tied behind her. She opens her eyes and everything is dark. She is inside of a truck. Cole's truck, to be exact.

"I really did like this truck. It's the closest thing to a home for over a year. Before that, it was a black truck," Dusty says before removing his seatbelt and turning around in his seat to look at her. He pulls the center console cover open and takes out a box of condoms.

"Do you really think you're the only one? You're just another one of his sluts. We go through a shit ton of them. If this truck could talk, the shit it'd be telling you...some of the stuff would sound like narration for porn," he says before getting out of the front seat.

The back door swings open. He reaches for her legs and she tries her best to kick at him, to keep him from touching her while she screams bloody murder.

"You love playing hard to get, don't you," he says to her.

He pulls on her legs, dragging her to him over the leather seats. He grabs her by the front of her sweater and sits her up. The backhand comes immediately, snapping her head sideways before he drags her out of the truck. It seems like they only walk a few feet before they go through a door into a dark hallway.

Her face is burning and her stomach is aching badly. She takes short breaths to ease the pain. She can't see very well in the dark but it seems he knows exactly where he is going.

They walk past several doorways and she gets a glimpse at one with light coming out of it. It looks like an old office of some sort. Dilapidated with trash and broken chairs everywhere.

He pushes her inside a large room lit up by a couple of dim lamps. There are desks, a couple of chairs along with trash, and wooden crates in the room. Behind one desk, she can see what looks like a mattress and some blankets.

He shoves her over to that area and shoves her down on top of the mattress. On top of the chair that faces the mattress, she sees her missing backpack and her old laptop.

"Let me go and I won't tell anyone what happened?" she tries to negotiate with him.

"Does that line ever work for anyone?" he asks. He pulls a phone out and looks like he's texting someone.

"Cole will kill you when he finds me," she tries to threaten him.

"Good thing I'll be long gone. Not sure what'll happen to you by then though."

He reaches for one side of her unzipped sweater and pushes it aside, off of her shoulder. She cringes, repulsed by him. His fingers trace down her neckline to the pendant of her necklace.

"Pretty sparkly piece," he says before tugging it off of her neck and putting it in his pocket. The sting of the chain cutting into her skin burns immediately.

He looks down at her hand and she tries to hide her ring from his view.

"Cole always did have good taste when it came to jewelry."

He flattens her balled fist and pulls the ring off of her finger too. Unable to control her anger, she spits in his face.

"Fucking bitch! You just want me to hurt you, don't you? Gets you wet, doesn't it?"

He raises his balled fist and brings it down like a hammer to the side of her head, almost completely knocking her out. She didn't even know the scream she heard came from her own mouth until the drumming in her ears begins to fade.

She's dizzy and it feels like she has no control of her limbs. She feels him further parting the front of the sweater before he disgustingly gropes her. What's left of her energy surges through her arms and legs and she tries her best to fight him off.

It only angers him more and he reacts by grabbing her by the hair, holding her in place as he slaps her across the face again and then repeatedly punches her stomach. She can taste blood coming from somewhere.

Dazed and confused, she feels him pulling her up off of the bed. Her legs don't have the strength to hold up her weight. The pain in her stomach causes her to gasp for quick, short breaths to keep conscious.

Holding her up, he turns her around to face the desk. He tries to pull her sweatpants off of her and now she's really scared shitless.

"NO! NO!! Stop it! Stop!" she screams.

She musters up some strength and sends her head back into his jaw as hard as she can. Within a second, she feels a searing pain surging from her bare shoulder as his teeth bite into her.

She screams as loud as she can, tears streaming down her face while she tries to stand up and away from his mouth. Her hands are on the desk, trying all she can to push herself up. Even through the pain, she's afraid that if she falls down, it'll be over for her.

He releases his teeth from her, only to kick down on her right leg with what feels like the weight of an anvil dropping on it. She feels her knee giving out and screams in agony, still trying to hold herself up on the table by her bound hands but flopping back down.

"Dusty! WHAT THE FUCK ARE YOU DOING?" A familiar voice booms from the doorway and she looks up.

Nick! Nick is here.

"Nick," she gasps.

His name escapes her lips with a few drops of blood. It lands on her hand. She's barely hanging onto consciousness and sees the crimson dots blurring in front of her.

Nick is here to help her now. She's going to be okay.

"Hey, man," Dusty says. He's still holding onto her head by her hair.

"Let her go," Nick says.

"Can't do that. She's kind of a cash cow right now."

She can hear Nick's booted footsteps getting closer.

"I wouldn't do that. Get too close and all her brain meat will get all over you," Dusty says. "I don't think you can beat the shit out of Cole for him forgive you for that."

Something cold is pressed against the back of her head.

"Put that away. I can get you what you want. You don't need her." Nick tries to bargain with the slime ball.

"Didn't know you had it in you to care about anything but the money," Dusty says. "She must have really sucked you off good."

"Shit," she hears Nick mumble.

"Finally! Took you long enough to get here," Dusty says.

She doesn't comprehend what he is saying anymore because everything is going dark quickly now.

"Tie him up before he causes trouble. We can use him."

It's the last thing she hears before succumbing to unconsciousness.

"You're supposed to be the tougher of the two, aren't you?" She hears a familiar voice speaking when she regains some semblance of consciousness.

She hears what sounds like someone slapping something. She opens her eyes and finds herself back on the mattress.

She quickly checks herself out to see if...if she has her clothes on. Thank god everything is still on even though every inch of her body is on fire with pain.

"Wake up." She hears the familiar voice again. "You're gonna make a phone call to your brother and you're gonna tell him to bring the twenty-five grand we know you have on hand."

"They easily have more than twenty-five, man!" Dusty exclaims.

"Do you want to wait until they can get to a bank to get it?"

She sits up slowly, trying to be as quiet as possible. Her knee is throbbing and she can't tell if she's able to walk on it.

Her watch! She sees her watch and swipes on it.

It has its own SIM card and that means she should be able to dial for help, right? She swipes to the phone interface. *YES!* She quickly dials 911 and shoves her arms under a bunch of blankets, trying to hide the ringing.

Someone answers but before she can say anything, Dusty is standing in front of her again.

Oh god! Please don't hang up! Please don't say anything! If the dispatch can just listen in, then no one will know that she's even on the call, right?

"She's up!" Dusty yells at his buddy.

He drags her to her feet and she feels her knee painfully give out even while she pulls her sweater sleeve over the watch. Her head spins and it takes a moment for her to focus on what's in front of her.

Nick is sitting on the floor. His hands are tied up and hooked onto something on the wall above him. It looks like he took a really bad beating and she can see blood. He hasn't said anything since she regained consciousness.

A guy is kneeling in front of him.

"*Donnie?*" she asks in disbelief.

He turns around to face her. He stands and walks over to her and she can't believe what she's seeing. Donnie shoves Dusty off of her and she falls into his arms.

"I told you not to hurt her!" he yells at Dusty.

"Can't be helped. She put up a fight, man." Dusty smirks. "Oh please! Like you spiking her drink with sleeping pills every chance you got, waiting for your chance to get a piece of her isn't just as bad."

Her head snaps up through the pain. "Donnie?" she asks again. "What are you doing? Why are you doing this? You...you know Dusty?"

"Oh, baby girl." He brushes a kiss to her head and sniffs her hair.

She still can't believe what is happening and still can't make sense of any of it.

"I told him not to hurt you. He never follows directions." He leans down and places a wet sloppy kiss on her shoulder and she squirms out of his grip.

"What are you doing?! No!" She tries to push him off but it only throws her off balance and he pulls her into him again. "You're holding me for ransom?" she asks loudly, hoping whoever answered her 911 call is still on and can hear her.

"It didn't start out that way, baby. I'm sorry. See, Dusty and I...we're kinda family. In a twice removed kind of way. I told him all I wanted was your laptop. He had one job to do that night. Get in and get out. But I should have known he would fuck that up."

"You? You sent him there?"

"Biggest mistake of my life. It brought Cole into your life and that bastard took you out of mine."

"Are you crazy? I was never in your life!" she screams in his face.

"Don't say that! YOU are the love of my life! For four years, it was you and me! You are everything to me. All the times we spent together, picking up the pieces of that fucking shithole bar. Remember?"

"That was work, Donnie. We worked together. That was all," she says.

"There's chemistry between us. At least there was until Cole came along."

"No. There was never anything between us other than the bar, Donnie."

"And now that's gone..."

"You did that? You burned down Vinny's Place?"

"I didn't plan for it to go that way. But it worked out. The old man wasn't supposed to be there but he was and he tried to confront me. I didn't have a choice," he says.

She hears Dusty slapping Nick around again and turns her head to see Nick stirring.

"He's coming around," Dusty says. "Fucking bastard. Not so tough now, are you?" Dusty throws another punch into Nick's stomach.

"Neither are you if you have to have him tied up!" she yells over at Dusty before snapping her eyes back at Donnie. "What did you do to Vince?" she demands.

"What I had to. I had to get rid of him."

She shakes her head at his answer, not wanting to even imagine what that could mean.

"Oh, come on, Frankie! He deserved it! After all the hard work you and I put into that place, we weren't even getting a piece of it! Did you know that he's giving everything to Karmen and her brats? That ungrateful bastard had it coming."

She tries to shove him off of her again.

"Let her go! I'll make the call," she hears Nick speaking clearly.

"Finally," Donnie says, helping her hobble over to where Nick is tied up.

"He has the cash and can get it here in ten minutes," Nick says. "You're gonna have to call Karmen's number and you're gonna have to tell him where to bring it. I don't know the area."

She peeks down at her watch quickly and sees that the call timer is still going.

YES! If they can get an address, help would be here soon.

Dusty pulls her out of Donnie's arms and Donnie digs in his pockets to pull out a phone. He begins dialing and puts it on speaker for them to hear the ringing.

"Yeah."

She hears Cole's voice. It's a tone that she hasn't ever heard coming from him before. Cold and detached.

She squirms and Dusty holds her closer to him. His stench makes her stomach roll. He brings his lips down to her shoulder where he bit her and she struggles to get away from him as if acid were scorching her flesh.

He purposely drops her onto the ground and he puts his foot on her knee, putting unbearable pressure on it, making her scream as she tries to pull her leg out from under him.

"Dusty, you don't need to do that to her!" Nick yells. "I'll tell him!"

Dusty removes his foot, leaving her whimpering in pain.

"They want twenty-five grand for her," Nick says loudly.

"Where?" Cole asks.

Nick looks up at Donnie, who pulls the phone to his mouth.

"Burnside and NE 122nd. You'll know which building. Pretty sure you don't want the cops involved." He hangs up before Cole says anything and puts the phone back into his pocket before shoving Dusty off of her and picking her up.

"Kill him," Donnie tells Dusty. "We don't need him anymore."

"NO!" she yells even through the fire in her knee. "Cole's bringing the money. You don't need to hurt him."

"That wasn't part of the plan," Dusty says to Donnie.

"Fucking chicken shit. Here!" Donnie tosses a small bag over to Dusty. "I'll take care of this."

Dusty pulls out a gun and hands it over to Donnie before he retreats into the dark corner. She begins to squirm in panic. There's no way she can watch Nick get killed in front of her.

"If you kill him, then there's no way for us to be together. You'll have to be on the run from the police," she tries to stall.

"Are you serious, baby? You think Cole will get the police involved? Seriously?"

"I'd be a witness. Do you plan on killing me too? Cole will spend the rest of his life hunting you down if you hurt us."

"Of course not. You're coming with me," he says, his voice softening. "Do you really think you're that important to him? The guy fucked you and shared you with his own brother. Come on, Frankie. Stop being delusional. You're much smarter than that."

Why does he think Nick had...Dusty? Dusty had to have assumed.

"I'm not going anywhere Dusty is going. You know he...hurt me first," she tells him, touching his face.

"I know. I'm so sorry, babe. Don't worry about him. He won't be joining us. Or anyone else anytime soon. I'll take care of him just like I took care of the other son of a bitch who put hands on you."

She looks at him, not comprehending.

"The motherfucker from the lounge. The one both your boyfriend and Sam did nothing to when he basically fucked you on the dance floor. See, Frankie? No one can love you as much as I do."

Not sure what he's babbling about, she keeps pushing to stall for more time. "Sam? Was that you? Please tell me you didn't."

"Fucking Sam. He was always in the way. Never letting anyone get close enough. Every time I had something planned for us, there he was." He pulls her closer. "Thanks for allowing me to pay him back. He didn't die as I wanted but I got him out of the way long enough."

He's lost his mind! He's crazy!

Stall, Frankie. Get that gun away from him.

She brings his face closer to hers. She needs to distract him and buy time. The gun is still in his hand and they are standing too close to Nick. She looks at him as alluring as she can, given that her face must look like a bruised tomato right now. Donnie leans down to kiss her.

Even with bile rising in her throat, she shoves it down and returns his kiss while her hand slowly travels to the hand holding the revolver.

She opens her mouth and licks his lip, inviting his tongue into her mouth. She nearly gags at the taste of old cigarettes but is able to maintain her composure and starts to lean her weight into him.

She manages to back him away from Nick and the doorway a good two feet before she inserts her thumb behind the trigger and then chomps down on his tongue, holding it between her teeth while she tries to yank the weapon from his hand.

"Frankie!"

Cole?

Startled, she lets go of Donnie's tongue, allowing him to step back and punch her harder than Dusty did, landing it to the side of her head.

She topples over, taking him with her. She can feel both of their hands holding on to the gun now, playing a deadly game of tug-of-war.

There's a loud sound like bodies colliding. Even with her currently fighting for her life with Donnie, she catches brief glimpses of Cole pummeling Dusty in the dark corner of the room.

She can hear the sound of scuffling and muffled voices in the background before two...no three...shots ring through her ears, echoing in the room. She sees Cole just behind Donnie, who is still struggling on top of her.

Cole pulls him off but Donnie has his arms in a vise grip around her, bringing her up with him. He has her standing with her face pressed into his chest, holding her like a shield in front of him.

"You! You ruined everything good between us." Donnie spews his hatred into those words at Cole. "Come closer and I'll snap her neck!" Donnie warns. "You don't deserve her. She's mine."

She shakes her head. "No," she whispers, trying to breathe through his tight hold. "I was never yours. I'll never be."

He kisses the top of her head and she can hear more footsteps and voices coming from behind her. She feels Donnie tense up and tighten his hold around her shoulders more.

"Let her go and we can talk about this, okay?" a voice she doesn't recognize speaks.

She sees more light in the room like someone is using a flashlight.

"This doesn't have to end badly, all right?" another voice says.

"You'll always be mine, Frankie. Always. You'll never have her, you son of a bitch!" he yells before she feels a searing pain burning into her right side.

She feels the gun slipping from her hands and hears it hit the ground before another searing pain burns through her again.

Her body slithers down Donnie's and he's struggling to hold on to her just like she's struggling to stand. There's a huge red stain in the middle of his shirt sprouting outward before she hits the ground. She sees him falling to his knees at the same time.

The sounds of rushing footsteps hurrying above her are fading, just like the light around her is dimming.

"Oh god! Baby! FRANKIE! Hold on! Stay with me!"

Cole.

- 71 -

cole

"Oh god! Somebody fucking help her!" he yells at one of the cops who comes over to him after cuffing Donnie.

Two more cops enter the room, one stopping to free Nick, who rushes over to him as soon as his hands are free.

"Someone call for a bus! NOW!" the cop next to him hollers while he tries to put pressure on her wounds. "I need some help here! Where is that fucking bus!"

He takes off his sweater and tries to put it over Frankie's wounds. The knife is still protruding from her but he knows not to pull it out. Right now, it's probably what's keeping her from bleeding out too fast.

He turns around and sees two teams of paramedics rushing in. One pushes him and Nick aside.

"What do we have?" the guy urgently asks the officer still holding the cloth over Frankie's stomach.

"She's got multiple stab wounds and a gunshot wound to the abdomen area. Visible trauma to the head and face. Something is going on with her leg too, I can't be sure."

Mother of God.

Nick is sitting next to him, hunched over with his hand holding his gut.

He wipes the sweat from the tip of his nose and he can smell her blood on it. He looks at both his hands. Her blood covers each of his palms.

"She's losing too much blood," the female paramedic says. "Where's that fucking gurney? Get that line started," she tells her counterpart.

"This one's done. Two to the stomach. Someone call the coroner."

He looks up and sees the other paramedics who were checking over Donnie stopping their chest compressions. They're starting to peel off their gloves.

"Hey! There's another one over here!" another police officer yells at the paramedics, who rush over to the corner.

"Dusty," Nick says quietly to him.

He looks over to the corner.

"He's done. He foamed at the mouth. OD?" someone asks.

Probably, because although he should have killed Dusty with his bare hands, he didn't have time. He was too focused on getting to Frankie and getting her away from Donnie.

A third team of paramedics arrives and pushes by him with a gurney.

He stands up and watches as the team of four hurriedly puts her on the gurney.

"I'm going with her," he announces because no way in hell is she riding alone.

"Fine. Sir, I need you to ride with the other van and get checked out." The woman instructs Nick.

"I'll ride with you and take your statement. We were able to hear most of what happened through the call but I still need to go with you," a cop says to Nick.

He looks over at his brother.

Nick waves at him. "Go," Nick says.

He's out the door running alongside the paramedics. He grabs her hand and holds on tight while they hop in the back. A third paramedic rides with them to help keep the pressure on her wounds. His sweater is still wrapped around the wound with the knife still sticking out. One of the paramedics wrapped tape tightly around the wad.

"We need to step on it up there!" she yells up at the driver.

"Frankie. Don't leave me. Please? Stay," he says to her.

She weakly squeezes his hand. He might have imagined it but he doesn't think so.

He slides over in his seat to be closer to her, pulling her hand to his lips. He wipes a strand of her hair away from her face and sees the magnitude of the beating she took and it breaks him into a thousand pieces.

"Stay with me, baby."

"We're here! Teams already waiting!" the driver yells after what feels like a cross-country drive.

He looks out of the window and sees they've arrived at the same ambulance bay at the same ER that he was just at with Vince less than an hour earlier.

"Shit!" the paramedic says.

He looks at her and sees her taking off her jacket.

"We need to start chest compressions now!" she hollers over the multiple urgently beeping machines.

She climbs on top of Frankie, careful not to sit on the leg that is kept between wedges just as the back door flies open. Both of the male paramedics pull the gurney out, forcing him to let go of her hand.

He jumps out after them and runs full speed behind them, listening to the lady count as she pumps into Frankie's chest. They clear in through the sliding doors, and he sees both Karmen and Alice looking at him wide-eyed. They're both on their feet and running to him before they realize who's on the gurney rolling in front of him.

"Oh my god! Frankie!" "Frankie!" they both yell.

A team of nurses and doctors rush over. Mick who is still in his work scrubs, stops and covers his mouth.

He reaches Mick and shakes his arm. "Help her! You gotta help her, man!"

"Mick! Do you know her?" one of the doctors asks.

Mick nods his head. "Oh god. She's a friend," Mick answers the doctor.

"Everyone, get your shit together!" the other doctor yells trading placings with the paramedic.

They head behind another set of doors and Mick turns around to stop the three of them.

"I'm sorry, guys, but you can't go back there. I'll be back to update you as soon as I can." He turns to leave but turns back and looks at them. "You need to get whoever should be here, down here ASAP," he says solemnly.

His legs nearly give out from under him.

He moves his feet, backing up against the wall, hoping it will hold him up but he slides down against it until he sits on the floor, knees bent and arms resting over them. His bloody hands dangle in front of him.

"What the hell happened to her, Cole?" Alice asks.

"I...I have to call David," Karmen says. "He can catch a three-hour flight here."

"Karmen, sit down. I'll call him," Alice says.

He sees the tears coming down Alice's face. The two women are a lot braver than he. He can't face David right now.

He watches as Karmen takes a seat, holding onto Alice who is on the phone, crying, and nodding her head at the same time.

The sliding doors at the entrance of the ER open and Nick is walking in with a paramedic and the officer next to him. His brother looks cleaned up for the most part. He still has bruising and redness around his face. The paramedic he rode with probably had to check and make sure nothing was more serious than it looked.

He must have had a devastated look on his face because one look at him and Nick is already running over.

"It's bad. Her heart stopped just as we pulled in and they were doing chest compressions while they were taking her back." He can hear his own words but can't really grasp what he's just said. How did this happen? How did he *let* this happen?

"I know this isn't the right time but I need to take both of your statements while everything is still fresh," the cop says.

He points over to the chairs and gestures for them to head over to the corner.

Nick leads the way to where Karmen is sitting and he's able to pick himself off of the floor and follow.

"Where do you want me to start?" Nick asks the cop.

"There was a mention of a fire. Start there," the cop answers.

"Our girlfriends work at Vinny's Place, a bar in Southeast Portland. At about midnight, she gets a call from the alarm company saying that the fire alarm was set off. We have kids so she sent me down there first until our sitter could get to the house," Nick starts.

"My girlfriend, Frankie, and I live down the street from the bar. We heard the sirens. It woke her up. I got dressed and ran down to the bar first. I told her to drive there once she could get ahold of Vince, the owner of the bar. I get there and the place was engulfed in flames. An ambulance was already there. They said someone pulled Vince out. They brought him here earlier."

"I'll check on that. What's Vince's last name?" the cop asks them without looking up from his notepad.

"Battaglia," both Karmen and Alice answer.

"He pulls up at the scene and I tell him I was going to ride in the ambulance with Vince. I asked him to go pick my girlfriend up at our place and bring her to meet me here," he continues.

"When I pulled into their parking area, his truck wasn't there but I spotted it moving the opposite direction about two blocks away. I called her phone and she didn't answer and I knew he didn't have a phone on him so I made the choice to follow the truck," Nick says.

"Did you call the police at this time?" the cop asks again.

"No. I thought she was driving. I just didn't know where she was going. I followed for over ten minutes and lost her.

"It took me almost ten minutes to find the truck parked behind that building. I've never been there before and I didn't know what she would be doing there, so I went in through the only set of doors nearby and followed the voices. I heard her screaming for help and ran towards the only room with light coming out. I saw one of them." Nick pauses.

"Who and what did you see?" the cop urges him to continue.

"The one in the corner. He was...biting her." Nick takes a deep breath and looks over at Karmen, who leans into Alice. "He stomped into the back of her leg and had a gun pointed to her head. Then his buddy showed up. He tied me up and they beat the crap out of me until you guys freed me."

"And you, sir. Cole. You're brothers?"

He nods his answer.

"How did you end up there?"

"I was here with Karmen." He points over at Karmen. "My brother called me on her phone and said he couldn't get ahold of Frankie and that he was following my truck.

"He doesn't know the area they were in but he turned his location on his phone and shared it with Karmen's phone. Still, it only gave a general vicinity, not an exact location, and we still didn't know if she was driving or not. I lost contact with him when he said he found my truck and was going inside."

"We might have to check your phone records." The cop looks at them.

"That's fine," they both say.

"So how did you find them?" the cop asks.

"Karmen's phone rings and Donnie's name and number show up so I answered it," he replies.

"He's the one that was holding her when we got there," the cop says.

"Yes, sir. He also works at the bar with the girls. I thought he might be calling about the fire," he says, and it's the truth.

"I think we can take it from there. We have the conversation recorded," the cop informs them.

"You got there minutes after I did. How did you find her?" he asks.

"She called on her smartwatch," Nick answers.

"Because of the GPS, we already had units heading to the vicinity. Luckily our dispatcher muted herself and listened to the situation. That was clever of you getting him to spill out a location," the cop says to Nick. "Other than the ransom he was wanting, was there anything else he might have said as to why?"

"It seems he thought they were in some kind of relationship and then Cole came in between that. He sounded kind of delusional. And the other one was related to him somehow and was just doing his bidding. Donnie was the one that tossed that baggie at the other one," Nick says, deliberately leaving Dusty's name out.

"Do you know if they were ever in a relationship?" the cop asks with an arched eyebrow.

"No," both Alice and Karmen answer. "We're her best friends. They only worked together. That was it," Karmen finishes.

"He also mentioned something about Vince. I think he might have been the one that set the fire. He said Vince deserved it and tried to catch him doing something," Nick informs the officer.

"Do you know what that would mean?" the cop asks.

"I might," Karmen answers this time.

"Frankie found evidence of some money being stolen from the bar. She recently told Vince about it. There's an open investigation that she filed at the precinct over the bar's jurisdiction. I'm not sure how far that investigation's gone. She handled everything."

"We can check on that and get the information," the officer says as he scribbles more notes into his pad.

"Excuse me." The paramedic who walked in with Nick joins the group. "The nurses will bring over the necessary paperwork for you to sign. I'm heading out."

She looks at everyone before speaking again. "Good luck with your friend. The hospital has a chapel if any of you need one."

"I'll need to get your phone numbers and I'll be out of the way. A few detectives may stop by later when they're finished at the scene. This is going to be one hell of a case with three crime scenes," the cop tells them.

"Unfortunately, there will be a team combing through your apartment since she was likely taken from there. Of the three vehicles at the scene, the truck is going to be processed for evidence. The other two can be picked up. The sooner the better in that neighborhood."

He nods at the officer and they each provide the officer with the information he requests.

As soon as the officer leaves, he gets out of his seat and walks over to the double doors that she disappeared through. He should be in there with her instead of out here doing nothing.

Nick comes comes to pace alongside him. "Cole. I'm sorry I didn't do more. I just didn't...I didn't expect Donnie to show up. I thought Dusty was the only one."

He nods his head. There isn't anything he needs to say. No one thought Donnie would be a part of this. Especially Frankie.

"You should be with Karmen. She's had a rough night," he tells Nick.

"There's something else. Donnie said that he was the one that gave Dusty instructions to go to her place that night. For a laptop but Dusty fucked up and brought us along with him. Fucking Dusty also said something about Donnie spiking Frankie's drinks with sleeping pills every chance he got."

Donnie set this up from the beginning?

He looks at Nick in disbelief, suddenly remembering the night he came home and she hadn't heard him even through the noise he was making.

"You need to know that so you *don't* blame any of this on yourself."

But he did play a part. If they hadn't brought Dusty with them to Portland, if only they had ditched him like Nick had wanted to long ago,

Dusty and Donnie would never have had the chance to play this insanity out. He would have never met her but she wouldn't be lying on a gurney fighting for her life right now either.

The doctor he recognizes from when they brought Vince in earlier walks through the double doors and looks at him solemnly. Karmen rushes over. The doctor takes his scrub hat off and stuffs it in his jacket before looking back up at them. Alice and Nick are standing with them now too.

"I'm sorry," the doctor says apologetically to both of them. "He never made it out of surgery. The wounds were too deep and caused too much damage to his vital organs." He looks at them, waiting for them to comprehend the news.

Karmen leans on his arm and he pulls her onto his side, putting his arm around her as she cries as quietly as she can.

"We did our best. I'm so sorry. One of our counselors will be out to speak with you and help answer any questions you may have about what happens now."

The doctor walks back through the double doors and Nick pulls Karmen away. He looks over at Alice, who's been silent and still. He pulls her into his arms next and she sobs into his shoulder uncontrollably.

"How is this happening? We were just celebrating with each other two nights ago," she sobs.

The double doors swing open again and this time Mick comes running out.

Both he and Alice rush over to the guy.

"They're taking her up for emergency surgery. They won't know the extent of her injuries until they do a laparotomy and see the damages. I won't be in the operating room with her but I can take you guys up to the waiting area and stay."

Nick and Karmen join them, reading to follow.

"Before I take you guys, I have to give you all some warning. Her heart stopped when she was brought in and they had to use a defibrillator. They've cut off all her clothes and she's under a sheet. But she was bleeding out fast so the sheet can look gruesome.

"The doctors have also intubated her to help her breathe and she's already on a ventilator. She's got a nasogastric tube. That's a tube inserted in through her nose to remove air and fluids from her stomach."

"You mean she's not breathing on her own?" Alice gasps.

"No," Mick answers her.

"Oh god," Alice says, taking the words right out of his mouth while she reaches for his hand to steady herself.

"Come on," Mick says. He punches the button on the wall and the doors swing open. He walks quickly through the department and they all keep up with him. "There," Mick says, pointing. "We won't be able to go up in the same elevators but we all can go with her most of the way. The set of elevators we use will be just around the corner," he points.

He and Alice are still holding hands as they run over to the gurney that is being pushed out of the room. Alice stops short just mere inches from Frankie. She loudly gasps and sobs. Karmen is crying audibly behind them.

The sight of her nearly brings him to his knees.

The knife is still protruding out of her side, though his sweater has been removed from around it and a nurse is now holding a large gauze to it with pressure. He steps around the nurse and picks up Frankie's hand. There's an IV with the line taped to the back of it.

Her hand is so cold. He looks at the tube in her mouth and watches as the ventilator moves up and down. He can see all the dark liquid flowing from the tube coming out of her nose.

"Baby, stay with me," he pleads softly, hoping she can hear him.

"I'm sorry, sir, but we have to take her now," one of the doctors tells him.

He nods and lets her hand slip out of his again as they roll her away.

"Come this way," Mick says, ushering them around to another set of elevators.

"Thanks, man," he murmurs to Mick.

Alice is clinging on to Mick now. When the elevator doors open, he lets them step in first with Karmen and Nick after. He walks in last before Mick pushes the appropriate button and the door closes.

"Karmen, you have to get something in you when we get to the waiting room," Mick tells her. "There are vending machines up there with a decent selection. Nick, please make sure she has something to drink at least."

"I will. Thanks, Mick."

"Were you in the room when they examined her?" he asks. He needed to know.

"Yes."

"I need to know. How bad is it?" he asks without looking at Mick.

A brief silence passes before Mick speaks. "I'm sorry, man. But it's bad. She was hit with a .38 caliber at close range with no exit wound. I didn't get to see the results of the X-rays to know where it strayed.

"The bullet probably caused her some internal bleedings and the knife wounds are just as severe and deep. Whatever she was bleeding internally came gushing out through those wounds. Her knee is dislocated and she's got a hairline fracture on her arm. Extensive trauma to her stomach before the gunshot and knife. She took some major blows to her head and face too. There's going to be a lot of swelling there."

"Oh god," the words slip through his lips.

He leans back on the elevator wall, letting the coolness of the steel fortify him and help keep his wits with him.

Dusty. That brutal beating had to have come from Dusty. He remembers what Nick told the cop earlier. He said he walked in while Dusty was biting her. He heard her screams through the phone. If the motherfucker wasn't already dead, oh what torturous things he'd be doing to the slimy bastard right now.

"Donnie? He did all of that to her?" Alice asks in disbelief. "How could he?"

"And her chances?" Karmen asks.

"I'm sorry. I can't even guess if I wanted to," Mick says. "She has a major fight to get through. This is exploratory surgery, which means the doctors don't even know her chances as of right now until they're inside and see the damages as a whole."

The elevator dings and the doors open.

"To the left," Mick tells them.

They all walk past a nurse's station and Mick stops to talk to them briefly before he points them to the big waiting room. It's dimly lit for this time of night. There are about fifteen chairs and four long couches. Some of the chairs are placed around tables with books, bibles, and magazines on top.

"Try and get comfortable. It's going to be a long night," Mick says.

- 72 -

cole

The first couple of hours of waiting was a struggle for him. He couldn't stop pacing and he jumped at the sound of every footstep whether it was coming in their direction or not. Mick had been helpful, getting up and trying to find out as much information as he could from the nurses' station.

They are the only group in the room and after three hours of waiting, a counselor joins them and speaks to Karmen about Vince.

Vince. The old man didn't deserve what happened to him. His bar was gone as well.

Nick held Karmen's hand as they speak with the counselor. Alice had fallen asleep and Mick didn't have the heart to wake her. He couldn't blame the man. It's too much to take all in one night. He isn't sure how Karmen is even doing it.

The counselor hands Karmen a folder filled with paperwork and her business card before she stands up. Karmen stands and shakes her hand before the lady leaves the waiting room.

Nick brings Karmen over to where he sits. "Can she stay with you for a few minutes? I need to get cleaned up and see if I can find a shirt down at the gift shop. I'm going to pick up David soon."

Mick walks over to them and sits. "I can stay with her. Alice is asleep anyway. You both can go wash up over there." He points to the restrooms. "Nick, I have an extra shirt in my locker. I'll run down and get it when you get back."

Nick stands up and pats the guy on the back. "Thanks, man. Come on, Cole."

He follows his brother to the restroom and heads over to the sink once he steps inside. He turns on the water and sticks his hand under the running stream, watching her blood wash from his hand and down into the drain.

"It's not your fault, Cole. You know that. You can't carry the burden of someone else's actions," Nick says to him from the next sink over. "Donnie was already in her life long before you and I or Dusty came along."

He knows what Nick says is true. Still, he can't help feeling responsible.

"I shouldn't have left her there. We knew someone was stalking her and I left her with no kind of protection," he says with a tremendous amount of guilt.

"Oh, come on. You know better than that. There's no way to watch her every second of the hour against someone who was that obsessed with her. They would have managed to get to her somehow, sooner or later."

Nick is right again. But it just isn't enough to make him feel better.

"What am I supposed to tell her dad? How am I supposed to even look at him?"

"You answer his questions as honest as you can. Just like we did downstairs with the cop."

They continue to clean up in silence, side by side.

It wasn't that long ago, they were doing almost this exact same thing in some run-down gas station bathroom while they were on the road, bouncing from one city to the next. Except he didn't have blood on his hands. He didn't have the blood of the love of his life on his hands.

Nick lifts his shirt and checks himself out in the mirror. Huge round bruises cover his brother's stomach and pecs.

"Jesus, Nick," he says. "You sure you're okay?"

"Looks a lot worse than it is. Dusty's way of paying me back." Nick pulls the shirt back down. "Nothing's broken."

"I'm guessing Dusty took his frustrations out on her too." He pauses and takes a deep breath before he continues. "Did he...?"

"No! He didn't," Nick exclaims. "He tried but she put up too much of a fight. Why do you think he hurt her as bad as he did?"

He nods his head, thanking God she didn't have to suffer through that too.

They finish cleaning up in silence before heading back to the waiting room.

After two more hours, two doctors and a nurse finally come and take a seat with them as everyone gathers around.

"She's out of surgery and they're going to be transferring her to the critical care unit in a few minutes," the female doctor begins.

"She's not out of the woods yet. She's lost a massive amount of blood. We were able to stop the bleeding and repair the damage done by the knife. However, the bullet tore through parts of her intestine," the male doctor follows up.

Mick exhales loudly, his hand raking through his hair before crossing his arms over his chest. That can't be good be a good sign.

"What does that mean?" he asks and then looks at Mick.

The doctor takes a deep breath and looks over at Mick, who nods. "The intestine holds human microbiomes that are good for us in the right place. However, when these bacteria spill into the bloodstream, we now have to worry about septicemia."

"Blood poisoning," Mick says quietly.

Alice looks over at Mick and he's holding her hand, pulling her closer to him. Karmen is leaning into Nick too, pale as the white walls of the waiting room.

"Does she have a chance?" Nick asks.

"She has a chance. Right now, she's heavily sedated and we're going to be keeping her that way so that we can try to stay ahead of the fever and administer high volumes of antibiotics intravenously to give her a fighting chance against the infection. She's got some swelling in her head as well that we've got to overcome. Her knee dislocation has been reduced and X-rays don't show any fractures. She's got a splint on for that and a cast on her fractured arm."

"I wish we had better news for you all, but it's good she's made it this far considering all the trauma that she's suffered. The nurses are cleaning her up as best as they can. Mick can take you to her once they have her in a room." The female doctor looks over at Mick, who nods.

"She's ready," a nurse says from the doorway of the waiting room.

The doctors and nurses stand up quickly and walk out as the rest of them follow. The nurse that just came to announce the news hands the doctors a tablet each and they scroll through quietly.

"They're bringing her out right now," the nurse says.

A minute later, he can hear the sound of a squeaky wheel rolling before a set of doors opens. A team of three nurses wheels her out and his own heart rate drops. The nurses roll her over to the standing group.

Karmen lets go of Nick's hand and picks up Frankie's small one. "Hang on, Frank. I can't lose you too," she says, unable to hold back the stream of tears.

"God," Alice says under her breath.

She rounds the gurney and stands on the other side of her friend. Wiping hair away and pinning it behind Frankie's ear, she leans forward and kisses her head. "You keep fighting, Frankie. We're here."

The sound of the machines beeping and the ventilator breathing for her echoes in the hollowness of his aching chest. He finally moves his feet and walks to her. Karmen steps away and places Frankie's hand in his. He holds on to it tightly, bending down to kiss her black and blue cheek right above the strap that holds her breathing tube.

He leans closer to her ear and chokes back the rock caught in his throat. "I love you, Frankie. Don't leave me. I can't go back to life without you," he whispers, not knowing nor caring whether she can hear him or not.

"Her unit is ready," the nurse says. "You'll be able to stay with her longer there."

They begin rolling the gurney away and he's left standing as her hand slips out of his yet again.

"The ICU only allows two visitors at a time to be in the room with her," Mick tells them. "But there's an additional waiting room close to her for us to use."

"Karmen, I'll take a cab over to pick up our car and head over to get David. Call and see if you can have the Camry towed here." Nick looks at him. "Hang in there, baby brother. Keep an eye on her for me," he says, pointing to Karmen.

"Of course," he says.

"Karmen, there's nothing you can do for her right now. If you're intent on staying here with her, at least get some sleep. Please?" Mick pleads.

"Karm, I agree. I can't have something happening to you or the baby too," Alice begs.

Karmen nods her head at her friend's plea.

"I'll have them bring a cot for you and some blankets," Mick says. "Come on. The waiting room is this way. Give them some time to set her up in her room."

They get to the waiting room and Mick runs off doing what he needs to do. The guy left his shift early and has been helping them for hours now. He's probably exhausted out of his mind too.

"Cole, can you stay with her? I have to call and let Katrina know what's happening. We were both scheduled to work today," Alice asks.

"Of course," he says, walking over to where she left Karmen. "And thanks, Alice."

He sits down next to Karmen and watches Alice pacing back and forth through the glass wall.

"It was Dusty, wasn't it?" Karmen asks him quietly. "Dusty did that to her, didn't he?"

"You know about Dusty?"

She nods her head.

"When I got there, I didn't see Dusty. It was just her and Donnie, fighting over the gun. But Dusty barrels into me out of nowhere. Because of him, it took me longer to get to her. When the gun went off, I didn't even know she was shot. Donnie was on top and when I tried to pull him off, he held her against him. I didn't see who got hurt."

"Is he dead?" she asks. "Are they both dead?"

"That's what they said at the scene. Sounds like Donnie gave Dusty a hotshot. And I heard them say that Donnie was hit twice in the stomach. It didn't stop him from trying to..." He can't finish his sentence.

"God! Why did this happen to her? She never hurt anybody in her life. That shouldn't be her in there." Karmen starts to cry again.

"If I could switch places with her, I would. In a heartbeat without a second thought," he says, holding her hand.

"I never knew my dad. Don't even know if he's dead or alive. My mom passed away when I was eighteen and I barely survived, living with shitty boyfriend after shitty boyfriend. I never knew much about pride and self-worth until I met Frankie.

"She showed me how good it feels to be independent. Before Nick came along, her, David, and Vince were as close to a real family as I was going to get."

She looks up at him, her eyes red and watery. "Cole, how do I go home and tell the babies that their Papa Vince is gone now and that their Frankie is hanging on to her life by a thread? How do I do that?"

"I don't know," he whispers.

And he really doesn't know. He pulls her into his arms and holds her there, letting her cry it all out. She's kept it together all night and for hours during Frankie's surgery. If she needs to let it out now, then he isn't going to stop her.

"Hey, her room is ready," Mick says softly from behind them.

"You two can go first. I'll wait for David to get here," Alice says.

"Alice, I'll be right back," Mick tells her. He leads the way.

"Thank you so much for everything, Mick. You've been so much help," Karmen says.

"I haven't been able to do much, Karmen. I wish there were more I can do."

"Thanks, man. You've done a lot more than I can ever ask." He pats Mick on the back.

They round the corner to her room and he sees Mick using the sanitizer on the wall by her door. Mick motions for them to do the same before they walk in.

The room is extremely cold. Colder than she would have liked.

Parts of her are extremely pale. Other parts of her are black, blue, and purple. Her beautiful long hair is tied messily beneath her head. She has multiple bags and drips running in and out of her from nearly every corner of her bed. The ventilator steadily moves up and down from the top corner, next to the beeping vitals monitor.

Mick pulls a chair closer to the bedside for Karmen.

He walks around the other side of her bed, sliding the chair on that side closer to her. Before sitting in it, he holds her hand and leans over to give her a kiss on her head, and runs his hand over her hair lightly.

What I would give for you to just open your eyes right now. Even for a few seconds.

"Baby, I'm right here," he tells her softly.

He sits with her for over an hour before David walks into the room. Nick lingers behind him and Karmen steps out.

He leaves Frankie's side to meet David for the first time, not knowing exactly what to say.

David reaches for his hand and pulls him into a hug, patting him on the back. "It's not your fault, son."

Those words became his undoing.

He holds onto the much smaller man tightly and the tears just flow out of him. He can't remember the last time he cried. She's brought so much love and light into his shitty life and now? She's barely hanging on to hers.

"She won't want to see you like this. To see *any* of you like this," David says, pulling back from him and looking at everyone standing in the doorway now.

David looked tired and weary but determined. Frankie was so good at taking care of everyone around her even when she is suffering and stressing behind closed doors. He sees where she gets it from now.

"Karmen, I need you to get some sleep. I mean it, young lady. When Frankie wakes up, she's already got enough bad news to deal with. She does not need to know that you didn't take care of yourself and the baby too," David says.

"Nick...you have a job to do, son. *They* are your job right now," David says, pointing to Karmen. "You both need to check in on the twins too."

"Yes, sir," Nick says and pulls Karmen back to the waiting room.

"Alice, thank you for calling her boss. You're going to have to be the strongest of the bunch right now. If you need some rest, I think you should go now. Otherwise, if you can take some of the burdens off of Karmen, that would be great. Vince is going to need a proper place to rest. Can you call around and see about that? I know it's going to be rough but I know you can do it."

Alice gives David a hug. "Whatever I can do, you know I will." She gives David a quick kiss before heading off as well.

David quickly uses the sanitizer on the wall and rubs it thoroughly around his hands.

"Now let me show my girl how much I've missed her," David says as he steadily walks into the room. He walks over to the bed. David kisses her head tenderly. "Oh, my love. You always have a way of bringing people together, don't you?"

- 73 -

Eight days have passed by already.

On day four of that time, three detectives on the case stopped by. One asked question after question in regards to Nick being a felon and wanted to know how they ended up in Portland.

He's been worried for his brother. They make it a habit to run background checks on themselves to make sure they haven't gotten sloppy somewhere and there weren't any outstanding warrants that they didn't know about. They'd stayed clean this far.

What also has him worried is the possibility that they could be linked to Dusty.

The other two detectives explained that Dusty was staying inside the adjacent vacant apartment next to Frankie's. They weren't sure how long he was there but it had to be a couple of days, at least.

They also released his truck back to him after collecting what evidence they could find. Their apartment is no longer a crime scene. He's been back inside to get cleaned up and pack a bag with a few changes of clothes and to grab his laptop. He brought David back with him once just after they picked her car up from the shop.

Mick has been in and out both during his shifts and when he was off. Alice had to go back to work since Frankie is out. When she is off, she's either right in the room with him or she's sleeping on one of the couches in the waiting room.

David just left him alone about half an hour ago. He had asked the man to go take a nap because he looked like he needed it. David didn't put up a fight and got up, patting him on the back before leaving.

Currently, he's sifting through all the information that Eric emailed him. They've been emailing back and forth since yesterday. He has yet to tell Eric about Frankie and thinks, for the time being, it's better this way.

There is a light tap on the glass, and he finds Sam standing in the doorway. Cast on one arm and on one leg, propped up by a crutch.

"Shit," he lets slip from his mouth and quickly puts the laptop on the table and hurries over to help Sam. "Have a seat," he says, watching the guy hobble uncoordinatedly with the crutch over to the seat he just pulled out for him.

"My God," Sam says upon seeing her more closely. "What animal can do this to her?"

"They're both dead now," he replies with pure ice in his tone.

"I heard. Some detectives came to update me on my case. Said Donnie was the one that tried to do me in."

"That's what Nick said he heard him telling Frankie too."

"That night. When I was crossing the street. Someone called my name. That's why I stopped in the middle of the road so abruptly. The car came straight at me from the middle of the road like a bull going for a red flag."

"You think he was waiting for you?"

"It's possible. Frankie and I walked. He left the bar before we did. He had time to get there by car. I just don't know how he would know that I'd be walking with her."

"I don't think it was you he was waiting for," he tells Sam, who looks up at him. "I think he was waiting for her. He knew I wasn't home."

"And the other guy, the one that took her. How the hell did he get in the building? I checked multiple times a day to make sure that the alarm is on, especially when I knew she was home alone. There hasn't been a single incorrect entry of the code."

"That part, I don't know either. She wouldn't have given the code out to anyone."

Sam turns back and looks over Frankie. "How bad is it? The detective didn't tell me."

"It's bad. She's still fighting. Gunshot to the stomach. Two stab wounds. Broken arm and dislocated knee, plus what you see. The swelling around her face has gone down a lot in the past week. She has a low fever but they've been pumping her with antibiotics."

"Motherfuckers. Why? Why would they want to do this to her?"

"Donnie had some sick fantasy that he and she were in love and that you and I were in the way. I think things got out of control when Vince tried to confront him."

"I heard about Vince too," Sam says.

"Vince caught him cheating the bar."

Sam stays quiet for a while.

"Do you mind staying with her while I grab some coffee?" he asks Sam.

"Go," the guy says.

He figures he can live with Sam sitting alone with her for a bit. Let the man say what he needs to say to her.

He checks his watch. 10 a.m. They are on Day 10 and he's in the waiting room with their normal bunch.

Both Mick and Alice stopped in before they each had to start their work shifts. David and Karmen are discussing Vince's service coming up in four days. A service that Frankie won't be able to attend. Nick had just walked in earlier.

Doctors and nurses had filed into her room for the usual rotation, forcing him to leave her side. By now, he knows the routine, as sad as that might sound. In less than fifteen minutes, he'll be able to go back into the room and sit with her again.

And right on the dot, her two doctors come walking into the waiting room, a nurse right behind them with her clipboard. They walk over to the couch and sit down, giving everyone time to take a seat close by.

"So...she's got some fight in her," the male doctor starts. "Today's the last day of her antibiotic regiment and she's responded extremely well to it. Her blood tests have been making very good progress with no trace of infection," one doctor speaks.

"The damage that was done internally is healing. Not as fast as we'd all like for it to heal but progress is a good sign," the woman doctor says. "I think she's ready to move on to the next step, which is to stop the heavy sedatives. We don't want to keep her in this state longer than is necessary to avoid muscle atrophy and other complications."

"So, you're saying she can wake up soon?" David asks.

"Correct. Though how soon is a little harder to determine. Each patient is different. It can be as soon as an hour after the meds are out of her system. It can be a week. There's no telling. But with her progress, we do think it's time."

"And when will you be taking her off the meds?" he asks.

"We can sign the order now and the nurses can remove it from her drip. After that, it's a waiting game. We're both on tonight and we'll be here as soon as she needs us," the woman doctor says to them with an encouraging smile.

"Let's do it," David says.

He stands and shakes both doctors' hands before the doctors sign some paperwork.

"All right, everyone. Here we go," the male doctor announces with a smile.

- 74 -

Frankie

Oh my god! I can hear again! Why can't I see anyone? Why is it so freaking cold in here? Where is here anyway?

Dad? Is that you? Why can I hear your voice?

She racks her brain trying to piece everything together.

Cole! He was pulling Donnie off of her. Is he okay?

She remembers the sound of gunshots. The sound still rings in her ear. Then there was the pain. Like someone stuck her with a hot fork and scrambled around her insides.

She opens her eyes slowly but the bright light is too much and her lids are too heavy. It gives her an instant headache and makes her want to sink back into the dark.

Just for a little while longer.

"Frankie. Baby, I'm here."

Cole? She can hear him so softly. No, not soft but from a distance, like he is blocks away.

"Open your eyes, my love. It's time, Frankie."

Dad?

She tries to wrap her arms around herself for warmth but her arms feel like noodles and she ends up just tightening her fists.

"Stay with me, Frankie." She hears Cole pleading from so far away now.

Stay with you?

Baby, where am I going?

God. My head just hurts too much. I just need to take a little nap. Yeah. That's it. Just a little itty bitty one.

cole

"What happened?" he asks the doctor.

"It's a pretty good sign. She just wasn't ready to wake up yet," the female doctor answers. "Her vitals are still good, no drop in blood pressure. These are all very good signs. We just need to give her a little more time." She continues checking Frankie over.

He looks over at David, who pats the back of his hand with encouragement.

For the first time in twelve days, she slightly moved her head. He saw her do it and was next to her in half a second. His heart leaped when he felt her squeeze his hand. It was a weak squeeze but it was enough to give him the hope that he was needing.

"Cole, can you step out for a second so we can check her out?" the male doctor asks. "You too, David. Give the nurses some room."

He reluctantly leaves, David walking next to him.

"What's wrong?" Nick asks once they make it to the waiting room.

"Nothing. She moved. It seemed like she was waking up and then she was out again. The doctors and nurses are checking her over right now," he answers anxiously.

"That's good news, right?" Nick asks. "That has to be."

"Yes. Yes, it is," David says confidently.

Three days later, and they are still waiting.

Yesterday, they'd mourned for Vince. He hated leaving her for the funeral, afraid that she would wake and not see any familiar faces nearby. But he couldn't not go and pay his last respects either. Luckily, Mick was able to stay with her for the few hours until he could get back.

And now he's sitting in the waiting room waiting for the nurses to finish their routine of moving her and cleaning her.

David is lying down on the couch, getting some much-needed rest. Alice and Karmen are both sitting together, making arrangements about who would be picking up Vince's ashes from the crematorium.

Two detectives he recognizes walk into the room with a large box, halting all conversation and activity.

"We heard about the funeral services yesterday and held off with these," Detective Garza says, bringing the box over to the table.

"We need some help identifying some of the evidence we found at the scenes. It seems those two had been squatting at that abandoned building for a while. These are still marked as evidence and we can't release any items until the case is closed."

"Squatting? But Donnie worked two jobs. He made decent money to afford a place to live," Karmen says.

"Seems he was heavy into gambling. Might have owed a lot of people money. And the other one was a junkie. Probably shot up every dime he had or made. They've already closed the case with the fire and the bar owner's homicide. Before they put him in the ambulance, Mr. Battaglia gave one of the paramedics a flash drive. It was a video from a hidden camera inside the bar right before the fire. You can contact the detectives assigned to that case for any information you might need. The bar owner, he had a probate attorney that may have all the information already."

"Yes, he's been very helpful," Karmen says while the detectives begin pulling evidence bags out of the box and setting them across the table.

"These two pieces here were found on Dusty Chambless at the scene. Do any of you recognize them?"

He sees her necklace and picks it up off the table. "I gave her this necklace as a gift and that's her engagement ring," he says, pointing to another bag.

The detective pulls his notepad out of his pocket and begins taking notes.

"This one, this is hers given to her by her mother." David picks up the bag and looks at it before handing it over to him.

He looks it over. It's the necklace that she wanted back. The one she thought she'd never see again.

"That one was found amongst Donald Hoyt's belongings," Detective Pearson says. "We recovered her laptop at the scene too. Because it was synced with her phone, our techs think they might have used it to track her. They most likely used it to read her messages and even her emails. Technology can do a lot of harm in the wrong hands."

"That's how they must have gotten the access code to our building," he says.

"Most likely. Unfortunately, that piece of evidence won't be released anytime soon. It's tied to her abduction case, the fire, and the ongoing investigation about the check fraud." He jots down some more notes. "Do you recognize any of these other things?"

Alice and Karmen look over all the bags, shaking their heads as they pass them over to either him or David to check out.

"No," they all say, handing each bag back to a detective.

Once all the bags are back in the box, the detective puts the items belonging to Frankie on top.

"Thank you all for your help. How is she doing? I read the report sent over by the hospital," Detective Garza says. "I know it won't sound like it but she's very lucky she's come this far. She's very resourceful in getting help."

"She's still fighting," David tells the man.

"She's one hell of a fighter then." The detectives stand and shake his hand. "We'll be in touch. We'll still need to talk to her when she wakes."

He nods his acknowledgment.

He heads back over to her unit once the detectives disappear.

The nurse inside is putting her knee brace back on. "I'm almost done here. You can take a seat. Has anyone shown you how to help her with the stretches and the knee strengthening exercises? This knee is going to need it to heal properly."

"Yes, but I haven't done it. The nurses have been handling it," he replies.

"Well, the next time one of them is here for it, let them know you'd like to try. They'll be watching and can help you along the way."

"Thank you, ma'am."

He walks to the other side of her bed and leans in to kiss her head. A double beep comes from the monitor and he looks over at the nurse.

She quickly finishes placing the brace back before walking over to the monitor. "We have some activity here," she says. "Try talking to her," she directs him while staring at the monitor.

"Frankie. I'm here, baby. It's time to wake up," he says softly to her.

He squeezes her hand before bringing it up to his lips.

Her heart rate picks up a little on the monitor. The nurse pushes the intercom button and tells the nurses' station to page the doctor before she places her knuckles on Frankie's chest and rubs.

The heart rate monitor picks up some more.

He can feel her fingers squeezing his hand.

"Baby, come back to me," he says into her ear. "I'm waiting."

Another nurse runs into the room to join the one already there. "Dr. Shah should be here soon," she tells them.

"Can one of you please go get her dad?" he asks them. "I don't want to leave her right now."

The nurse that just came in nods at him and runs out of the room. The other nurse rubs her knuckles to her chest again. Firmer this time.

"Frankie, can you hear me? Come on, gorgeous. Let me see those beautiful eyes," he pleads to her.

She turns her head in the direction of his voice. Her eyelids squeeze tightly and her fingers tighten around his hand stronger.

David rushes into the room and the nurse moves closer to the machines to let him hold the other hand. "I'm here, my love. Wake up. It's time to give your old dad a sweet hug, baby."

The doctor walks quickly into the room.

Alice and Karmen are standing just outside, looking through the glass, holding hands.

"Baby," he calls her. He watches her eyelids slowly lift only for them to shut quickly.

"David, I'm sorry. I need to get in there," the doctor tells her dad.

David moves over to stand next to him.

"Frankie, it's time to get up, sweetie. You have a lot of people here waiting to say hi," the doctor says.

She rubs Frankie's chest with her knuckles firmer than the nurse did. "Come on," the doctor says, looking back at the monitor. The doctor nods at the nurse, who unclips something from the IV line.

A minute passes and she's definitely squeezing his hand. A lot harder and stronger than before.

"Baby, wake up. We have a wedding to plan and a farm to start working," he says. "Open your eyes, Frankie."

He holds his breath, watching her eyes open until the most beautiful green eyes he's ever seen peeks at him in confusion.

She moves her head and looks over at her dad with the same confusion.

"Frankie? Is that your name?" the doctor asks her.

She slowly turns her head in the direction of her voice.

"Is your name Frankie?" the doctor asks again.

She nods once. Her free hand comes up to her mouth slowly and touches the tube coming out. Her heart rate rises again and the doctor holds her hand away from the tube.

"You're in a hospital, sweetie. That tube is helping you breathe, okay?" the doctor gently informs her.

Frankie looks around the room before resting her eyes back on him, the look of confusion still written all over her face. She's scared. He can see it in the way she's looking at him. He can feel her struggling to move her hand to his face and can see more confusion at her inability to do so.

He leans forward into her palm. He'd give all his breaths to be able to comfort her.

"Is Dr. Patson on his way?" the doctor asks the nurse, who nods her head, eyes not leaving the monitor.

"Cole. David. I need you both to step out and let us take a look at her, okay? It'll be just a moment. I promise," the doctor says to them.

"I'll be right outside, baby," he tells her.

She shakes her head, gripping on as tight as she can in her weak state, her eyes wide with fear.

"I'll be right back, Frankie." It guts him leaving her side when she clearly needs him.

She looks over at her dad, pleading with her eyes.

"We're not going anywhere, my love. But they have to make sure you're okay," David says and pulls him away from her side just as the other doctor enters the room.

Half an hour passes before a nurse ushers them over to the waiting room.

"It may take a little longer for them to check her over," she explains to them. "She's responding well so that is a *very* good sign. Let's just give them a little space to work, all right?"

He paces and cuts a trail into the rug for another half hour before Mick walks into the waiting room. "She's doing good, man. She's doing really good. Just be a little patient, okay?" Mick announces.

Before he can get a word out, Nick rushes into the waiting room to join them. "She's up?" he asks, out of breath.

"She's up," he answers. "They kicked us out. Said they have to check her out first."

Nick rushes over to Karmen and gives her a big hug and kiss.

Alice and David are already sitting down and talking to Mick.

He walks over to the wall and places both palms against it, frustrated that he can't be in there with her. After fifteen days of waiting, he's given a minute and he needs more. He needs to know she's going to be okay. He needs to see her move, see her eyes open with clarity, and he needs to feel her hand squeezing his again.

Two hours past eternity flies by before the two doctors and a nurse join them in the waiting room. He practically jumps out of his seat to get to them.

"How is she?" he asks.

"She's doing great," Dr. Shah says with a smile. "I know we kept you waiting but there were procedures that we needed to follow. She's awake, alert, and responsive. We had to wait for the respiratory therapist to get here too. She was adamant about extubation."

"So, she's been extubated already?" Mick asks them.

"Yes. And her breathing is right where it should be without the ventilator," Dr. Shah answers him.

"That's amazing!" Mick says.

"Yes. It is. She's still on oxygen but we're happy to say she's breathing on her own now. She'll still be a patient of this ward for a while because she'll still need around the clock care to make sure her wounds are healing properly and to make sure she's clear of sepsis."

"When can we see her?" Nick asks.

"In a few minutes, the nurses are still setting her up. She's still somewhat groggy and weak and she might fall in and out of sleep. We still have to keep her on the tube diet for now until her damaged intestines give us a sign they can handle more."

"She's going to be very hoarse and might not be able to say much. Don't be alarmed. She's probably got a really sore throat. She should take small sips of water if she can handle it," Dr. Patson takes his turn to speak.

"She might not remember everything about the event. I recommend you not push her right now. Give her a day or two. It's still two visitors in the room at a time so she doesn't feel overwhelmed so soon," Dr. Shah instructs.

He nods and shakes their hands.

"She should be ready," the nurse says.

He and David head in first.

Even in her hospital bed, with her disheveled hair and frail body, she's the most beautiful sight his eyes have ever seen. The bed is slightly inclined and she taps on the cast on her arm and wiggles her toes on the side with the knee brace.

"Dad," she says, barely audible.

David walks over to her bedside and kisses her head. "My love," David replies.

"Sorry," she tries to tell him.

He pats her hand lightly.

"It's not your fault. It's in the past now. We'll get through," David says.

"You've met Cole," she says with a weak smile and a very strained voice.

"Yes. Yes, we've met."

"One minute?" she asks her dad in a whisper, holding up an unsteady finger.

David nods and leaves the room, walking with more confidence than he's ever seen the man with since they met.

Frankie turns her head to him, tugging on his hand, and he sits down on the edge of the bed as best as he can.

"You're okay?" she asks, her hand coming up slowly to touch her throat.

"I'm okay. Even better now."

"*Sorry,*" she tries to say but no sound comes out.

"It's not your fault, baby."

"Not yours either," she manages to get out.

He isn't sure what to say to that. It isn't the time to unload all of his thoughts on the subject to her.

"I'll spend the rest of my life making this up to you," he vows.

She weakly shakes her head and closes her eyes. "*No.* Don't make me feel like you're only with me out of guilt. Again." She smiles at him and tries to laugh but she flinches. "Bad?" she asks.

"You mean for being shot and stabbed?" he teases her.

"Eck," she says, making a disgusted face.

"Are you having a seizure now?" Nick asks from the doorway.

Frankie rolls her eyes and he smiles, getting off the bed and sitting down in the chair right next to her.

"You lived?" she whispers. "*Eck*," she says again.

"No thanks to you," Nick says, walking over to her.

He watches quietly while Nick squeezes her hand. He sees her squeeze in return, rubbing her thumb lightly against the back of his brother's knuckles. This moment is probably as good as it's going to get between the two of them. There seems to be an unspoken understanding there that he isn't going to question but he's glad they can finally come to some kind of terms.

"I know I owe you a bullet. You think I can just get a tattoo of one and we call it even? That shit looked like it hurt," Nick says.

"*Asshole*," she whispers in return and rolls her eyes again.

"Guess you're a hundred percent back to normal already. I'm going to get out of here then and get dinner started. Thanks for that Instant Pot, by the way. I love it!" Nick leans over and kisses her hair.

"Eww!" she says very loudly and clearly.

It puts a huge smile on Nick's face. Nick's hand lingers around her hand a little longer before letting go and leaving the room.

"Should have let him take the bullet," she says.

He can't help but laugh. Something he hasn't been able to do in too long a time.

- 75 -

cole

The fourth day after she had awakened, Karmen and David broke the news to her about Vince's passing. It was a hard decision to come to but she kept asking about him and no one could prolong the inevitable anymore. She was devastated, shaking her head in disbelief and crying uncontrollably. David held onto her while Karmen tried her best to console her best friend.

It took almost three weeks for Frankie to be moved off of the ICU ward and into a normal room. She's getting stronger every day yet is still fighting through the pains of her wounds.

In the three weeks, he barely left her side and only because she insisted that he get out and get some sun and some laps in.

He can tell she's getting restless as well. Many times, it took David a lot of fatherly persuasions to convince her to pace herself and try not to push too hard too fast. And after David had to return home, she was back to pushing herself again. They'd had many moments of bickering when it was clear she'd been overexerting herself.

She carefully swings her feet off the side of the bed and sits up. He can tell the movement hurts her. He caught her slight wince.

"You should tell me when you want to stand," he says, coming to stand in front of her.

"I didn't want to stand. Just wanted to sit. My knee feels like it needs to pop or something."

He rolls up her hospital pants leg and takes the brace off of her knee. "Lay back," he tells her.

He begins bending her knee and straightening it out again as the nurses taught him. Her physical therapist says she should be able to start light exercises to help strengthen it quicker. There wasn't any ligament damage but because she has been immobile for so long after the dislocation was reduced, the healing has been slower than the norm.

"Do you know when the cast comes off?" she asks, tapping her forearm.

"Probably another week or two. They'll put you in a soft cast after that."

"That's better. Thank you," she says.

He helps her sit back up so she doesn't put too much strain on the muscles in her abdomen region.

She slides her arms around him and he pulls her closer. Face against his chest, he smells her hair. He brought her toiletries for her after hearing her complain about the stuff the hospital provided. She's starting to look and smell how he remembers her more and more each day.

"I love you," she tells him.

"You know you are everything to me," he says, holding her tighter.

"Ahem," someone says from the doorway.

He looks up *and of course*, Sam is standing there. He's ditched the crutch and is in a short leg cast now. His arm cast is already in a soft one which he can bet that Frankie will be jealous of. Sam has a blueprint carrier hanging around his shoulder.

"Sam!" Frankie exclaims.

"You're looking a lot better than the last time I saw you," Sam says, walking in.

Frankie looks up at him. "He visited you while you were..." he answers her.

"Oh. Thank you, Sam. I didn't know."

He watches as Sam walks over to her, moving him out of the way in that Sam-passive way he has.

Frankie leans into his outstretched arms and hugs him. "You scared the shit out of me," Sam tells her.

"Can't be any worse than seeing you flying over a whole car," she answers in his arms. She moves out of his arms. *Finally.*

"I didn't know we were trying to outdo the other."

"Is that what I think they are?" she asks, pointing to the blueprint carrier on his back. Sam nods and he can see the excitement in her eyes.

"Cole, can you get Karmen and Nick in here? The twins should be fine in here too."

He eyes her suspiciously.

"Please?"

"Don't let her get off that bed without some help," he growls to Sam before reluctantly leaving the room.

It takes him about 2.5 minutes to wave at Nick and Karmen before he walks back into the room to see her and Sam laughing about something. It's great seeing her smiling and laughing again but with Sam? *Come on!*

"They're coming," he announces.

"Thank you," she says, pulling him in for a quick kiss. "Can you pull that overbed table over here, please?"

"What's going on?" Karmen asks when she walks into the room with Nat holding her hand. Nick is right behind her with Nic.

"Remember before all this happened and I said I had an idea about something for the farm? I asked for an acre or two?"

Sam takes rolled-up blueprints out of the carrier and lays them on the table. "Frankie came up with a great idea and asked me to help her get it on paper. We had been working on this before...you know. But I finally got the chance to get the renderings completed just a few days ago."

And for the next hour, everyone was wowed by Sam's drawing and Frankie's business ideas for the farm. Frankie is fucking amazing and they might make a life doing legit business after all.

"Frankie, how the fuck do you just pull amazing shit out of thin air like this? Like you woke up one morning and said 'Shit, I think I wanna make a restaurant out of shipping containers.'" Karmen slaps Nick on the chest, shaking her head.

"It'll definitely give me and her something to do to bring in some income," Karmen says. "But how much is it going to put us in the hole before we turn a profit?"

"I have someone at the office putting together a budget and working the numbers. Honestly, I don't think it's an unattainable amount. The grants should help out a ton," Sam says in all seriousness.

"What are you thinking? I know it's probably not what your grandpa had in mind for his land. I don't want to step on his legacy and you don't have to agree to do any of this. It's just an idea," Frankie says.

"It's an idea that you invested a lot of thought, a lot of time and energy. And I think it's actually amazing. If this is what you want to do and if everyone else is on board, then so am I," he says before kissing her cheek.

"Really?" she asks. "No pressure at all. I'll still love you either way," she says.

"Really," he tells her sincerely because it's an absolutely amazing idea and he's willing to put in the work to make it happen.

"So, we're in business?" Sam asks everyone.

"We're in business!" she says, giving Sam a high five.

"Sorry to interrupt," a man's voice comes from the doorway.

They all turn around and look to see who it could be.

"Gary," Frankie and Karmen say at the same time.

"Sorry, I'm late."

"Guys, this is Gary Steinman. He is...was Vince's attorney," Karmen introduces him.

"Gentlemen," Gary nods at them. "Frankie, I'm sorry I couldn't get here sooner. My old bones can only move so fast nowadays. Plus, everything that's going on with Vince."

The man walks over and gives Karmen a pat on the hand before leaning over and giving Frankie a familiar hug as best as he can with her lying down in bed.

"I'm so sorry for your loss, Frankie. Twenty-four years, I've known Vince. I didn't think things would end this way."

Frankie nods her head. He can tell she's putting on that brave face again and fighting to keep her composure. He squeezes her hand, letting her know that he's here, right by her side.

"Gary, this is Cole. He's my fiancée. That guy over there is Nick. He's Cole's brother and also Karmen's fiancée. And this is our friend Sam."

"Again. Gentlemen. Pleasure meeting you, even under these circumstances."

"Is everything okay?" Karmen asks.

"Well, other than the tragedy? Yes. Everything has been moving along smoothly. But it's time, girls. I'm here as executor of Vince's estate and it's been over thirty days since his passing. I need to update you both and let you know what's been happening.

"First, I need to read you the legal jargon and have you both sign off on some paperwork. Frankie, are you okay to do that?"

"Yes," she answers. She must already know what he's talking about.

"What do you mean 'both of us'?" Karmen asks.

"It'll all be clear by the time we finish up," Gary answers.

A younger woman enters the room and they all turn around.

"Ah. You made it. Everyone, this is my paralegal, Wendy. She had to find parking." Gary speaks directly to Wendy, "I'm about to read the legal stuff to them and have them sign off. Can you get the next set ready?"

Wendy nods and digs in her bag.

They sit through about five minutes of legal jargon before he hands the two-page document for Karmen to sign first, giving him time to help Frankie up for her turn to sign. Sam was asked to sign as a witness with Wendy notarizing his signature immediately afterward.

"Okay, ladies. I'm going to basically tell you the short version of his final wishes and then give you each a copy of the legal one so that we can go over it together."

Karmen is now sitting on the bed next to Frankie.

"In short, you both have been named as the beneficiaries to his estate with his assets being divided as follows.

"He has two life insurance policies to the sum of $500,000 to be divided equally between the two of you. We already filed the paperwork and have recently sent in his death certificate along with all police and hospital reports to the insurance company on your behalves."

He sees the stunned look on Karmen's face, a tear visibly sliding down her cheek. Frankie reaches over and holds her hand.

"To Frankie, he has bequeathed you his house, with all properties and belongings within the structure and on the land; this includes his car and boat. These assets are yours to do with as you see fit.

"In addition to the property, he has bequeathed you all his personal cash-on-hand. This includes his personal checking accounts, his personal savings accounts, and all his personal investments. The current estimated amount totals $108,439.19."

Gary looks over at Frankie, speaking directly to her. "I say the current estimated amount because, in the state of Oregon, probate takes a minimum of four months. In that time, I have to notify all his creditors and they have to respond to me of his debt to them. So that amount can increase or decrease depending on who responds with what.

"This amount has also taken into account the cost of his burial and services. As of right now, a month has gone by since the notification and the public announcement as required so we have three more months to go. Does that make sense?"

"Yes," she replies, her voice a mere squeak.

"Moving forward. To Karmen, Vince has bequeathed to you one hundred percent ownership of Vinny's Place and all assets umbrellaed under the business."

He looks over at Karmen, who's covering her mouth, trying to control her crying. Nick walks over to her and rubs her back.

"Karmen," Gary addresses her. "This is a little tricky. I've spoken to the insurance company and have sent them everything they've requested along with the police report. It doesn't seem like they are going to fight the claim being that there was video evidence, but these guys can be tricky so it's a waiting game for now.

"The bar has a value of $275,000 but his policy has a maximum fire coverage of only $250,000 and that's including property damage to any nearby buildings too. It will be completely up to you to rebuild or walk away.

"Along with the bar comes all cash accounts which is currently to the sum of $189,133.42. Unlike Frankie's situation, you are responsible for paying the balances on any credit accounts now. Should you decide not to rebuild the business, the creditors will have to be paid off with the available cash from those accounts or they will have the right to file suit. Does that make sense?"

Karmen nods her head. "Frankie, the bar should have been yours. You worked day and night to get it to where it was. I shouldn't have gotten any of this," Karmen sobs.

"This is what Vince wanted. He wanted to make sure you and the kids will never be in a situation like the one you were in when we met," Frankie tries to soothe her friend.

- 76 -

Frankie

It's just her and Cole in the truck on the ride home. Karmen and Nick are driving closely behind them. It seems like she's waited far too long for this day to get here and now that it's actually happening, she's beginning to feel apprehensive.

Her physical recovery is going really well. Only every now and then she can still feel some pain, usually when she moves too fast. Her knee has been doing great also and she uses the brace less and less.

Up until this point, she never had to put her emotional recovery to the test. Being in the hospital for over eight weeks, she felt a sense of security that she hasn't been able to admit to anyone. Especially to Cole.

She couldn't even tell him that once she was taken off of the sleep meds, the nightmares began. She can't really call them nightmares though. They're more like revisits of what happened. The nurses leave her monitors muted at night otherwise, Cole would have probably noticed the rise in heart rate.

"Do you want to have that sized down?" he asks, breaking the silence.

She faces him.

"Your ring. You've lost some weight. I was asking if you wanted to have it sized to fit."

She looks down at her hand, not realizing that she was fidgeting with her returned engagement ring. "No, babe. It's fine. I'm sure it'll fit just fine once I can start eating my normal stuff again. My diet right now is kinda...bland," she says. "I can use a ring sizer." She touches her necklace. "You're okay with me wearing this, for now, right?"

When her belongings were returned, the first thing she reached for was her mom's necklace. It isn't expensive or extravagant like the one Cole gave her but it brings her comfort and some feeling of normalcy.

"Of course. I know how much you love it."

They pull onto their street. "Cole, can we stop at Vinny's first? Please?"

"Are you sure? There's really not much left there."

She nods her head. "Yeah. I'm sure."

He slowly pulls to stop at a spot directly across the street.

The street isn't packed this early in the afternoon. Vinny's Place would have just opened its doors for the lunch crowd. But now, there are no cars in front of the place. The spot where the bar used to stand is eerily and heartbreakingly empty except for the rubble.

Vince isn't here anymore. There's such a heaviness to that knowledge. Heaviness and a hollowness all the same. It hurts and it's numbing.

Flowers and old candle jars lined the sidewalk. Teddy bears and deflated balloons are tied on what's left of the building.

She opens her door and steps down, careful not to land too hard on her still recovering knee. Cole steps out of the driver's side as she walks around, looking both ways before crossing the street. Wrapping her jacket tightly around her, she sees from the corner of her eye that Nick is pulling up behind the truck.

She reaches the sidewalk and observes the magnitude of the devastation. The fire burned everything to the ground. Even after two months with several weeks of light snowfall, the ashes can still be seen mixed with the dirt, dust, and mud. Various metals shining and gleaming, reflecting off the light of the sun.

Vince could have been a part of the ashes here if someone hadn't walked by and pulled him out. That was Donnie's intention.

"I already scheduled a company to come and clean the debris and clear out the lot next week," Karmen says from beside her.

"This is all because of me," Frankie says quietly.

"No. This is all because of some sick guy who fucked up and was trying to cover his tracks," Karmen says vehemently.

"And if I hadn't opened my mouth and told Vince what happened, he would have never tried to confront Donnie alone."

"Frankie, Vince leaves a lot of choices and decisions up to you but that doesn't mean he's deaf and blind to what happens in and around his business. By the time you told him, he probably had his suspicions; otherwise, he wouldn't have confronted Donnie. *You* didn't even suspect Donnie."

Karmen puts an arm around her shoulder and a hand on her upper arm, "Come on. Let's get you home," she says, pulling her backward before turning her around and helping her step over the threshold that used to be the front entrance to Vinny's Place.

Home?

Cole is holding the door open for her to get into the warm truck. He kisses her lightly before shutting it.

Through the side mirror, she can see Karmen getting into the SUV, her belly bump now pretty obvious at...*how far along is she already?* Karmen has been a rock through all of this. She should be enjoying the pregnancy and yet she's spent countless days and nights at the hospital, tending to her.

"Ready to get home?" Cole asks.

Home? That word causes a shiver to run through her.

The truck shifts into gear and they are moving down the street. *This street.*

Her palms grow clammy and she absentmindedly fidgets with her ring again as they approach the building.

She zooms in at the middle of the street where Sam had been lying because Donnie tried to kill him. He tried to kill Sam because of *her* and though he didn't succeed, Sam suffered. He suffered greatly. He nearly died.

"We're here," Cole tells her.

There are several cars parked. Her car is back. She recognizes one as Sam's. The renovations had to be done by now, which means that Sam is probably here to welcome her home.

Home. She looks out the windshield at the building. Everything looks exactly the same, except it isn't the same. She can't put her finger on it but she feels uneasy and reluctant to move.

Cole opens the door for her. "Let's get you inside. I'll come down for the bags later."

He helps her out of the car. Nick parks directly behind the truck and then helps Karmen get out of her side too.

The building's door swings open, causing her to jump. Sam and his assistant, Josh, are standing in the doorway with smiles on their faces, even as her heart is pounding so fast and too loud.

"Welcome home!" Josh says as Sam pulls her into a bear hug and out of Cole's hold.

"God, you're even tinier now," he says.

Sam releases her and steps into the hallway to let her inside.

She sets foot inside and looks up at the staircase and freezes, unsure whether her legs have frozen on their own or if her brain is telling them not to move. Her throat feels dry but at the same time, her mouth feels watery. Her sweaty hand holds on to Sam so tight she's sure he'll be able to feel the moisture from her palms.

She looks down at that hand, staring at the neon pink soft cast around most of it and her arm.

"Do you need help getting up the stairs?" Sam asks her.

The stairs. Home.

She faces the stairs again. Her senses are on overdrive. Her feet finally move. Cole's hand is on her back and she can feel Sam still holding her as she takes her first step onto the stair.

A loud thud startles her. Sam's leg cast hitting the step. She can hear a few other footsteps coming from behind and then they soon fade out. They reach the top landing and Sam releases her to open the door.

She freezes, breath caught in her throat as the scene plays before her eyes as if she were watching a movie.

There was no beeping from the keypad, just like there wasn't that night when Dusty came in. She looks over to the bedroom doorway, to where she stood when he first set eyes on her. She can feel the fear creeping inside of her again this very second, can see the excitement in his eyes as he kept punching her stomach.

She clutches her stomach at the imaginary pain. She takes a step back into Cole.

"Frankie, what's wrong?" she can hear him ask through the ringing in her ears.

She opens her mouth to answer him but the scene just keeps playing before her eyes. She flinches as if Dusty had slammed her head into the doorframe again. Her heart pumping rapidly.

"I...I..." That is all that comes out of her.

A solid set of arms comes around her, enveloping her in warmth and security. Cole. She'd lived her whole life being independent and headstrong. Until Cole came into her life, she'd never needed or wanted security from anyone.

Her breathing slows down and her heart isn't pounding in her ears anymore. She shuts her eyes to stop another round of replays, shaking her head.

"I can't..." she says. She isn't even sure if anyone can hear her but she's not sure she can repeat herself.

"Okay, baby," Cole softly says.

She turns in his arms, hiding her face, ashamed that she let the likes of Donnie and Dusty destroy the peace that she called home for so long. These people are here supporting her and here she is, crying and sobbing. Weak. Ever since she woke up in the hospital, all she wanted to do was leave and come home. Now that she's steps away, she can't even walk through the door.

- 77 -

Frankie

"Mmm...I think I definitely needed that," she says to Cole.

They're currently entangled with each other in bed, returning from utopia, after an amazing reintroduction to learning each other's bodies.

He was extremely gentle. Maybe even too gentle. It almost reminds her of their first time together that one September night. She isn't blindfolded tonight though. Her arm is in a cast instead of being tied but the chemistry is definitely still there. Stronger. Much, much stronger.

"I love you," he tells her again as if he needed to remind her as often as possible.

"I love you too."

She stays in his arms and in less than ten minutes, she can hear his steady breathing and can see the rise and fall of his chest. This is the first night he's sleeping in an actual bed in the past two months and he was exhausted even before their lovemaking.

She looks around their hotel room. It's a few steps up from the Oasis Inn Motel. She objected to something fancier because she simply isn't sure what she's going to do yet.

She loved her apartment. It'd been home for so long but it just doesn't feel like home anymore. Too many bad memories outweighing the good right now. Except for Cole. He's been the one good thing to come out of all of this. He's her everything right now; he's her home.

He stirs and she moves her head off of him, giving him space to sleep comfortably. She moves onto her side, facing the window, and looks out into the night.

His arm immediately drapes over her hip, pulling her closer against him without even waking up.

"NO! No! Stop it!" *she screams at Dusty.*

He's trying to pull down her pants. She can feel her head swing back, hitting him. Pissing him off. She screams when he bites down on her bare shoulder. It feels like he is ripping into her flesh with his bare teeth.

"Frankie. *Baby.* Wake up!"

Her eyes shoot open and Dusty fades away. The feeling of his teeth sinking into her shoulder lingers and her hand immediately reaches up to touch the bare area.

Cole. He's next to her. They're in a hotel room, she remembers now. It's just a dream. Another nightmare.

Daylight is breaking and the signs of a new day are creeping into the room, filling it with light. It isn't hard for her to see the concern on his face. She reaches for his cheek and brushes her fingers over his lips.

"I'm sorry," she says. "Did I wake you?"

"How long have you been having these nightmares?" he asks.

"Just a couple of nights. Since I stopped taking the sleep meds," she replies.

"Stop being sorry. None of this is your fault. You don't have anything to be sorry about." He brushes the hair from her face tenderly even though his jaw is set tightly. "You should have said something about them, Frankie."

"Cole, it's something I have to work through."

"I know. But you don't have to work through it alone. I'm here," he says, looking into her eyes. "Don't shut me out."

"No. No...I didn't mean to make you feel that way, babe. I would never shut you out. It's just...you've already been there for me night and day. You deserve a break too."

"Stop worrying about me. What good is a break when you're going through this alone? It doesn't speak much about what you think of me if you think I can't handle all of this."

"You know I think the world of you. You're everything to me. You're the only semblance of a home left for me." She turns onto her side, moving her head on top of his arm, snuggling into him. "My haven, that's what you are."

"I love you. Every part of you," he tells her before kissing her bare shoulder where minutes earlier she'd felt Dusty chomping down on her.

"He bit me there," she says quietly into the hollow of his neck. "That's what I was dreaming about tonight. I felt it like I was just there."

She's quiet for a minute, trying to work through her feelings. He remains quiet too, pulling her closer into the safety of him.

"He had me bent over a dirty rotting table and he was trying to get my pants off but I head-butted him and he bit me. And out of everything that happened that night, it was the most..." She pauses. "I was scared. I was beaten. I was hurt all over. And when he bit me, I felt...degraded. I just felt...he made me feel beneath him and worthless."

"Baby, you're not worthless. What he did was a coward's way. *He's* the one worthless. Try not to hold on to that feeling. I know it's easier said than done right now, but you are *my* everything, and worthless is something you'll never be. You have so many people in your corner. You're not alone, Frankie."

"I'm so glad it was you that night," she says quietly, her fingers moving over to touch his hand. "I'm so glad it was you I ran into," she says again.

"And I don't know what shitty hole I'd be in right now if you hadn't wrapped your arms around me that night. My lifesaver," he says before picking up her hand and placing a kiss over the finger with his ring.

"You sure you're ready to sell this place?" Cole asks her.

It took them a whole week to clear out Vince's house. She decided to donate almost everything except for the pictures that Vince had in frames and various albums. Some are pictures of his family members, including his parents and grandparents. Most are pictures of him at the bar. The ones in frames are mostly of her and him. There are many of Karmen and the twins before their first birthday as well.

She packed everything into a rubber tote along with some of his jewelry they found and other things that Vince found sentimental. Along with those items, she chooses to keep all three of his Fender electric guitars, Karmen choosing to keep the Gibson acoustic one.

And today, the real estate agent had come by and grounded the For Sale sign in the yard.

"Baby, are you okay?" Cole asks her again.

She turns away from the window now and faces him.

"Yeah," she replies. "I'm sure. Without Vince here, it just doesn't feel right anymore. Like this isn't his home anymore."

"I've hitched the boat to the truck already. Do you want to ride with me and drop it off?"

"Yeah. I can use a drive," she says, grabbing her jacket from the floor.

Cole holds the door open for her.

Both the car and the boat are being donated to the women's shelter. A volunteer already picked up the car and returned the plates to her. The titles to both are in Gary's possession and she already called to speak to him about the donation and her wishes for having the house listed.

She gets into the truck and waits for Cole to lock up the house.

Where would she be without him this past week? He's worked hard and tirelessly helping between her and making sure Karmen isn't overdoing herself while Nick is away. He's also doing what he needed to do to help Nick over the phone in between.

"Be honest with me, babe. How many women have you left brokenhearted across the country in your travels?" She reaches for his hand. "You're amazing and I don't know where I'd be if it weren't for you."

"Didn't we already talk about not asking questions you really don't want answers to?" He laughs as she smacks his arm.

He flashes her one of his gorgeous smiles before he returns his attention to the task at hand. He pulls the truck out of the driveway carefully and they are well on their way to the drop-off.

"Since we're in between homes at the moment, how would you feel if I said that I was ready to pack and leave for the farm?" she asks, breaking into the silence.

He turns his head to look at her for a few moments before returning his eyes back to the road. "You know I wouldn't object to that."

"I don't know when I'll be able to feel like I can go back to the apartment. Karmen wants to have the baby there anyway. And I can start working there. So what if I just went on ahead and got everything ready for her?

"It might give me some time to run things through my noggin and clear things out of my head," she tells him before leaning back into the seat with resignation.

The truth is...she is tired. Not physically tired but emotionally drained and she isn't sure what she needs to snap out of this funk.

"If that's really what you want to do. When do you think you'd want to do that?"

"As soon as you guys can get my things at the apartment packed. I'll have to talk to Katrina and let her know I won't be returning to work and I'll let Gary know that I'll be leaving, but he can always reach me and I'm just a flight away if he needs me for anything."

"And your follow-up doctor's appointments?"

"I can request a copy of my records and try to find someone to take over in the area or I'll just make the trip back."

"You seem to have thought about everything already," he says as they approach the drop-off location.

"Not really. I'm just giving you answers, thinking out loud, as you're asking me the questions." She looks at him and smiles. "How about we have dinner at Katrina's later tonight so I can talk to her and Oscar."

"We can do that," he says. She watches as he tries to unsuccessfully hide his grin. "Do you think Nick will be okay with us being there first?" she asks.

"If you haven't noticed, my brother is kinda at your feet. Sometimes I wonder if he's actually in love with you too."

"Eck! Don't ever say that again. Makes me gag." She actually gets the wiggles from the statement and he laughs at her loudly from his side of the truck. She gives him a good smack to the arm again.

"Sometimes I feel like the two of you have this secret thing going on behind my back. He barely speaks to me without mentioning you anymore," he says.

"Cole!" She shoves him playfully.

- 78 -

cole

"What in the fuck is going on around here?" Nick asks, taking the words right out of his mouth. "She's only been here a week, right?"

He looks around, just as astonished as Nick. He had to double-check the screen on the navigation to make sure he didn't make a wrong turn somewhere.

Things in Portland had taken longer than he expected. There were a ton of details to go over before Eric was happy enough to hand off his part of the agreement for their legal team to look over. He was supposed to meet Frankie here two days after her move. That didn't happen.

"She's been here two weeks technically," he tells Nick.

They had driven down the road to the house and saw the shipping containers sitting in the yard. She never mentioned that she was already moving forward. The last he heard was that she needed everyone's signature for the permit application. And now they are pulling into the driveway, where backhoes and a bulldozer sit close to the house. Major digging is clearly evident.

He gets out of the truck the same time Nick does and looks around to see if anyone is nearby for an explanation.

It's April and the sun is shining bright. He unzips and takes off his sweater, not expecting for it to be as warm as it already is this early mid-morning.

"She tell you what she's been doing?" Nick asks, looking around. "Look! Something is going on around the barn too." He points off into the distance.

He shields his eyes from the rays to see what Nick is pointing at. Sure enough, there is definitely something going on over there. Two trucks are there and he assumes that's where Jake, Lucas, and Nelson are too.

"She didn't say a word, Nick. I would have told you." He looks around again. "Let's get inside and see what's left of the house," he mumbles.

He heads in through the side door, not even bothering with his bags.

"Frankie! You here?!" he yells, opening the door.

Instead of her voice, he is greeted by a low, warning growl. The kind of growl you know not to fuck with.

He quickly slams the door shut and looks back at Nick. His brother shoves him out of the way, turning the knob and opening the door only to be met by not just the low growl but some really, really big teeth.

"Basil! Down!" Frankie hollers from somewhere inside the house.

The dog closes its mouth instantly and trots over to his commander.

He looks up at the voice the same time Nick does. "Cole!" Frankie says with a big smile from the dining table.

"Are we allowed to come in?" he asks.

Damn! She's so fucking beautiful. Her long hair braided loosely, hanging over one bare shoulder. She's wearing perfectly fitted jeans and one of those off-the-shoulder shirts that he loves seeing her in. Before he takes a step past Nick, another dog rounds the corner from behind the kitchen island and glares at them.

"Did we just walk into the wrong fucking house?" Nick asks.

He waits for her to glide through the house and into his arms. "I missed you," she says.

He leans down to kiss her, eyes never leaving the vicious animals. "Are you sure about that?" he asks.

"Oh, the boys are harmless. Come in!" She pulls on his arm and shuts the door behind them. "Boys! Look! Daddy's home!" she says.

A dog runs over to her excitedly and faithfully. It comes over to sniff him while Nick carefully shifts out of the way and behind the island.

"He's Basil. He's a blue heeler/German shepherd mix," she introduces him. "He's about nine years old now."

He kneels down, her arm settling around his shoulders, and the dog licks his face and hands. So much for the vicious teeth and growling.

"The other shy guy over there is Jaxon. They're brothers." She sits on the floor next to him. "Jaxon, come here, boy."

Jaxon comes immediately to her but is a little apprehensive about smelling him.

"Are they good around kids?" Nick asks.

"They're great around kids. Some family was moving away and dropped them off at the vet's office to be put down. Poor boys were scared. Imagine that. They've been with the family since they were babies and were going to get killed just because they couldn't make the trip. These boys are loyal, fully trained, and housebroken."

"And now they're your minions just like everyone else around here," he comments.

Jaxon leaves him and heads back to her side.

He stands and helps Frankie up too. He pulls her back into his arms, holding her to his side. *Cuddle.* That's what he wants to do with her right now.

"So, you've been...*busy*," he states.

"Might be an understatement," Nick says as he opens the fridge and grabs a bottle of water.

He walks over to the island with Frankie still attached to his side, kissing the top of her head, getting a good whiff of the scent of her shampoo.

"An empire doesn't build itself," she says.

"That's what we're building?" He looks down and the dogs are lying down, one on each side of them.

"The shipping containers for the project just got dropped off on Saturday. I got them well below the budget. They were in Montana so they got delivered quickly."

"Okay," Nick says. "So, what's with the backhoe and dozer out front?"

"Oh...those? They're for the house," she says nonchalantly.

Nick chokes on his sip of water.

"Come on...I'll show you guys." She walks over to the dining table where apparently, she has set up shop. Her laptop and various stacks of folders and papers are laid out along with a printer at the corner. The dogs are already at her heels like they are on some unseen leash.

"Cole told me I could do whatever I wanted to the house."

"I don't think he meant for you to demolish it, *Frankie.*"

"No shit, *Nick*. I'm just making a little addition."

Nick chokes on his water again. "What kind of *addition*?" Nick asks.

"Baby, so...uh...can we start from the top here?" he steps in.

"I love this house. I really do. But it's not practical for all of us here. The master bedroom doesn't really have space for a nursery, Nick. And if you use the adjacent room as a nursery, the only two rooms left for the twins are downstairs. They're too young to be down here alone right now. The only option is for them to take Cole's room."

"Then we can renovate the house and adjoin the two rooms down here and make it a second master for us," he tells her.

"We can. But it'll still be impractical for when we want to start our own family."

"Exactly *what* do you have in mind?" Nick asks.

"Like I said...just a little addition."

"Why do I get the feeling that your *little* is from a different dictionary than mine?" Nick asks her.

She gives his brother a dirty look.

"How little are we talking about, Frankie?" he asks.

"Just another thirty-four hundred square feet."

"Thirty-four hundred square feet! Baby, that's *not* a little addition! That's almost the same size as this house! How are we going to afford that?"

"Have faith, Cole," she says, much too calm.

"So, we're going to pray it happens," Nick says sarcastically. "You want to build a whole house on prayers?"

"Look, I wouldn't be doing this if there weren't a way to make it happen."

She rummages through her stack of papers and pulls out a folded sheet that looks like a large blueprint. She unfolds it and lays it on the table facing them.

"Shit but that's fucking beautiful. And here," Nick points on the paper, "this is where the house connects? Basically, by a hallway?"

She nods.

"It's beautiful, baby. It really is. But the time and money needed for that might be out of our reach right now. Nick's got a kid coming. Karmen and the twins are moving out here soon. We have the project to build and we don't really have an income coming in yet. Everything we have will barely keep us afloat *and* get our end of the deal ready for Eric."

He doesn't like to disappoint her. It really is a beautiful house or *addition to the house* but it's just out of their price range for now.

She shakes her head, unfazed. "Can you guys hear me out first before freaking out? Because it's already too late to stop the train right now."

"Oh Jesus," he says. His hand rakes through his hair.

Nick is doing the exact same thing.

"You might have noticed debris has already been cleared away and space has already been dug and flattened. Jake and Lucas accomplished that with Jessie's help and supervision along with Sam's blueprints and instructions."

"Jesse? My buddy, Jesse?" Nick asks with arched brows.

"Yup. Apparently, he just so happens to be in the cement business. I subcontracted to him so he was able to use his license to rent us the equipment at a much better rate than I would have been able to get. The three of them were able to get the job done in a day."

She hands over the receipts for both equipment rental and for Jesse's services.

"Woah! He's doing all this for fourteen grand? Including the equipment rental?" Nick asks.

"Yes. I've already paid him upfront and told him that if the cost of the equipment rental changes, he can come to me about it. He'll be coming back tomorrow with two guys to lay the slab foundation. You two can help if you want to partake or not. Doesn't matter. But it would be nice if you did. Maybe it'll save us a couple dimes," she says with an optimistic smile.

He stares at her in disbelief.

"Sam already got us the permits that we need and he's my acting general contractor. We're subcontracting the work as we go and he's got an established list of reliable subs out here.

"The plumbers and electricians will be here tomorrow as well to work alongside Jesse's crew. These guys were recommended by Jesse and gave him a really decent deal according to Sam."

She hands him two more receipts together totaling almost $9k.

"These guys are only bringing one other person each to help and say they can get the work done in a day. They'll be back to finish the job once the framing of the house is put together."

"How? Please don't tell me you took out a loan?" he asks his girl.

"No. Vince's insurance policy was dispersed," she says quietly.

"I know it was," Nick says. "But you didn't need to spend all of it on any of this. We had time to work it out, Frankie."

"I don't intend on spending all of it. I have a budget and I'm pretty sure I can stick with it." She holds up her hand to stop them from saying any more. "Just let me finish."

She pulls out a bunch of paper from the folder.

"So, while I was shopping for the shipping containers, I came across this."

She puts a standalone picture of the finished addition on the table.

"This house was custom designed for a client who, after placing the order with this company, didn't have the funds to pay it off. Their loan didn't come through or something. The company specializes in prefabricated custom log homes within Montana. Being that their clients all want custom work, this project which was already cut and ready to be picked up, just sat in their storage facility for almost two years.

"I ran across their ad. They were asking thirty-three grand for it and I was able to talk them down to twenty-seven grand plus delivery."

"You're telling me that you paid under thirty fucking grand for a thirty-four-hundred-square-foot house?" Nick asks incredulously.

"I'm sure they still made a tiny profit from whatever their original buyers had already paid. And if not, it's probably better to let it go for twenty-seven grand than have it continue to sit there doing nothing. We got lucky," she says with a shrug.

"I can't even believe this," he says to which she hands him another printed receipt.

It's the receipt for the purchase of a "Log Cabin Home Package Kit - 3,400 sf Home." And there is the proof.

He hands the receipt over to Nick.

"What in the holy fuck?" Nick stares at the paper.

"It gets delivered a week after the foundation is laid. AND included in the purchase of the kit comes one of their contractors who will help us put together the house. We just have to provide him with enough crew members.

"Jesse said he can find four carpenters who will work by the hour easily plus you two if you're around and possibly Jake and Lucas if they're available. The estimated time from start to finish of the house itself is two to four days because everything's been precut. After that, we can slowly put the interior together depending on how you'd like it to look, Cole."

"I don't even know what to say right now," he says, looking over at Nick.

"Like I said before...how do you pull this shit out of thin air?" Nick asks.

"So, you're really going to do this?" he asks.

"No, babe. WE are really going to do this. It might be a lot more blood, sweat, and tears than you bargained for. Sorry in advance for that," she says, coming around the table and wrapping her arms around him.

"Woman. You are never going to stop surprising me, are you?"

"This is really happening, isn't it?" Nick asks. "Why did Gramps make it sound so hard when he built this place? She just made it sound like it was a walk on a treadmill." Nick continues flipping through the receipts and looking over the floor plan.

"When do you have to pick Karmen and the kids up from the airport?" she asks Nick.

"Not for another three and a half hours."

"Let's go down to the barns. Maybe you two can help out down there," she says with a smile.

"What's going on down there?" he asks her.

"You'll see," she says. "Jaxon! Basil! Let's go, boys!"

The dogs are immediately at her side.

"By the way, they know most verbal commands. They know whistle commands too but I'm not good at whistling so I haven't tried it. I believe it's one short whistle for them to go ahead and scout, two short whistles for them to halt, and one long whistle for them to return. You guys can try it out."

They walk through the kitchen and she picks up a basket of tennis balls from the corner by the door while he holds the door open for her.

"How's your arm?' he asks her.

"It's healing. Slowly but surely," she pouts. "The past two days I've left the brace off most of the day and put it back on only after dinner before I go to sleep."

"And the nightmares?"

"They still come and go," she says quietly.

He pulls her next to him and kisses her head while they walk across the gravel onto the trail heading to the barn.

Wait. *Barns?* She said barns, didn't she? Barns as in more than one barn.

"Here," she says, handing him and Nick each a tennis ball. "They'll probably love how far you guys can throw them. Freaking Jake lost one in the trees the other day. Jaxon was out there for over an hour looking. I thought a coyote got him or something."

He and Nick look at each other with grins a mile wide. They never had dogs before, let alone ones that know how to fetch. They both pitch the balls out as far as they can but look down at the dogs only to find them still walking beside them, looking anxiously up into their faces.

"They're not going anywhere until you tell them to," she says with a giggle. "Try whistling. One short whistle."

Both he and Nick let out a good short one and the dogs are running full speed ahead already. They know exactly where they are going.

"Before they get to the balls, make them stop. Two short whistles. Loud," Frankie instructs.

He watches as they get closer before he lets out two short whistles and they immediately stop and lie down. "That's fucking awesome. People were really going to put these guys down?" he asks.

"Yeah," she says, hugging him. "I couldn't just watch it happen. We have space."

Nick gives a loud short whistle and they run at full speed again.

"They're good around the other animals in the barn too," she tells him.

Nick gives them one long whistle and they both return at full speed with the tennis balls in their mouths as if they are in a race.

"You said you got them at the vet's office. What were you doing there in the first place?" Nick asks after he takes the ball from Jaxon.

"You'll see," she replies.

They walk the rest of the way to the barn while playing with the dogs. The closer they get the more noise can be heard. Lucas's country music plays along with the sounds of hammers and power tools.

Frankie leads them past the opening of the barn and off to the side and behind the barn a good twenty yards. Jake and Lucas are working on building what looks like one of those small barns you can pick up from Home Depot.

"Look who decided to finally show up!" Jake hollers.

Jaxon runs over to Jake excitedly. "Hey, boy!" Jake greets the dog.

"What's going on here?" Nick asks once they reach the two.

"Frankie didn't tell you how hard she's making us work?" Jake asks.

"She picked up these two barns so we can move the goats and the pigs out here," Lucas answers. "The chicken coop is already done over there," he says and points.

"We have chickens now?" Nick asks.

"Yeah. Ten of them and about a dozen chicks. Frankie collected the first dozen eggs this morning," Lucas replies. "They'll probably lay more once they get used to the place."

"The barns are almost done. We just have to get the pen up before we can bring them out. I'm sure those goats will figure a way to get out anyway," Jake grunts.

"And why are they being moved out of the barn again?" he asks in confusion.

"She didn't tell you?" Jake asks.

Both he and Nick shake their heads.

"Come on. Nelson's in there right now. You'll see," Lucas says with a huge grin.

"Oh god. What now? I'm still in shock about the house," Nick says.

"The house is going to looking fucking amazing, right?" Jake asks. "Ten years from now, I'll be able to say I had a hand in laying the foundation to this place."

They round the barn and Frankie slips her hand into his before they enter. They all walk in past the office just as Nelson walks out of a stall with a beautiful brown horse. His white blanket looks amazing, highlighting his muscles perfectly.

"Are we breeding?" he asks Nelson.

"Uh...no," Frankie answers. "Don't be mad," she says, squeezing his hand.

"God, I don't know if I like the sound of that," he retorts.

"This is Oliver," she introduces the horse.

He looks down at his tiny fiancée and not a clear thought forms.

"He lives here now," she says quietly.

"You bought a horse?!" Nick exclaims.

"No, not exactly," she says, fidgeting with her necklace.

"She bought four," Jake answers with a smirk like he's watching a good show.

"WHAT?!" he asks, stunned. "Frankie!"

Frankie can visibly be seen shooting daggers with her eyes at Jake.

"Oh, don't be mad," Nelson says when he finally reaches them. "She made some great choices. Hear her out first."

"Gotta admit, this one's fucking gorgeous," Nick says and takes the lead rope from Nelson's hand.

"Oliver's a yearling Appaloosa. He's pretty gentle. He's easy to handle and lead. He's about fourteen hands now. Should mature to about fifteen, maybe sixteen hands. Gorgeous, isn't he?" Nelson asks, patting Oliver gently. "I've gone over him and done the tests to make sure he's in good health. He's doing great but he needs a lot of training."

"Please tell me you didn't overpay? Frankie, you really should have talked to me about this first," he says, trying his best not to sound like he's scolding her.

"I'm sorry. I didn't mean to overstep. But I didn't pay anything for him except for the three-hundred dollar adoption fee."

"WHAT?!" This time, it's Nick asking loudly.

"Yeah. He was ditched at the vet's because he's unregistered. His dam is unregistered so I'm not sure what whoever had him was thinking but they tossed him," Nelson says. "He doesn't have any saddle experience but we can work on that. I've saddled him a few times since he's been here but I think we need to pick up a better one for him."

How did she get so lucky? Oliver is definitely a looker.

"A yearling?" he asks, petting the horse and taking the lead rope from Nick. He leads the horse back and forth and Oliver follows gently.

"Yeah. His papers say he's eighteen months old," Lucas answers. "We haven't introduced him to the herd yet. Nelson wants to wait until all his tests come back. Make sure he doesn't have anything underlying."

"And the others?" Nick asks. "Are they here too?"

"Yeah." Nelson leads the way while he still has Oliver's lead rope in his hand. "His stall is the second one there if you want to put him back."

Nelson walks past the second stall and opens the door to the third stall. He waits for Oliver to be lead into his stall before leading out another one.

"This beautiful palomino here is Bella. She's seven years old now but she's experienced and level-headed," Nelson tells them.

"She's my favorite," Lucas says. "I've taken her out the past three days. She's athletic. Stamina and speed. She does obstacles like a pro too. I've been working on introducing her to the herd. She came with papers, AQHA registration, the whole nine yards, and she goes to the same vet we use so her records are up to date."

"She's amazing. Damn beautiful," Nick says, taking the lead rope from Nelson again and walking her out of her stall.

"She's gorgeous," he tells Frankie.

"I know. Reminds me of you," she responds with a wink.

"I can see why you like her," Nick says, looking over at Lucas.

"Lucas and I picked her up from a handler that couldn't care for her anymore. He was losing his land. I gave him three thousand dollars for her. Lucas said that was a good deal. Just about half of what he was asking," Frankie tells him with a nervous look on her face.

"Hey, I told Frankie that if you guys didn't want to keep her, I'd like to buy her off of your hands," Lucas says.

"She's a good choice for sure," he replies.

"Really?" she asks, her eyes lighting up.

"Yeah. I can't complain," he reassures her. "Lucas, you're more than welcome to continue working with her when you have free time. Nelson's probably going to need the extra hand with a full house."

"You have no idea," Jake says with a chuckle.

Frankie slits her eyes over at Jake again.

"So, who else do we have?" Nick hands Bella over to Lucas, who leads her into her stall again.

Lucas points to the next stall and they all follow Nelson.

"We have Lily over here in the next stall. She came from the same handler as Bella. She's a dunskin tobiano filly. She's got papers and vet records too. This one is going to have speed. She's solid," Nelson tells them.

"She's just as beautiful as Bella, isn't she?" Frankie asks, petting her.

The filly leans into her small hand.

"I gave the guy a thousand dollars for her," she says and looks at him.

"Not bad, baby," he tells her. "Does she have any training?"

"Yeah. Not as much as Bella, of course, but she's a sweetheart. Might be good for the kids," Lucas says.

"'*Not bad,*' he says. Wait until you see the last one," Jake chortles from behind everyone.

"Where?" Nick asks curiously.

"Very last stall on the other side," Lucas points.

Nick walks over to the stall door.

"That's Wade," Nelson says, hurrying over like he's walking on hot coal and stepping in front of everyone.

He strides over but can feel Frankie holding on to him to hang back a little.

"He's a four-year-old. Painted horse," Nelson says quickly.

"He's an asshole, that's what the fuck he really is," Jake announces.

"He's got problems?" he asks.

"Not physically, but he can use an attitude adjustment. Probably why she got a good deal on him. The guy who owned him couldn't handle him," Jake replies.

"You guys let her buy a wild one?" he asks, looking at them.

"It's not like that," Nelson starts. "Wade is athletic, experienced. He's strong and big. He's only four years old and he's at sixteen hands high and about twelve hundred pounds already. He's good on trails, he's good in the mountains, an arena, or wherever. He's papered and his vet records are immaculate."

"So, what's the problem?" Nick asks.

"He's kind of an asshole like you," Frankie mumbles.

Lucas and Jake are trying hard to cover their chuckles.

He moves closer to the stall door where Nick is standing.

Nick tries to approach the horse but can see that he is agitated. Nick steps back and looks at Nelson.

He tries to approach Wade from the left and makes it close enough to feel his nostrils sniffing at his hand before the horse turns around and kicks the stall door hard, not once but twice, showing his disapproval.

"Other than his attitude, he's beautiful. And he knows it. A bit of a show-off," Nelson says. "Chestnut with the overo markings. She paid a good chunk for him. Didn't think he would turn out like this."

"How much did you spend?" he asks her.

"Umm...four thousand?" she replies, not meeting his eyes.

"It's not a bad buy at all if he can be worked with," he says, trying to soften the blow for her. She did so well up until now.

"So how have you guys been handling him then?" Nick asks.

"Well, he lets me handle him when he's in a good mood or when he just wants out," Nelson tells him. "Let's see what he thinks of me right now."

He and Nick step aside to see if Wade is going to let Nelson approach. He immediately sees the rapid swishing of his tail and the pawing of the front hooves.

"Well, guess he's not liking me too much right now either. He hasn't been out the past two days. Probably upset," Nelson says.

"Well, how do you guys get him the exercise he needs if no one can handle him?" Nick asks.

"We have a secret weapon," Jake says.

Nelson steps out to the left side of the stall door and Frankie rolls her eyes before she walks over.

"Might want to move back," Lucas tells them. "He's not a happy camper."

Frankie reaches for the stall latch and he pulls her out of the way.

"Baby, what are you doing? He'll trample you!"

The irritated horse paws at the stall door loudly, neighing and stomping his foot hard enough to feel the ground move.

"Babe, he's fine. He's just...being Wade," she says before pulling her arm out of his hand.

She unlatches the stall and opens the door.

"Come on, Wade! You're making yourself look bad and they're gonna send you away, you big jerk." She grabs his bridle and tugs on it, not in the gentlest way, to lead him out of the stall. "I wouldn't stand behind him if I were you guys," she tells him and his jaw-dropped brother.

"See? Secret weapon," Jake says smugly.

"Holy shit," Nick says.

He's speechless and walking alongside his brother a good distance away from Wade, who shows his teeth at Jake and Lucas as Frankie leads him by them.

"By the way, she's not very good at leading either," Nelson says. "I think that's what makes him mind her. She's just as unpredictable as he is."

- 79 -

cole

Nick finally makes it over to join them at the house. "Frankie, those horses are fucking awesome. I'm not going to even ask how you managed to find them," Nick exclaims.

"I wasn't really looking. I was looking for something else and found them, just like I did with the house," she says.

Funny how things work out like that.

"I just got off the phone with Jesse. He's coming over tonight for dinner and he's bringing me the quote that I asked him for. I might go ahead and have him start the digging on the site for the containers. As far as that goes, Sam says we don't need a permit, so we might as well get it out of the way," Frankie informs them.

"Sounds good. Karmen and I are only here for a week though, but I'll be glad to pitch in where I can. Eric gets here in two days and tomorrow we have to meet our attorney who's going over the lease to try to get it ready before he gets in."

"The four of us need to go down to the bank and establish a couple of corporate accounts. They require all four of us to be present to sign. We should also separate our personal accounts from our investment accounts."

"We can do that," he tells her. "We need to send Liam his payment anyway."

"I'm going to unhitch the truck and start unloading our stuff from the U-Haul into the garage," Nick says.

"Our stuff is pretty organized and labeled in there already," Frankie calls out after Nick.

Nick gives her a thumbs-up and leaves the house with Basil trotting over.

She turns and kisses his lips. He deepens the kiss, wanting more of her. Needing more. "I'm never gonna get enough of you," he whispers.

"Mmm..." she says, sounding content. "You're stuck with me, so you really don't have a choice now, cowboy."

"I know where I'd love to be stuck right about now."

"I miss you too, cowboy. How do you manage to make a T-shirt and joggers look so freaking sexy?"

They walk into the kitchen, hand in hand.

"Need some help?" he asks her.

"Belinda helped me already. Did you check on Karmen?"

"Yeah. She's up but laying on the couch and on her phone. Said she'll be done soon."

He looks around the kitchen. "The boys are still out with Nick and the kids?"

"Yeah. They're throwing the balls around. They're going to be hungry soon," she replies with a smile.

The boys. Interestingly, Frankie understood he was talking about the dogs and not the males that are working on the farm.

"What do you feed them?" he asks.

"Just the stuff Lucas grabbed from the vet's office. Their bowls are right by their tub of food over there in the closet by the back door if you want to make their dinners. I usually give them two cups and mix in a raw egg to each bowl. For breakfast, I scramble the eggs."

He heads over to the closet and grabs the bowls off the floor before opening the tub. Did other people feel this kind of tingling excitement at something as normal as feeding their dogs? Because he'd never done such a task before. He puts the food into the bowl and brings them over to the counter before searching for the eggs.

"Cole," she calls out pulling on the back of his shirt.

He turns around and she wraps her arms around his waist. "There's something different about you today."

He kisses the top of her head, arms coming around her. "Really?" he asks. "Maybe we've been apart too long." It's true. Every minute away from her is too long though. So there recent time apart, although for a legitimate reason, was equivalent to an eternity.

"Yeah. You're sexier than normal," she says with a grin. "You're the most relaxed I've ever seen you. It looks good on you, babe."

Now that she mentions it, he does feel different. Lighter. He doesn't feel like he's this six-five and standing in a room full of people...alone. Now, it just feels like he's...*home*.

He leans his back on the counter and turns her with him, placing her between his legs, his arms still around her.

"It does feel different. You're here and every time I've walked in and out of that door today, I knew one hundred percent that I'd be coming home to you. This is what normal is like, isn't it?"

"I don't know. You're the first guy I've gotten to come home to. But I love it," she tells him. "I love it as much as I love you."

She tiptoes and he leans down to meet her halfway so their lips can scorch and sear. He can feel cool air feather his abs as she pulls his shirt up enough to slide her hand under it.

"Mmm..." she hums softly into their kiss.

"Can we just call it a night? I missed you," he says after she ends their kiss.

She grins at him with her beautiful twinkling green eyes.

He tilts her chin up and places a gentle kiss on her head. "I love you," he says.

"Ahem..." Karmen says as she waddles into the kitchen. "Having dessert before dinner again?" she says, teasing them. She walks over to the fridge and looks inside. "Where is everyone?"

"Belinda brought dinner back to her place. And the guys are still outside," Frankie answers.

Some commotion is heard by the back door and then dogs trot in to greet their mama and the twins can be heard loudly running in after.

"Jaxon. Basil. Come on. Let's get you boys some dinner," he calls the dogs. To his surprise, they actually follow him. "Where do you feed them?" he asks Frankie.

"In here, by the window. Makes it easy to clean up after they're done," she answers from behind the island.

It takes them a solid fifteen minutes to get the dogs fed and everyone's dinner plates in front of them at the dinner table.

"Thanks," Nick tells Frankie once he gets settled in after getting the twins washed up.

"Frankie, you've been busy," Karmen says after a bite.

"I'm just trying to get everything ready for you and the baby."

"Babies don't need all that much. Remember when we had the twins in your apartment? That worked out fine for six months."

"I know. But you have a growing family. I'm sure you guys want your own space and privacy."

"I know you've always been good at handling money. Just...don't leave me out and tell me if you need help. You have that annoying habit of taking care of me without me knowing it," Karmen says with a scowl.

"I think she has a habit of doing that for everyone," he retorts because it's true.

"When we go down to the bank tomorrow, I'm paying you back half of what you spent on those containers. From now on, we split everything that has to do with that place evenly down the middle, all right?" Karmen demands.

"Okay! Jesus! Calm down before your blood pressure peaks."

He laughs at his sweetheart while she takes a bite of her food.

"By the way," she says between chews. "There's something we should talk about while we're all here."

"Now she wants to talk *after* she's done everything else on her own," Nick says with a mouthful.

Frankie rolls her eyes at Nick. "When Sam sent over the application for the permit, it was filled out incorrectly."

"Sam made a mistake. Probably nothing new," he retorts.

"Cole!" she scolds him. "Anyway. He didn't know that you two didn't legally own the farm yet so he listed your names on the application. I was going to have him make the proper changes but I wasn't sure what it needs to be changed to."

"Liam personally owns this farm. He didn't incorporate it and he didn't umbrella it under his current company," Nick tells her.

"Well, I didn't know that and I happened to ask Liam about it when he came out to visit me. He had to know what we had planned anyway. I know you guys already spoke to him about leasing the space out and by the time that was to happen, you probably would be the rightful owners.

"As for this project, we need those permits as soon as we can get them. So I showed him our plans and told him about the idea. I was hoping he would allow us to use his name on the permit application so we can get the ball rolling."

"He turned you down," Nick says, wiping his hand on a napkin.

Karmen looks at Frankie with disappointment.

"I'm sorry, baby. We can wait until it's ours to start," he says, patting her hand for encouragement.

"Well, he didn't exactly say no," she says.

She puts her taco down after another bite and wipes her hand on a towel before getting out of her seat. She heads to her stack of paperwork and pulls the very nice-looking file folder out.

Unhooking the clip, she flips through and pulls out a document, and hands it to Nick. She hands stapled sheets of paper to him as well and before he can wipe his own hands, Nick jumps out of his seat, pushing the chair a good distance behind him

"This is the deed to the property with Liam's signature!" Nick exclaims and looks over to Frankie.

He snatches the papers and quickly flips through the paperwork, reading it as fast as he can. He recognizes it as their initial contract from ten years ago except it has an extra page now. The page states that the contract has been paid in full and that transfer of deed has taken place.

He looks at Frankie, astonished because how the fuck did this happen? Liam never mentioned a word of this to them.

"Wait! Don't get too excited yet," she says. "Yes. He signed the deed over to us and gave us all the paperwork required for us to transfer the property. We can meet with the attorney as soon as you guys can get us there. But he still expects us to finish making his payments to him and he's putting in blind faith that our words hold up.

"He didn't want to hold our project up. He said that if we run into any issues down at the permit office, let him know and he can help us."

Karmen stands up and holds his brother. She whispers something into Nick's ear and he nods. Nick pulls out of her arm and looks down at the piece of paper again, walking over to Frankie, his eyes never looking up from it.

"Frankie..." Nick says before he wraps his arms around her shoulder.

Nick holds her close, his brother's tears falling over his arms and onto the back of her shirt, unashamed and unfiltered.

"Thank you," Nick says. "I don't even know what to say."

Nick pulls away from her and looks down at the document again. "There were times when I wasn't sure I'd ever see this again let alone hold it in my hands."

He's speechless himself, standing stoically with the contract in his hand. Before he can put another thought together, Nick pulls him into a hug. He wraps his arm around his brother's shoulders, looking down at the piece of paper.

"Wow," he says, staring down at the deed.

Ten years and it's fucking done. Ten long fucking hard years and it's finally done.

"Baby brother, it's here. It's home, man. It's finally home," Nick utters. Nick gives him a huge pat on the back, one that he returns.

"Gramps would be happy," he tells his brother. "He'd be really happy."

It doesn't take another thought before he's at Frankie's side, his arms wrapping around his girl's petite frame. His eyes captured by her sparkling gaze and his heart captivated by her whole being.

"I love you, Frankie. There's no one else like you. Home is where you are."

"I love you back, Cole. Home is right here. In your arms."

Fate is a funny thing. All the bullshit he's done, everything Frankie went through. All of that led them both here.

Home.

Finding home

Finding Home

Dear Readers

As always, THANK YOU for finishing this read with me.

Finding Home was previously released in December of 2019 and the trilogy was quickly complete by Valentine's Day of 2020. Here's the thing about authors. No matter how many novels are published, we still get extremely nervous about a launch. These truly are our book babies and we always want them to do well.

Though I absolutely loved the Home Trilogy and Cole and Frankie's story, it wasn't as well-received as I had hoped compared to the murder and mayhem of my other series. The reviews were wonderful from the readers that did give it a chance though. When I asked a few booklover friends why they feel like it would be overlooked, the common answer was that the book may seem too long at first glance, and in the market today, readers keep busy and may not want to commit several days to finish one book when they can read two to three shorter adventures in the same amount of time.

I absolutely should apologize for that. I LOVE detail. And I love Cole and Frankie along with their bunch of friends and family. I could go on and on about them, especially since this trilogy was technically my first novel even though it was released after The Kings and the Knights. I love the fast-paced yet slow-burn and the small-town romance with a hint of suspense. And cowboys...enough said about that!

I loved this trilogy and the characters so much that I actually went up to Montana to visit a small town just like my fictional Colt Springs. And I fell in love with Montana too. My heart lives there. It truly does. I plan to return there as often as I can so don't be surprised if there are giveaways Montana-related.

With that said, I revisited Cole and Frankie's story to give it the love it deserved. I want you all to love them as much as I do. I've gone through with an editor for another pass through. We've shortened it down some more and I'm giving it a completely new look as well.

So for those of you who are giving this a second chance...THANK YOU! I hope that you'll love them the way I do. Cole and Frankie's unconventional meeting is amazing to share and oh what a great beginning it has been. I can probably go on and on forever with these two and their friends but I'll focus on tidying up the next installment in this trilogy and then the final. *Breaking Home* and *Coming Home* are now both available.

ON TO THE NEXT!

Sincerely,
Ami Van

About the Author

Ami Van is a crazy cat lady residing in Las Vegas, NV, with her children and, of course, her cats. As a child, she held her cats hostage in a room as she unleashed her imagination, boring them with countless stories of fire-breathing dragons and heart-shaped dandelions floating into space. Stubborn and defiant, she disregarded her tutors', teachers', and mentors' advice to explore creative writing and instead graduated college with an Information Technology degree. It took many twists and turns for her to start writing. Since she's a firm believer that it sometimes takes a little more time to find one's path, it took her nearly 16 years to finally take the step.

Please visit my website at www.AuthorAmiVan.com for my social media hands and my newsletter subscription to keep up to date with me, my projects, giveaways, and new releases.

Other Books by Ami Van

All links are for Amazon's US Market. Please check your respective markets for availability.

The King Family Series

Becoming His
Finding Her
Until Her
The Coin
Losing Her

Knights of Havoc MC

Dakota
Maddox

The Home Trilogy

Finding Home
Breaking Home
Coming Home

Printed in Great Britain
by Amazon

77891562R00243